# THE
# 13T
# PILLAR

Troy,
I hope that
(I hope this!)
you enjoy this!
All the best,
V.Bill

# THE
# 13TH
# PILLAR

## William F. Mann

NORTH STAR PRESS OF ST. CLOUD, INC.
St. Cloud, Minnesota

## DEDICATION

To Marie, William, and Thomas,
for their inner strength and love

First Edition: December 2012

Printed in the United States of America

Published by
North Star Press of St. Cloud, Inc.
P.O. Box 451
St. Cloud, Minnesota 56302

www.northstarpress.com          Facebook - North Star Press

# ACKNOWLEDGEMENTS

This novel is another one of those carved stones in a multi-storied building that may never be completed. Indeed, it could very well be the keystone to it all. Building upon a richly layered composition created through the real application of signs, seals and tokens by such true initiates as the renaissance masters, Nicolas Poussin and David Teniers the Younger, *The 13th Pillar* presents a fabric of intrigue first woven by the Sovereign Order of the Knights Templar and the Norse and Davidic families who first came together in Normandy in the eleventh century A.D.

Following in the footsteps of Lewis and Clark across the vast American wilderness, the modern-day explorers entered another world, where Native North American traditions and ceremonies most certainly mixed with earlier European Masonic rituals and customs amongst the shadows and dancing light of the fire.

It is also most appropriate that this novel is first published during the 200th anniversary of the War of 1812, when the American indigenous people and their British allies so desperately sought to take back what they believed was rightfully theirs.

As such, when creating a novel of this nature, an author is required to immerse himself into the pages so deeply that at times he forgets to acknowledge those most dear to him. I, therefore, wish to first and foremost acknowledge the inner light and warmth of Marie, my wife, without whose support and critique, this novel would never have taken shape. I also wish to thank my two sons, William and Thomas, for allowing their father to escape at times into what they refer to as his "other world."

Many friends and close family members also deserve a fair amount of credit in providing much-needed outside feedback to the many earlier editions. Included in this group are Niven Sinclair and Steve St. Clair, John and Cheryl Fitzgibbon, Vicki Derouville and Rob Mann, Scott and Janet Wolter, Joe and Marla Clark, George and Carina Karski, Mark and Wendy Phillips, and Michael Thrasher. Without good friends and family, this novel, and life in general, would never be complete.

Thanks must also go to the Louvre Museum in Paris, the Trustees of the Chatsworth Settlement, the Trustees of the Dulwich Picture Gallery, the National Gallery, London, the National Museum of Scotland, the Ashmoleum Museum, the Cluny Museum, the Metropolitan Museum of Art, the Cloisters Museum, the University of Toronto Press, the Staatliche Museum in Berlin, and the U.S. Library of Congress for their kind and generous research assistance and various use of copyrighted materials.

Along these lines, it must be noted that the hand-drawn illustration on the back cover of *The 13th Pillar* has been produced by the author himself and is the copyrighted intellectual property of the author. As to how it developed in the author's mind, readers will have to delve into that other world for themselves.

It must also be noted that all latitudinal and longitudinal positions stated in this book have been verified through Microsoft's TerraServer USA, which is sponsored by the USGS.

Finally, I wish to thank the staff at North Star Press of St. Cloud, Inc, specifically Corinne, Seal, Anne, and Brandon. Their editing and publishing skills have created a wonderful, fast-paced adventure novel, which will surely cause many to pause and think. Some readers will most definitely ask the question: How much truth is contained within the novel? That is truly for the reader to decide.

The clue is to always look beyond!

# CHAPTER 1

President Helen Jefferson-Rose, the first female president of the United States, stood in the Oval Office gazing out the bay window, her hands entwined behind her back.

Sitting opposite her desk, wearing identical expressions, were the only two men she completely and absolutely trusted—her husband, William Rose, and the director of the Secret Service, George Artowski.

The two men waited for the president to make the first comment.

"The Antient Meridians!" President Jefferson-Rose murmured. "Now there's a term I've never heard before. I never thought in my wildest dreams, I'd ever see that as the subject of a top-secret presidential file."

Artowski cleared his throat. When the president didn't comment, he said, "To be fair, Madam President, the file was first compiled by George Washington himself and was considerably added to by your own great-great-great grandfather, Thomas Jefferson. It seems to me to be more than mere coincidence it's been handed down to you."

The president turned to face the two men, looking from one to the other. "Tell me something: Why is the file labeled 'Antient' instead of 'Ancient'? What's the reason for the spelling difference?"

Her husband spoke up quickly. "You're aware that Francis Bacon was one of the leading scientists and Utopian freethinkers of his time?"

"Yes," Helen said firmly and with an element of "we've been here before" in her voice, not wanting to encourage him to go into a long history lesson just so she could get an answer.

"Well, he was a practicing alchemist, mystic, hermetic philosopher, and chancellor of England during King James I—the Scottish Stewart King. There's evidence Bacon was part of a secret society—"

"Yes, yes, the Knights Templar. Please make this short, Bill."

"Well, it was known as the Order of the Rose Croix, or Rosicrucian, for short." Bill paused, his eyes locked on Helen's. She sighed, and he continued. "In *The New Atlantis*, published in 1627, Bacon writes of an 'Island Solomon House . . . in a New Jerusalem . . . whereby concealed treasures now utterly lost to mankind shall be confined to so universal a piety.'"

"Bill . . ." President Helen said, her patient wearing thin.

Bill nodded rapidly and finished quickly. "He theorized that the original treasure of the Temple—the original wisdom—came from the 'Antients,' the race that existed before the Great Flood, and that this wisdom was preserved on brick and marble pillars that survived the flood."

That answered the president's question. She nodded.

Then Bill said, "We also need to tell you about something that happened just yesterday. It adds to the overall mystery."

The president cocked her head and almost purred, "What, pray tell, would that be?"

"Yesterday, at exactly noon, Paris time, America's long-time ambassador to France, Michael St. Jean-LeNeuf, suffered a massive brain aneurism and died. We're waiting for the autopsy, but we're suspicious. We think he died of something more than natural causes."

"Murdered?" the president said. "That's a shame. He was such a gentle man."

"What you may not know, my dear," Bill Rose said, "is that George and Michael did three tours of Vietnam together as Navy Seals on special ops. Apparently, Michael was as much a warrior and hero as our George."

The president looked to her Secret Sevice director.

"He always said he had big shoes to fill," George said quietly. "His great-great-great grandfather, one Michel LeNeuf, fought for the Colonies during the Revolution and for Napoleon after that. Then he returned to America and was involved in a number of things, including the War of 1812."

The president said, "There's a brief mention of a Michel LeNeuf in the Antient Meridians file you handed me."

Bill Rose said, "Well, that's the thing. It's one short line. Thomas Jefferson received a report from him noting the sad news that Captain Meriwether Lewis had taken his own life."

"The Lewis and Clark Lewis?" The president's eyes switched from Bill to George and then back to Bill.

Bill and George both nodded solemnly.

"George, let's cut to the chase. I can see you both are working up some grand thesis on this, but I just don't have the time. Give me the *Reader's Digest* version," Helen said.

"Well," George began, "in 1784, Jefferson was appointed ambassador to France. Nothing's ever been proven, but it appears he became a member of at least one secret society there because, when he returned to the States, it appears he came into possession of some sort of secret knowledge. We at least know that Jefferson became obsessed with everything from astronomy to native Indian legends."

"Yes, yes. History has documented that Jefferson was definitely an esoteric scholar," Helen said. She sighed. It always took so long to get to the meat of a subject with these two.

George continued unabashed, "It seems Jefferson somehow learned of the series of 'antient longitudinal meridians' established around the world well before Christ's time. This knowledge would have been closely guarded because it allowed control of world trade. Rumors say these same meridians allowed King Solomon to gain immense quantities of gold, not from Africa, but from the New World."

President Helen quirked her mouth and rolled her eyes. "Really, guys?"

"This knowledge was either lost or suppressed in early Christian times by the Romans and the early church," Bill said, jumping in. "Some say it was lost when the Library of Alexandria burned or when Jerusalem was sacked in 70 AD by the Romans. We can skip forward a thousand years to when the knights of the Temple of Solomon excavated below the Holy Temple. These Knights Templar, as they came to be known, rediscovered this sacred knowledge, along with material treasure. For the next three hundred years, the Templars controlled the seas and formed the most advanced maritime fleet in the world at that time."

"Hold on a minute." The president said, raising her hand. "Come on, guys. I've heard all this before. This is *National Treasure* fluff and coming straight out of Hollywood? Is this where you want to go? Really?"

"You gotta admit it's a great story," Bill said grinning. "But within all the conjecture and speculation, I believe there's a grain of truth to it."

"Here's something you may not have heard." George said. "Shortly after Friday the 13th, 1307, the night that King Philippe of France conspired with Pope Clement X to eradicate the Knights Templar, groups of Templars popped up in all sorts of places—Denmark, England, Portugal, and Scotland."

"Okay. What has that got to do with—?"

"A group of Templars sailed to Scotland," Bill said. "Legend has it that major portions of the Templar treasure went with them. Legend also has it these same Knights Templar helped Robert the Bruce defeat the English in 1314 at the Battle of Bannockburn. In return, the knights were able to secure a sanctuary for the Temple in Scotland for at least the next one hundred years."

"So, what's the point?" the president snapped impatiently. "I have a Joint Chiefs of Staff meeting in ten minutes. If you two modern-day Masonic Knights Templar tell me you're in possession of this 'antient knowledge,' then I swear I'll shoot you both with George's gun."

"But, but, here's something I know you don't know," Bill said slowly in order for the full weight of the subject to be understood. "In 1398 A.D., the hereditary grand master of the Scottish Knights Templar, a Prince Henry Sinclair, sailed to what is now Nova Scotia with five hundred of his trusted knights, some of their families, and a number of Cistercian monks, in order to extend their sanctuary into the New World."

The president stared at her husband. "In 1398? A century before Columbus?"

Bill nodded rapidly and continued merrily. "Supposedly, Sinclair, with his band of knights and support staff, including the Cistercian monks, who acted as clerks, and even women and children, moved inland after wintering in Nova Scotia. Over the years they established sanctuaries and permanent relationships within the Algonquin Nation, which once stretched from the eastern seaboard to the foothills of the Rockies. The final refuge of these Templars was their New Jerusalem. This is what Francis Bacon was alluding to in *The New Atlantis*."

"Bill . . ." President Jefferson-Rose said warningly. She looked again at her watch and shook her head. "Five minutes more."

4

"Out of these strategic relationships and liaisons were intermarriages and offspring, of course. And those people could claim they were descendents of the original Sinclair family."

"Which is important . . . why?" the president asked.

Bill grinned. "The Sinclair family's tied to the legend of the Holy Grail."

Helen rolled her eyes. "And now we're up to *The Da Vinci Code*." The president shook her head.

"Helen, you have to look beyond the far-out notion that direct descendents of Jesus Christ are running around today," Bill implored. "Think of the 'antient knowledge' Sinclair supposedly had in his possession. Native North American lore speaks of a wise old man who came from the east, dressed in garb similar to that of a Templar, who around 1400 AD traveled across North America teaching and learning about, among other things, the earth's forces and a higher level of spirituality anyone could attain if they practiced the liberal arts and sciences. This wise old man supposedly rests in the foothills of the Rocky Mountains, *with* the sacred knowledge. This is the point. This is what Thomas Jefferson really sent Lewis and Clark to find on their epic trek across America. And, not only were they to find Prince Henry Sinclair's crypt, but the relics and hidden sacred knowledge of the earliest prophets who lay with him. "

Helen opened her mouth.

"Masonic scholars have always speculated," George hurredly said, taking up the ball, "that thirteen of the earliest prophets rest with Prince Henry Sinclair, and the Thirteenth Pillar is the one who provides the greatest knowledge because it relates to the thirteenth degree of the Ancient and Accepted Scottish Rite. The thirteenth degree presents a moral allegory of when workmen discover a crypt some nine levels below the ruins of the First Temple in which a great secret is hidden."

"Okay, okay," Helen said, holding up her hands. "I can see you two have your teeth sunk deep into this stuff. Why are you so interested in this fairy tale all of a sudden?"

"Three reasons!" George held up his fingers and counted. "First, a solar eclipse travels across the continent in ten days, and the sun is seen as the key to finding the crypt in some way. Second, during our stint in

Vietnam, in a rather dark and hopeless moment, Michael St. Jean-LeNeuf confessed to me that he inherited some of Meriwether Lewis's secret messages to Jefferson passed down through his family. He told me his family always maintained that Meriwether Lewis's Masonic apron possessed documents—*The Lewis Parchments*, which alluded to what Captain Lewis secretly discovered. And, third and most important, we've just received information from our Masonic brothers in Canada that a Scottish and York Rite Mason with longstanding Templar family connections to the Order, going by the rather interesting name of Thomas Randolph, has unlocked the mystery. Coincidentally, in the early nineteenth century, a Thomas Mann Randolph was the son-in-law of Thomas Jefferson, having married his oldest daughter, Martha. We don't know yet if there's a direct family connection to this Randolph from Canada."

The expected knock on the door from the president's executive assistant finally came, signalling the end to the discussion.

President Rose started walking around her desk but paused. She gave each man a measuring look. "Okay, dig into it. I must go deal with the Palestinians, the Israelis, and the Syrians . . . and you two nuts want me to also disturb our Canadian neighbours. Great. But when you give me the follow-up to this nonsense, please, please, make it brief."

She smoothed her skirt and brushed the hair away from her face as she walked toward the door. "And, my two precious knights, keep your quest quiet or I'll deny I know either of you!"

# CHAPTER 2

By good fortune, Thomas Randolph found himself right on time for his breakfast meeting and took the first available elevator up to the eleventh floor of the Fairmont Royal York Hotel. Curiously, no one else got on the elevator with him, even though the main lobby was packed.

At the *ding* and the number eleven glowed, and the doors to the elevator opened with a soft *ping*. A very large, middle-aged man in an ill-fitting suit and crew-cut hair stood in the hallway, half blocking his way. Thomas noticed the earpiece with the extending wire leading into the back of his suit jacket.

Thomas was certainly taken aback. *What the heck's going on? What's this big monkey doing blocking my way?*

"Mr. Randolph?" The gorilla-man said. "This way please. Standard security sweep. Please empty your pockets." The man didn't even extend his hand. Instead, he just stood there, stone-faced, like a gargoyle as Thomas hurredly complied. "Your breakfast meeting is down the hall and to your right, suite eleven eleven. Someone will greet you and show you to the door."

"That's fine," stammered Thomas, as he made his way past the man, who made no effort whatsoever to give him any more room to maneuver than necessary.

The hallway was echoingly quiet, strange for such a large and well-attended hotel. *Has the whole floor been cleared?* Thomas wondered.

Rounding the corner of the hallway, Thomas saw almost a twin to the man at the elevator—the same stocky build, ill-fitting black suit, and cropped hair with matching earpiece. *Who the heck am I meeting for breakfast?*

Thomas came to an halt in front of the second giant, who said, "Mr. Randolph? If you would follow me, sir. Your party is waiting."

Thomas followed, assuming if he diverted in any manner that he might be shot or thrown out the nearest window.

As they came to the double doors of suite 1111, the guard lightly knocked three times, then opened the right door to usher Thomas in.

Thomas found himself standing before two men slightly older than himself and smartly dressed in well-tailored dark suits. They were sitting on settees arrangement before a huge fireplace with a gilded mirror above it. Both poured over a file spread on the oversized coffee table between them.

As the first man looked up, Thomas thought he looked somewhat familiar. Thomas immediately warmed to his smile as the red-headed man stood to cross the floor to greet him, warmly taking his hand. The second gentleman, in his early sixties, judging from his gray hair and lines around the ice-blue eyes, possessed the build and raw energy of a starting linebacker. His handshake came close to crushing Thomas's hand.

"Brother Thomas?" The one with the red hair said. "I'm Bill Rose. Maybe you recognized me already because of my famous wife, the president of the United States." Thomas stared at him, awestruck. "And this fellow is the director of the Secret Service, George Artowski. He's also currently the grand master for the state of Minnesota, but we don't let this go to his already rather large head."

George Artowski said, "We're all Scottish and York Rite Masons and Masonic Knights Templar here, and we're delighted you could find the time to meet with us to discuss some common interests. You come highly recommended."

"In other words, George thoroughly checked you out." Bill Rose laughed. "On a more solemn note, we're sorry to learn that your wife passed away recently."

"Thank you," answered Thomas.

"Please, sit," said George. "I've taken the liberty of ordering breakfast, which should be here any second."

Bill Rose pointed rather to the nearest couch.

Just then, the same three knocks came. It softly opened without delay and a nondescript, uniformed waiter entered, pushing a large silver cart laden with the usual breakfast fare—juice, coffee, tea, and a huge platter of assorted muffins, fruit, bagels, and croissants and various toppings for them. George jumped up to marshal the cart, and the waiter departed as quietly as he had arrived, without once looking up.

Thomas was having trouble focusing. All he thought about at the moment was that two of the most powerful men in the world ate the same things for breakfast that he did.

George pushed the breakfast cart towards where the three men would be sitting. Suddenly he stopped, his attention seemingly fixed on the tea pot. All Thomas saw was that its lid was rather firmly in place. George said in a low voice, "Bill, take Thomas and lock yourselves in the bathroom."

A gun suddenly appeared in George's right hand as he flung open the door to the suite.

Bill had started to move immediately, though Thomas didn't. Bill grabbed his elbow and hustled him across the room into the bathroom. Thomas, looking back, caught a glimpse of one of the huge guards propped up against the far wall, sitting with legs crossed, staring blankly across the hallway. There was no blood, no sign of a struggle, just a slightly odd, confused look on the obviously dead man's face. If Bill hadn't been pulling at him hard, Thomas probably wouldn't have gotten into the bathroom at all.

Bill then shut and locked the bathroom door, blocking out the macabre scene. Bill quickly pulled Thomas to the back of the bathroom, as far from the door as possible. And, as this was a large suite, that meant going through a wash-up area with sinks, through a door to a tub and shower, and into the shower stall.

It was the various inner doors of that bathroom that saved them when, a few seconds later, the breakfast cart disintegrated in a blinding flash as the fragmentation device concealed under the linen detonated. The cart itself—thousands of tiny shards of hot metal—hurtled in all directions, embedding themselves into anything and everything, including going through some of the bathroom doors and walls.

# CHAPTER 3

I t took exactly sixty-four seconds for the two back-up Secret Service teams to arrive. With their automatic pistols drawn, the two four-man teams secured the entire floor and were communicating with central command—a black van parked in the service alley behind the hotel—within another fifty-six seconds.

Two minutes—that's all it took to restore order out of the chaos. Thomas shuddered, as he was tended to by a rather efficient-looking paramedic for a slight bump on his forehead he received while being half-dragged by Bill Rose into the bathroom. The paramedic assigned to the first team carried out his business with military precision, as Bill Rose stood over what was left of the suite's doors lying on top of the unconscious body of George Artowski.

The man in charge of the back-up teams, Robert Ross, barked orders alternatively at the paramedics and to nobody in particular. At least that's what it seemed to Thomas.

Bob Ross—mid-forties and slightly more slender than the standard Secret Service body-type—was, without mistake, in charge of the scene. By his order, the doors were lifted off George Artowski by two paramedics.

Unbecomingly, George was spread eagle with his head firmly buried in the lap of the dead agent sitting against the wall. Yet it took only a few seconds for the hulk to awake with a shudder and rise to his knees under his own power.

"Thank God you're alive," exclaimed Rose. "You had me worried for a moment, you big ox! Are you okay?"

Artowski sucked in a huge gulp of air. "Just had the wind knocked out of me. The doors exploded outward. What was it? A fragmentation bomb?"

"Yes, sir," Robert Ross responded immediately. "By the looks of it, the bomb was professional—small enough to conceal, and designed to use the cart to inflict maximum damage. I'd say the three of you are more than lucky to be alive."

Artowski had righted himself and was taking off his jacket with the help of the two paramedics. "Thank you, Mr. Ross, for your candid and efficient observations. I take it the scene is secured and that the local authorities are on their way?"

Ross immediately put his hand to his ear and responded in a clipped, military tone, "Yes, sir, we estimate their arrival time at four and one-half minutes. What is your command?"

"My suggestion, Mr. Ross," Bill Rose said, "is that the three of us along with your teams, who aren't supposed to be here in the first place, leave immediately via the service elevator, and your paramedics stay and make the scene as plausible as possible. I think we're going to have to stage the two dead agents in order to make it look like a construction accident. Do we know how they were killed?"

"It appears, sir," one of the paramedics said, "that both of them were killed by a technique I've seen before, in Iraq. The killer stands at close quarters, usually conversing with his victim. He carries a concealed stiletto in one hand and quickly brings it up to the chin and thrusts the blade upward, so that it penetrates the soft underbelly of the chin, then the nasal cavity and into the brain—instant death—almost no blood, no sound. "

Thomas was absolutely stunned at this rather casual explanation, but there was no time to absorb everything around him. Ross once again put his hand to his ear. "The service elevator is secured, sir. It's time to go!"

Artowski, aided by one of the Secret Service agents, moved quickly down the hall. Thomas could tell that Artowski was trying to flex his shoulder blades, as if trying to work something out of his back. Thomas also noticed that Artowski's gun had returned to its holster.

Two agents awaited the party's arrival at the service elevator, expressionless but with their collapsible sub-machine guns still at the ready. As the elevator doors closed, the tension and nausea hit the pit of Thomas's stomach.

Thomas could feel the eyes of the entire Secret Service team staring right through him, almost willing him to vomit or to try to run away.

The elevator jarred abruptly and the doors opened to a flurry of activity. Van side-doors with tinted windows flung open, and Thomas found himself half-flung into the third row seat along with Ross. The door shut as soon as Bill Rose and George Artowski deposited themselves in the middle row, and the convoy of three black vans pulled away, first to the end of the alley and then merging into normal traffic heading south.

Bill Rose let out a sigh and then spoke, once again with the calm, midwest accent that had greeted Thomas just moments before, "Mr. Ross, please inform the president there was a *slight* incident at the hotel, but that both George and I are fine and we're returning immediately to the White House."

Thomas thought, *What about me?*

Bill Rose rather innocently responded to the silent question, "Mr. Randolph, under the circumstances, not knowing yet who the real target was meant to be, may I suggest you fly back to Washington with us, since it might be the safest place for all three of us for the moment."

Thomas thought again a moment . . . *So, it's Mr. Randolph now. Am I suspected in some way? Once in the bowels of the White House, I won't be able to escape even if I try.* "Of course, sir," he said, "but I'm going to have to explain my absence at work." Thomas shifted his weight back and forth next to Bob Ross.

Bill Rose responded immediately with a casual wave of his hand, "Don't worry about that. It'll all be taken care of . . . maybe a sudden death in the family or something of that nature. I seemed to have read from your file that you haven't taken a holiday since your wife passed away. Your office'll suspect you've finally met someone and flown off for a few days of romance."

*What else is in that file he has on me? What's going on here?*

Just then a cell phone rang at the front of the van, and the agent riding shotgun examined the display and then passed it to Rose without comment.

Bill Rose eyed the display, gave a big sigh and flipped open the phone, pressed "RECEIVE" and then spoke. "Yes, dear . . . now calm down . . . everything's fine. We're heading straight back to the airport. We'll be home in less than two hours . . . yes . . . unfortunately, Tommy Webster and Brent Madison are both dead."

Two men dead. Thomas wanted to exit the van right then and there, even though it was picking up speed.

"Yes, it was a fragmentation bomb," continued Rose. "Apparently, according to Ross, quite sophisticated. Yes, everything will be kept under wraps."

Rose made a face with the next question posed to him. "Unfortunately, yes. Well, it might just have had something to do with the file. George and I were meeting with this Randolph fellow we told you about when it took place. And, yes . . . once again, George saved my life."

Rose listened to the phone, the words not quite audible to Thomas.

"Yes, dear, your precious George is fine. Perfectly. Okay, okay, he'll have a bruise in the middle of his back for a day or two. Well, a door hit him. No, really, he's fine."

George rolled his eyes at that comment.

"It's a long story, dearest. We'll brief you when we arrive at the White House . . . yes, I love you too. Goodbye."

Rose hit DISCONNECT and handed the phone back to the silent agent in the front seat who stared straight ahead. Then Rose lay back against the seat and closed his eyes. Thomas noticed that Ross appeared to be whispering into his sleeve again before announcing, "Two minutes to the island airport, sir. The Gulfstream's waiting at the end of the runway, and all other local air traffic will be diverted to Pearson International for the next five minutes."

The convoy bounced over the bridge into the airport, and then sped the length of the runway to where several men in blue, bulging coveralls waited. In seconds, the party transferred to the jet and the plane was in the air, winging itself south across Lake Ontario.

Only then did George Artowski appear to relax. "Bob, see if you can find some good scotch in the bar. I'll have a tumbler full, no ice. I know that you shouldn't drink before noon but the knot in the middle of my back feels as though a moose hit me."

Ross said, "Anything for you, Mr. Rose?"

The president's husband said, "Maybe a small rum and coke, just to settle my nerves and to clean the dirt from the back of my throat. How about you, Thomas? Can Bob get you anything?"

*Thank goodness, we're back to Thomas.* "I'm sorry, sir. I don't drink alcohol, but I could do with some orange juice, if you have it?" replied Thomas, as he just realized he hadn't eaten since the previous evening.

Bill Rose responded, as if again reading Thomas's mind, "Bob, can you also see if we have anything like those little sandwiches I like so much or other snacks in the fridge back there? I just realized that our breakfast is embedded in the walls of our hotel suite."

George chuckled as Bob Ross dutifully made his way to the back of the jet where the bar was situated. Then rubbing the side of his nose with his thumb, he leaned in close to Thomas, who sat wide-eyed opposite him and Bill Rose. "Now then, Right Eminent Knight Thomas Randolph, we have about an hour to kill. Why don't you tell us what you were going to tell us this morning before we were so rudely interrupted?"

# CHAPTER 4

Thomas just sat there and stared at nothing in particular.

George immediately recognized the delayed stress in Thomas's face and moved forward. "Thomas, I know what happened back there is bouncing around in your mind like a ping-pong ball, but I need you to concentrate. The first time something of this nature happened to me, well, I can tell you I soiled myself. There's nothing to be ashamed about . . . you reacted much better than most people would have in a similar circumstance. But I need you to focus right now. We need to understand whether the bomb was an act of terrorism against the United States or if it had something to do with what you've uncovered. Do you understand?"

Thomas mustered up everything he had and stammered back, "Yes, I think so . . . it's just the way your men went about their jobs . . . no emotion whatsoever."

"It's what they're trained to do. They're all ex-Navy Seals, experienced in covert operations." George smiled reassuringly. "Now, back to the business at hand. Thomas, tell us what you've discovered."

Thomas cleared his throat and tried to focus. It wasn't easy, but he began. "Over the past ten years, I've had so much information swirling about in my brain about Masonry that I had to get it organized. My wife, Sharon, suggested I lay it out in book form. I'm sure you know I've written two books, *The New World Knights Templar* and *The Antient Meridians*."

"Thomas," Bill Rose said, "both George and I and many like-minded others have read your books several times over."

Thomas blinked. "Really?"

"Absolutely. The story of Prince Henry Sinclair, the hereditary Grand Master of the Scottish Knights Templar in the late fourteenth century and his supposed voyage to the New World is relatively unknown except in certain inner circles. Your second book, surmising there's a system of 'antient longitudinal meridians' spanning the world and that Sinclair was in possession of this knowledge is just mind-boggling. How on earth did all of this come to you?"

"Well, you'd have to know my background—"

"We do," said Bill Rose. "At school, you went from business, engineering, and architecture to finance and public administration. You have an aptitude for geometry, calculus, and surveying. But what impressed us most was your interest in the arts—classic literature through art history."

Rattled off like that, Thomas thought his education sounded scattered, unfocused. "I guess I'm a sponge of sorts. I see connections where no apparent connections exist.

"When I was thirteen, my great-uncle showed me his Masonic ring. It had a secret compartment with a hidden symbol. The symbol was two intertwining circles forming the *vesica picese*. Within the center fish shape was a carved jewel, a purple amethyst, which resembled the Star of David—the Seal of Solomon. This was set on a pale-blue background, which suggested water."

"Amazing!" George couldn't contain himself. "So, so, after reading a background piece on Sinclair's voyage to Arcadia, you somehow fitted that symbol to a map of mainland Nova Scotia and used it to pinpoint an archaeological site, which has proven to be a Celtic earth fort. And then you determined there are stone circles at this location that would have been used to determine astro-alignments that would have allowed those inhabitants to determine both latitude and longitude. Am I correct?"

Thomas nodded. Just then he felt the plane slowly bank to the left. Bob Ross, who had sat in on the conservation with his mouth half-opened, was now speaking into his shirt cuff once more and then announced, "Gentlemen, please fasten your seatbelts. We will arrive in Washington in exactly four minutes. Mr. Rose, sir, I'm informed that the three of you are due for a private lunch with the president at noon. We're to avoid all press. The motorcade is parked in the hangar in order for your transfer to be unobserved."

Bill Rose checked his watch. "Thank you, Bob. I trust what you've heard here today will remain with you for the rest of all of our lives?"

"So mote it be!" Bob Ross intoned.

"Thomas, this is all very fascinating." Bill Rose smiled as he fastened his seat belt. "We know the best is yet to come, but I want you to spring it on my wife, the president. Understand that she is very much a black-and-white person. The fuzzy gray she leaves to George and me. But before we land, I want you to tell us the punch line. Where is all of this heading?"

Thomas, who had also fastened his seat belt, sat back and cleared his throat. "To be honest and straightforward, sir, I believe I've determined that Prince Henry Sinclair and his followers brought with them the treasure of the Temple to North America. And, I believe, I've discovered the required methodology to pinpoint the exact resting place not only of Prince Henry Sinclair but of the sacred knowledge buried along with him."

"Thomas, how can you be so sure you can find the very spot?" George questioned.

"Because I've discovered the treasure map painted close to four hundred years ago, before the knowledge went underground for good," Thomas stated.

"Did you say 'painted'?" Bill Rose almost choked out the words.

"Yes, painted, and it's been in front of the whole world all this time!"

# CHAPTER 5

The jet-black motorcade pulled up to the east entrance of the White House, and, under close observation, the occupants emerged.

Bill Rose took the steps into the White House two at a time, just to indicate that no harm had befallen him. He knew his wife was monitoring his arrival from the Oval Office. George Artowski moved a little slower, as the lump in his back had stiffened.

Bill Rose was greeted just inside the doors by an impeccably dressed marine lieutenant who sported a chest full of medals, "Good morning, sir, or should I say, good afternoon? I hear your little vacation in Canada went off course a little."

"You could say that, Lieutenant. Any word from Toronto?"

"Everything is secure, sir. Local authorities are cooperating with the construction accident explanation. It's a shame about Webster and Madison though. Both you and Director Artowski should know we've been monitoring the usual airwaves. There hasn't been any mention of the incident or a spike in digital traffic. The Bunker's initial opinion is that neither of you were the intended targets. The forensic guys are working on the make and type of bomb used, but they already knowthis guy was good, whoever he is. The bomb almost totally disintegrated upon detonation, so there's not much to examine."

Bill Rose glanced over his shoulder to make sure Thomas wasn't within hearing distance. "Then it appears as though our guest, Mr. Randolph, may have some uninvited admirers. Do me a favour, Lieutenant? Let's not scare Mr. Randolph, but make sure he's buffered, if you know what I mean?"

"Yes, sir. Of course, sir. We'll make him as secure as a bug in a rug. May I ask who he is, sir?" Lieutenant McCormack looked in Thomas's direction.

18

"Just a nice, innocent Frater who possesses something of immense value but has no idea what's he in for, if you catch my drift?" Bill Rose smiled.

"Yes, sir!" The lieutenant flashed Bill Rose a crisp military salute even though he knew it was unwarranted, as the president's husband held no official status.

George and Thomas had caught up to Bill Rose just in time for the president to arrive.

To everyone's surprise, President Helen Jefferson-Rose rushed over to her husband and gave him a fervent kiss on the lips. Then she turned to George Artowski, smoothed her skirt and assumed her leadership role. "Director, I understand we're in your debt, once again, for sparing me from being a widow while in office. Thank you. You know black makes me look too pale for the cameras."

George chuckled at the quip delivered to lighten the mood. "Madam President, everything is fine. As usual, your husband responded to the moment as trained. That helped. Madam President, we would like to introduce you to Thomas Randolph. He's quite the sharp fellow and has a very interesting story to tell."

The president extended her hand. "Mr. Randolph . . . Thomas," she said with a smile, "I welcome you to the White House. I hope your little escapade this morning with your two fellow knights didn't ruin your appetite. We've set up a special private lunch in your honor in the Green Room.

"Madam President, it is indeed my honor. I hope I won't disappoint you in what I have to say," Thomas said.

"Now, off we go to lunch." Bill Rose said, clapping a hand on Thomas's shoulder.

\* \* \*

The lunch was simply amazing. The lobster was fresh from Maine, along with a crème caramel, Thomas' favorite dessert. *Once again, my file! They must have my complete diet outlined.*

All the while they ate, the president made small talk about everything from the Canadian prime minister to how badly the Toronto Maple Leafs were playing. George even recounted the events of the morning, which now seemed so far away. The service was quiet but efficient, and Thomas hardly noticed when the last plate was cleared from the small round table that had been set up in the Green Room.

The president caught his attention, a cup of Earl Grey in her hand. "Thomas, did you know that Thomas Jefferson was the first president to live in the White House? Of course it's changed a great deal since then. I think that this is appropriate for what we're going to be discussing."

Thomas accepted his cue. "Madam President, I assume you've been briefed to the basic background to the story." The president nodded. "Therefore, I'm sure you know, one of the instructions Jefferson offered to Lewis and Clark was to establish, as accurately as possible, the latitudinal and longitudinal positions of prominent natural features within the landscape, starting at the mouth of the Missouri River where it joins the Mississippi. Outwardly, this is not unusual, as one of the stated purposes of the journey was to be able to construct an accurate map, given the surveying technology available at the time. In fact, Jefferson himself instructed Meriwether Lewis in the art of establishing both latitude and longitude. The striking thing about this is that I independently determined a pattern of 'antient longitudinal meridians,' separated by eight degrees—the number eight actually represents infinity—which span the globe. I've determined many of the points where Lewis and Clark took longitudinal readings and they correspond directly to these meridians."

Thomas took a deep breath and continued, "A number of currently existing communities across North America named Meridian or some derivation of that name—such as Merida, Mexico—continue to mark these meridians, which I used for the title of my second book, *The Antient Meridians*."

The president's eyes widened. "Thomas, how did you come up with the title, *The Antient Meridians*? Did you read somewhere about these 'antient meridians'?"

"No, Madam President," Thomas responded. "I just came up with the term in my head. You see, I just surmised that this was part of the 'antient knowledge' that the Templars discovered under the Temple of Solomon— earlier charts and maps that were highly accurate from latitudinal-longitudinal positioning.

The president leaned back, studying him. Then she laughed. "Well, here's one for the books. Thomas, I'm about to tell you something that you must promise will never leave this room. I must have your word as a Mason, or whatever. I can have you swear on the bible, if necessary."

"Madam President, my word is my bond," Thomas said solemnly.

She leaned toward him. "There's a top-secret, presidential file, first written by George Washington and added to by Thomas Jefferson, who just happens to be my great-great-great-grandfather as well as yours, I believe? Subsequently, small facts have been added by other presidents to corroborate the story. Indeed, it tells the same story you've developed through your two books: That the real Templar treasure, if discovered, contains a large amount of 'antient' knowledge. But Jefferson was unsuccessful in recovering it through Lewis and Clark. He, in fact, suspected that Meriwether Lewis, though he did, indeed, stumble across its exact location, for some reason kept the secret and committed suicide, or was killed, because of it. Now the really interesting aspect of all of this is that Washington first titled the file, 'The Antient Meridians,' over two hundred years ago."

Thomas sat dumbfounded. "They used that term?"

"They did indeed."

"Madam President, I have no explanation for this odd coincidence. The only thing I can think of is that, as I explained to Mr. Rose and Mr. Artowski, these things just keep coming to me out of the blue. It's as if I'm a lightning rod for all of these connections. I've even asked some of the most high-ranking Knights Templar I have come to know, and all they can tell me is that it's in my blood and not to worry about it."

"It's in your blood*line*!" George laughed before exclaiming, "That's an interesting way to put it!"

"Oh, George, stop with all of this holy bloodline nonsense," the president said with mock frustration.

# CHAPTER 6

The three men had ridden hard for close to six hours. They had encountered no one along the trail the entire time. It was as if the whole world had stopped. Even the birds were quiet. The only sound beyond the dull clops of their horses' hooves was the constant pounding of a steady rain through the forest.

Meriwether Lewis, in spite of his bearskin slicker, was thoroughly soaked and miserable. And though he continually drank from the canteen that hung from his saddle, his mouth remained parched and dry. He feared he was getting ill. He was definitely uncomfortable in the company of LeNeuf and St. Jean as they rode staring straight ahead into the darkness. Yet Lewis believed they were completely aware of their entire surroundings, as they should. After all, they were professionals. After a while, traveling with these two men, Meriwether found himself uneasy. There was something almost eerie about the way they traveled the trail, like ghosts flitting through the forest night. His brain slipped into hesitancy. *God, I wish I had never set out to meet with Jefferson.*

Lewis saw a clearing up ahead through the morning mist. He could just make out what looked like a cluster of old barns, which appeared to be completely boarded up.

But as the riders rode into the clearing, the main door to the smaller barn swung open. Several lanterns glimmered, revealing men beckoning them on. They rode directly into the barn, and the door swung shut to envelop them into a netherworld of shadows and flickering light. Meriwether thought it might have looked like they had just disappeared.

Michel LeNeuf was the first to dismount. He handed the reins of his steaming mount to the nearest fellow. He shook the hand of a man hidden by the shadows. "Greetings, Brother," he said, weariness in his voice. Lewis noticed another man beside him stand up. He took his cue to dismount, and was greeted by another dark stranger. St. Jean also dismounted. Their puffing horses were led away to be tended to.

Lewis noticed a dozen other horses unsaddled and tethered in the stalls. Six men tended to the horses, and Lewis noticed that every man sported a military sword. It certainly was not hard to recognize the military toughness that years of war could bring to a man.

"Come, Brother Lewis," LeNeuf said from the darkness behind him. "A special sunrise ceremony within the field lodge of the St. Tammany Lodge No. 29 of Nashville is about to begin. This morning, with the weather as it is, we'll be holding this lodge meeting inside the larger barn."

LeNeuf then clapped a hand on his shoulder and started to lead him toward another door. As they walked, LeNeuf leaned close to his ear and said in a half-whisper, "Please remember, Brother Lewis, what is said this morning in secrecy will determine if we are to take you further on your journey to meet with President Jefferson. Do you have your apron?"

Lewis gave a quick nod and submitted to the pressure on his shoulder and walked on. *So, this is how it's going to work? I'm to be judged if I'm worthy enough to be passed along.* He had the impression his life depended on his answers.

Jean St. Jean appeared at Lewis's other side and patted him on the back as if to reassure him and then said, "Brother Lewis, it is indeed an honor to share this lodge with you this morning. I shall be your guide, if I may?"

Lewis took some comfort in the familiar camaraderie. "Of course, Brother St. Jean. Please lead the way."

The group ran through the downpour to the larger barn. As if by some magical signal, a small door swung open to allow them entry. Once inside, to Lewis's amazement, he saw what looked like a barn built inside the larger barn. Only then did he realize, by the pale light cast by two stationary torches, that the dimensions of the inner barn portrayed Solomon's Temple. Lewis stood for a moment in awe. LeNeuf and St. Jean urged him on.

Lewis had no doubt that only the initiated would make it this far. St. Jean steered him toward one of the doors in the west wall of the inner structure.

After passing through a number of doors, they entered a fully-arranged lodge room with a checkerboard pattern painted on the rough plank floor and an altar constructed of barrels and planks. And, although the room was only illuminated by a few stationary torches, Lewis could just make out three seated figures along the east wall.

"Brother Lewis," one of the three seated men said. "Esteemed Master Mason, we are honored to have you present at this sunrise meeting of a special field lodge of St. Tammany Lodge No. 29, of Nashville, Tennessee, so sanctioned by the Grand Lodge of North Carolina. Officially, we are now known as Harmony Lodge No. 1, sanctioned under the recently formed Grand Lodge of Tennessee. As we are opened in the third degree, I would ask you and your escort to approach the altar, place your hand on the bible and pledge that what we are about to discuss will remain within this lodge, until such time you are able to convey what has been discussed through another lodge."

Lewis started forward, feeling a slow creep of dampness climb his back. St. Jean's hand on his arm guided him toward the altar. As he passed the seated figures, he recognized LeNeuf sitting to the right of the grand master. LeNeuf nodded slightly and smiled. Lewis also recognized the man who sat to the left of the grand master as Andrew Jackson. Jackson also smiled and nodded. The only person who Lewis didn't recognize was the grand master himself.

He attempted to clear his jumbled thoughts. The dark ride, lack of sleep, and prior alcohol consumption in the inn were starting to work on his concentration. St. Jean noticed his uncertain movement and gently lowered Lewis to his knees in front of the altar, placing his right hand on the open bible and compass and square, which lay on top of the altar.

"Brother Lewis, I have been informed by other officers here during this special lodge meeting that you have requested a meeting with President Jefferson. I understand you desire to discuss certain things that are only known to you but which most likely concern the Brotherhood. I would ask that you now share this information with your fellow brothers. It will be kept in the strictest confidence. We will judge how best to help you on your journey."

Time stopped. An angry flush rushed to Lewis's face. He could not believe the treatment these free men were giving him. *They want my secret?*

*It's mine!* Then he had a further thought, and it chillded him. *After everything, they want to keep it buried!*

Lewis's eyes snapped open at this terrifying thought. He jumped up and pointed to the east. "How dare you!" he screamed. "After I spent years of my life half-starved and feverous, challenged beyond all endurance, you dare in the name of the Masonic Brotherhood question my intentions? By Solomon's judgment, I have been an upright Freemason and maintained my life on the square ever since I was first initiated. Now I'm treated like a rank candidate! You ask me to swear on the bible, state my intentions and reveal the secrets only I know!" Now accusatory, he said, "You want the glory! You want the treasure!"

Jean St. Jean wrapped his arm around Lewis in a partial bear hug, but Lewis's arms flailed. He seemed to have gained the strength of ten men and sent the larger St. Jean sprawling.

He turned towards the three seated men and raised his finger in their direction. "And the three of you, like the wise men of old, look to control the destiny of the one person who has found that-which-was-lost." He reached into his pocket and pulled out the knife he had secreted from his trunk before they left the inn.

With this statement, the three men in the east, as if in silent unison, sat upright and quickly glanced at the other brothers in the shadows to determine if they heard the same thing.

LeNeuf knew he had to try to calm Lewis in order to gain what he so badly desired to hear. "Brother Lewis, esteemed Brother Lewis, no one in this lodge room doubts the extreme sacrifices you have made for your country and, while doing so, have brought great honour to Freemasonry. We, who are your Brothers, salute you. But, please, let us help you. What, pray tell, is this demon that chases you?"

Lewis slumped across the altar, his head in his hands. "Brethren," he said from between his hands in an entirely new voice, "I have seen the light. I have been a good man, a good Mason, and a good American, and now I am being asked to reveal a secret that would affect everything. And, you sit here ready to pronounce judgment on me as to whether I can or cannot reveal all. You have no right!" Lewis choked out the last word as a sob.

Andrew Jackson cautiously rose to his feet and approached the younger man, who was still holding his dagger.

Lewis sprang to his feet with the knife in his hand. His eyes had lost all ability to see. His sudden movement took everybody by surprise, even an old soldier like Andrew Jackson.

In a similar movement, St. Jean let the concealed stiletto in his sleeve drop into his palm and swept it upwards, piercing the underside of the chin of Meriwether Lewis, killing him instantly.

The room froze.

St. Jean then deftly yanked the stiletto out and caught Lewis as he fell again across the altar, lowering him gently to the floor.

Many eyes glittered in the low light as every man left their seats and formed a protective circle around the limp body of Meriwether Lewis.

"Brethren!" Andrew Jackson broke the silence, causing a few starts from the assembled men. "Before us lies a great man, a great Mason. Let us not judge him over the last hour but by the deeds he performed throughout a lifetime of service to God and Country, which ultimately led him to us. It remains obvious he was a tormented soul. We ask that the Supreme Being grant him peace." He looked around the circle, meeting eyes.

"I know none of you will reveal what happened here this new morning," Jackson said, a hint of deadly control in his voice. "I also know the president will want the highest honors bestowed upon this great American but we cannot have this morning's ritual linked to his death. Therefore, I suggest that several of us arrange to take the body back to Grinder's Stand and make the death look like a suicide. Brothers LeNeuf and St. Jean, as soon as you're able, please report to President Jefferson that, unfortunately, Brother Lewis has taken what he found to his grave. The middle pillar remains broken. Are we all in agreement, Brethren?"

The circle as one declared, "So mote it be!"

# CHAPTER 7

The president's limousine sat off to one side of the cemetery by itself preceding the state funeral for Michael St. Jean-LeNeuf. Inside sat Helen Jefferson-Rose, her husband, George Atrowski, and Thomas. Continuing an ealier conversation, the president inquired about St. Jean-LeNeuf's family.

"He met his wife, Monique, while he was ambassador to France," answered Bill Rose.

"Did they have any children?" Helen asked.

"Two," Bill replied. "The oldest is a daughter, Marie Magdalene. She's about thirty and a brilliant scholar in medieval history with a PhD from Yale. She chose U.S. citizenship over France. The son is a bit more of a rebel. His name is Jean Baptiste. Now twenty-eight, he became a French paratrooper when he was twenty-one until honourably discharged about two years ago. Rumor has it he may take a run at French politics, since he confirmed his French citizenship. Apparently, he's quite the linguist, fluent in five languages."

Helen smiled sadly and seemed to visually collect herself. "Now, George," she said, turning to the director, "what can you tell me about the French situation?"

George shifted his weight and said, "Certain circles tell us the father and son had a falling out when Jean Baptiste turned twenty-one. It's rumored it was over something within the families' past. Anyways, Jean Baptiste, for whatever reason, rebelled and enlisted in the elite French paratroopers against his father's wishes. Having been through 'Nam, I think Michael came to question the purpose of war. The family has a long military history, stretching back past the first crusades and the formation of the original Poor

27

Knights of the House of Solomon. It certainly is reasonable to conclude this family history is what attracted the daughter to study medieval history but the persistent rumour is the son is heavily involved in a secret society—The Order of the True Rose Croix—although we cannot prove this."

The president once again stared out of the limousine window, now watching the funeral procession of cars approach. "George?" she questioned, as if she hadn't listened to what he conveyed previously. "Could you let your people know we're going to walk from here over to the gravesite? It's such a lovely day, and I hate it when I show up at the last minute, as if the queen is arriving by carriage."

\* \* \*

BILL ROSE, GEORGE ARTOWSKI, and Thomas Randolph took up their assigned positions in the second row just in time to witness the president perform a rather extraordinary feat of personal diplomacy. As the family's limousine pulled up to the adjacent curb, Helen Jefferson-Rose walked forward and seamlessly wrapped her arms around Michael St. Jean-LeNeuf's daughter.

Marie Magdalene was certainly striking. With shoulder-length, dark brown hair and a slim figure, she made the simple, black knee-length dress and matching jacket appear rather elegant. Thomas had pictured a rather dry, scholarly looking woman, but here she was in the flesh, possessing almost Native American features, including a dark-reddish, glowing skin tone. In a very French way, Marie Magdalene swooped in very close and kissed the president on both cheeks.

Bill, George, and Thomas shared a ghost of a smile at the picture the two women made. They chatted for a moment and then reluctantly broke away from one another. Marie Magdalene certainly appeared genuinely touched by the president's condolences. The three men watched in awe as if her grief had been lifted off her shoulders. Marie Magdalene then just as suddenly introduced a man who must be her brother. The nod he offered the president was definitely frosty.

Jean Baptiste was in every inch of his six-foot-two frame a French aristocrat. Slender and tanned, but with broad shoulders and thick, black hair, he carried a quiet but forceful presence. Jean Baptiste turned and looked over at Thomas, standing next to Bill Rose and George Artowski. His eyes were icy and distant.

What he did see were Thomas's eyes meeting Marie Magdalene's. In response, her mouth curled ever so slightly at the corners, as if she was recalling a meeting in a previous life.

As the president moved back to stand beside her husband, she also noticed the rather intimate exchange between Thomas and Marie Magdalene. As a result, it was the president's turn to meet Thomas's eyes with an all-knowing twinkle.

Finally, when everyone was in their seats, the president turned and nodded to the priest stationed at the head of the coffin. The ceremony could formally begin.

It was precisely noon. Thomas let the priest's words wash over him, as he thought about the sunrise ceremony held that same morning. It was a ceremony that he, Bill, and George had all attended, along with several hundred other high-ranking officials representing the seven pillars of the Knights Templar—Canada, the United States, Portugal, Britain, France, Belgium, and Germany. There were also representatives from the sister countries of Sweden, Norway, Denmark, Spain, Italy, and Brazil. Thirteen pillars in all! To Thomas, it was an incredible experience, even though it was a sad occasion.

At that time, Thomas recognized that even though several members of the extended St. Jean-LeNeuf family attended the ceremony and were obviously Knights Templar themselves, Jean Baptiste was not in attendance. What George Artowski earlier outlined about the son, perhaps taking a different path within the True Rose Croix, would certainly explain his absence.

Thomas's thoughts were abruptly interrupted by the barking of orders and crack of rifle fire, as the twenty-one gun salute startled him back to reality.

Afterwards, the crowd broke up, and Thomas found himself following Bill Rose back to the limousine. The president stayed to mingle and offer further condolences, with George staying close to her, along with several of his best agents.

"Well, Thomas," Bill said quietly once they were seated in the limo. "I believe, as Winston Churchill once said, 'Gentlemen, we have met the enemy.' Did you get the sneaking suspicion you've met Jean Baptiste once before?"

"No?" Thomas's head snapped around to meet Bill's gaze. "I've never met him before!"

"Oh, but I think you have," Bill responded slowly. "But that time he was wearing a waiter's uniform and was hunched over." Bill Rose watched Thomas's reaction but before he could reply, the president and then George entered the car and the motorcade moved off without any prompting.

Thomas was simply stunned.

"I thought the funeral was a fitting tribute to a fine gentleman." The president conveyed the sentiment with a bit more formality in her voice than previously. "Wouldn't you say so, Thomas?"

But before he could reply, she continued, "Jean Baptiste is quite the cold fellow, don't you think? Maybe it's his French superiority. He carries it quite well, don't you think? Marie Magdalene told me the St. Jean-LeNeuf family owns a small estate in Virginia, quite close to Jefferson's Monticello, actually. Surprisingly, he invited us all to a small reception there this evening. I'll have to have my office do a mad dash with my calendar but, given the circumstances, I don't think any of us would miss it for the world. George, you can arrange things can't you? I think it should be a very interesting evening."

# CHAPTER 8

The president's motorcade departed the White House at 5:30 p.m. sharp. Everyone seated in the president's armored limousine was dressed rather conservatively for the funeral reception, including Thomas. Though he had come with only the clothes on his back, the White House staff had produced an impeccable wardrobe for him.

As the motorcade made its way down Interstate 66 West, the president turned her attention to the three men accompanying her. "Okay George," she said, "you hinted that you've found some interesting information this afternoon."

"Well, Madam President," George began, "apparently, Major Michel LeNeuf and his adjunct and longtime friend, a Sergeant Major Jean St. Jean, were granted a small track of land by Thomas Jefferson just on the outskirts of Fincastle, Virginia, in 1815 . . . for services rendered."

"For services rendered?" Bill Rose asked. "What on earth would that have related to, do you think?"

"We're not really sure," George said, consulting a folder in his lap, "but it may relate in some manner to Lewis's suicide. Major LeNeuf and Sergeant Major St. Jean reported the death to Jefferson at Monticello in October of 1809. The "for services rendered" tag line was found on the back of the original deed to the property, deposited in the land registry files, which can still be found in the archives of the Fincastle courthouse. The handwritten note found on the back of the deed is, indeed, in Thomas Jefferson's own script."

"Hold on!" Thomas said sharply. "Just who were Major Michel LeNeuf and Sergeant Major Jean St. Jean? They're French by name, but I've never heard or read about them in any of the history books."

31

"Exactly, Thomas," replied George. "The only other place they appear is a brief mention in that highly classified file the president mentioned earlier. At the very least, no other written document with any mention of them exists, at least that we know of."

"Thomas," Bill Rose interjected, "it's speculated that both LeNeuf and St. Jean were not only Masons belonging to the French Blue Lodge but also Knights Templar. So, we're somewhat sure both LeNeuf and St. Jean were young free-thinkers who first fought for the Americans during the American Revolution."

George continued, "We've tried to follow these two across the hidden history pages only folks like us have access to, but we have only come up with faint third-hand references and suspicions that both LeNeuf and St. Jean were not only involved in the American and French Revolutions but also in the War of 1812 between the Americans and British North Americans and Native Indians. They appear to have been the Knights Templar's personal trouble-shooters and secret emissaries at the time in both Europe and North America."

"My God!" the president exclaimed, her eyes wide. "That's a span of about forty years. They must have been over sixty when they received the land grant from Jefferson. The average lifespan was about thirty-five years of age at the time, and they survived at least three major wars and must have also each fathered offspring for the families to intermarry. Incredible!"

"George," Thomas said suddenly. "Would you happen to know the latitudinal and longitudinal coordinates of the St. Jean-LeNeuf estate?"

George took out his BlackBerry, and typed a bit. After a simple Internet inquiry, he received the answer, "The estate is positioned at 37 degrees, 29 minutes and 58 seconds north latitude, 79 degrees 52 minutes and 36 seconds west longitude."

"The Antient Meridians," muttered Thomas.

"Thomas, what did you say?" The president's eyes once again focused on Thomas.

Thomas turned a deep red, as though he had just been caught with his fingers in the cookie jar. "I'm sorry, Madam President. As I suspected, the estate is located along an antient longitudinal meridian. These are the longitudinal meridians—roselines, if you like—were established around the world since before the Great Flood. In the granting of the land by Jefferson to the two French Masons, a clue was being left for any initiate who could recognize the sign. They were telling future generations to follow the antient longitudinal meridians.

Thomas continued, "The pattern is defined through the number eight, with eight degrees, between each meridian. With the estate being located along one of these meridians, it's obvious Jefferson and maybe even LeNeuf and St. Jean knew of the secret pattern and what supposedly lay along one of the roselines."

"Do you think Lewis and Clark discovered what Jefferson sent them to discover?" the president asked, somewhat excited by Thomas's revelation.

"I imagine that only Lewis was really in on the secret, as he was a Mason prior to the expedition, whereas Clark became a Mason afterwards. I think Lewis discovered the final resting place of Prince Henry and the depository of sacred knowledge but I also think he was hugely conflicted because of his Masonic vows, which refer to the ultimate penalty for exposing that-which-was-lost to non-initiates. At the very least, I imagine Lewis recorded in some manner what he found, perhaps in order to return later and to recover it alone. The one thing I know for sure . . . is from Jefferson's instructions to Lewis."

Thomas thought for a second and then started to recite a passage from a letter written by Jefferson to Lewis prior to the journey west. "Beginning at the mouth of the Missouri, you will take observations of latitude and longitude, at all remarkable points on the river, and especially at the mouths of rivers, at rapids, at islands, and other places and objects distinguished by such natural marks and characters, of a durable kind, as that they may with certainty be recognized hereafter . . ."

"Thomas," Bill said, pausing to chuckle before continuing, "I don't imagine you know this, but while teaching at the University of Virginia, I spent a great deal of time going through Jefferson's original letters. And, let me tell you: Jefferson was a prolific writer. A great many of the letters were addressed to his son-in-law, Thomas Mann Randolph. You reminded me of Jefferson himself just then with your train of thought."

"Bill, I think we're going to have to continue this conversation later. We're coming up onto the turn-off." George interjected.

"Yes, I agree," the president said, "no more talk of this until after the reception."

"Thomas," Bill interjected once more. "If I may, I'd like to leave you with a warning . . . Jean Baptiste St. Jean-LeNeuf would not be holding this reception this evening if he's already in possession of that-which-was-lost.

Bill's eyes went steady as he reiterated his point, "Jean Baptiste's attitude toward the president is only being held in check by the fact that he doesn't possess the treasure yet. I'm sure he now possesses more pieces to the puzzle than we do but he doesn't possess, as yet, the key. However, I'm sure he believes we all are on the same trail."

Thomas's eyes grew larger as he took in the implications of Bill Rose's comments.

The president sighed and gently patted her hair. "Ah, Thomas," she said. "I see you're nervous. You should be. With so much at stake, I'd be careful this evening with Marie Magdalene, especially after the way she was eyeing you at the funeral."

# CHAPTER 9

Marie Magdalene St. Jean-LeNeuf was waiting for them under the front portico. The main house, although not as big as Monticello, reflected the neo-classical architecture common to a number of early Virginian designs. However, it was the magnificence of Marie's intense energy and beauty that stood out the most, as she bounded down the steps to personally greet the president and her entourage.

President Jefferson-Rose wrapped her arms around Marie once again and gave her a kiss on both cheeks. "Thank you for your hospitality," the president said. "It certainly is an honor to pay one last tribute to your father. He was such a great man."

Marie responded in kind, her voice almost cracking at the president's sentiment, "You are so kind to have made the trip all the way from Washington."

Marie then seemed to cast about for another subject, and her eyes landed on Thomas and widened as he exited from the limo.

"Marie," the president said, noting Marie's gaze, "I would like to formally introduce Mr. Thomas Randolph, a newly-discovered cousin of mine and formidable student of medieval history in his own way. I do believe that is also your own specialty?"

Marie extended an elegant hand to Thomas and he took it and bowed slightly "Ms. St. Jean-LeNeuf," Thomas said nicely. "It is with such sadness we meet at a time like this. You have my sincere condolences. If I may be of any service, please let me know."

The president took in the scene and quickly moved onward. "Marie, I would also like you to formally meet my husband, Bill Rose, and the director of the Secret Service, George Artowski."

"Gentlemen," she said with a glint of a smile. "It is indeed a great privilege to have two companions of my father present. It would mean so much to him. He could not keep secrets from his only daughter, so I am fully aware of your Masonic fraternity." Her smile took on a slightly angelic quality.

"And, Mr. Artowski, my father told me about some of your shared exploits during the war. You saved him from certain death on a number of occasions. Ah, so much history. Please come into the house. My brother would like to greet all of you."

Marie led them into the central foyer where her brother was holding court with several foreign dignitaries, who widened their circle as the president and her group approached. Jean Baptiste extended both arms as the president approached and smiled broadly. "Madame President," he gushed outwardly, more as a show for the people who mulled around than for the president herself. "It is indeed a great honor to have you grace my sister's home."

Jean Baptiste unabashedly grasped the president's two hands and spread them wide in a grand gesture. "And, may I be so bold to say you absolutely look radiant tonight?"

The president slightly winced at the over-the-top compliment and gracefully extricated herself from his grasp, in an attempt to introduce the rest of the group.

"Yes, yes, of course, welcome gentlemen." Jean Baptiste extended his hand first to Bill Rose and then to George Artowski, who addressed Jean Baptiste, "It's a shame we didn't see you at the private service held for your father at sunrise this morning."

"I'm afraid," Jean Baptiste shrugged, "that I haven't shared my father's penchant for mysteries and the like."

With formal introductions complete, the entire entourage moved on to the majestic east room, which had been cleared of its central furniture for the occasion. The room was laid out proportionately in accordance with the golden mean and most of the floor depicted the checkerboard pattern common to any Lodge room. Great vases of fresh flowers had been placed around the room, as were small banquet tables laden with light food of all kinds. In the middle of the east wall stood three magnificently ornate, high-back chairs with plush red seat covering—a bouquet of red roses lay on each chair.

"The French like to go over the top sometimes to prove their cultural superiority," Marie said, as she effortlessly slipped her arm through Thomas's. "I wouldn't think this is your cup of tea, though, being Canadian? Canadians are much more reserved than Americans, I think?"

"Yes, you're certainly right about that." Thomas said.

# CHAPTER 10

Two of the brethren were busy harnessing horses to the wagon, which would bear Meriwether Lewis's body back to the farm. A third was in the loft scampering for something to cover the body during the journey, just as St. Jean and LeNeuf ducked into the barn and out of the rain.

"Brothers, if you don't mind," LeNeuf said in a hushed tone, "I ask a favor of you. Would you be kind enough to leave us for a few moments, so we can say a prayer for Brother Lewis?"

The men nodded and scuttled out.

"*Mon Dieu!*" exclaimed St. Jean. "What are you trying to do, raise Lazarus from the dead?" For as soon as the three men were out of sight and ear shot, LeNeuf jumped up into the wagon bed next to Lewis's body and began to pat him down.

"Be quiet!" LeNeuf responded. "Didn't you see the way Lewis was fidgeting with his apron all that time? It was as if he was making sure of something! And here it is!"

LeNeuf produced a small packet wrapped in a waterproof skin and tied with thin leather string. The major held it up to the diffused light just for a moment before tucking it inside his own jacket. As he struggled to re-adjust the apron on the corpse, he whispered to St. Jean, "Did it occur to you that Lewis kept a more personal record of his journey, other than an official log? Remember what he said about Clark not being made a Mason until after their return from the wilderness. Meriwether Lewis was a dedicated army officer and surveyor, as well as a Master Mason. He surely secretly recorded what he discovered, either in code or signs and symbols— or more likely, by latitude and longitude."

LeNeuf made one final gesture by wrapping Lewis's stiffening right-hand fingers around a sprig of wild acacia and then beckoned St. Jean to follow. "Come on, Jean, let's get going. Jefferson is waiting for our return to Monticello. There'll be time enough on our journey to examine the packet in safety."

# CHAPTER 11

The corner of the large room provided a tiny place of sanctuary for their quiet conversation. For over two hours, Thomas and Marie talked about the medieval Knights Templar and their real purpose. Thomas was reserved in his comments, but Marie was animated, even speculating that the true treasure of the Templars was the bones of Jesus and his family.

Marie was also certain that with the modern-day science available to determine the DNA of those bones, specific aristocratic families around the world would be able to claim to be direct descendents of the holy family.

Thomas, on the other hand, put forward his theory that the Templars had rediscovered a sacred knowledge, which had been preserved since before the great flood.

"Thomas?" Marie questioned, her eyes dark and brooding. "Do you really think the Templars made their way across the Atlantic and settled in North America, all the while intermarrying with the natives and forming blood alliances?"

"Marie, wherever did you ever get such an idea?" Thomas tried to appear surprised.

"From your books, you silly fool! I must have read them at least ten times."

"I'm sorry," he said, attempting to control his thinking in the presence of such beauty. "Yes, I believe there was two-way trans-Atlantic trade going on between a circle of secret societies and the Native Americans for thousands of years. The idea that the first North Americans crossed a massive ice shield stretching across the Bering Strait is just unfathomable to me. How did those Clovis people survive the frozen wasteland without a secure food supply?

"When I was a little girl," Marie said, "my father told me a story about two of my ancestors who lived in the late eighteenth and early nineteenth centuries. I'd never heard anything about them before. Apparently, they were two soldiers—Michel LeNeuf and Jean St. Jean. Apparently, my two ancestors were Masons and Knights Templar. My father indicated that they were something like secret agents between the French and American governments, always performing rather nefarious tasks because they really reported to an inner Templar circle.

"Anyways, the story is that the two ultimately found themselves out west for several years, where they both took native wives. Upon their return, the families were given this very land by Thomas Jefferson. Ultimately, the two lines intertwined and now here I am!"

Thomas smiled as the pieces started to fit into place. "The funny thing is I have some native blood in me, too. We had always suspected it, my sisters and I, but my mother was too hesitant to talk about it. My mother's family was from the Ottawa Valley, along the Ottawa River, north of the capitol of Ottawa. My mother always had claimed that we were Black French. Have you ever heard of such a term?

"No, I'm afraid I haven't," Marie said.

"Well, when my first book came out, I had to provide a photo for the back cover. I really didn't think anything about it until I got a call from a Native Algonquin elder who was pretty blunt, asking me how I knew the things I wrote about within my book. I couldn't understand what he was talking about. He suggested I was revealing some of their ancient Midi 'win secrets and wanted to know how I came to understand these. I responded by telling him that I had read a lot and had done a great deal of research, but it was primarily related to Masonic and Templar ritual."

Thomas paused, thinking, and then continued. "The long and short of it is I've been going to native ceremonies for ten years now and have not only discovered that my mother was pure Algonquin but that her family had intermarried with the Templars and guided them inland, which corroborates portions of your story.

"Now here's a really interesting thing," Thomas said, staring out through the windows into the night. "The Midi 'win rituals are mirror images of the Templar rituals I've also been initiated into. When I revealed this to the native elders, it blew everyone's mind. The fact that the signs, symbols, and tokens of the Templars were also present within the Midi 'win culture was unheard of before I made the connection."

"Thomas, there's no way they could have developed independently," Marie said. "They have to share a common origin."

Thomas said, "Well, this is what I'm hoping to find. I'm hoping to find the common antient knowledge still protected by the natives Prince Henry Sinclair and his knights found sanctuary with!"

At this moment of realization, they both turned to see Jean Baptiste walking towards them, with the president and Bill Rose next to him. Both the president and her husband had a gleam in their eyes but Jean Baptiste seemed somewhat perturbed. He surely sensed what the two had been talking about for so long.

"Marie, you must not tell family stories to complete strangers, especially authors who more than likely spill secrets without even knowing so." With that, Jean Baptiste pulled Marie to her feet and rather roughly led her away off up the stairs without even saying goodnight.

"I think it's time we headed back to Washington," the president said firmly.

# CHAPTER 12

The drive back to Washington was eerily quiet until Thomas broke the silence.

"Ahem!" Thomas said into the darkness, startling the others, each of whom were deep in private thoughts. "I've been going over my conversation with Marie. The thing that struck me was her comment that LeNeuf and St. Jean retired quite wealthy. This could mean only one of two things: Either they discovered a treasure of some sort that translated into a vast quantity of money, or they were paid very handsomely for keeping something quiet."

"Would that even have been possible, let alone probable?" The president frowned, uncertainty in her voice for the first time.

"Actually, it may very well have been the case," Thomas replied. "You've heard the expression: Let sleeping dogs lie? Well, the strength of the Templars' power came from the fact they were able to blackmail the Catholic Church only as long as they concealed what they maintained in their possession. If it was lost or exposed, then their power would vanish. This is actually what I think happened. As soon as Prince Henry Sinclair sailed with the treasure to America, it was removed from the sphere of European conflict, if you like. The church had effectively driven the secret so far underground and at the same time decimated the Templar ranks that even if for some reason a holy heir came forward with a claim, the Roman Catholic Church could easily dismiss it without substantial proof. Or, better still—just make the whole problem disappear."

"LeNeuf and St. Jean," Bill began quietly, "their true loyalties lay within the inner circle of the Templars—men who had manipulated whole countries for centuries. They would have wanted to possess the treasure but

43

keep it secret. Then they would be able to once again hold it over the church and state. If I have to guess, I would think Jefferson's instructions to LeNeuf and St. Jean were to rediscover the secret and to ensure its safety. Now what better place to ensure its safety than its present resting place, out in the wilderness somewhere, guarded by Native Indians who probably considered it sacred also?"

"It definitely makes sense," George said.

"Do you know what the symbol is for 'peace' in the Algonquin Nation?" questioned Thomas, but to no one in particular.

"The right hand open, palm forward?" Interestingly, it was the president who jumped in and answered.

"No, no, that's what many people consider to be the universal sign. I think that was promoted more through old cowboy movies. In fact, the Algonquin symbol is a white eagle feather with a long thin strip of deer leather, which is dyed red and wrapped around its stem. There you have it—red and white—the colours of the Templars. So, if a group was approached by another unknown group, the holding of the eagle feather was the symbol declaring they come in peace."

"Okay, say you're right," said the president. "Let's accept for the moment that LeNeuf and St. Jean actually uncovered the secret but determined it was best to leave it where it was and to secure it even further. Do you really think they would have been rewarded so handsomely?"

"Helen, if this is true, if they had sworn allegiance to a higher calling," Bill interceded, "then those powerful men who controlled the ultimate secret surely possessed the means to see that LeNeuf and St. Jean were more than handsomely rewarded. The granting of a parcel of land in Virginia at the time would have taken nothing more than a stroke of a pen."

# CHAPTER 13

Thomas slept late the next morning. The bed at the White House was definitely more comfortable than his own. When he did finally awake, the Marine guard at his door escorted him to an adjacent room where he found brunch laid out buffet-style. He fixed a huge plate and sat looking out over the impeccably groomed lawn.

Thomas ate and watched with interest as the president's helicopter landed and four gray-haired gentlemen exited from its interior. He couldn't quite make out their features, but it was obvious they were very special guests, judging by the way the Marines, Secret Service, and White House staff scurried around. What Thomas didn't realize was these four gentlemen represented the world's three greatest religions: Christianity, Judaism, and Muslim. The fourth member of the group was the world leader of the modern-day Knights Templar, a group once again looked to unite the world in peace and harmony.

A knock on the half-open door startled Thomas. Lieutenant McCormack approached. "Are you ready to go, Mr. Randolph?" he asked quietly.

"Of course." Thomas said, smiling back.

McCormack led Thomas down the hallway to an elevator, which automatically opened as they arrived in front of it. Once inside, the doors slid shut and the elevator descended. It was unnecessary to push any buttons because there were none. Thomas was impressed but still tentative.

The Marine Lieutenant ushered Thomas into what looked like a standard boardroom with an oval table and eight chairs that displayed the seal of the United States. The president, who sat at the far end of the table, silently indicated for him to sit at the other end. On the one side of the table, already seated, were Bill Rose, George Artowski and one of the gray-haired gentlemen who had just arrived by helicopter. The opposite side of the table was taken by the other three men. Surprisingly, no introductions were made.

The president started right in, "Mr. Randolph, from your conversation last night with Marie Magdalene, you were able to confirm that the two revolutionary soldiers, Major Michel LeNeuf and Sergeant Major Jean St. Jean, undertook a very important mission on behalf the inner Templar circle, the ultimate result being they retired into relative luxury. Is this true?"

Thomas nodded. "I think what Marie told me verifies there was a longterm strategic alliance between Prince Henry Sinclair's Knights Templar and a specific entity amongst the larger Algonquin Nation, which stretched from the Eastern Seaboard to the foot of the Rockies.

"I can also confirm Jean Baptiste and Marie Magdalene St. Jean-LeNeuf are products of the union between the families of Major LeNeuf and Sergeant Major Jean St. Jean. I certainly now believe these two Templars confirmed between themselves that the secret was secure, so they left it where it was. I imagine, though, they would have taken a few gold and silver trinkets in order to prove that the secret actually existed. A fourteenth-century Templar sword would also have done the trick"

One of the gray-haired gentlemen stirred at the reference.

The president, along with the others, appeared to ignore the reference to the sword and continued unfazed, "George reports to me that Jean Baptiste left the house at 11:00 p.m. and drove to a small private airstrip near the estate," said the president. "His flight plan indicated he was going to New York. George's contacts thought he appeared quite jovial and excited as he raced out of the house."

It was Thomas's turn to react, but, though he opened his mouth, he didn't have time to say anything before George abruptly cut in.

"Yes, Thomas," George spoke up. "I've had a number of men watching the grounds since we left last night. Jean Baptiste's behavior was surprisingly upbeat, and my men confirmed he continued in the same manner when the plane landed in New York around midnight."

One of the gray-haired men interjected, "Mr. Randolph, we've been told you believe you've discovered the Templar map. Would you like to explain?"

"Of course, sir. If the lieutenant would be kind enough to load my memory stick onto the laptop?" Thomas handed his memory stick to the Marine.

Lieutenant McCormack took the small device and loaded it into the computer. "Done, Mr. Randolph." Lieutenant McCormack cracked a smile.

"Okay, Mr. Randolph, the floor is yours," said the president, as she stared at the blank screen appearing on the wall behind Thomas. "But please be direct. I haven't got much time. I don't think any of us do. Riots have broken out in the streets of Jerusalem and other Middle East capitals."

Thomas cleared his throat and started his presentation, "How did royalty and Masons alike hide secrets from the non-initiated over the centuries? They became patrons of the arts and sponsored the painting or litho-printing of several masterpieces that contained secret signs, symbols, and tokens incorporated into them. But the art was good in its own right, put on display and accepted for what it was.

"One of the documents referenced in *Holy Blood, Holy Grail*, written by Michael Baigent, Richard Leigh, and Henry Lincoln, is an inscription found on the gravestone at Rennes-le-Chateau, *Et in Arcadia Ego*, referencing the painting by Nicholas Poussin, and *St. Anthony and St. Paul*, by David Teniers the Younger. These two paintings are two of the main references found within the gravestone inscription.

"According to the authors of *Holy Blood, Holy Grail*, the documents included a number of genealogical charts and Latin texts that contained amazingly complex codes. Now, if you believe the story, the texts were deciphered, along with a rather enigmatic inscription on an important gravestone in the churchyard of Rennes-le-Chateau. The inscription reads in French:

"Bergere, pas de tenation que Poussin, Teniers, gardet la clef, DCXXXI. Par la croux et ce cheval de dieu, j'achieve ce daemaon de gardien a midi: pommes bleues.

"In English it translates as:

"Sheperdess, no temptation, that Poussin, Teniers, hold the key, peace 681. By the cross and this horse of God, I complete—or destroy—this daemon of the guardian at noon: blue apples."

Thomas picked up the remote control to the projector. "Madam President and distinguished guests, the hidden layers of the two paintings, which I am about to show you, depict an amazing level of latitudinal and longitudinal accuracy to an area, which could only be derived from a surveyor who possessed the sacred knowledge in a time prior to the paintings being completed."

Thomas looked around the room to ensure his audience was still interested and then continued, "I propose that these two paintings' compositions were based on information provided to their patrons—the King of France for Teniers, and the Spanish Archduke for Poussin—by early North American explorers. By this time, though, the Jesuits had been sent to New France by Cardinal Richelieu, the ultimate puppet master, and they knew what they were looking for because they bypassed Montreal and headed straight inland to the native villages. Their cover was to convert the savages but the only thing they were successful in giving the natives was a deadly strain of small pox. The Jesuits knew the natives held the key to the location of the Templar secret but it was never revealed."

Thomas pushed the remote's button and the first sequence of slides appeared on the screen. The room was quiet, except for the slight humming of the LED projector. At the same moment, the president got up to leave. "Mr. Randolph, unfortunately, I cannot stay for the history lesson. I must meet with my Joint Chiefs of Staff at 2:30 to be brought up-to-date on the Middle East situation."

Thomas just stood there for a moment, not knowing what to make of the president's hasty exit.

# CHAPTER 14

For four days after taking their leave of Andrew Jackson, LeNeuf and St. Jean took turns sleeping in the woods during the daylight hours and traveling the trail by night.

In Nashville, it was relatively easy enough to make contact with other Masons who offered them food and comfort without questioning their purpose or motives. Once the signs and tokens were exchanged, men of all profession and rank united as one to provide any support requested of them. In this case, LeNeuf and St. Jean were granted lodging in a widow's home.

At noon, they found themselves alone at a dining room table with a hot beef stew and a steaming hot apple pie cooling on the nearby pantry hutch. The widow, whose late husband was a high-ranking Mason, had politely excused herself and indicated she would be out most of the afternoon, so they had the whole house to themselves.

Only after assuring himself that everything was secure did Michel LeNeuf finally take the packet from his jacket and lay it on the table in front of him. Both LeNeuf and St. Jean stared at the packet they had taken from Meriwether Lewis's apron.

"Before we open this packet, we must ask ourselves," said LeNeuf, "is it true or is it false? Does it point us in the right direction or is it meant to throw us off the right path?"

With this agreement between them, Michel LeNeuf unraveled the waterproof packet before him. Inside, they found two folded parchments. As Michel held up one of the two parchments, he whistled. "This is old. Jean, I think I can already say that these are authentic. As to where they lead, that's another matter altogether."

"How can you be so sure?" questioned St. Jean, who was trying to read the parchments upside down.

"First of all, the two parchments are identical in quality and color and contain the same script, which means that they were penned by the same man. Secondly, the first parchment contains the prose Thomas Jefferson made me memorize when we visited in the summer—the same prose he made Meriwether Lewis not only memorize but write down before his departure into the interior. It's in French, which is another clue as to its authenticity. The president referred to it as *Le Serpent Rouge*—The Red Serpent. He indicated he was given a copy in Paris by some mystery man. The prose contains thirteen verses, each relating to a sign of the Zodiac."

"Wait a minute," interjected St. Jean. "I thought there were only twelve signs in the Zodiac?" interjected St. Jean.

"I as well. However, this list holds a thirteenth sign—Ophiuchus, named because he's the Keeper of the Secret. It lies between Scorpio and Sagittarius. Jefferson was told by his mysterious contact in France that the unraveling of the riddle within the verses would lead to the antient secret!"

Jean impatiently reached for the one parchment. "I can't read upside down. Here, let me see it!" Jean flipped the parchment around and held it up to the light.

"I didn't know Meriwether Lewis could speak French. This will take some translating." St. Jean turned the parchment over and upsidedown, as if searching for something. "There doesn't appear to be any hidden symbols or codes. I don't see any watermarks either."

"I think the message is in its text. There's probably a numerical sequence or cadence to the verse. On the other hand, maybe its hidden meaning is on a different level of understanding. Or maybe it's an astronomical chart, for all we know. There are references to historical figures in the seventeenth century. I recognize the classical painter, Nicolas Poussin. I know that his most famous painting is *Et in Arcadia Ego* . . . oh, and Nova Scotia was once known as Arcadia or Acadia.

Meanwhile, St. Jean scooped up the second parchment and was examining it intently. "I think I've found our signs and symbols, even a code."

"Here, let me see it, Jean." LeNeuf gently placed the first parchment on the table and reached for the second one.

"*Sacré bleu!* Lewis outdid himself. I've never seen anything like this. Jefferson will have to translate it. Maybe you were just a little too quick with that stiletto of yours, Jean!" LeNeuf repacked the two parchments in preparation for the end of their journey.

# CHAPTER 15

Thomas had definitely gotten everyone else's attention with mention of the two paintings. He shrugged a little at his own confusion as the first image flashed on the screen, **Poussin's *Et en Arcadia Ego,* 1629** . . . otherwise known as *The Shepherds of Arcadia.*

Thomas started a little hesitantly, "I'm sure you know that art critics generally regard Nicolas Poussin as the greatest neo-classical French painter of the seventeenth century. In 1629, he gained the attention of some very important people when he completed his first version of *Et in Arcadia Ego.* This first painting is an idyllic scene of the three biblical figures who first stumbled upon the empty tomb of Jesus, with Jesus observing the scene from afar. The theme of the painting is that Jesus has ascended to Arcadia, the blessed otherworld of Greek myth."

Thomas pushed the button on the remote control for the projector and the second image appeared. He said, "In 1640, Poussin traveled back to Paris from Rome on the express orders of Cardinal Richelieu, King Louis XIII's right-hand man. After receiving specific instructions from the cardinal, Poussin then painted his most famous version of *The Shepherds in Arcadia,* which you now see on the screen. The woman and the two men examining the empty tomb are meant to represent Mary Magdalene, St. John the Baptist, and St. Peter. The fourth figure, sitting off to the side, clad in white and sporting a crown of thorns, represents the risen Christ.

"The first hidden clue you should notice is that the shepherdess, who appears to be supported by the figure dressed in red and sporting white sandal straps, is obviously pregnant."

"Now here's a really interesting aspect to the painting: I believe it also is a chart going backward in time, and, therefore, should be read counter-clockwise. The kneeling figure, dressed in green, represents Neolithic man, who believed in the forces of nature and earth. The female figure represents the pre-Christian, Pan-Hellenic period when the Egyptians and Greeks worshipped the goddess. Notice that the figure is dressed in the gold of Egypt and the blue of Greece. The third figure, dressed in red, represents the Celts, who originated in the eastern steppes, and who worshipped many gods, especially Mars, the god of war. And the fourth figure represents the Roman-Christian period, as depicted by the white tunics and the veneration of one God."

"Thomas," Bill Rose said, seemingly struggling with what was swirling in his brain. He narrowed his eyes and pointed at the painting in question. "Are you telling us Poussin was not only secretly conveying that he had been given esoteric information, but his painting . . . the painting itself is meant to lead us to the exact resting spot of the Templar treasure?"

Thomas started nodding rapidly. "Yes, sir, . . . yes, sir, that's exacting what I'm suggesting." Thomas grinned. "What we're talking about is the final refuge that Prince Henry Sinclair and his followers established after first landing in Arcadia in 1398 A.D. But let me finish this quickly. I don't want to get off topic because what I'm about to show you is the first part of the treasure map, if you want to call it that."

Thomas flipped to the next slide, and the group leaned forward in anticipation. He waited a few seconds for the full effect to sink in before continuing. Already Bill Rose was looking excited and pointing. Thomas was pleased he had seen the point so quickly.

"What you see here," Thomas said, "is Poussin's painting broken down to its basic outline elements—five, if you like, in perfect harmony in Arcadia, which stretched from Nova Scotia to Lower Quebec by the 1640s. Notice how a modern-day depiction of the area neatly juxtaposes itself in relation to the four visible figures. In one way, it's the alchemical 'completion of the square.' To me, this is simply amazing. Nicolas Poussin definitely achieved a higher level of enlightenment when he developed this painting. The grid pattern equally divides the painting into eight segments, based upon the proportions of the golden mean.

"The horizontal line that divides the painting exactly in half represents 45 degrees north latitude, exactly halfway between the equator and the north pole. The three parallel north-south lines represent ancient longitudinal meridians, separated by 8 degrees. The first meridian, piercing the female figure, the goddess, is located at 58 degrees west longitude and corresponds to the coordinates of present-day St. Anthony, Newfoundland. The second meridian, which splits the painting again in two, allows us to pinpoint the exact center of the painting, corresponding to the latitudinal/longitudinal coordinates for Prince Henry Sinclair's secret refuge in Nova Scotia. And the third longitudinal meridian at 72 degrees west longitude divides the Christ-like figure and locates him on the St. Lawrence River at Montreal and the Isle de Jesus.

"But this is only one of many pieces to the puzzle. What the Poussin painting depicts was the geographical information available at the time, as presented to the King of France by Champlain. By 1632, Champlain had developed an alliance with the Algonquin Nation, allowing him to travel and explore an area west to the eastern edge of Lake Huron, which you will notice as corresponding to the left or western edge of the painting. Here's the 80 degree west longitudinal meridian."

"Thomas, if I may," Bill interrupted, "can I suggest we take a break and have supper in the Green Room in order for us to absorb what you've just shown us?"

"Yes, absolutely," Thomas responded without hesitation. He knew he needed some time to get his remaining thoughts together.

# CHAPTER 16

Jean Baptiste St. Jean-LeNeuf lay back on the plush sofa and sipped his champagne. The elegant surroundings of the suite reflected the best New York City and the Plaza had to offer for someone of his stature.

Lounging around the room with him were Jean Baptiste's most trusted friends and comrades, all ex-paratroopers and French patriots.

They were the brightest and the toughest, and all firm believers in the resurrected Ancient Order of the True Rose Croix.

Jean Baptiste knew things were starting to come together and that his personal sacrifice had been well worth it. *Slipping the stiletto into my father's ear really cleared the way. He just couldn't accept the facts, but now I am the last remaining guardian of the sacred knowledge.*

For a moment, the rush of power and the simplicity of his discovery turned his face red. Not to mention there were several young and beautiful women curled up next to him on the oversized sofa.

One of the leggy, blonde beauties was Jean Baptiste's fiancée, Michele Laguarde, who purred as she basked in Jean Baptiste's glow, "*Mon Cheri*, please tell us again what you've discovered."

The room full of people seemed to hold a collective breath. Even the two young men who sat at a nearby table, cleaning their automatic pistols, paused to listen. Jean Baptiste had told the story many times previously, but its fascination never dulled.

"My two ancestors, Michel LeNeuf and Jean St. Jean, were more than just comrades-in-arms." Jean Baptiste smiled and settled into the familiar words of this tale. "They shared *l'esprit de corps*, the spirit one can only share after having saved each other's life. Once you do this, they say your life belongs to the other."

All of the ex-paratroopers nodded in unison.

"But these two men not only shared a life together, they shared a common ancestry, for they represented two branches of the same ancestral tree. They were of the true Rose Croix. Because of this sharing of blood, they were entrusted to carry out the inner circle's quest to once again recover the Templar treasure."

"But we must remember that there is treasure, and then there is *real* treasure. In this case, it is the antient knowledge that is the real treasure—knowledge first realized centuries before the Great Flood—knowledge that will allow the inner circle once again to control the three greatest religions of the world."

Jean Baptiste's eyes took on the cold steady intensity of the assassin he truly was. "And those few unwilling to conform to this new world will once again feel the wrath of God!

"Coming full circle," he continued, standing up and meeting eyes with every man in the room, "we know for certain Jean St. Jean and Michel LeNeuf were members of a number of secret societies, each possessing different clues to the puzzle. Indeed, Thomas Jefferson possessed the genius to fit most of the puzzle together and was the one who instructed St. Jean and LeNeuf to secure the final resting place of the sacred vault after Meriwether Lewis rediscovered it. Unfortunately, Lewis did not understand its true meaning outside of his basic Masonic teachings and looked to use it as a bargaining chip with Jefferson. But St. Jean silenced him before he could reveal that-which-was-lost. St. Jean and LeNeuf then confirmed the location of the vault and, with Jefferson, determined that it was safe where it lay until a more appropriate time."

"But here's the most interesting part of this history: My two ancestors didn't tell Jefferson exactly *where* the vault is located. Instead, they produced just enough evidence to assure Jefferson that it *did* exist. As Jefferson was content with this outcome, he granted them land in Virginia and made sure they were handsomely rewarded. And when the time is right, as secretly decreed by the inner circle, the direct descendants of these two men will take their rightful place as the possessors of this treasure and become one of the most powerful families in the world!"

# CHAPTER 17

T he seven men enjoyed a wonderful dinner in the Green Room. The two hours it took for the meal to be completed passed quickly, and Thomas found himself refreshed when they returned to the boardroom and ready to continue with his presentation.

As the lights dimmed once again, Thomas started to speak from the half-shadows. "I left off describing how I developed a longitudinal and latitudinal grid pattern relating to Poussin's most famous painting and how it pointed exactly to the geographical location of the first refuge of Prince Henry Sinclair and his followers in Arcadia—Acadia. It appears this refuge was too exposed to the agents of the Church, and it caused the Knights Templar to move inland, establishing temporary sanctuaries in relation to the antient meridians. In most instances, it's logical to assume these settlements related to existing Native Indian encampments at the time, as the Templars and their entourage were passed from one Algonquin tribe to another. Of course, this happened over many generations."

Thomas clicked the remote control and a new painting was displayed. "This is the painting entitled *St. Anthony and St. Paul*. It depicts the story of the two original monastic priests, St. Anthony and St. Paul, who took to the Egyptian wilderness in the fourth century in order to find the true meaning of God. The official Church-sanctioned version of their lives conveys how the purity of their thoughts was sustained by the raven, who once a day delivered manna from heaven." He used his pointer to indicate the raven arriving.

"So, Thomas," Bill Rose said slowly, "how does the Teniers' painting relate to the latitudinal and longitudinal positioning you discovered in the Poussin painting?"

"Here," Thomas said. The next image showed the same painting with a grid superimposed over it. "Here we have the second latitudinal and longitudinal pattern. I know you might not see it yet, but this painting actually covers the territory of the larger Algonquin Nation, from Nova Scotia and the eastern seaboard to the foothills of the Rocky Mountains. The longitudinal meridians extend from the right edge of the painting, which relates to 56 degrees west longitude, with the present-day St. Anthony, Newfoundland, located in the upper right-hand corner."

Thomas pressed the "forward" button on the remote control once again. "This next slide reduces Teniers' painting to its basic outline elements like I showed with the other painting and inserts the Poussin piece of the puzzle into the larger picture. Poussin's earlier painting, centered on Acadia and New France, fits perfectly, once the grid pattern and relative scale is established."

Murmuring had begun around the room. Everyone easily recognized the eastern seaboard of the United States, along with the Great Lakes and the Mississippi and Missouri rivers.

"My God!" exclaimed Bill Rose. "It's right there! It was there all the time. Right in front of us! This is simply amazing!"

"I think, gentlemen, we have just witnessed pure genius," said the gray-haired man who sat off by himself, a man known simply as James. "This is the application of the two basic tenets of Freemasonry—sacred geometry and moral allegory—on its most perfect level, in perfect harmony with one another. Thomas, I commend you."

Thomas smiled and thought, *I think the Supreme Grand Master of the Inner Council just revealed himself to me.*

"I just want to ask one last question, Thomas," George said. "Exactly seven days from now, a solar eclipse will travel across North America. Do you consider it a sign of sorts?"

Thomas held George's eye contact for a moment, and then took a deep breath. *How did he know? How did he put it together so fast?*

"Yes," Thomas said slowly, "it will allow us to pinpoint the exact location of the vault of sacred knowledge. Seven days from now at the time when the sun is at its meridian, twelve noon, I'm expecting that the source of an underground stream will be revealed, *if* we are in the right location."

"Thomas," Bill Rose said, "I seem to sense you know exactly what is to be found and how it can be found. Is this true?"

Again, after a moment's hesitancy, Thomas nodded and said, "Yes, I suspect that I do."

James then pulled a sheet of paper from his suit pocket and handed it to Thomas. "Then I want you to have this. It may just help you in your quest."

# CHAPTER 18

J ean Baptiste sat at the breakfast bar in the suite watching CNN. On the counter were the two original parchments and horse-skin wrapping of the Meriwether Lewis packet. Once sharp and crisp, the parchments were now brittle and yellowed, though the skin had maintained its softness. But the script wasn't faded, even though each generation of his family had examined the parchments hundreds of times over the years.

Jean Baptiste was still mesmerized by the clues they contained.

His all-too-familiar sinister smile formed as he sorted out the past few days' events in his mind. *Thanks to Mr. Randolph's obsession with my sister, Marie, we now have confirmation of our family's entire story.*

As Jean Baptiste took a sip of the steaming, thick espresso he had just prepared, he studied the second parchment. He had the first one memorized in both English and French—Le Serpent Rouge—and knew he would recognize the physical and metaphysical clues contained within the verse when he encountered them. But the second parchment was different. As far as he surmised, no one presently living had been able to fully decipher and locate the eight symbols lying in sequence across the parchment. But he was sure that if anyone could, it was Thomas Randolph.

As Jean Baptiste was pouring himself another cup of the fine Moroccan brew, there was a soft knock at the suite's door.

He tightened his robe and ran his hands through his hair as he walked over to the door. Without first confirming who it was by peering through the peephole, he undid the latch and swung open the door. "Dear sister, do come in. You are right on time, as usual. So predictable!"

Marie Magdalene, looking very chic for so early in the morning, embraced her brother and kissed him on both cheeks. "I see our father's

59

death has not affected your plans at all," she said, holding back her own wicked smile.

"Have you heard the news about Jerusalem?" he asked.

"Of course," she responded, as she took a seat at one of the breakfast stools. She noted the two parchments spread out on the breakfast island's surface. "I see you're still deliberating over those. Have you come any closer to deciphering the exact position of the vault?"

"Yes, big sister," Jean Baptiste said, as he mockingly grabbed his sister's arm."I've discovered a new key to deciphering the signs and symbols of the second parchment."

"Really? Tell me, what is it?" Her voice filled with a mixture of excitement and skepticism.

"Big sister, it's quite obvious. It's your new friend, Mr. Randolph."

Jean Baptiste winced at his own joke, as he continued to prod his sister's arm with his right thumb. "Please tell me, though, that you're not developing a genuine affection for someone close to twice your age?"

Marie Magdalene yelped just slightly as he applied greater pressure. "Don't be silly. Blood is thicker than water. Now tell me everything about Jerusalem. And let go of my arm!"

"The riots are growing ever worse. Our hired Palestinian agitators are certainly earning their money this time. Robert is performing magnificently, as usual; but enough of this!" Jean Baptiste waved his free hand in the air in a gesture of dominance. "I want you to understand that Mr. Randolph is completely expendable, as soon as he provides us with the information we require to finish our quest."

Marie Magdalene glared at him. "You promised you wouldn't hurt him. He's just a nice man who recently lost his wife. He's curious, but I don't think he knows anything really beyond what he's already written in his books."

"Ah, now, Marie, that's for me to decide. You play your part in this, and do what I say, and everything will turn out fine."

Marie, rebellious at his words, turned away, but he grabbed her arm in the same place as before, adding to the bruising already starting to appear.

# CHAPTER 19

O nce he was back in his room, Thomas stared for nearly five hours at the piece of paper handed to him before he fell into an exhausted sleep. Yet he was neatly showered, shaved and dressed when Lieutenant McCormack knocked at exactly 0800, as if his senses were kicked into overdrive.

As before, Lieutenant McCormack guided him through the labyrinth of corridors to the elevator.

Thomas's stomach dropped as the elevator—with no buttons—descended once again. Lieutenant McCormack led the way into the boardroom, where only Bill Rose and George Artowski were present. Both of them were dressed rather casually in jeans and flannel shirts and looked as though they were about to embark on a fishing trip.

Bill Rose stood and greeted the two men, "Thomas, it's good to see you this morning. As you can see, the president is occupied, but she wishes us well on our little quest, while the other four gentlemen have left to fly to Jerusalem to see if they can help with the Middle East crisis. I don't think that Dunk—Lieutenant McCormack—has filled you in on what's been decided?"

Thomas shook his head. *Lieutenant McCormack is now called Dunk? He appears to have taken on a different level of importance.*

Bill Rose was obviously in charge of the mysterious mission. "Well then, Lieutenant McCormack, why don't you go change into some less-obvious civilian clothes while George and I fill Thomas in on the last-minute details?"

Dunk spun smartly on his heels to leave, but not before he shot Thomas another wicked grin.

"Thomas," Bill Rose laughed in response to the lieutenant's theatrics before continuing, "whether you like it or not, you have been conscripted into what we are calling the *Templar Express*."

George Artowski rolled his eyes. "Thomas," he said, "I can see by the look on your face that you're worried. There's no need to be. We're on our home soil and have the best in electronic surveillance and security backing us up. We can't have a platoon of army specialists running around the United States digging holes in every state, can we? No. As far as anyone who encounters us is concerned, well, we're just a bunch of fraternity buddies out for some R and R and fishing. Even the president's husband and her director of the Secret Service need some down time, right?"

"The only problem is we don't know where to start our knights' quest." Bill said. "But we all think that you do."

"Can you call up my PowerPoint presentation once again?" Thomas asked.

The task easily completed, Thomas started, "This is a painting completed by Good King René D'Anjou in the 1400s, titled *The Green Knight*. The King was obviously privy to a great deal of underground information relating to the Templar treasure. It depicts two knights on their Grail quest, one standing at a stone marker denoting an underground stream, the other lying on the ground, a tree in front of him. In effect, his body is bisected by the tree, suggesting one of the penalties that we as Masons recognize for revealing a secret. As you can see, the scene also depicts an eclipse along the center of the painting—a meridian of sorts.

"Gentlemen, here we find several clues as to how we're going to trace the antient meridians and what they're going to lead us to."

"But Thomas, where do we begin?" asked George Artowski impatiently.

Thomas laughed out loud. "At the St. Jean-LeNeuf estate in Fincastle, of course! I don't know if you noticed, but there's an obelisk in the middle of the front yard pond. I believe it's the first clue St. Jean and LeNeuf left for us to follow. Of course, it's a meridian marker."

# CHAPTER 20

The contrast of the large black and white horses was easily recognizable by Thomas Jefferson as he stood on the front porch of the magnificent estate. He smiled and sighed in relief. He shielded the setting sun from his eyes with his hand as the two riders pulled up in front of him. "Gentlemen, you are indeed a sight for sore eyes. I'm most anxious to hear your report. But first I suggest you take a moment to wash up and collect your thoughts." Jefferson then ushered them into the house, where they were greeted by servants who saw to their immediate needs.

While the president waited patiently in the drawing room, he lazily poked at a small fire burning in the hearth with a brass poker. He looked up and smiled as the two companions quietly entered the room and hour later. "Well, Major LeNeuf, Sergeant Major St. Jean, I see the two of you clean up rather nicely. I imagine it will take a few days to get the grit out of the back of your throat after your long journey?" He waved them to seats.

Major LeNeuf, ever impatient, jumped right in with his information. "Your instructions were to find Captain Lewis," LeNeuf said, "to assess his mental and physical state and then to determine whether it was prudent to guide him back to Monticello. Is this correct, Mr. President?"

"Yes, yes, of course. And what condition did you find him in?" The president leaned in towards the pair, quietly anxious to hear the result of the knights' journey.

"Captain Lewis appeared to be possessed, either by the alcohol that clouded his brain or by some other demon that haunted him. We were on his trail for some time and finally tracked him down at Grinder's Stand in Tennessee. We had been informed earlier that it was his intention to travel to Washington with information in his possession concerning something

63

discovered during his journey with Clark. We tried first to calm him and then encourage him to come with us and arranged for his belongings and horse to be prepared for the next morning. It was the very same night, October 10th, which I am sad to say, he took his own life."

"I was afraid of this," Jefferson sighed.

Major LeNeuf paused and then withdrew Lewis's packet and placed it on the table. "We recovered this from, of all places, a hidden pocket sewn into the backside of Lewis's Masonic apron.

"Fascinating!" The president was indeed intrigued by what lay before him. He, however, did not touch it.

"May I open it, sir?" LeNeuf asked.

"By all means, Major LeNeuf."

LeNeuf untied the leather packet and spread out the two parchments on the table, making sure they faced the president so he could examine them. "I'm sure you'll recognize Captain Lewis's own hand, Mr. President? The first parchment is, of couse, the prose you had me memorize before we left for our journey—Le Serpent Rouge."

The president nodded and then picked up the parchment and examined it, holding it up first to the light of the lamps. St. Jean chuckled. "That's exactly what I did when I first saw the parchments, Mr. President. Unfortunately, we can detect no hidden signs, seals or tokens. By this, we assume the clues are in the directions referred to in the verse."

The president gently placed the first parchment down on the table and picked up the second one. It displayed a mathematical or symbolic progression. As he had done with the first parchment, the president leaned back and held the parchment at an angle above his head to catch the most light. The contents of this parchment appeared almost transparent.

"This is a complicated lunar-solar sequence charting both the movements of the moon and the sun in relation to one another! I taught Meriwether Lewis myself to calculate the lunar distances in order to establish longitudinal meridians. This is a multi-level code, which symbolically and mathematically illuminates the antient meridians established long ago across North America. The chart must be read from right to left, from east to west. The 'M' at the lower right, therefore, stands for meridians, while the 'D' on the lower left suggests degrees. I can't quite understand the meaning of the letters positioned under each meridian—O., U., O., S., V., A., V., V. Gentlemen, we have a riddle on our hands."

The president certainly displayed a level of esoteric knowledge unknown to either knight. But they were confused.

"Mr. President," St. Jean questioned, "are you telling us that you can't completely decipher the parchment?"

"Exactly, Sergeant Major St. Jean," Jefferson sighed. "However, I know a man who will definitely be able to help us. He's in Montreal at this moment, though."

The president appeared to be weighing something in his mind.

"I know I've asked the two of you so many times over the years to risk your lives in order to further our cause of justice and freedom, but I'm afraid I'm going to have to ask you once again. The gentlemen's name is Monsignor Lartique. He's the head of the St. Sulpician's in Montreal. Will you consent to the journey?"

LeNeuf and St. Jean looked at each other, paused for a moment, and then nodded in unison.

"Mr. President," LeNeuf said formally, "it will indeed be our honor and our privilege to serve you."

"You must be in a position to locate the vault on exactly September 17, 1811, as a solar eclipse is predicted for that very day across all North America. I think this is the meaning of Lewis's eighth and last symbol. This gives you roughly two years to rediscover and trace the meridians to the west. I'm positive that Monsignor Lartique will point you in the right direction."

# CHAPTER 21

**8:00 P.M. • SIX DAYS AGO**
**JERUSALEM, ISRAEL**

Archeologist Philippe Chevalier didn't care who paid for his services, as long as he was able to retain the academic rights to any of his digs within the Old City of Jerusalem.

And so it was when he stumbled upon the old Templar tunnel, which ran directly under the Dome of the Rock. He couldn't believe it at first but later confirmed the Templar signs and symbols, which led him beyond an ancient underground cistern into the bowels of the Temple Mount itself. The relics that presented themselves for his taking would establish him as a pre-eminent medieval scholar to the world, and their monetary value was beyond comprehension.

Luckily, he was able to keep his latest find to himself, or so he thought. In this manner, he was extremely surprised when a young man visited him in his Paris apartment one evening.

The young man possessed a haughty, aristocratic air about him, yet treated the professor with distinction and honor. Open to flattery, it didn't take long for the young man to cast a spell upon the professor, regaling him with stories of his own ancestors' Templar history. The young man spoke of how the professor wasn't given the professional recognition he truly deserved because of his sometime-dubious sponsors. Then the young man offered Chevalier a small fortune for just showing a friend the tunnel.

The professor agreed happily and made arrangements to meet the friend, Robert Dumas, at his apartment in Jerusalem in two weeks' time. However, on the night of his return to the Old City, prior to the pre-arranged date, he opened his apartment door to find the strapping, young initiate standing there. Rather surprisingly, he was dressed in typical Israeli army gear with a high-powered sniper rifle and a heavy backpack supported by a large aluminum frame strapped to his back. "*Bonsoir*, Professor," he pronounced in a thick Parisian accent. "I am Robert. Are you prepared to go?"

"Robert, you seem to be early. I thought we were to enter the tunnel tomorrow evening?"

"The Palestinians have created a nice diversion over the past few weeks. The riots in the streets are forever escalating. If we wait until tomorrow evening, we may not be able to enter the tunnel undetected."

"Then isn't it dangerous to be out in the streets?" The professor was openly agitated.

"Don't worry. I'll be able to handle anything we encounter."

The professor seemed to calm down after Robert's assurance. After all, Robert's mysterious friend with the odd glasses had already paid handsomely for the professor to be Robert's guide.

"In that case, let me get my supplies." The professor quickly made his way into the apartment's bedroom and returned looking like an overweight Indiana Jones, complete with a worn, salt-stained leather hat and coat, and carrying a small knapsack over one shoulder.

Over the next hour, they made their way on foot into the Old City via the eastern gate. Robert presented such a formidable presence he was non-ceremoniously waved through the many checkpoints the Israelis had established in an effort to prevent several small groups of roving Palestinians to come together. For all intents and purpose, it appeared that Robert had been assigned to protect the professor, as he made his way to his latest archaeological dig.

The professor was certainly well-known in this area. It appeared to be common knowledge that the archaeological team headed up by the professor had recently made a number of new and exciting discoveries underneath one of the older homes, located within the Arab neighborhood of Silwan in annexed East Jerusalem.

It was also common knowledge that the Old City Imans and Keepers of the Dome of the Rock were paranoid of any archaeological digs in and around the mosque. Indeed, it was generally believed the professor's discoveries were somehow the cause of the general unrest Jerusalem was presently experiencing.

It was shortly past 2130 hours when they arrived at the unlit, now-vacant home.

The only security for the entire site was the front door lock and a large padlock on a sturdy iron gate, which had been secured to the basement wall.

The first part of the tunnel to the cistern was rigged with electric lights, but afterward, in the still-secret tunnel, glow sticks were required. Over the past few months, experts had marveled at the cistern and its intricate system, not thinking to look beyond. Fortuitously, it was the professor who accidently discovered the false wall late one night when he leaned against itl only to find that it was positioned on pins to swing outward.

Finally, they stepped into the central cavern and both of them fell silent. The powerful glow sticks cast a myriad of greenish shadows and diffused light off the limestone walls and ceiling. The cavern itself was empty but the long-ago polished-marble floor still showed a fantastic inlaid mosaic of a Templar cross. It was obvious this cavern once held something of immense spiritual value, judging from the skeletal remains of the thirteen knights who still solemnly guarded the cavern from their individual, man-made grottos.

Robert crossed himself instinctively in silent deference to the ghostly warrior-monks before unfastening his knapsack and setting it at the heart of the cross. The professor's eyes widened as Robert removed a device and placed it on the floor. The device was clearly a sophisticated miniature bomb—a weapon of mass destruction of some sort.

"What's going on here, Robert?" shouted the professor, his voice echoing in the cavern.

Robert ignored the professor and worked on the timing device, even as the professor struggled to stop him. It was probably the only courageous act the professor attempted during his entire life. As Robert let the professor spin him around, the ex-paratrooper extended the silenced gun, which had been hidden in the front of his knapsack.

# CHAPTER 22

**12:00 P.M. • SIX DAYS AGO**
**THE WHITE HOUSE • WASHINGTON, D.C.**

The two white vans pulled out from the White House at high noon like two conestoga wagons heading west. In the lead van, *Templar Express 1*, Thomas sat in the passenger seat with a sleek new laptop with roaming Wi-Fi capability on his lap. Driving the lead van was an amazingly relaxed Lieutenant McCormack, while Bill Rose and George Artowski occupied the middle seats.

Dunk looked as though he had just stepped out of a fishing magazine. He sported a fly-fishing vest, plaid shirt, the latest wrap-around sunglasses and a Minnesota Vikings ball cap. The funny thing was the lieutenant actually was from Minnesota and had spent his youth fishing and hunting.

Following at a remote distance was a second white van. However, it didn't have the wrap-around tinted windows like the first, because it served a different purpose. It was the group's communications center and, as such, housed a variety of the latest military grade equipment, including a small arsenal of weaponry.

Secret Service agent Danny Bishop was driving *Templar Express 2*, all the while mumbling to himself. He had grown up in New York City and was completely out of his comfort zone on this adventure. Beside him, riding shotgun, was Bob Ross, who constantly pressed the ever-buzzing earpiece deeper into his ear, trying to keep in constant contact with the Navy Seal teams shadowing the small convoy. *Some fishing trip! We're exposed out here like sitting ducks.*

"Thomas," Bill Rose asked, as the small caravan started moving, "please tell me why we have to recreate Lewis and Clark's journey. Why can't we just fly to the site you've pinpointed?"

"Well, I could tell you it's the journey itself and not the end result that's important, but I imagine George would shoot me for that." Thomas looked squarely at George through the rear-view mirror and smiled.

"But the real reason is we have to re-collect and re-assemble certain signs, signs necessary to open the vault."

Everyone in the lead van seemed to understand and nodded.

"There's just one problem," Thomas said.

"And, what's that?" Bill Rose retorted.

"Well, according to the diagram James gave me, Fincastle lies on the fourth meridian, so, we've skipped the first three signs," he said sheepishly.

"Wait just a second, Thomas!" George was clearly beginning to become agitated. "Are you telling us we've skipped over the first three stages of our journey even after you just told us that we have to duplicate the stations?"

"Please don't worry too much. I'm pretty sure I know what the first three elements and their signs are. They're on the paper James gave me. I just need to find the fourth element, or its sign, at the St. Jean-LeNeuf estate in order to verify my hunch."

"Thomas, I swear . . ." George's temper subsided a little before demanding, "If you don't prove your hunch . . ."

"Give Thomas a break, will you, George?" Bill interjected, trying to lighten the mood. "We're all Masonic Knights Templar here. On the other hand, it would be a shame to disappoint the president of the United States."

At that revelation, Dunk cast another of his wicked grins at Thomas, as though to say he was extremely happy he wasn't in Thomas's shoes at this moment.

"Listen, here's what I know." Thomas recovered nicely. "The four figures of Poussin's painting are the first four elements, earth, wind, fire, and water, with the unborn child of the shepherdess as the hidden fifth element."

Thomas pulled up Poussin's painting on his laptop once again and held it up for the occupants in the second row to see, "Okay, remember that this painting was created on many levels. Starting with the pregnant shepherdess, she represents the element water, and the 56 degree longitudinal meridian.

"The knight in red—the figurative fire element who's somewhat hiding behind her but also supporting her, represents the first Templar settlement located at the 64 degree longitudinal meridian splitting Nova Scotia. The figure in white, the Christ-like figure who represents wind, is located at the 72 degree longitudinal meridian, which splits the Isle de Jesus—the one-eyed island, in Montreal, in the middle of the St. Lawrence River. And, the fourth element, earth, represented by the kneeling Green Man, is located at Fincastle, Virginia, along the 80 degree meridian."

"Okay, Thomas, we're with you so far," Bill Rose acknowledged, trying to ease the tension a little.

"In order to expose the hidden fifth element, represented through the coming together of man and women, which creates the unborn child, all four elements must line up in harmony. We find the child along the 88 degree longitudinal meridian." Thomas then flipped over to David Teniers's painting of St. Anthony and St. Paul. "And here we have St. Anthony and St. Paul, the sixth and seventh elements who represent logic and reason and the relative 96 and 104 degree west longitudinal meridians. Only when we can align the seven elements in their perfect alignment both metaphorically and physically, will the eighth element, the 112 degree longitudinal meridian expose that-which-was-lost."

"Thomas, are you telling us the Templars ultimately sought refuge among the Native Americans in the foothills of the Rockies?" George had finally come around to Thomas's thought process.

"It's exactly what I'm telling you."

71

# CHAPTER 23

Thomas stood at the edge of the oval pond at Fincastle, staring intently at the obelisk positioned in the centre of the front-entrance pond when a black BMW pulled into the driveway.

Marie Magdalene exited the car, took in the scene and rather too-innocently exclaimed, "Thomas, what on earth are you doing?"

"Well, I was certain this obelisk has some sort of sign or symbol carved into it." Thomas scratched his head as if in deep thought.

"I'm sorry . . . what's going on here?" Marie's voice sounded utterly bewildered.

Thomas glanced over her shoulder to where Bill Rose was standing. Bill gave a slight nod, as if to say it was okay to tell her everything—well, almost everything.

"Marie, you'll remember our conversation the other evening about your ancestors, Major Michel LeNeuf and Sergeant Major Jean St. Jean, and how they received this piece of land?"

She nodded.

"Well," Thomas continued, "I believe they rediscovered the Templar treasure transported by Prince Henry Sinclair to the New World and secured its final resting place. As a result, they were handsomely rewarded for that final deed by an inner circle of the Founding Fathers. Because of that, they were able to live out their lives in relative luxury right here. This estate lies on one of the antient meridians I've identified. I was positive this obelisk marked the meridian and would lead us to the next marker. I tried to call and get permission to come, but they said you were out. We came anyway, and now it appears I've got it all wrong. I hope you don't mind us showing up the way we did?"

"Of course I don't mind your arriving unannounced. And you weren't that far off the mark after all!" Marie glowed.

"Marie," Bill Rose said, "what do you mean?"

Although Marie directed her answer to Thomas, the answer was really for everybody's benefit, "Thomas, you've been reading too many books about lost symbols, obelisks, and Washington conspiracies. The solution to your problem is so simple . . . you should have asked where Michel, Jean, and their families are buried. That would have told you what you need."

Thomas smacked his forehead with his right palm. "Marie Magdalene, you've been playing all of us for fools! Where is the family graveyard?"

She pointed. "Out back in the forest on top of the hill."

With this revelation, the entire group took off around to the back of the house, where Marie showed them the well-worn path leading up to the wrought-iron fenced graveyard.

There they found about twenty-five gravestones lined up in rows of five from east to west, and each was adorned with a flower vase and fresh cut roses and small patches of red cloth for the native graves. There were fresh offerings of tobacco, sage, and cedar on top of them, along with circles of sweet grass. Obviously, the graves were lovingly kept.

Marie knelt down in front of the first row of five marble gravestones and crossed herself. "Gentlemen, please meet Major Michel LeNeuf and his wife, Marie, and their stillborn son, Michael, along with LeNeuf's longtime friend and companion, Sergeant Major Jean St. Jean, and his wife, Angelique."

The men were mesmerized. It was the lieutenant who broke the spell by quietly whispering, "Earth to earth, dust to dust."

"What did you just say?" Bill Rose questioned in a loud voice.

"Earth to earth . . . don't you get it?" Lieutenant McCormack said. "Here are Thomas's fourth and fifth elements. They're buried in the earth. The stillborn child amongst them is the fifth element, the essence of God if you like, created through peace and harmony between a man and a woman. And, five markers all in a line, going from east to west."

"And here I thought marines were only blunt objects? Lieutenant McCormack, you amaze me sometimes!" George Artowski laughed.

"Be quiet, you two!" Thomas demanded. "I'm trying to concentrate and prove to Marie that I'm more than just a pretty face."

Marie moved to his side and stroked his arm in response to his remark.

Thomas then read the markers, one by one, "Here lays Major Michel Charles LeNeuf—Gallant Knight – August 3, 1750–August 8, 1822 – Beloved Husband of Marie – As above, So Below . . . Here rests Marie – Cherished wife of Michel LeNeuf – Of the Blackfoot – died August 8, 1822, while giving birth to Michael . . . Here lays Michael – beloved son of Michel and Marie LeNeuf – born August 8, 1822–died August 8, 1822 – May the Spirit of God be with you . . . Here lays Sergeant Major Jean Baptiste St. Jean – Gallant Knight – December 14, 1850–December 21, 1830 – Beloved Husband of Angelique – As Above, So Below . . . Here rests Angelique – Cherished wife of Jean St. Jean – of the Blackfoot – died August 25, 1870, St. Louis."

Upon reflection, he commented to no one in particular, "It's interesting Major LeNeuf died on the same day his wife did, following the birth of her stillborn son. It's pretty amazing both of the men lived so long."

"Hold on a minute . . . there's something odd going on here." Thomas was scratching his head. "Marie, how could the two families have intermarried if Marie LeNeuf died in childbirth along with her child?"

Marie again crossed herself, almost subconsciously this time, before answering, "There was an identical twin, the first born by a minute or so. His name was James Louis. He married Jean and Angelique's daughter, Catherine Marie. From that time forward, the family name became St. Jean-LeNeuf. The grave markers of Jean and Angelique's five children—Martin, Louis, Marie Anne, Marguerite, and Jeanne—form the second row of markers. My brother and I and our spouses will occupy the sixth row with our mother."

Bill Rose pondered for a moment and then commented to Marie, "Angelique must have been quite young when she married Jean Baptiste St. Jean, to have lived until 1870?"

Marie Magdalene knew the comment was thrown out as bait, but she took it anyways, "Actually, I came across some old records suggesting she was eighty-eight years old when she died."

"Hold on, Marie. Are you saying Michel was seventy-two, Jean was eighty, and Angelique was eighty-eight when they died? The next thing you'll be telling us was that Marie was sixty-four, reflecting four of the antient meridians longitudinal location in degrees west . . . no, that can't be right. She died at a young age during childbirth. Right?"

Marie gave one of her wicked smiles. "Yes, the birth and death dates have always seemed a little odd, compared to what little records we have of the front row. There really isn't much to go on, other than the dates that you see here. We've tried to find out more, but it's like Michel and Jean just appeared in France one day out of nowhere, although the LeNeuf and St. Jean families can certainly be traced back to the First Crusade and earlier. A lot of birth certificates were lost during the French Revolution. Of course, there were only oral records among the Native Americans."

"The clues are still there, carved in stone," Thomas chirped in. "The French King, Louis IX, a Capet, led two crusades and was the patron saint, Saint Louis, of a number of things, including the crusaders. He actually died in the Holy Land of dysentery while leading the Seventh Crusade."

The rest of them nodded. This was known information.

"You know I am a professor of medieval history," Marie said. "I have to tell you before you ask the obvious that the king was born on April 25, 1214, and died August 25, 1270."

Thomas had no idea he had just been manipulated for a second time. "Hold on. Angelique's date of death is reflective of Saint Louis's death, just 500 years apart. I'd be really surprised if she died in St. Louis and not here at the estate. Whoever was responsible for her grave marker was paying tribute to the Crusader King. I have a feeling Major LeNeuf and Sergeant Major Jean St. Jean left definitive instructions as to what Angelique's grave marker would say, regardless of when she died, or where. They're probably all rolling around in their graves right now laughing up at us."

Bill Rose had been quiet and taken in the whole scene but it was his turn to ask a question. "Thomas, why would you say such a thing?"

"It's because Angelique, even in death, is telling us where to go next." Thomas stood there and pointed west, feeling more and more like a fool in front of the crowd as the silent seconds passed. "Don't you remember the Teniers's painting? At exactly the center of the painting, lies the 88 degree west longitudinal meridian bisecting the small cross of Jesus, which rests atop the rock, along with a skull. Of course, this represents Golgotha, the 'place of the skull,' where Jesus was crucified, just outside of the Old City of Jerusalem. Well, gentlemen . . . and lady . . . we need to head west to a place named after another king, St. Louis. I happen to remember I read somewhere that Lewis and Clark first believed the mouth of the Ohio River at the Mississippi fell along the 88 degree west longitudinal meridian. More likely, it related to the St. Croix River, which flows southerly through Minnesota from the western tip of Lake Superior. It really doesn't matter at this point."

George Artowski remained quiet, studying the interaction between Marie Magdalene and Thomas. In George's mind, he believed that what had just transpired between the two was just too bloody convenient. But he kept his thoughts to himself for the moment.

Bill Rose slapped Thomas on the back. In return, Thomas beamed like an idiot. Marie was beaming also but for a different reason. *Bravo, Thomas. Keep following my lead and we'll be there in no time! It's up to you to pinpoint the exact location of the vault, though.*

"Gentlemen, in light of the hour," Marie said, "may I suggest I arrange for an early supper here at the estate and then we can be off by 7:00 p.m.? By my calculations, if we take turns driving, we can probably make St. Louis by 7:00 or 8:00 in the morning. This will give Thomas enough time to figure out where exactly we should be looking for the next marker."

Nobody seemed to dispute Marie's assertion that she was now part of the quest. Alternatively, she debated about showing the group the backs of the five gravestones. If they had bothered to stop and think, they might have thought of looking for themselves. What they would have found carved into the stones in the proper order were the first five symbols of Lewis' second parchment. Marie just shrugged as they made their way back down the hill to the house. *Silly boys . . . playing a game they don't quite understand. Oh, well, some secrets are better left unrevealed!*

# CHAPTER 24

**6:00 P.M. • SIX DAYS AGO**
**THE PLAZA HOTEL • NEW YORK CITY, NEW YORK**

Jean Baptiste anxiously waited for his BlackBerry to ring as he and Michele sat at the suite's bar. He was nursing his Napoleon Brandy. Michele knew enough not to disturb him when he was like this. She knew he would relax after he received the eagerly anticipated call and only then could they enjoy the rest of the evening.

In fact, he had already received one call this morning and another one this afternoon, which kept him satisfied up until now. The second long-distance call had been from Robert's scrambled phone in Jerusalem, so there was no probability of being overheard.

Now he waited somewhat impatiently for the third call of the day from his sister, once Marie knew the intentions and timetable of the esteemed group of knights. They were taking a calculated risk, he knew, but he needed the expedition's timetable in order to put his own shadow team in motion. From a military perspective, he knew the advantage of knowing the enemies' schedule, to be one step ahead of them all the way to the very second Thomas pinpointed the exact location of that-which-was-lost.

Indeed, Jean Baptiste was picturing the little pipsqueak and his fellow knights being blown away by Jean Baptiste's paratroopers when his BlackBerry rang. Michele jumped at the sound, but Jean Baptiste remained calm, first verifying the caller and then pressing the button to receive. "Hello, big sister! Did you get the information?"

Marie Magdalene sounded calm but a little out of breath. "Yes, but I haven't got much time. I told them I had to powder my nose. Now listen carefully . . . I innocently as possible exposed the graveyard clues to them, so they would actually think that they solved the riddle. As we planned, all of us are now off to St. Louis, driving through the night in order to arrive early in the morning. They appear to accept I'm going along. With a little gentle prompting, I'm sure that the good Mr. Randolph will uncover the next marker. If everything goes well, I suspect we will arrive at the 112 degree longitudinal meridian some five or six days from now, giving Mr. Randolph plenty of time to fix the exact location of the vault and to await the eclipse. Your team will be ready?"

"Of course. I'll see to it personally." Michele could see the tension leaving Jean Baptiste's face. "What about their security?"

Marie thought just for a second before answering, "If you exclude Director Artowski, there are three others, a smartass marine lieutenant and two quieter Secret Service agents. But there's also a shadow team—Navy Seals, I suspect. They must be somewhere out there in the dark."

Jean Baptiste was elated at the news. "You've done well, now take care and be mindful. We are so close to the prize I can taste it." With everything in motion according to plan, Jean Baptiste terminated the call and turned to his fiancée, "Michele, my darling, you're as jumpy as a cat on a hot tin roof this evening. I apologize but I must call together the team for a short briefing. Then just the two of us will go out and have a fabulous meal and maybe some dancing. Afterwards, I will have to see what I can do to sooth your nerves. I can think of a few different things right now but I'll wait and surprise you."

# CHAPTER 25

Monsignor Lartique was almost hallucinating as his feet shuffled through the gently falling snow, making their own way through the deserted streets back to the relative comfort of a small fire and a straw bed.

The monsignor's thoughts slowly drifted across the deep snow. *Thank God for small mercies! My simple dwelling is at least more than half of what the occupants of Montreal will have this evening. I will pray for their souls and ask God why He has forsaken us.*

If the monsignor wasn't half-starved himself, he would have appreciated the harsh beauty around him. The moonlight was shining off of the hard-packed snow, and the frost that clung to everything shined and sparkled. Even the mist from his breath enveloped his head and created a halo-like glow, as he reached the seminary and fumbled for the large skeleton key to the side door.

That's when two ghostly apparitions appeared out of the frosty mist. The relatively smaller one extended his hand in comfort and said to the priest in Old French, "Here Father, let me help you with your key. It appears as though your hands are frozen."

The father sighed and gave in to his dreams. Before him stood two rather large and gruff voyageurs, all decked out in layers of rough spun wool and soft buckskin. He envied their heavy fur mittens and fur caps and outer woolen coats, fastened with the common red sash. The one noticeable difference with these two ghosts was the paleness of their skin and sunken eyes. If these two ghostly beings before him were indeed real, their skin would have the darkened, leathery look of those who spent most of the year on the rivers and lakes of the wilderness.

The priest stumbled, attempting to cross the threshold. This time, it was the other ghost who helped him, taking his arm and gently guiding him to the simple chair beside the unlit hearth. The ghost exclaimed, "*Sacré bleu*, he is half-dead. I'll see to the fire, Michel, while you do what you can for him."

The ghost named Michel knelt before the priest and dipped his hand into the deerskin pouch which hung from his shoulder. He produced a thick piece of salted deer meat and handed it to the priest, who wrapped his hands around it and brought it to his lips. "Ah, I can taste the salt," the priest whispered, as if to confirm he was still alive. Michel then produced a soft-skinned flask and held it up to the priest's lips. "Here Father, drink this! It's apple cider mixed with wine to prevent it from freezing. I believe the saints will forgive us for drinking alcohol, as this season has produced the most snow and cold I've ever seen."

The priest switched to English upon hearing this. "Ah, that explains it. I was wondering how you and Sergeant Major St. Jean were going to cross over from the south. The St. Lawrence River must be completely frozen over." Monsignor Lartique's mental faculties were coming back as he thawed.

The sergeant major was getting the fire going but stopped when he heard what the priest said. "You know who we are?" he questioned.

"Yes, I received a coded message from Thomas Jefferson to expect you. He described the two of you pretty accurately, right down to the sunken eyes and pale skin. If you want to continue to pass as voyageurs, I suggest you rub some dirt on your faces." Lartique certainly had an inner spirit to him, even though he was half-starved.

Major Michel LeNeuf laughed out loud. "Father, that's a good suggestion. I must say that the voyageur's winter garb is quite warm. It's no wonder they look the way they do."

The priest gently replied, "Yes, but the one thing they don't carry is a Templar sword. I suggest you leave those here if you want to go anywhere in the city. The English sentries are quite efficient and well trained in spotting things out of the ordinary."

Michel continued to chuckle. He immediately took a shine to the priest. "That's good advice. Jean and I will take it under advisement. I see you recognize the Templar sign of the cross on my sword's handle?"

"Yes, Sir Knight, I do indeed." The priest felt a little bit more refreshed after the food and drink. "Here, if you would continue your kindness, I will ask for your help in seeing me to my meager bed and blanket. I apologize, but I must sleep. We will talk about the things you desire to learn when I am stronger."

\* \* \*

MICHEL AND JEAN LET THE PRIEST sleep for twenty-four hours. It was obvious he was suffering from mental and physical exhaustion. But when he finally woke, it was as though a burden had been lifted from his shoulders. Although still physically weak, his mind had once again returned to its razor-sharpness. The physical weakness was due to the lack of food, Michel told himself. The two Templars also easily recognized why Thomas Jefferson instructed them to see this man. He possessed an inner spirit and strength that only came from a person who possessed a higher level of understanding and knowledge.

Besides, both the major and sergeant major enjoyed the opportunity to relax and contemplate their journey together. The only thing concerning them was that they left their horses with a fellow Brother who ran a stable in upper New York State. They assured themselves, however, as they sat at the small table in the kitchen area, that they would be well taken care of while they traversed the frozen St. Lawrence.

Their outfits and snowshoes also cost a fair amount, but the gold and silver sewn into their heavy wool shirts like a knight's armor was more than enough. Michel had even ventured out while the priest slept and stocked up on food for at least a week. Not to attract attention to himself, he left his sword behind and had rubbed some red clay, mixed with black dirt, all over his face. The major even consented when Jean suggested he buy some heavy rum cake, maple sugar squares, and a malted wine in celebration of Christmas.

Back at the seminary, both Major LeNeuf and Sergeant Major St. Jean were pleasantly surprised to see Monsignor Lartique walking towards them without any assistance, although it was quite evident he was still weak. Major LeNeuf stood to assist the priest, who accepted the major's chair, the one closest to the fire. "My friends, I am indeed in your debt. I'm afraid if you did not show up when you did, I might not be sitting here looking forward to celebrating the birth of Our Savior. I see the two of you have been hard at work in making the seminary a little bit more comfortable."

Major LeNeuf smiled at the priest. "Father, it's indeed an honor and a pleasure to serve you in your time of need. Sometimes the Supreme Being has a funny way of providing for those who provide for others. If I may ask, where are all of the other priests and servants?"

Monsignor Lartique returned the warmth of the major's smile and nodded as if in agreement. "When I learned you would be appearing around this time, I sent everyone away on assignment."

Jean St. Jean had been busy, filling up a big bowl of hot potato stew. It was full of big chunks of potato and deer meat, along with some turnips, all of which the major had purchased at the corner market. He plunked the bowl in front of Lartique, who gratefully accepted it. All three went quiet, as the priest said a silent prayer and then dove into the soup. The two knights looked at each other and shrugged, as though to say they might as well join him, since they realized they wouldn't be able to get a word in while the stew was so hungrily devoured.

Once everyone was satisfied, Major LeNeuf took the Lewis packet from his inner shirt and placed it on the table. Michel then untied the skin and carefully unfolded the parchments and laid them side-by-side before the priest. Monsignor Lartique's eyes narrowed to slits as he considered what he was looking at. He then held the two parchments up to the light of the fireplace, searching for any hidden codes or watermarks. As none was evident, he put the two parchments down on the table and closed his eyes.

Jean looked at Michel with an inquisitive nod, who reciprocated in the same fashion. The answer, when it came, was earth-shattering.

Monsignor Lartigne opened his eyes, which were slightly moistened, and addressed his visitors, "I have been waiting for this moment all my life and now it's arrived, I can hardly find the words. So, please bear with me if I stumble a little . . . what I'm about to tell you must remain with you well past your deaths. Agreed?"

Major LeNeuf spoke for both of the knights, "Father, you have our absolute trust as Knights Templar."

"This second parchment is the more interesting one to me. I understand it was created by Meriwether Lewis during his expedition to the

Pacific. I'm sure you were told by Jefferson, if you didn't know it beforehand, that it's a multi-layered lunar-solar chart depicting the distance of the moon and sun at the antient meridians, which extend across North America?" Monsignor Lartique held the parchment as though he half-expected the various stages of the moon to jump off the page.

Jean interjected, "This much we know Father. What we don't know is the mathematical sequence and the resulting coordinates depicted by the letters."

"Ah, then you'll have to remain as my guests at least for another twenty-eight days. I'm going to have to teach you how to track the stages of the lunar cycle and how to measure its distance and the distance of certain stars and the sun in order to calculate longitude and latitude. I can already tell you the third circle in the chart falls across Montreal. By the time I'm through with you, if you are good students, you'll be able to follow this chart to the exact location of what appears to be the final resting spot of Prince Henry Sinclair and that-which-was-lost. I would be most proud if you take along my sextant for that historical moment."

# CHAPTER 26

Thomas Randolph woke with a fright. *Where am I? What's going on?* Then he heard an angel's voice quietly say, "Good morning, sunshine! It's about time. I thought you would sleep through the whole night." It was Marie Magdalene's voice, coming from the driver's seat of *Templar Express 1*. Thomas faintly remembered her taking over the driving duties from Dunk around midnight.

They had departed from the St. Jean-LeNeuf estate right at 7:00 p.m. the previous evening. It was obvious this was no fishing trip as they seemed to be working to military precision. The small convoy, consisting of the two vans, had first headed west and now was traveling on I-64, just about to make their way out of Indiana and into Illinois, on their way to Missouri. In the middle row slept both Bill Rose and George Artowski, looking quite comfortable in their captain's chairs, and tucked into the fetal position across the third row bench seat was the marine lieutenant, looking rather content. Marines possess a habit of being able to sleep anywhere.

Following the taillights of *Templar Express 1*, but keeping its distance, was *Templar Express 2*, with the coffee-laden Secret Service agents Bishop and Ross, blurry-eyed but forever alert.

Thomas rubbed his eyes and finally came awake enough to ask Marie, "You okay? I could drive if you wanted to sleep."

Marie turned her head sideways to face Thomas for a split second and fluttered her eyelashes at him. "No, I'm fine. What I need you to do, now that you're rested, is to think hard about where we should stop in St. Louis. Come on, Thomas. Think! Where do we go next?"

Thomas raised his eyebrows in response to Marie's rather abrupt command. "I'll fire up the laptop. It always helps me in my thought process."

Thomas first tapped the combination of words into the search engine, "St. Louis, latitude, longitude," and then read the results out loud, "38 degrees, 38 minutes, 53 seconds north latitude, 90 degrees, 12 minutes, 44 seconds west longitude. Hmmm, this is interesting. St. Louis and your estate at Fincastle share roughly the same latitude but we're two degrees beyond the 88 degree west longitudinal meridian. Where did you say we are, Marie?"

"We're coming up to the border of Indiana and Illinois, at a small place called Grayville. We first have to cross over the Wabash River."

"Wait, slow down for a minute." Thomas became quite animated. "Stop at the side of the road at exactly where we register 88 degrees west longitude on the GPS."

Marie did as she was told, first crossing the bridge over the Wabash and then pulled into a hotel called the Windsor Oaks, which was very close to the interchange. Thomas busily typed away at his laptop, calling up several Internet sites, saving the ones he believed to be important.

By this time, both Bill Rose and George Artowski were awake and trying to take in what was happening. Bill Rose spoke up first. "What's cooking?"

Marie responded, "I'm not quite sure. Our amateur Sherlock Holmes is acting as though he just had a sudden revelation."

Meanwhile, *Templar Express 2* pulled in behind the first van. Both men had caught the conversation via the hidden intercom and Bob Ross had hopped into the back of the second van, hitting "record" on the bank of electronics sitting in front of him. He also notified the Navy Seal teams of what was happening, "Seal Teams 1 and 2, please hold your position. Situation is normal. We're just allowing our hound dog to follow his nose. I repeat, hold your position."

Somewhere in the dark, two non-descript, white cube vans pulled off to the edge of the highway, not noticing the shiny new black truck and trailer blowing past them.

Everyone was waiting for Thomas's mind to unfold. "I think I've got it!" he quietly exclaimed.

"Got what, you ninny!" George Artowski did not like to be wakened from his dreams, especially when he didn't absolutely control the situation.

He spied the Windsor Oaks Hotel illuminated sign. *Boy, what I would give for a hot shower and warm bed right about now.*

Thomas ignored George's comment. "Let me try to consolidate all the connections. First of all, we have Lewis and Clark hooking up at roughly the spot where we're presently sitting. The Wabash and the Ohio converge just a stone's throw from here. Why did the French secretly position a trading post and then a fort at the spot they did? Because it fits the 88 degree west longitudinal antient meridian the Indians instinctively recognized as one of nature's powerful forces! Secondly, the latitude reflects a tangent running due west from the Fincastle estate to St. Louis, forming a cross of sorts. Thirdly, when I search the surrounding area, I see a number of things labeled with the 'oak' name, which suggests that a prominent stand of oaks was at one time sitting on the banks of Wabash River, acting as a signpost. We are sitting here in front of the Windsor Oaks Hotel. The Oakgrove Cemetery isn't far away. Jefferson's instructions to Lewis and Clark were to observe and record all prominent natural formations that would still be recognizable to future explorers. The key here is that natural formations and old oak stands don't really move. Granted, the oak stands may get harvested eventually, but we're talking centuries and they regenerate themselves. Anyways, one of the most dramatic natural formations on the Wabash River is a limestone formation known as the Wabash Hanging Rock. It's a National Natural Formation Landmark. All of the clues point to this spot as being one giant signpost."

Bill Rose scratched the stubble on his chin. "Okay, Thomas, I'll give you there are a large number of coincidences, but all of it is still pure speculation. How can you be sure it means that we're on the right trail?"

"Well, here's the kicker. Think back to the David Teniers's picture of St. Anthony and St Paul. The exact middle of the painting falls right on the 88 degree west longitudinal meridian. It also bisects a rather large rock with a smoothed surface, which supports an hourglass, a skull, a cross depicting the crucifixion of Christ, along with three small bottles of liquid. I happen to think that the bottles represent the convergence of the three rivers, the Ohio, the Mississippi, and the Missouri. We've determined that the name 'St. Louis' harkens back to the sacrificed crusader king, Saint Louis, where Lewis and Clark started to time their movement west in accordance with the sun, moon, and the stars. The shaped stone upon which Jesus' crucifixion occurred was Golgotha—'the place of the skull.' George, can you tell me what the predominant stone the Temple of Solomon was made out of, which naturally occurred at Golgotha, and which forms the predominant stream bed to the Wabash River; and which extends all the way to St. Louis? It's quite evident in the hanging rock, where we have another reference to deathly torture."

George had given up at this point trying to refute Thomas's summations. "Limestone! Okay, you've convinced me, Thomas. But where to next, Einstein?" George portrayed a gruff outer manner but deep down inside he was continually amazed at Thomas's logic and reasoning.

"We head due west along I-64 until we get to St. Louis where, I suggest, we stop for a nice breakfast. Then we'll check out the Lewis and Clark Interpretative Center, which is positioned quite close to the site of Camp Dubois, where Lewis and Clark spent the winter of 1803, waiting until the ice thawed on the Missouri River the next spring. This is their official point of departure."

*Templar Express 1* and *2* moved out in tandem. Bill Rose yelled to the back of the van, "Dunk, you lunkhead, wake up, we're almost there!"

Marine Lieutenant McCormack sat up wide awake and ready for action, asking, "Did I miss anything?"

The rest of the van's occupants broke into laughter.

# CHAPTER 27

The two white vans containing the group of seven stopped at a large truck stop just outside St. Louis on the east side of the Missouri River. It was Marie Magdalene's two-sided suggestion that they try to blend into the native scenery by eating at a real American truck stop. So, as the vans pulled up in front of the diner and stopped, Lieutenant McCormack donned his Minnesota Vikings ball cap and ambled into the diner to check it out, while the others stayed in the vans.

Thomas was amazed at how Dunk assumed the exact persona of a Minnesotan outdoorsman. Both Bill Rose and George Artowski had donned their fishing vests and fly-fishing caps while still in the van, but everyone knew they would still stand out to a certain degree amongst the truckers who were coming and going.

Dunk casually came ambling back to the van and stuck his head in the passenger window. "I think we shouldn't have much trouble in there if we keep a low profile. Mr. Rose, if I may, I suggest you keep your hat pulled down, though I'm sure most of the truckers will be paying full attention to Ms. St. Jean-LeNeuf and couldn't care less who's with her. I also suggest you also wear your hat and jacket, Ms. St. Jean-LeNeuf. Some of these guys look like they'd just love to throw you in the back of their trucks for the rest of their trips, if you know what I mean? Now a really nice young waitress by the name of Sally is saving us a large table in the back corner. Man, I tell you, I could learn to dig this life."

Everyone laughed at Dunk's comments, and then proceeded to enter the diner and quickly make their way to their table without attracting too much unwanted attention. Thomas even brought his laptop along in order to continue unraveling the puzzle.

St. Louis, some two hundred years after the Lewis and Clark Corps of Discovery, was still the gateway to the west, and the number of eighteen-wheelers running idle in the massive parking lot attested to this. This was exactly the beauty of ex-paratrooper Angel Hollande's scheme. While his ex-paratrooper companion, Godfroi Beaufort, drove ahead in the small black van containing the main communications hub, a larger tractor-trailer perfectly blended in with the interstate traffic. As a result, amongst several hundred anonymous rigs, a brand new, all-black eighteen-wheeler sat idling while its driver had breakfast inside. The odd thing about this particular truck was that within its trailer a team of French ex-paratroopers lounged away the time by monitoring the conversation amongst the group of seven, thanks to the tiny transmitter sewn into Marie's jacket.

The beauty of the whole scheme was that none of the occupants of the two white vans, nor the two white cube vans shadowing them, had any idea what the black tractor-trailer was really up to. Angel even added himself to the ruse by indulging in his passion of driving the big rig. It was no surprise to any member of the French team when he suggested he assume a position at the diner's counter before the two vans arrived. He had used the excuse that he needed to size up the immediate opposition. Besides, he was thoroughly enjoying the Hungry Trucker Special—two eggs, an eight-ounce steak, hash browns, and all of the coffee and toast he could wash down. He knew the others back in the truck were equally enjoying their fresh croissants with fruit and jam and thick Moroccan coffee, but this was heaven to him.

What he didn't know was that the thick, muscular trucker with the Green Bay Packers' cap who sat three seats down from him also had an interest in the fishing party sitting in the far corner. Phil Bloomer was in reality a Navy Seal lieutenant, originally hailing from Dallas, Texas, but who was now assigned to NAB Little Creek.

It had been George Artowski's idea to have two levels of Seal teams shadow the *Templar Express*. The two Seal teams and their white cube vans parked out front were supposed to be just conspicuous enough to lull the opposition into a false sense of superiority. The real fire power sat in their own red and white eighteen-wheeler parked some ten rigs down from the French one.

Director Artowski had previously learned this little trick while in Vietnam. It was a real-life cat-and-mouse game. Artowski definitely knew Marie was wired for sound. What he didn't know yet was where the enemy was hiding, but he had surmised that the first shadow team would eventually draw them out. What they in turn didn't know was that a second shadow team would pounce once they exposed themselves. Anyways, this was the plan.

The pretty twenty-something waitress, who had immediately taken a shine to Lieutenant McCormack, ambled over to the group with a fresh pot of coffee after she saw them put down their menus. "Hi there, my name is Sally. Welcome to the gateway to the west. Can I take your order?"

The lieutenant assumed his role perfectly. "Now, Sally, what's a pretty girl like you doing in a greasy place like this?"

Sally blushed before responding, "Well, I'll tell you." Her eyes locked onto Dunk's. "I've actually been accepted into the Master's of Business Administration program at Ohio State but took a year off so I could pay for it. I can make three times the amount of money just on tips here than I could working in some office in St. Louis. Besides, you meet the most interesting people at these truck stops. You'd be surprised at the background of some of these guys. I could write a book with just the one-liners I hear all day."

"Is that so?" Dunk laid it on just a little thick, but the waitress didn't seem to mind. "I imagine someone as pretty as you receives a lot of intriguing proposals? Anyways, I propose we all have the breakfast special, with lots of toast and juice and keep the coffee coming. We've been driving all night long, as we only have a few days to catch some big ones. Thank you, Sally."

As Sally made her way back to the counter, both Bob Ross and Danny Bishop laughed and shook their heads in unison. Marie even got into the act by quietly saying, "Smooth, real smooth, Dunk. I imagine you go over big in places like Iraq and Lebanon? If I wasn't so hungry I'd also chastise you for being so presumptuous in ordering for all of us."

Dunk threw his hands wide and responded, "Ms. St. Jean-LeNeuf, one thing I've found in my travels is that any lady, no matter their nationality, loves to be complimented. Is this not so, Mr. Rose?"

Bill Rose had watched the exchange with a certain admiration for the younger spirit. "It works for me every time, Lieutenant."

This unexpected comment certainly lightened the mood around the table. Even Director Artowski had no immediate complaints, since he knew that even though the lieutenant was acting like a buffoon, he was constantly scanning the dining room, as were Bob Ross and Danny Bishop. George Artowski had recognized Phil Bloomer at the counter, in spite of the greasy long hair and scraggly beard, though he was careful not to make any sign of recognition.

At the same time, Thomas was listening to the exchange around the table while trolling on his laptop. He stopped, however, when he came to the official website of the Camp River Dubois historical site, owned and operated by the Illinois Historic Preservation Society. Sally interrupted his train of thought just for a moment when she arrived back with a huge tray of food. She could see that the group was hungry so she hastily beat a retreat, but not before slipping a card to Dunk with her home phone number and address.

Thomas took a bite of the bacon and washed it down with the strong black coffee before saying, "I don't suppose anyone would be interested to learn that Camp Dubois, the camp where Lewis and Clark spent the winter of 1803 before departing up the Missouri River in the spring of 1804, is located on the east side of the river in Illinois?"

Everyone kept on eating but also turned their attention to what Thomas was saying. Bill Rose knew something was coming. "Please go on, Thomas. What have you found?"

Thomas took time to swallow another bite of his food before responding, "At Camp Dubois, over the winter months, Lewis and Clark took a number of latitudinal readings using a meridian observation of the sun method. George, I'm not going to go into how this method works other than to say that both captains only made small mistakes in calculating latitude from an observation with the sextant even while using the artificial horizon. I think we can generally rely on Lewis and Clark's latitudinal reckonings but, on the other hand, his longitudinal readings were consistently off by about two degrees."

George quickly responded, "Okay, so what you're trying to say is, as we drive west, we'll be trying to follow the Missouri River as much as possible and be using Lewis and Clark's positioning as a guide only?"

"Well, in a way that's exactly what I'm saying: We can rely on Lewis and Clark's original latitudinal and longitudinal calculations, if we make certain adjustments. But don't forget what I showed you earlier. We should be coordinating the Lewis and Clark positions all of the time with the grid pattern demonstrated through the Poussin's and Teniers's paintings. The underlying information the two painters earlier based their compositions on were far more accurate."

Thomas once again called up the simplification of the two compositions he had created on his laptop. He turned the screen to the group in order to make his point.

"Thomas, I'm going to ask you one more time politely because you are a fellow Mason. Just what the hell are you saying?" George pointed at Thomas and his face reddened.

Thomas responded the best he could under the circumstances, speaking slowly as a result. "What I'm saying is we need to go view the replication of Camp Dubois at the Lewis and Clark Interpretative Center just outside of Hartford, Illinois. According to my calculations based on the paintings, the treasure falls at exactly 46 degrees, 18 minutes north latitude. Lewis and Clark wanted to be at this latitude exactly. This is what the fifth symbol tells us." Thomas again scanned the copy of Lewis's second parchment, the one that James had given him previously. "All of this tells me that at the very least Meriwether Lewis was given a secret map, which accurately depicted where they were heading, showing the same latitudinal and longitudinal grid pattern the earlier paintings were based on."

Bill Rose leaned forward, looking quite satisfied with the decision he and his wife had made in private, to put their trust in Thomas. "Whoever created the earlier map certainly possessed a higher level of knowledge and understanding than Meriwether Lewis had to be able to map North America to the accuracy you're suggesting. Who were these earlier mapmakers?"

"I could tell you I think it was the Recollet priests, who disappeared for some time in the wilderness in the early 1600s, but I also think they were just following earlier maps. The question really is, as you say: Who created the original maps?" Thomas was beaming again.

Marie Magdalene had followed the conversation quite intently. By now, she reckoned, the information was already conveyed to her brother. "My goodness, look at the time. We've been so enthralled with eating and listening to Thomas that it's close to noon. Can I suggest we check out Camp

Dubois and then find a nice quiet motel for the evening? I don't know about you, but I'd like a hot shower and soft bed this evening. I'd also like to get to bed at a half-decent hour."

As the two white vans pulled out of the parking lot heading north, they were followed at a distance by one, then the other, of the white cube vans. Their occupants had satisfied their hunger by stopping at the fast food restaurant a couple of miles up the road before they pulled into the truck stop.

About half an hour later, the non-descript black rig pulled out of the parking lot and headed due west into St. Louis. The tractor-trailer didn't have to keep up with the *Templar Express* because of the GPS signal tracking Marie. The agreed-upon strategy was that Godfroi, in his own black van, would be the lead vehicle, always in front of the convoy, and the real fire power brought up the rear. Besides, Jean Baptiste had just text-messaged the truck that he would be arriving outside of St. Louis at a private airport by 5:00 p.m. local time and he expected to be greeted and brought up-to-date by Angel and the team. They all knew their special skills would not be required any further this day.

The other, yet-unknown, red-and-white tractor-trailer was still sitting in the parking lot. Phil Bloomer had accessed the trailer via the truck's cab. Sitting with him were another seven Navy Seals, all loaded for action. The inside of their long trailer wasn't as fancy as the French one, but it contained most of the same military equipment. The group was listening to a playback of the seven's conversation in the diner, thanks to the tiny transmitter sewn into George Artowski's fly-fishing vest. They were also tracking *Templar Express 1*, thanks to the GPS micro-chip embedded in Bill Rose's shoulder.

# CHAPTER 28

*Templar Express* 1 and 2 moved via Thomas's laptop directions towards the Lewis and Clark State Historic Site and Visitor Center. As Thomas flipped through the saved files relating to the journey, George interrupted his thoughts.

"Thomas, there's something I've been thinking about. You mentioned the notion that part of the treasure Prince Henry had in his possession were possibly members of the so-called Holy Bloodline?'

"Yes, I did mention this but also said not to get hung up on the notion." Thomas didn't quite fathom where Director Artowski was going with this line of reasoning. Neither did Marie, who sat up straighter at George's question. Her movement didn't go unnoticed by anyone in the van.

"I know, I know," responded George nonchalantly. "I was just thinking: I read somewhere that Thomas Jefferson was descended from King Edward III of England. I believe this was through the Randolph family. Thomas, do you think Jefferson believed he was also a descendent of the Holy Bloodline?"

Before Thomas could respond, Marie joined in, "Jefferson was also descended from King Henry II of England, through the St. Clair family. This would make Mr. Randolph here not only a Knights Templar but another potential candidate of Jesus' descendents."

With this pronouncement, the occupants of the van fell silent until they reached Camp Dubois. Nobody would dare suggest, since President Helen Jefferson-Rose was also a direct descendent of Thomas Jefferson, that she was also a direct descendent of the Holy Bloodline.

\* \* \*

THE TWO VANS PULLED into the parking lot adjacent to the Lewis and Clark Visitor Center. The last comment by Marie had caused everyone in the van to reflect on what had been insinuated. Dunk was certainly looking at Thomas just a little differently, not with admiration exactly but certainly with mild curiosity as to what Thomas really possessed in his brain.

Bill Rose knew he needed to bring everyone back to earth and away from interest in Jesus' purported descendants. "George, I won't be much help to you inside the visitor center other to attract unnecessary attention. Tell agents Bishop and Ross I'm going to wait in the van . . . maybe take a little nap. My bones are getting a little tired in my old age. Besides, I better check in with the boss or she'll be worrying about us. Is this okay?"

George seemed a little concerned about his friend's general wellbeing but said, "Of course, Bill. You'll be milking the poor-old-me until the day you die. Come on, people, let's go see what Thomas wants us to find."

The lieutenant, the director, Thomas, and Marie made their way down the path to the visitor's center, while the others stayed in the vans, some to sleep, some to go over details of their assignments. Once they paid the admission fee, they stood just inside the main foyer, waiting for Thomas's instructions. "Okay, here's where we break up," Thomas said. "I need everyone to take a section and meticulously go through the exhibits. We're looking for something resembling a crossed stick with gradations on it, almost like the Celtic cross. I know this sounds like a long shot, but I think Lewis was not only in possession of some ancient map, but also somewhat trained with an antient knowledge, which allowed him to pinpoint both latitude and longitude accurately on both land and water. If you don't find anything, let's meet back here near the replica of Lewis and Clark's keel boat." Thomas pointed over to the central foyer.

Off the four went, each one of them reading and studying the various exhibitions as they went. At one point, Thomas happened to cross paths with Marie, who pulled Thomas into an alcove and planted a spine-chilling kiss on his lips, lingering just long enough for him to register the smell of her perfume. Then she was gone again. This totally flustered Thomas, causing him to be late by the time he met back up with the rest of the group, who were already standing next to the central display.

George Artowski eyed Thomas as he approached them. Dunk had a faintly quizzical look on his face, but Marie Magdalene gave no hint of their brief encounter.

Thomas just shrugged, looking completely defeated. "I don't understand it. I was sure we'd find some sort of clue to a hidden knowledge conveyed to Lewis prior to the expedition. I know Thomas Jefferson had an inkling of where to look for the vault, but from the copy of the parchment I was given, it appears Lewis located the *exact* resting place. How could this have been without some hidden knowledge?"

Thomas was staring up at the keel boat, feeling disappointed and confused. That's when it struck him . . . what they had been looking for had been right in front of them all along. The replica of the keel boat showed an upper viewing platform at the back of the ship with a single-mast sail located to the front—a single-mast sail supported by an upper cross beam, a beam that could be hoisted and lowered to any height and tilted at any angle—a Templar cross of sorts. This allowed the sailors to capture the wind, even if it was blowing in the opposite direction, similar to the Arab lanteens. Yet the crossed sticks could also be used to chart the relative distance of specific constellations or the moon in relation to the distance traveled in the boat.

When, with a shaking finger, Thomas pointed out the now obvious feature to the trio, they stood and stared. Eventually, George Artowski made the rather understated remark, "Well, I'll be damned."

As it was coming up to closing time, the foursome made their way back to the vans, where Bill Rose greeted them with the rather simple, "What's up?"

George just shrugged, "You won't believe it when I tell you, Bill. However, I'm hungry and tired, so let's find an out-of-the-way motel where we can regroup for tomorrow."

With no objections from anyone, everyone took their seats in the vehicles and fell silent as the vans moved out. The dynamics amongst the group of seven appeared to have changed with the events of the day but nobody could put their finger on how or why.

The low-key motel they decided on was next to a strip plaza with a number of take-out restaurants. Again, Dunk made the arrangements and came back from the motel office with four room keys. Marie would take Unit

#1, with Dunk and Thomas sharing Unit #2, Bill Rose and George Artowski getting Unit #3, and Bob Ross and Daniel Bishop in Unit #4, all of them having two double beds. It had also been collectively decided when Dunk was in the motel office that the group was exhausted from the last twenty-four hours, so Dunk was again called upon to go up the road to the strip mall and purchase seven take-out dinners. Everyone was content to eat in their rooms, agreeing they would get a good head start at 6:00 a.m.

Before retiring to his room, George instructed Thomas to work his magic on the laptop during the evening in order for them to know where to head next. Thomas was more than happy to obey the order, as it was obvious George had turned into a believer. George also needed the time to make a few calls to the shadow teams and welcomed the quiet time with Bill Rose so he could get caught up on his call to the president. Marie also quietly excused herself as she wanted to make a call of her own.

After devouring the surprisingly tasty take-out chicken dinner, Thomas trolled the Internet for a few hours before Dunk declared lights out. Thomas still hadn't figured out their next move, but he was resigned to getting some sleep.

Suddenly, there was a faint knock at the door. Dunk rolled over in his bed and whispered to Thomas, "Go ahead and answer it Thomas, I imagine it's for you."

Thomas was confused. "What do you mean? Who could it be?"

"All I'll say, if I'm right, is that you shouldn't stay out all night. Director Artowski will have your hide. And, remember, the walls in this place are pretty thin." Dunk used his pillow to muffle his laugh.

By this time, Thomas had padded across the room in the relative darkness and as quietly as possible opened the door. On the other side was Marie Magdalene, wearing a short coat over an even shorter nightgown. She looked Thomas up and down and whispered, "Nice pajamas . . . Thomas, I need to talk to you. Can you come with me to my room?"

Thomas was dumbfounded but nevertheless stepped out of the room and shut the door, following Marie back to her room like a lost puppy dog. Dunk snuggled up to his pillow and thought of Sally, the waitress.

This evening, four out of the seven slept with loaded pistols under their pillow.

# CHAPTER 29

ontrary to their original intentions, Major Michel LeNeuf and
Sergeant Major Jean St. Jean spent just over 100 days in Montreal,
succumbing to Monsignor Lartique's gentle persuasion and rationale.
The Sulpician priest had rightly argued that the two knights needed to
perfect their astronomical and native linguistic skills, and they were certainly
better off canoeing across the Great Lakes as real voyageurs when the ice
broke up on the St. Lawrence River and beyond, rather than having to make
the trip to St. Louis by horseback. Besides, the Sulpician priest immensely
enjoyed the company of the French-speaking Knights Templar, for they
exhibited a tremendous intellect and higher understanding.

As a result, with the priest acting as their go-between, the two
knights found themselves signing a contract with the Northwest Company
to paddle inland to the present-day location of Thunder Bay on Lake
Superior, known then as Fort William.

The Northwest Company's agent in Montreal initially couldn't
believe his good fortune at having two strong, silent bodies who could paddle
with the best of his regular men. Added into the bargain was the odd request
that the two only wanted to go inland, against the current. The incentive of
only having to pay half the normal wages without the usual bonus, and that
he would have more room for furs on the way back in the fall certainly sealed
the deal. Nobody minded when he thought that the two were criminals
looking to escape to the wilderness. What with their sunken eyes and
paleness of their skin, the agent surmised they had recently escaped from a
British jail.

So, on May 1, 1810, Major LeNeuf and Sergeant Major Jean St. Jean
found themselves shoving off in a giant birch-bark canoe from the north

shore of Montreal, heading west into the unknown. Both of them had that morning said a silent prayer to St. Anthony, but also made doubly sure their bedding concealed their swords and other weaponry. Their heavy woolen shirts also held their remaining gold and silver coins, making swimming almost impossible if the canoe turned over. Major LeNeuf and Sergeant Major St. Jean pushed this thought out of their minds.

The major also held in his deerskin pouch the original Lewis packet—a translation into English of Le Serpent Rouge, which the three had completed over the winter; Monsignor Lartique's prized sextant; and, much to the two knights' sheer delight, a mysterious map that the priest had given them just before they left. The priest had confessed that he had obtained the map from the great French explorer Pierre Gauthier, Sieur de la Verendrye, whose real name was Pierre Saguirou. This secret map, generated from La Verendrye's explorations in 1738 to the Rocky Mountains, reached to the farthest extent of the larger Algonquin Nation.

Lartique had also arranged, with the help of a few of the knights' silver and gold coins, for a young French Mason to collect the knights' two horses in Upper New York State and to deliver them all the way to St. Louis. On the way, the Brother would stop in at Monticello and report their progress to Thomas Jefferson, with the black and white horses providing an appropriate calling-card. If the young French rider happened to also report to Thomas Jefferson on some of the British preparations for war with the Americans, so much the better!

As a direct result, following in la Verendrye's footsteps, the voyageurs found their canoe darting swiftly up the Ottawa and French rivers, accessing first Lake Huron and then Lake Superior, always hugging the coastline to avoid the danger of sudden storms.

For two French knights in their early fifties to be sharing a canoe with thirteen younger men, who were mostly Algonquin, the scene was almost surreal. The beauty of the Canadian wilderness was tempered a little by the back-breaking work, but every morning the two knights felt as though they had ascended to a heavenly paradise. Even when they had to leave a young paddler to die on one of the portage trails due to a hernia, the peace and harmony of the wilderness triumphed over all obstacles. No one would have expected the unusual bonding between the two knights and their surroundings.

It was, therefore, with a great deal of sadness that they parted company on Lake Superior at Fort William, after spending a major portion of their wages on a smaller two-man canoe, cooking equipment, and food supplies. From there, with the use of the secret map and sextant, they crossed the tip of Lake Superior and traveled the length of the St. Croix River to the south, where, at the appropriately-named St. Anthony's Falls, they portaged a small distance to the mighty Mississippi River.

Similar to Lewis and Clark's expedition that came before them, they spent a number of days at the confluence of the Missouri and Mississippi rivers taking longitudinal and latitudinal readings under the night-time summer glow of the stars. They then made their way up the Missouri River to the giant trading post dubbed St. Louis, arriving in early September where they met up with their Masonic Brethren and the young French rider who had so ably taken care of their prized horses, all the while conveying a secret message to Thomas Jefferson.

\* \* \*

MAJOR LENEUF LOOKED UP at the ceiling and said from his bed, "Well, sergeant major, what do you think of our journey into the wilderness?"

Sergeant Major St. Jean was casually lying on the other bed, which along with the major's, occupied most of the room they had been provided. He thought for a moment, and said, "There's something I must share with you, Michel. I was just waiting for the right moment to tell you. Do you remember when I went back for that last load at the portage and put the poor young fellow with the blown hernia out of his misery?"

The major drew himself up on his side and propped his head up with his bent arm. "Yes, I do remember. You shouldn't feel badly though. He surely would have died a slow and horrible death if you hadn't assisted him."

"Yes, my conscience is clear, for we are on a holy mission, are we not?" The sergeant major didn't expect an answer and continued, "The funny thing is that in spite of his obvious distress, he appeared resigned to his fate. When I bent over him to dispatch him to Arcadia he held up his hand as though I should wait for a minute. It was then he whispered to me that he and the other voyageurs knew what our real purpose is because the native prophecies told of our coming. Then he went on to explain that his Algonquin brothers and sisters, the Blackfoot, were given the task of guarding the secret until we came along. But that's not all! He told me that our purpose is just to make sure that the secret is secure, for it is not to be revealed for another 200 years. He also told me that he felt blessed he had been chosen, in a rather odd way, to convey this message to us. Finally, he closed his eyes and sighed, as though he knew what was coming next. As I plunged the stiletto into his chin, I swear I heard him whisper, *Merci!*"

Major LeNeuf was silent as he reflected upon what he had just heard and then responded, "Yes, Jean, I believe in a strange way we have been sent as the angels of mercy."

At this moment, there was a faint knock at the door and the owner of the house where the two knights rested poked in his head. The owner, a Jean Dubois, was a Mason and old army colleague of both knights during the French Revolution, before he came to America. He also ran the trading goods store on the main floor of the house and welcomed all visitors since the death of his wife pneumonia about two years previously. "*Pardonez moi, mes amis.* You asked me to disturb you when it was time for Lodge to begin. I know you'll be most welcome in St. Louis Lodge #111, as we are accustomed to having any number of visitors. Tonight, we will be conducting the third degree for a new candidate. It will be most illuminating for sure, as will be the lecture given afterwards. I don't know if you know this but when the Lodge came into light some four years ago, our first Worshipful Master was Meriwether Lewis himself. It is in remembrance of him that Brigadier General William Clark will be speaking on their expedition to the west coast. It is certainly fortuitous you have arrived when you did."

Both the major and sergeant major arose together. The major was reaching for his apron and at the same time raising his eyebrows towards the sergeant major. In reply to Jean Dubois, he made the simple comment, "Yes, Jean, very fortuitous indeed. Please show us the way."

# CHAPTER 30

St. Louis Lodge #111 was packed with Masons of all sizes and shapes, creed and color. Most sported the same weathered look, as St. Louis was the rallying point where those seeking their fortune in the west rested over the winter while awaiting the spring thaw on the Missouri River. The exaggerated stories of gold and silver just lying in the streams waiting to be harvested certainly had generated an unusual electricity in and around St. Louis.

There were roughly 120 men present and many of them attended Lodge this evening to specifically hear William Clark's presentation. What lay up the Missouri River and beyond was still relatively unknown and any advantage one could gain beforehand would hold him in good stead.

After conducting the usual business, which included the welcoming of esteemed visitors and guests, the Worshipful Master opened the Lodge in the third degree and conducted the initiation of an extremely nervous gentleman who hailed from Connecticut. After the newly initiated and relieved Master Mason was congratulated and shown to a seat, the Lodge was formally closed. After his introduction, Brigadier General Clark took to the floor and regaled the audience with tales of the western Native Indians and their customs, geological formations and the natural environment, the presence of precious metals, and exotic flora and fauna.

Major LeNeuf and Sergeant Major St. Jean listened quietly to the delivery of the third degree and General Clark's presentation. Although they were esteemed Masons themselves, they chose to remain somewhat anonymous and, as such, occupied seats in the back row and far corner of the dimly-lit room. It was only after the assembly started to break up that they approached Clark. Most of the other Masons were already heading to the bars for some light refreshment.

Major LeNeuf extended his hand in greeting to the brigadier general. "Brother Clark, please allow me to introduce myself as well as my fellow Frater. I'm Michel LeNeuf, and this is Jean St. Jean." Jean also extended his hand in greeting. "We hail originally from France and are here, like many of those among us tonight, seeking information on the west. We'll wait out the winter here in St. Louis and will move up the Missouri come spring."

William Clark quickly sized up the two knights as being much more than common fortune seekers. "Ah, Major LeNeuf and Sergeant Major St. Jean, it's indeed a pleasure." Clark looked around, checking that no one was within ear shot. "Please, rest assured your rank remains a secret between us. I was told by Thomas Jefferson himself that we may meet sometime. I was to offer any assistance required. Tell me, Brothers, do you desire anything?"

Michel quickly looked at Jean, who held his usual stone face, and then turned back to Brother Clark. "No, sir, we want for nothing. Brother Dubois has kindly seen to our accommodation and comfort. Indeed, you provided us with all we require through your lecture. I must say I found your presentation of the customs of the various Native Indian tribes quite illuminating."

General Clark was certainly pleased with himself. Since talking to Jefferson about the two brethren now before him, he had wondered what their western mission actually was, but he knew not to ask too many questions. "Ah, then, all's well! If you gentlemen do require my assistance, Brother Dubois knows how to reach me. I hope to see you in Lodge over the coming months. At some time, I'd also be most honoured to introduce you to my wonderful wife, Judith. Are you gentlemen married?"

Major LeNeuf smiled at the question. "No, unfortunately the sergeant major and I are addicted to our work and to each other. On many occasions though, after witnessing the bond between a man and a woman, I must confess I get a pang about not having chosen a wife. To have children carry on one's legacy is a blessing indeed."

"Yes, I count my blessings every evening, after they're fast asleep." General Clark chuckled at his joke.

Major LeNeuf had one more thing on his mind. "I was going to ask you the one thing puzzling me. Both the sergeant major and I read yours and Captain Lewis's published accounts of your journey. We were most fascinated with your encounters with the various Native Indian tribes and their customs. As such, Brother St. Jean and I recently debated a philosophical question concerning whether the Native Americans are the remnants of the lost tribes of Israel. I read somewhere that the hieroglyphics of some of the tribes were similar to Egyptian hieroglyphics. What we're interested in is the question as to whether any of the Indian customs remind you of our Masonic rituals. We know you're recently initiated and were not a Mason when you made your journey with Brother Lewis, but something afterwards may have struck you as being beyond coincidence?"

William Clark stood there a little puzzled. *What a strange question for two gruff army officers to be asking.* "I'm sorry, Major LeNeuf. I lost my train of thought for a moment. I must say the two of you are fascinating. I see you are most learned. Tell me, where on earth did you receive your education?"

Major LeNeuf chuckled before responding to the question, which he knew deflected the answer to the prior question for the moment, thus allowing Clark to gather his thoughts. "I know it's highly unusual, but I was educated by the Jesuits in my native France. I even studied Latin and the classics before I received a higher calling, if you like. The sergeant major here is self-taught in rather more rudimentary things, but we've found the companionship formed over the years to be a most pleasant, yet challenging. It's as though he's my mirror-image, challenging my every thought. Now, I must ask you again, Brother Clark, has anything struck you in terms of commonality of ritual or custom between the Native Americans and Freemasonry? I understand President Jefferson asked you to study the habits and customs of the Mandan Indians in particular?"

Suddenly, William Clark thought that he may have some sense to the real purpose of the two Brothers before him. "Ah, the White Indians, as the president first called them. No, nothing unusual has struck me about their manner relating to Freemasonry. I must say I found all of the native customs quite unusual, but nothing stood out in particular."

"The thing I found odd about the Mandan Indians is that their lodges, although built out of wood were round, not unlike the Plains tepee but similar in construction to the Ojibwa wigwam. I myself read somewhere that all the European Templar churches and towers were round. No matter, perhaps you would have better luck talking to Sacagawea herself?"

"I'm sorry? Are you telling us the native woman is here, herself, in St. Louis?" The two knights just stood there, elated but puzzled at this news. They both registered Clark's reference to the Templars but let it go for the moment.

"Yes, of course, she and her son, Jean Baptiste Charbonneau, are taking up residence with my wife and myself." The brigadier general was just as puzzled by their reaction. "I thought it to be common knowledge around St. Louis that Sacagawea is staying with us?" *Where on earth have these two been over the last couple of years?*

"This is most interesting. We would very much enjoy speaking with her." It was Jean St. Jean's turn to interject.

"Then it's settled. I'll have Judy arrange a splendid meal, and Brother Dubois will notify you of the date. Until then, Brothers, may the Supreme Architect of the Universe bless you!" General Clark then took his leave.

Major LeNeuf and Sergeant Major St. Jean were careful to conceal their aprons before they left the Lodge and headed towards their lodgings. It had been a most interesting evening. The two foresaw a rare opportunity to learn a great deal about the western Native Americans. Running into William Clark and Sacagawea was certainly a stroke of luck!

Major LeNeuf was in a splendid mood as the two knights made their way up the street, and he slapped the sergeant major on his back to show his obvious pleasure. "Jean, the gods are with us this evening. I was afraid the secret went to the grave with Lewis but between what we learned while in Montreal and now what we will learn in St. Louis, I have no doubt we will find what we're looking for."

# CHAPTER 31

President Helen Jefferson-Rose had just been informed that her call to Jerusalem had been put through. She pressed the flashing button on her phone and spoke into the receiver, "Hello, James, how are things in Jerusalem this morning?"

James sighed before responding, "Unfortunately, Madam President, things are not going well. The four of us have met with the leaders of all three religions here in Jerusalem and they are adamant each of the other religions is trying to eradicate the other two. Rumors on the streets of the Old City and beyond speak of the apocalypse coming with the next solar eclipse, in four days time."

"The age old prophecies of the second coming of the messiah and the necessary building of the third temple are being touted in response. The Christian right is even predicting a new holy crusade. To make matters worse, an unidentified Israeli soldier last night started sniping at groups of Palestinian youth roaming the streets, killing three boys before vanishing. In Egypt, there was even the car-bombing of a Christian church, which was full of the faithful. The result is that all groups are ready to boil over."

The president's head sagged. "I saw the official reports. The Hezbollah staked their claim for the car-bombing in Egypt. With respect to the sniper in Jerusalem, although eye witnesses claim he was an Israeli soldier, we can't confirm it."

"Yes, Madam President." James felt a sudden pain between the eyes, as the sun started to rise. "It really doesn't matter who's responsible. Do you have any news about your husband and Thomas Randolph?"

"I talked to my husband this afternoon, as a matter of fact." The president was trying to sound upbeat, although it wasn't coming out that way. "They're unraveling the puzzle and are at the antient 88 degree west longitudinal meridian, meaning they're about to enter the dark half of the painting. Bill knows how imperative it is to retrieve that-which-was-lost in time. I just cannot imagine how something, either tangible or intangible, will be able to stop what's happening. The world's three greatest religions have been on this collision course for the past two thousand years."

"Yes, Madam President, you're correct, but we cannot lose faith. Without it, the dark forces will win. We promise we will do everything we can to quell the flames, but I'm afraid that, without the sacred knowledge, which my Templar ancestors rather foolishly removed from the Temple, I am not so confident. I'm afraid we've left things too long and in the hands of too few. I'll pray for their success."

"Thank you, James. And I'll pray for you. I'll say goodbye now. Please keep me apprised of all of your endeavors." The president hung up the phone before James could respond. Then she stood and with hands clasped behind her back, continued to stare into the night. *Please Bill, don't let us down. For the love of God!*

# CHAPTER 32

The alarm in Lieutenant McCormack's and Thomas's room went off at 5:00 a.m. sharp. The lieutenant rolled over in his bed to check on Thomas but he wasn't there. Dunk jumped up quickly, only to hear, "Good morning, you jarhead. Aren't you afraid of shooting yourself during the night?" This remark came from Thomas, who was sitting at a small round table with his laptop open. Immediately, Dunk was fully awake and took in the fact that his gun was showing slightly from beneath his pillow. "No way, man. The safety's on!"

Thomas laughed, obviously in a good mood this morning.

Dunk caught the effect of the light-hearted air in the room also. "So, Thomas, what time did you return to the room last night?" Dunk already knew the answer but he wanted to check whether Thomas would tell the truth.

Thomas didn't take the bait. "Oh, it was at about 2:00 a.m. You were snoring to beat the band."

*Good man, Thomas. Always tell the truth.* "It comes from having your nose broken about four times. I'm going to have to get it fixed for good one day." Lieutenant McCormack was pleased Thomas passed the test. "Now tell me, what happened between you and Ms. St. Jean-LeNeuf, and don't leave out any juicy details."

Thomas sat there for a moment, staring intently at his laptop. "Well, you really shouldn't be asking, but I'll tell you anyway. What you were expecting to happen . . . it didn't . . . remember, I'm old enough to be her father. However, I can tell you she told me where we're to go today!"

Dunk just sat on the edge of his bed with his mouth open. He didn't expect a reply quite like this. "What do you mean, she told you where we're going today?"

108

"That's what I said." Thomas was pleased with the opportunity to confuse the marine. "Don't look so dumbfounded. Actually, I was the same way last night. Marie sat me down and chastised me for thinking like a man. Two-dimensionally, she said. She told me I had to start thinking beyond just two dimensions. In other words, I had become too fixated on latitudinal and longitudinal coordinates. What I really needed to do was add another dimension—height or depth—'w,' 'y,' and 'z' coordinates. I also needed to think in terms of time, in order to complete the square—the eighth symbol on Lewis's parchment. Time and space, Dunk, time and space!"

"What the hell are you talking about?" The marine was scratching his head by this time.

"Well, I didn't get it myself until she pinpointed exactly where we're to go to next. We have to find the spot where Lewis and Clark stopped at 40 degrees north latitude, 96 degrees west longitude, in order to relate it to the grid." Thomas swung the laptop around to display a topographic map he found of the area through the USGS website.

"On Friday, July 13, 1804, Lewis and Clark camped for several days at the mouth of the Nemaha River, where it flowed into the Missouri. This location is as close as one can get to 40 degrees north latitude and 96 degrees west longitude. If I follow this antient longitudinal meridian to the south, lo and behold, there's the small town of Meriden, Kansas. Anyway, close to their camp lay the ancient burial mounds of the Indians, which afforded them a clear view of the great plains to the west. Part of the group, including Clark, actually took one of their smaller boats—a pirogue—up the river to the mounds, where it's presently known as Mound City, Missouri."

"Okay, I'm following you, but I still don't follow you." Lieutenant McCormack was sharp but obviously didn't have the history background.

"Don't you see, Dunk? Friday the 13th is the infamous day when the Templar Order was first smashed by the king of France and the pope. Eighteen plus 4 equals 22. One plus 3 plus 2 plus 2 equals 8—8 degrees of separation. It's a sign! Everywhere we've gone, there's not only been a reference to sacrifices, torture, death, and burials, but also to life everlasting—infinity. These burial mounds were first created by the ancient native peoples, not only as burial mounds but celestial viewing platforms. If you follow the antient 96 degree west longitudinal meridian southerly, it also pierces Merida, Mexico."

"So, what we're following is a grid system established around the world by an antient society that understood astronomy and other such things relating to the infinite transit of the stars and planets?" Dunk was finally starting to put the pieces together.

Thomas pointed his finger at him. "Exactly! This is part of what the medieval Knights Templar rediscovered. And, what we're ultimately looking for is a vault or crypt positioned in accordance with this antient grid pattern—a burial vault containing the remains of Prince Henry Sinclair and who knows who or what? Now the question is, how does Ms. St. Jean-LeNeuf know all of this and why is she telling me this now?"

Dunk spread his arms. "Why don't we go ask her?"

There was suddenly a hard knock at the door. Dunk grabbed his gun from under the pillow and swiftly moved to the door where, after checking through the peephole, opened it. Bob Ross stood there, fully dressed, exclaiming, "She's gone!"

Thomas stood up and responded, "Who's gone?"

Bob Ross just shrugged. "Ms. St. Jean-LeNeuf, that's who, Mr. Randolph! I went to see if she was up, and she didn't respond to my knocking, so I naturally tried her door. It was open, so I went in. The room is clean, as though she hasn't been there at all."

"But this is impossible. I was with her until two o'clock this morning." Thomas was starting to panic at this point.

"Excuse me?" Bob Ross just knew something like this was going to happen. *Damn amateurs! Every time you involve them, trouble follows!*

Dunk quickly interjected, "I can attest to that, Bob. Mr. Randolph was with her in her room between 10:00 p.m. and 2:00 am."

Bob Ross just lifted his eyebrows and asked, "Is this correct, Mr. Randolph?"

"Yes, absolutely, and before you jump to any conclusions, we just talked." Thomas felt as though he was being accused of something—that somehow he was responsible for Marie's sudden disappearance.

"Talked . . . about what?" Bob Ross had assumed the role of the inquisitor.

"We talked about where we're to go today?" Thomas was starting to feel the heat.

Bob Ross was incredulous by this point. "You mean to tell me you spent four hours with her and all you did was talk? And the only thing she showed you was exactly where we're going? And then she disappeared, leaving her room as she had found it? I can't believe I'm hearing this crap."

"Yes, I know it sounds rather odd but that's exactly what I'm saying."

"Man, I can't wait until Director Artowski and Mr. Rose hear this one." As soon as Bob Ross said it, he instinctively knew that George Artowski was close by.

George, along with Agent Bishop and Bill Rose, had reacted to all of the commotion, apparently through the thin walls of their rooms, and had come out to see what all the fuss was about. "Mr. Ross," asked George, "what's going on here?"

Bob Ross just glared and pointed at Thomas, who took Ross's silence as his cue. "It appears as though we have a problem, Director Artowski. Ms. St. Jean-LeNeuf vanished sometime between 2:00 and 5:00 this morning. I was with her up to this time and can attest that nothing seemed out of the ordinary, other than her telling me where we should be heading next and what we should be looking for."

George stopped dead in his tracks, trying to consolidate and analyze the information. It was a good thing it was before 6:00 in the morning or the group would have attracted a fair amount of interest. Everyone was dressed except for Thomas, who was still in pajamas, and Lieutenant McCormack, who was in boxers.

Pondering the implications of the situation, George said, "This tells me she's already obtained everything she needs from us and she's done a runner with her brother. How far ahead of us they are now, I have no idea. In light of this new information, my recommendation is that we call everything off, get you to a safe place and let the military handle the rest."

Bill Rose did his own quick analysis of the situation and then responded to George directly, but loud enough for everyone to hear. It was apparent he wanted everyone to be in on the decision, which had already been made during his latest discussions with his wife. "No, George, you know we can't do that. Since we're all Masons and Knights Templar, I want everyone to hear this because everyone should know what they're in for. When I spoke to the president yesterday, it's become obvious that what we're doing here is somehow tied into what's happening in the Middle East. Riots have broken out in the various capitals, especially Jerusalem, which is pitting Jew against Muslim, Muslim against Christian, and Jew against Christian. The world's three greatest religions sense that something affecting all three of their very beings is happening. Gentlemen, I believe in my heart that what we're doing here somehow ties in with this whole convoluted mess involving the Antients, Thomas Jefferson, Lewis and Clark, Prince Henry Sinclair, the Knights Templar, the Native Americans, the St. Jean-LeNeuf family, all of us . . . and, specifically, Thomas, and what he has subconsciously stored in that brain of his."

Everyone else just stood there, the awe showing on their faces. They weren't used to Bill Rose making the speeches.

Bill Rose continued, "Gentlemen, I have specific instructions from the president on this. We must find whatever is concealed and do it as quickly and quietly as possible. This means we can't call out the army, although we do have our Navy Seal teams as backup. But I can tell you Jean Baptiste has his own team consisting of some very nasty ex-paratroopers, which probably stack up to our Navy Seals."

"Now I can't tell you what happened to Ms. St. Jean-LeNeuf—whether she went off on her own or was forcefully removed. We do know her telephone conversations appear to indicate she's one of the bad guys, but if this is the case, why would she tell us where to go next? When Thomas pulled up on his laptop, the copy of the Lewis parchment while we were in the diner yesterday, she didn't flinch. I think we can surmise that she and her brother have the original or a copy and have already deciphered the symbolic progression."

"But if they somehow figured out exactly where the vault is situated, why wouldn't they just allow us to flounder around out here in the midwest?" Bill Rose looked at Thomas and put his hand on his shoulder. "I'm sorry, Thomas. I didn't mean it like it sounded. You've more than surpassed our expectations. It's just apparent you have a lot of things happening in that head of yours."

"No offense taken." Thomas didn't quite know if what Bill Rose said was a compliment or not. "Uh, Bill, there is one other thing, which Marie Magdalene showed me."

Five sets of eyes bore down on Thomas. Bill Rose dropped his hand from Thomas's shoulder. "And what would that be?"

"Well, she gave me a copy of a translation of a second parchment she claimed was written by Lewis, which goes with the other parchment." Thomas inadvertently stepped back a little.

George Artowski couldn't believe what he was hearing. "If this is true, Bill, then she's feeding Thomas in order for him to pinpoint the exact location of the vault. You're absolutely right, we're still in the game! Gentlemen, in light of the present situation, may I suggest we get ready to move out in ten minutes? Thomas, you can tell us what specific direction to head towards when we're in the vans. Lieutenant McCormack, I would be most obliged if you make sure Mr. Randolph has his laptop and that piece of paper with him. Agents Bishop and Ross, I suspect we're being followed. By the end of the day, I want to know how they have us on their radar. Now let's move!"

# CHAPTER 33

Everybody traveling in *Templar Express 1* was a little on edge, especially Thomas Randolph. After the events of the previous evening and that morning, he didn't know whether to laugh or cry. Marie Magdalene had inexplicably shown him how to piece together the puzzle running through his head and then disappeared. Thomas still couldn't quite comprehend the events, along with George Artowski's and Bill Rose's summation that they were still in the game.

To Thomas, there was new electricity in the air. He didn't completely realize it before, but it was now officially confirmed that Thomas's brain held the missing piece of the puzzle as to where the hidden vault lay. Thomas himself just didn't know how they were going to extract it.

In accordance with the instructions conveyed to him by Marie Magdalene, Thomas directed the small convoy to first take I-70 towards Kansas City, and then head north on I-29 towards Council Bluffs, Iowa. The entire route ran somewhat parallel to the Missouri River, but they would be stopping before Council Bluffs at somewhere around Mound City, Missouri, because it was there that Lewis and Clark established a camp on Friday, July 13, 1804.

Thomas had told this much to Lieutenant McCormack just after 5:00 a.m., when all of the confusion started. At first, even Thomas didn't get the true significance of the Friday the 13th date until he compared the 40 degree north latitude and 96 degree west longitude coordinates with the Teniers—Poussin composition he had stored in his laptop.

The point where the antient latitudinal and longitudinal meridians were shown within the painting, as resting in the bend in St. Paul's elbow, depicted the rather sharp bend in the Missouri River. This rather unusual

114

ox-bow was noted by Lewis and Clark in their journals and in several diaries of the individuals accompanying them. Two thousand or even two hundred years ago, when the major overland highways didn't exist and the rivers were the only highways of their time, a unique feature of this nature was sure to be noted on any map. This feature was definitely significant enough for David Teniers the Younger to note, some four hundred years ago, within his multi-layered painting.

As the two white vans rounded the bend of the highway, which followed the Missouri River ox-bow, the cut-off sign to Mounds City loomed ahead. The sign, aside from a friendly welcome, listed a number of local attractions and public facilities including the Meridian elementary and high schools. Dunk slowed down and pulled to the side of the highway, with the second white van pulling in behind.

Thomas was desperately searching the Internet on his laptop; hunting for the answer he knew was just a website away. "One thing Marie indicated to me last night, which just came back to me, was that she was surprised none of us had bothered to look at the opposite side of the grave markers back at the St. Jean-LeNeuf estate. She said something about men not being able to see beyond the obvious. Apparently, if we had looked into it, we would have discovered the five grave markers had the first five symbols of the Lewis parchment carved into the back of them. Marie said the symbols, as we suspected, fell along the antient longitudinal meridians and they could be found carved or painted on specific natural outcrops or stone markers close to the various grid coordinates."

"In my Internet search, the closest site I find fitting the requirements of being close to the desired coordinates, being a rock or natural landform, and being a site of ancient Indian activity is just up ahead on the highway near the next town, Brownville, and across the river. We can access it, Dunk, by turning west on Highway 136. It's called Indian Cave State Park, and I see it's near the rather appropriately named Lewis and Clark Camp Site."

Dunk pulled the van back onto the highway and gleefully exclaimed, "You're the man, Thomas!"

# CHAPTER 34

4:30 P.M. • FOUR DAYS AGO
INDIAN CAVE STATE PARK • NEBRASKA

The vans found the entrance to the park without any difficulty and parked at the far end of the main visitor's parking area. Before they left the van, Lieutenant McCormack looked over his shoulder at Bill Rose and commented, "Mr. Rose, sir, did you see the way the park ranger was staring at you, as though he recognized you from somewhere?"

Bill Rose had noticed. He was a little concerned about his presence being discovered by the public and the media but they had their story down pat: The president's husband and some of his friends were off out west on a fishing adventure. Helen Jefferson-Rose had even quipped that, if discovered, Bill might catch some of the Cornhusker vote for her, as the primaries were coming up soon.

Bill Rose thought about it for a moment and then commented to George Artowski, "George, I think Dunk's right. Maybe we should have Danny Bishop stay back with the vehicles just in case somebody decides to snoop around. What do you think?"

George was quick to respond, "Bill, that's a really good idea. From the map the park ranger provided us, the cave is just a short hike." George exited the van and shouted over to Danny, who had the window of his van down, "Danny, stay with the vans. You can even have a short snooze if you want. We won't be long." George knew full well the Secret Service agent wouldn't dare take a nap, but Danny Bishop was more than happy to stay behind.

The small party of five made their way over to the start of the trail that slowly ascended to the Indian Cave via a boardwalk, which had been constructed against the edge of the sandstone outcrop. It was obvious the Missouri River was quite a bit wider at the time the petroglyphs were first painted and that the Native Indians could easily access the site by canoe.

Luckily, the group was the only one on the trail at this time, as the park was closing soon. The heavily forested area was quiet except for the various chirping of birds and gentle rustling of the trees in the wind. The men reflected on the beauty of the area as they made their way up to the petroglyphs. The area was certainly a sacred spot to the natives and still exuded an atmosphere of serenity and solemnity.

Lieutenant McCormack was in the lead with Thomas following and, for the first time, Thomas noticed the bulge under his fishing vest at the small of Dunk's back. He knew instinctively it was the same gun Dunk kept under his pillow at night. Thomas tried to tell himself that it was normal to have some sort of security, given that the president's husband was along for the trip, but he had little love of weaponry.

Lieutenant McCormack suddenly whistled, causing the ad-hoc conga line to momentarily stop in its tracks. Bob Ross, who was bringing up the rear and wearing a similar bulge to Dunk's, yelled, "Hey, Dunk, what's up? Why did you stop?"

Lieutenant McCormack was staring at the petroglyphs. "Man, you have to take a look at this stuff. It's gorgeous!"

Thomas just shook his head. *There's a chance for you yet, Lieutenant McCormack!*

Then George Artowski spoke up, "Over here! I think I've found what we're looking for." He had moved off to one side of the sandstone face towards a small crevice in the rock. In response, Bill Rose bent down and angled his head to get a better look. "By God, George, you've got good eyes. We may have found it! Thomas, come and take a look for yourself."

Thomas came over and looked. He felt a thrill run through him. There it was—a faintly-painted square, divided into four equal parts, within a circle with a diagonal line running from the southeast corner of the square to its northwest corner and from the southwest corner to the northeast corner—the sixth symbol. It was right there for those who knew what it was.

Thomas pulled out his BlackBerry and took several different, angled shots of the sign. He then stood back to think for a moment. "If I were trying to follow in someone's footsteps, and knew when and where to look for the sign, it would have told me to continue to the northwest up the Missouri. I would also have known I had reached the sixth stage of my journey by the design of the sign itself. I don't know whether Lewis was responsible for this symbol, or if it was the antients themselves, because it blends in with the rest of the petroglyphs so well, but I can tell you if you were being pursued and were lost and finally came across this symbol, it must act like a beacon of hope hitting you right in the middle of the forehead."

Bill Rose patted Thomas on the back. "Well said, Thomas. And, well done, everyone. We're on our way. I have no doubt, now we know what to look for, that we'll be able to pinpoint the vault in plenty of time to position ourselves for the eclipse. I'll have to let my wife know we've had a breakthrough. I hope the attempt at détente in the Middle East can hold on for another week."

This last comment sobered everyone a little, but the group still made their way back to the parked vans feeling somewhat elated. Thomas was more confident than he had ever been. They were on the right track. The presence of the hidden sixth symbol on the cave's overhang presented further confirmation that both the ancient natives and the antients considered this area sacred.

But as they made their way down the slight incline to the parking lot, it was obvious something was very wrong. The second white van containing the communications and surveillance equipment and weaponry, as well as Secret Service agent Danny Bishop, had vanished. George Artowski broke into a run, exclaiming, "Damn it, where the hell is *Templar Express 2?*"

Lieutenant McCormack and Bob Ross arrived a second later with Dunk quickly saying, "Danny wouldn't have left the van for anything and he wouldn't have left this spot by his own will. If somebody wanted to steal the van, they would have had to drag him out of it. Bob, see if you can get hold of him on your BlackBerry."

Bob Ross already had his BlackBerry out and had quick-dialed Danny Bishop's BlackBerry. There was no answer. Ross tried again but there was still no answer. Bishop's BlackBerry was dead.

Thomas and Bill Rose finally caught up with the rest of the group. Bill Rose exclaimed between breaths, "I can't believe it. I'm going to surmise that Jean Baptiste has captured—taken, our white van and Danny Bishop. There's no other explanation."

Thomas asked quietly, "What do we do?"

George Artowski, just disconnecting from his last call, said, "We do nothing. We suspect the worst but can't prove it and it hasn't been twenty-four hours, so we can't even file a missing person report. Jean Baptiste has just upped the game, that's all. He's keeping us on the defensive and telling us he's watching our every move. We can't call in the marines or Danny Bishop is dead. Okay, this is the way we play the game. We're going to stop for supper and regroup while we have some down-time. My recommendation is that, if need be, we drive all night to the next antient longitudinal meridian. Thomas, you'll have to figure it out during supper. We have just a little over three days left to be in position. Come on, everybody, get in the van. Let's go!"

Thomas was definitely taken aback by the director's abrupt seizure of the situation but hopped into the remaining white van as he was told. Bob Ross was now riding in the back seat and Thomas noticed he had pulled out a rapid-action shotgun from under the seat and was ramming home a shell, ready for action.

George saw him watching and said, "The first thing you learn as a Secret Service agent is to constantly be on the move. It's more difficult to hit a running target!"

# CHAPTER 35

After spending the fall and winter months in St. Louis, Major Michel LeNeuf and Sergeant Major Jean St. Jean traded their two-man canoe for what they knew best—their trusty horses, Pegasus and Icaria. The sensation that both horses and their riders felt when they embarked from St. Louis the early morning of April 15, 1811, was certainly one of comfort and familiarity. They did not regret, however, the time they were forced to spend in St. Louis due to the weather, as they gained invaluable information with respect to the obstacles they would face. Indeed, on several occasions, they seized the opportunity to enjoy not only William Clark's and his wife's company, but the engaging company of Sacagawea. Both LeNeuf and St. Jean also found immense satisfaction in playing with Sacagawea's son, Jean Baptiste, who took a particular shine to the big and rough sergeant major, who just also happened to have been baptized as Jean Baptiste.

And, while William Clark regaled them with stories of his and Meriwether Lewis's western adventures, the two knights were cautious not to expose the real purpose of their mission. As far as they were concerned, Brigadier General Clark had not been apprised of Thomas Jefferson's hidden instructions to Meriwether Lewis. Therefore, the topic of Templar signs, symbols or tokens, or antient longitudinal meridians, for that matter, was never discussed at the Clark dinner table.

Instead, under the guise of being generally interested in the western plains and its native history, LeNeuf and St. Jean gradually gained the trust of Sacagawea to the point where each could confide in the other. What the two knights hadn't realized was that, at their first meeting, Sacagawea had already guessed the true purpose of the knight's presence in St. Louis this winter, since she too was familiar with the native prophecies regarding the protected secret. When the two knights first showed up at the Clark residence for Thanksgiving, they were dressed in their newly cleaned army uniforms, complete with their Templar swords, out of respect to William Clark's territorial position. Sacagawea recognized these accoutrements as she was related to the presently assigned native guardians, who awaited the coming of those who once again wore the Templar cross.

In addition to her charming beauty, the two knights were equally amazed at Sacagawea's intelligence and sense of honor and trust, and her amazing linguistic abilities. Aside from speaking English and French and her native Shoshone, she spoke any number of Algonquin dialects, from Blackfoot to Ojibwa. Michel LeNeuf even suspected that Sacagawea was of the Holy Bloodline herself, but kept this suspicion to himself.

It was, therefore, not surprising when Sacagawea presented them with a unique gift at the time the two were about to depart. Wrapped in a soft skin was a gift of tobacco, cedar, sweet grass, sage, and a square piece of red cloth, along with a beaded necklace of Sacagawea's. She indicated that when the two knights arrived at the Mandan village they should seek out the eldest tribal statesman and show him the gift. They would then be passed on to the Shoshone and then to the Blackfoot guardians, who would take them to what they desired.

In return, Sergeant Major St. Jean presented to the boy, Jean Baptiste, the gold cross and chain he'd carried around his neck since he was a boy, and Major LeNeuf presented five gold coins to Sacagawea, telling her they would forever be in her debt. He suggested that, if desired, she should use the money to return to her tribe.

Clark was certainly not privy to what had taken place previously when Major LeNeuf turned over a copy of Le Serpent Rouge to Sacagawea. Michel had thought long and hard about conveying the message the two knights and Monsignor Lartique spent many long winter evenings translating into English. But he finally decided to do so, once he was convinced Sacagawea was in on the secret, so to speak.

Sacagawea was indeed honored, immediately recognizing the importance of the document, as Meriwether Lewis had also taken her into her confidence during the Corps of Discovery. Lewis's parchment was the French version of Le Serpent Rouge, and Sacagawea conveyed to Major LeNeuf that she had some difficulty with the French subtleties. The major asked Sacagawea to examine the document in English, in the hope she would recognize something that could help them.

121

Alas, the only reference she highlighted was contained under the zodiac sign of Sagittarius, the Archer, and its comment of the white hill. Sacagawea noted to the two knights that at the source of the Missouri River, past the Mandan village and into the foothills of the Shoshone and the Blackfoot, there was a prominent limestone outcrop, which shone for miles when the sun first rose.

Both Major LeNeuf and Sergeant Major St. Jean were overjoyed when they heard this comment, since they quickly realized this was one sign of the Antients—Taliesin, the Shining Brow. Many ancient fortresses had been built atop natural limestone outcrops, which acted as natural beacons to those coming from the wilderness.

* * *

THE LAST OF THE SNOW was melting in the early morning sunshine, as Major LeNeuf and Sergeant Major St. Jean rode out to the north from St. Louis on April 15, 1811. They had said their thanks and goodbyes to Brother Dubois the night before and indicated that most likely they would be passing through St. Louis again within the next couple of years. In turn, Brother Dubois indicated he was most grateful for the company and reluctantly took the silver and gold offered to him for the accommodation and fresh supplies. As usual, the knights rode light, carrying everything they required within their saddle bags and bedding.

To anybody who happened to observe the two knights leaving town, they appeared as just two of the many heading west in search of fame and fortune. If anyone bothered to take a second look though, they may have noticed the small Templar crosses on the handles of their swords or the striking horses that they rode, but the signs and symbols meant nothing except to a few of the initiated.

The two knights spurred their horses to the north, with the intent to follow the old Indian trail running along the top of the east bank of the Missouri River.

Major LeNeuf and Sergeant Major St. Jean found themselves making good time on the trail, in part due to the steadfastness of their horses. The horses themselves were feeling a sense of relief and freedom, having for the most part spent the last six months confined to a stable. On the odd occasion, the two knights took them for a run in the deep snow, but the spring air was obviously stirring the sense of adventure that even the two horses felt.

At noon, the two riders decided to stop for lunch and a small rest by a shallow brook. Major LeNeuf pulled Lewis's packet from his pouch and opened up the second parchment.

Sergeant Major St. Jean waited for the major to get comfortable and then asked, "What do you think, Michel? Are we on the right track?"

Michel nodded and responded solemnly, "*Oui*, Jean, the saints have been very good to us. With the information we've gathered and the invitation card provided to us by Sacagawea, I'm quite confident indeed! Look here. We're heading towards the location of the sixth symbol, representing 40 degrees north latitude and 96 degrees west longitude. After this, we only have two ancient longitudinal meridians to acknowledge in order completing the square."

The sergeant major became a little melancholy himself. "Michel, after we find that-which-was-lost, do you think we could settle down on a small piece of land somewhere? I have to admit, my bones are getting tired. And after seeing the happiness between the Clarks and between Sacagawea and that little rascal of hers, I've suddenly realized what you and I have missed all these years."

"I know. I know. Jean, I too long for a simpler life. But remember our vows: We are warrior-monks of the highest degree. Our stay in St. Louis, I think, has caused us to go a little soft. What we need are a couple of months in the saddle. I'll tell you one thing: This is going to be our last mission in the name of the Supreme Being. My bones are starting to ache also."

Major LeNeuf raised himself up and then lent his hand to help Sergeant Major St. Jean rise up, as if to speak to the uncommon bond between the two. The two horses also lifted their heads in recognition that they were about to depart. The knights surmised it would take about two months of nighttime riding and of taking celestial readings before they arrived at the location of the sixth symbol—the Indian Cave, where at the very same location, the Corps of Discovery spent several days during the middle of the month of July 1804, some six years ago. The ultimate objective was to be in a position at the eighth symbol—the ancient longitudinal meridian of 112 degrees west, by September 17, 1811, so that they could observe the predicted solar eclipse, which was required in order to expose the Thirteenth Pillar.

# CHAPTER 36

After grabbing a quick bite to eat at another non-descript roadside diner, the consensus around the table was to get moving, and to keep moving. George Artowski had made some phone calls to the Bunker and to the shadow teams, so he was fairly confident most avenues were covered. But the mysterious disappearance of *Templar Express 2*, Danny Bishop, and most of the communications equipment and backup firepower, didn't bode well for the future. Even the GPS system linking *Templar Express 2* to the Bunker was dead.

Within their immediate reach, between George Artowski, Duncan McCormack, and Bob Ross, they still possessed three standard SIG Sauer P229s, one Remington Model 870 shotgun, and two MK MP5 sub-machine-guns. Their communications consisted of five BlackBerrys, two cell phones, and Thomas's laptop. A link-up with state or military authorities was ruled out, as George knew their every movement and outside communications had somehow been compromised.

The director didn't want to say anything in front of the civilians but he knew if Jean Baptiste wanted to take any or all of them out, he could do so at any time. It would be like swatting a fly. The one thing they still had in their favor was that George Artowski was as skilled as a military tactician as Jean Baptiste was, perhaps even better.

With this in mind, *Templar Express 1* assumed a military-style hierarchy. George Artowski was the colonel-in-charge. Whatever he said was to be followed to the last breath. Dunk McCormack and Bob Ross were his lieutenants and joint seconds-in-command. If one of them went down, the other would assume the second-level position totally. The assumption was, if the director went down, then everybody would be down. Bill Rose

124

was deemed non-expendable, so it was both of the seconds-in-command's responsibility to protect the "asset" at all cost. With respect to Thomas, he was now deemed expendable.

Fortunately, Thomas hadn't been told any of this. He was given the responsibility, though, to determine the van's direction, since it was decided they would push on through the night. It was also assumed that it was better to remain conspicuous, and, therefore, they would stick to main interstate highways.

Hence, the van headed north along Interstate 29, on which they would eventually hit I-94, running west towards Mandan, North Dakota, where the highway once again traversed the Missouri River.

Thomas calculated with the help of his laptop that sometime the next morning, if they pushed hard, they would reach their destination. In the meantime, George suggested that both Thomas and Bill Rose try to get some sleep and that Dunk and Bob Ross share the driving duties.

By 11:00 p.m., *Templar Express 1* had pushed northward on I-29 past Sioux City, Iowa, and was making good time. This leg of the trip up until this time was uneventful, with both Thomas and Bill Rose sleeping like babies. Dunk drove, with Bob Ross constantly checking out the rear window to ensure they weren't being followed.

But they were being followed. The two white cube vans carrying the eight Navy Seals were traveling on the same I-29 about half an hour behind *Templar Express 1*. They were in constant contact due to the van's GPS system, which was also constantly triangulated with the shadow teams' system and the mother system located in the White House Bunker.

The small convoy had just logged in digitally that they passed through Sioux City at exactly 11.30 p.m. and crossed into the state of South Dakota with all systems quiet.

Suddenly, as the two cube vans rounded a bend in the highway, the men saw up ahead what looked like a partially jack-knifed tractor-trailer. Its running lights were on but there was no apparent movement in or around the truck. It blocked the entire northbound lanes.

The driver of the lead van reacted calmly and forewarned all of the two cube van's occupants in enough time for the teams to grab their gear and to prepare to exit the vans when they stopped. Even though the incident up ahead might be nothing more than a real-life accident, the teams were trained to take no chances. In the split second it would take for the vans to stop at the required strategic angle, the teams would disperse from the back of the vans and assume a defensive perimeter.

The problem was that the split second never came. The stinger missiles aimed at the two vans were already on their way. Angel had set up the killing field perfectly. The lead stinger shot from the grassy knoll, which lay to the right side of the highway in the shadows, took out the lead van. The second stinger was positioned along the same knoll except it was some two hundred yards south, intercepting the second van out from behind. The vans went up like roman candles, vaporizing all within them.

Angel stood casually beside the truck's cab admiring his strategic handiwork. The two stinger marksmen had already run back to the truck. It was obvious that no mopping up was required, so with all the men loaded back into their home-away-from-home, Angel jumped up into the cab and started to head north once again.

The entire operation took less than two minutes. Angel chuckled to himself since he knew Jean Baptiste would find something negative to say about the operation. He always did, but it didn't bother anyone. It was just the perfectionist in him.

If Angel hadn't been chuckling, he may have noticed the red-and-white eighteen-wheeler bearing down on him from the south with its lights turned off. Phil Bloomer was approximately five minutes behind Navy Seal Teams 1 and 2 and witnessed the whole deadly scene. Instinctively, he made the decision not to slow down and instead shifted into a higher gear as he swerved around the two burning wrecks. As he did so, he yelled into the intercom for the team in the rear to brace themselves for a head-on collision. The seven Navy Seals caught the entire scene via a close-circuit monitor linked to a camera on the truck's dashboard and braced for the collision even before the warning was given. As the truck-trailer was expertly guided around the wreckage, the smell of burning flesh seeped into the rear trailer.

The Texan aimed his own truck at the very spot, just behind the black cab's door, where he knew it would cause maximum damage and hopefully flip both truck and trailer. Phil Bloomer hit the gas at the same time he hit a higher gear and looked up just fast enough before his own airbags deployed to witness the pure horror in Angel's eyes.

The sound of the crash, mixed with the high-pitched screaming of tearing metal, was actually secondary to the main event. The black tandem truck-trailer was at its maximum vulnerability. The direct result was that it flipped not once but twice. Phil Bloomer, although saved by the airbags, managed to burst an eardrum but the rest of the team had been cushioned from the blow to the point they deployed before their truck came to a full stop. The side door of the lead trailer swung open even before the skidding black truck-trailer fully stopped. One acrobatic Navy Seal looked as though he was riding a giant bronco, as he vaulted onto the side of the trailer and lobbed two stun grenades into the pitch blackness. Pulling down his night goggles, he then leaped into the void and loosened off a barrage of automatic fire, with absolutely no return fire from within.

By the time "John Wayne" popped his head up out of trailer and signaled "all-clear," Phil Bloomer was already being tended to by one of the other Navy Seals. As they both examined the headless body of the Frenchman called Angel lying on the side of the road, Phil Bloomer felt an immediate sense of deep satisfaction.

At the same time, that energetic first Seal ran over to Lieutenant Bloomer for his orders. "Master Chief Wayne, listen to me now: Get on the blower and tell *Templar Express 1* what happened. But make sure you only talk to Colonel Artowski. Then get in touch with Little Creek and let them know what took place here, so that the state troopers can shut this area down immediately. Have them say it was a major truck accident. And have the police form a two-mile outside perimeter. Get our military clean-up crew moved in as fast as possible. We need this mess sorted by sunrise. And I want my truck fully operational by then! As of this moment, *Templar Express 1* is totally naked without us backing them up."

The medic was trying to see to Phil Bloomer's ear with a long cotton swab but he was bouncing around too much. "Ouch! Dammit, watch where you're sticking that thing."

Lieutenant Bloomer continued with his orders, "Wayne, you smirking idiot, also get on to Admiral Drake. Tell him personally what happened here and that we need complete containment, authorized by the president herself. Although we're not supposed to tell the president anything, do I make myself clear?"

Master Chief James Joseph Wayne, out of Houston of all places, grinned from ear to ear, since the Seals rarely got to fight on their native soil. "Sir, yes, sir! I have two additional observations the lieutenant may appreciate."

Phil Bloomer shook his head and replied, "Okay, master chief, what are your observations?"

Master Chief Wayne stood erect and to attention, "Sir! . . . The first is that none of the enemy survived, unfortunately. Sir! . . . Have you noticed the driver's severed head still has a toothpick stuck in its teeth, sir?"

Both the paramedic and Lieutenant Bloomer did a quick one-eighty and stared at Angel's severed head in disbelief. Master Chief Wayne was right, of course. There was a toothpick still sticking out of the teeth.

The lieutenant picked up a small piece of fender lying beside him and hurled it at the retreating Navy Seal, who was guffawing as though he had just rung the bell at the county fair.

* * *

DIRECTOR ARTOWSKI'S BLACKBERRY started to vibrate, bringing him back from a place not quite awake but not asleep. He looked at his watch. It displayed 1:00 a.m.

Before answering the call, he looked around the van and, through the dim light, tried to discern if anyone else had been startled awake. Bill Rose and Thomas were still asleep, and Lieutenant McCormack was concentrating on the road, although it was obvious his ears had perked up. George didn't turn around but he knew that Bob Ross was sitting in the third row seat, stone-faced and alert, also listening for any information.

The director pushed the receive button and spoke as quietly as possible into the phone, "Yes?"

The voice on the other end sounded calm and efficient, "Colonel Artowski, sir, this is Master Chief James Wayne, sir, attached to Shadow Team 3. I have important news for you, sir, courtesy of Lieutenant Bloomer."

George sat a little bit straighter in his captain's chair, immediately becoming alert. "Yes, Master Chief Wayne. Go on . . ."

James didn't pull any punches in his report. "Sir, Seal Teams 1 and 2 have been eliminated. Eight of our men have been lost—taken out by stinger missiles, of all things. It was a well-crafted ambush, on I-29, just north of Sioux City."

George just stared ahead for a few seconds before exclaiming, "Shit!" He then regained his demeanor. "Excuse me, master chief. Go on."

On the other end of phone, the master chief could picture the director's face. "Sir, yes, sir! Shadow Team 3 was lucky enough to come onto the scene just after the altercation. Although we were too late to save Seal Teams 1 and 2, we eliminated the perpetrators. We eliminated eight of their team. I guess you can consider it as payback, sir?"

The director's mind rushed about in a number of directions. "Master chief, were there any survivors on their side?"

"No, sir!"

George sighed as he rubbed the bridge of his nose with his left thumb and forefinger. A slight throbbing started right between his eyes. "Yes, I understand perfectly, master chief. Tell me the rest."

"Sir, Lieutenant Bloomer is slightly injured . . . a blown eardrum, but aside from this little complication, we'll be completely operational once we replace a front bumper. The state troopers just sealed off a two-mile radius and a containment unit is on its way. The scene will be completely sterilized before sunrise . . . Shadow Team 3 has already surveyed the equipment in the opposition's trailer . . . It's the latest communications equipment and armaments money can buy. The boys at Little Creek will have a field day tearing the stuff down . . . Jesus, sir, they even had the truck rigged to detonate. Luckily, we discovered the guts of the system and disarmed it."

By this time, the entire van was awake and listening intently to the director's muffled conversation.

George thought long and hard over the next question before asking it, since he knew the van's occupants were listening intently. "Master chief, is there any sign possibly indicating the presence of an American Secret Service agent?"

This question took the master chief by surprise, since only Lieutenant Bloomer had been briefed on Danny Bishop's disappearance. "Sir. Nothing, sir!"

George Artowski breathed a small sigh of relief before continuing, "Very well, master chief. You and your whole team must be commended. I'm sorry to hear about your buddies, but you've dealt a good blow to the enemy on our home soil. Tell Lieutenant Bloomer I want Shadow Team 3 on the move as soon as possible. By my calculation, you should be back in position behind us by noon at the latest. I don't care if you have to break every speed limit to do it. Have Admiral Drake clear it with the state troopers and make sure they understand they're to keep their distance . . . This fight is between the government of the United States and some nasty little secret organization. Do I make myself clear?"

The other end of the conversation became quite serious, and George pictured Master Chief Wayne snapping to attention. "Sir, yes, sir!" Then the connection was broken.

Just then, Director Artowski's BlackBerry started to vibrate once again. George Artowski frowned when he looked at the call display. The caller's name and number was blocked.

George pressed the receive button and held the BlackBerry up to his ear and said, "Yes?"

The voice on the other end was easily recognizable: It was Jean Baptiste St. Jean-LeNeuf's.

# CHAPTER 37

Director Artowski remained calm. He had half-expected Jean Baptiste to call. Jean Baptiste was as cool and collected as George Artowski because in a macabre way, it was all just a game—a very serious and deadly game—but nothing more. Jean Baptiste had been slightly rattled when he first learned the fate of Angel and seven of his closest friends and allies, but he quickly shrugged it off. His philosophy gave him some comfort—in war there are casualties and blood is thicker than water.

"Good morning, Director Artowski. Did you manage to get any sleep this evening?"

George thought he knew how this conversation was going to play out even before it really started. "Not much. Actually, none in fact." There was no sense in denying the obvious. "I understand our teams were involved in a slight altercation just a while ago?"

George could hear Jean Baptiste chuckling. *This fellow is obviously deranged. He just lost eight of his fellow paratroopers and he can chuckle?*

Jean Baptiste became serious again, as though he read the director's thoughts. "Yes, Mr. Artowski, bravo to your military tactics. Having a third back-up team is really quite ingenious. Unfortunately, we are on your, how do you say, home turf? Your resources are certainly greater than mine. Are they not? I will remember what you have done. You can count on it!"

"Thank you for your observations, Jean Baptiste. Now may I ask the nature of your call so early in the morning?" George had an uneasy feeling swelling up in the back of his mind.

"Ah, I see you are a typical American—abrupt and to the point. Very well, Director Artowski. I too can be abrupt. As I'm sure you've very quickly realized, all of you are quite vulnerable right now. I know exactly

131

where you are and where you're heading. I also now know your Shadow Team 3 will be out of position to defend you for the next twelve hours."

George looked around the van. Its occupants hadn't moved.

George was silent and reflective. *The bastard's right. We're sitting ducks because he somehow is tracking us and he knows I have no idea of his additional strength and resources.*

Jean Baptiste saw an opportunity to press his advantage. "Director Artowski, are you still there?"

"Oh, yes, Mr. St. Jean-LeNeuf, I'm still here." George definitely didn't like the way the conversation was going.

"That's good, Director Artowski. For a second there, I thought maybe you had disappeared. That is certainly a lovely thought but for now let us concentrate on the task at hand. I think we all realize the president of the United States' first love is not for her country but for her husband. It certainly would be a shame if anything happened to him. You must believe me when I say I have no real animosity for her or for your country. What I want is to make the world a better place. Ultimately, it will also make the United States a stronger and safer place to live . . . Here, therefore, is what I propose: I need Mr. Randolph to help me pinpoint exactly the final resting place of the Templar treasure. We both know he possesses this knowledge, even though he may not realize it himself. We also both know once he's done this, well, then, he no longer is of any use to either of us . . . I'm, therefore, proposing you swing west at Fargo onto I-94 and continue on to Bismarck. Once you arrive there, I will call you again and direct you to where you can drop off Mr. Randolph. You have my word that you and Mr. Rose can then return to Washington and your beloved president unharmed. However, I cannot promise that your Shadow Team 3 will not come to harm, as I have a bone to pick with them."

George didn't have to ask what the alternative would be if they didn't accept the proposal, but he also realized, as long as they had Thomas, they held the trump card.

"That's quite generous of you, Jean Baptiste." The tone of George's voice did not change but the sarcasm was evident. "I'll have to discuss it with my group. You already know we're heading in that direction anyway, so why don't we agree you'll learn of our decision as we come up on Bismarck, North Dakota, when you call me back?"

"*Trés bien. C'est la vie.* I am a patient man, Mr. Artowski. I can wait a little while longer. By the way, Agent Bishop says hello!"

With this unnerving last comment, Jean Baptiste broke off the conversation.

George Artowski put down his BlackBerry and sighed. *The guy's definitely suffering from a grand delusion. What a friggin' megalomaniac!*

Bill Rose had been following the conversation carefully and saw the opportunity to interject, "George, what is it? What's happening?"

George looked over at his oldest and dearest friend and then focused in the direction of the rear view mirror. "Lieutenant McCormack, can you pull over at the next convenient spot? We need to stretch our legs."

Dunk recognized by the glint in the director's eyes that something was wrong. "Of course, Colonel Artowski. There's a spot just up ahead."

Thomas picked up on Dunk's reference to the director as colonel. *What the heck's going on here? I thought George was just the director of the Secret Service? Was he a colonel in the army coming out of Vietnam? Is he still a colonel?*

Dunk slowed the van down and pulled off into a rest stop. The air was fresh and cool and, as nobody else occupied the area, George suggested they get out and stretch their legs and sit down at one of the many picnic tables situated around the grounds.

Bill Rose and Thomas did as George suggested, with Thomas not really noticing how both Dunk and Bob Ross assumed positions at their small perimeter, guns at the ready.

Bill Rose sat across from both George and Thomas. He focused his gaze on his longtime friend. "George, you and I go a long way back. I can tell when something's shaken you and can tell when you're conflicted. Now, be honest with both of us. As fellow Knights Templar, where do we stand?"

George thought about cracking a joke, saying they obviously were sitting at a rest stop, but then he thought the better of it. "Well, I'll tell you exactly where we sit. The bastard, Jean Baptiste, is deranged. But he's also one clever little weasel. He knows exactly where we are at any given moment and what we're up to. He also knows I'd do anything to protect you, Bill, and he's confirmed he has Danny Bishop."

George conveniently left out the fact that eight of his Seal team had just been killed and what was left of their back-up was indisposed for awhile.

Bill Rose rightly sensed there was more. "George, what's the other side of the coin?"

George was tired and figured it wouldn't make any sense to pull any punches. "Fraters, here's the gist of what's happening. Jean Baptiste has the upper hand, and he knows it. For the life of me, I can't figure out how he's so on top of us. I had Bob Ross scan the van when we were inside the diner a while ago. Everything's clean—no tracking devices. Nothing! . . . Well, here's what he proposed, Bill: Your life for Thomas's"

That silenced both men. Thomas, especially, couldn't believe what was happening.

Bill Rose quickly assured Thomas, "Brother Randolph, I see this has come as a complete surprise. I suspected it might somehow come to this. It's quite obvious Jean Baptiste is a madman. But don't forget our vows to one another. Outside of our own family, we have pledged to safeguard one another above all else."

Thomas couldn't think of anything to say, but his thoughts were running wild. *It's easy for you to say! You're married to the president of the United States, and George is your best friend, which means when push comes to shove, I'll be the first one thrown out of the boat.*

Both George and Bill rightly imagined what Thomas was thinking at this moment. Luckily, George suddenly picked up on something that had been nagging him all along. "Thomas, where's your laptop?"

"Back in the van. Why?" Thomas said, perplexed by the question.

"Thomas, I was thinking. When Bob Ross scanned the van back at the diner, your laptop was with you inside. Am I correct?"

Thomas nodded.

"When you met with Ms. St. Jean-LeNeuf the other evening in her motel room just before she disappeared, did you have your laptop with you?"

Bill Rose and Thomas looked at each other, both realizing where the line of questioning was going.

Thomas quickly responded, "Yes, I remember grabbing it at the last minute and taking it with me, thinking she might want me to call something up on the computer or to search something over the Internet . . . And yes, if I follow your reasoning, I did use her washroom at one point, leaving my laptop on the small table in her room."

George nodding knowingly. "Would you mind getting your laptop from the van?"

"No problem. I'll be right back." Thomas was more than happy to oblige, thinking this may just be the advantage they needed.

Thomas retrieved the laptop and returned to the picnic table, where George held his finger up to his lips. Then he retrieved a small Swiss Army knife from his vest pocket and gently turned the laptop over. Using the small screwdriver attachment, he quietly unscrewed the bottom plate and gently lifted it to expose the laptop's electronics, including an accessory that shouldn't be there.

George Artowski examined the extra bit of hardware closely at a variety of angles, again holding his finger to his lips. He then just as quietly replaced the bottom plate and screwed it back into place. Then he handed the laptop back to Thomas and, through silent gestures, indicated to Thomas he should return the laptop to the van and return to the picnic table.

The director waited patiently until Thomas was once again seated and whistled for both Dunk and Bob Ross to join them at the table. When they did so, Thomas for the first time noticed the deadly looking shotgun cradled in Bob Ross's arms and the futuristic-looking sub-machine gun Dunk was sporting. The stakes had definitely been elevated.

The colonel spoke in a clipped, military way, keeping his voice low, "It's now obvious how we're being tracked. Thomas's laptop is bugged, both for positioning and voice recognition. No wonder the bastard is one step ahead of us. He hears all of our discussions, knows where we are at all times. Well, he's not hearing us now, so we'll use Thomas's laptop to our advantage. Here's what I've planned . . ."

George Artowski outlined something really quite simple, but, if beautifully executed, could result in the odds flipping in their favor. Thomas wasn't as confident but realized it might be the only way he might come out of all of this with his life.

Bill Rose reassuringly patted Thomas on the shoulder as they rose from the picnic table. "Now remember, Thomas, the next couple of hours of conversation in the van is crucial. Jean Baptiste will be wondering why we stopped and why he lost our conversation. We'll resume as though we just took a pit-stop to stretch our legs and to have a washroom break. He's no dummy. He'll have heard already and figured out we must have responded to his conversation with George while we stopped, so we'll have to work this into the conversation naturally. Do you understand what we have to do?"

"Yes. I just hope I don't blow it." Thomas wasn't as confident as the other four. Bill Rose knew he needed to generate more confidence in Thomas in order for the plan to have any chance of succeeding. "Thomas, I want you to know that whatever happens, George and I have no regrets in contacting you. What you've done for us and for the United States is proof this country was indeed founded by men who possessed a higher understanding of what they wanted to achieve and did achieve—not only for the United States but all of North America. I now understand why the Native Americans consider this land to be their sacred Turtle Island. Besides, there will always be ambitious men like Jean Baptiste. We're on the verge of a priceless discovery of hidden knowledge that, if not for you, might be lost forever. In making this discovery, you're solidifying my faith in the ideals of Freemasonry and Templarism and it will do the same for millions, which is certainly a legacy you can be proud of."

Thomas was feeling a little bit better as the group of five loaded into the van and once again headed into their own dark abyss.

# CHAPTER 38

Robert Dumas arrived at Charles de Gaulle airport on the morning flight from Israel brimming with self-accomplishment. He knew that within the next few days all of the Middle East would be in turmoil. The riots were escalating, not only in Jerusalem, but in Cairo and Tunis as well, with the cry for "democratic republics" spreading like wild fire. The story of the young Israeli soldier who shot and killed the three young Palestinian protesters was certainly the spark lighting the flame.

Dumas went through customs without incident, as his Israeli work visa, which identified him as an archaeologist's assistant, was all in order. Thanks to the web of connections he constantly developed amongst the French military and police, Robert was personally escorted by the head of airport security out a side door to a waiting limousine. Within half an hour of his arrival, Robert was being whisked away to a small luxury apartment located next to the Sorbonne. Here he was to be reunited with his long-time girlfriend, Angelique Martine.

He spotted Angelique bounding down the steps of the apartment building, as the limo pulled up to the curb. Robert barely had enough time to straighten up from the opened car door before Angelique embraced him and planted long and rough kisses all over his face.

"*Mon cher*, Robert, my darling, I was so afraid you would not return." It was quite obvious Angelique had been crying.

The limousine driver quietly emptied the car trunk of Robert's luggage and, after being slipped a healthy tip, discreetly exited from the curb.

"Angelique, *ma cherie*, why are you crying?" Robert gently disengaged himself from Angelique's embrace and proceeded to wipe the tears away with a brush of his hand.

"Oh, Robert, I'm so silly. I couldn't help but watch the news, and I had in my mind that somehow you were caught and torn to shreds in the street."

"Oh, Angelique, it is indeed a silly thing to think about. The operation went off like clockwork. You and I should be so proud in being part of the establishment of a New World Order. Our children will carry with them this pride and the knowledge their bloodline is of the Merovingian kings."

Angelique's face took on a radiant glow. "*Merci*, Robert. I needed to hear this from your own lips. You are so good for me. Now, let's get you upstairs and into bed where you belong, my beautiful French man-god. My heart and body aches for you!"

\* \* \*

ROBERT HAD NEVER EXPERIENCED erotic intensity similar to what he experienced over the next four hours. It was as though Angelique melted into Robert's body to create one androgynous being. The metaphysical level they achieved was in reality due to the ecstasy pills they took when they first got into bed—washed down by a beautiful bottle of 1965 French Merlot, but this was besides the fact, because in three days they were to be part of a world revolution.

Angelique propped herself up on her elbow, her naked body's contours outlined by the white silk sheets. She purred and stared into Robert's sleepy eyes and played with the soft, blondish hair on his chest. "Robert, tell me again about the bomb."

Robert lay still and drank in Angelique's perfume. "It's quite simple, really, my dear. The beauty of it all is that in addition to the physical destruction the bomb will cause, the psychological damage will be overwhelming. Every Middle Eastern facet of all the religions will be involved, either being wrongly accused of planting the bomb or accusing someone else."

Robert started to feel the excitement building up inside him once again, but he continued, "The dirty little bomb itself was supplied by a little known Middle Eastern sect, still believing the real target is the Israeli Mossad headquarters. Given that the bomb will be linked to the Mossad, their idea was the Israelis themselves would be blamed. It's amazing they couldn't care less if the contamination fallout killed a million innocent Israelis and Palestinians."

"Now, when the site of the Old City Temple and Dome of the Rock is obliterated to dust instead of the Mossad headquarters, the same Middle Eastern sect will be scrambling to absolve themselves of any responsibility. Muslim will be accusing Muslim. Muslim will be accusing Jew. Muslim will be accusing Christian, and vice-versa. The result will be a void in true leadership, justice, and faith. The three greatest religions will see it as a sign from God that their selective principles have not resulted in peace, just war and bloodshed. This point is exactly where Jean Baptiste will come in."

"In three days time, he will possess the secret knowledge and understanding that demonstrates he was chosen as the direct conduit to God and his desired will. As leader of the Order of the True Rose Croix, he will be able to demonstrate to the masses that God has chosen to cleanse his House, and only by following the Order will mankind be allowed to share the Order's direct relationship with the one, true God." Robert had played the scene over and over in his mind several hundred times.

Angelique started to purr once again. As she reached out to grasp Robert, she whispered, "And, our children will take their rightful place at the high altar alongside Jean Baptiste's and Michele's children."

# CHAPTER 39

Four months after embarking on their journey, the two knights arrived at Fort Mandan, North Dakota, on the Missouri River. All along the way, they paid special attention to the sun, stars, and to the lunar cycles, recording the measurements. Upon reaching the nearby Native Indian village, their immediate objective was to establish friendly relations with the Mandan Indians in order to be passed on to the Shoshone and Blackfoot and meet the September 17th eclipse deadline.

As the two men rode through the distinctive corn patches cultivated by the Mandan and into the centre of the village, the chief and elders came out of the main lodge and stood tall in front of them with their arms crossed. The chief held a white-and-black eagle feather with his right hand, hiding the red leather binding within his fist. Major LeNeuf immediately recognized the sign and held his right hand up, palm forward, as the two pulled up and dismounted. Major LeNeuf then slowly withdrew his sword from its scabbard and extended it to the chief, held horizontally in both palms.

The chief, Bull Bear, spoke first in French, asking the two knights, "Do you come in peace?"

Major LeNeuf responded in kind, "We come in peace."

The chief extended his left hand to touch the sword's blade, all the while holding the eagle feather with red leather binding high for all of his people to see. The chief declared, "Then come in peace." To which a piercing whooping went through the crowd, all the more welcoming as villager after villager recognized the Templar cross on the major's sword.

Before returning his sword to its scabbard, the major handed the sword to the sergeant major, who in turn held it up by the blade with both hands, handle high, for all to see. By this time, a murmur spread through the entire village, as the prophecies told some two hundred years before were about to be fulfilled.

Bull Bear then invited the two knights to join him and his council inside the main lodge for food and a conference. The two knights accepted and left their horses attended to by two young braves.

As they made their way into the wigwam, Sergeant Major St. Jean whispered to the major, "Michel, are you seeing what I'm seeing? The outer wooden palisades and wooden wigwams are all constructed with circular walls. It's a European Templar design, that's for sure!"

Major LeNeuf nodded slightly and replied, "Yes, Jean, it's obvious an earlier Templar influence has been at work here. Now let's rekindle this friendship."

After thanks was given to the Creator for delivering the two unharmed, and the knights' presentation of the gift of tobacco to the chief and elders, a number of Indian women appeared, bearing all kinds of meat and other foods. The meal was delicious, especially after the diet the two knights had reluctantly been enjoying for the last four months, mostly consisting of small game, fish, roots, and berries.

After everyone ate their fill and the ritual pipe ceremonies were completed, Chief Bull Bear addressed all those present, first in his native tongue and then in French, "My people, my brothers, and sisters, when the two white men named Lewis and Clark first came amongst us many moons ago, we thought they were the ones that the prophecies spoke of. However, they were not the chosen ones. They did not show us any of the signs, symbols, or tokens we had been taught to look for. Instead, they asked for our assistance to travel over the mountains. We provided that to them, as we are people of the earth, and it was the right thing to do. But now I tell you the prophecies have delivered us the men of the red cross, who first came amongst our grandfathers' grandfathers. Our elders tell us the stories of how these warriors did not challenge us but learned many things from us, and we learned many things from them. They married among us and we married among them. So, they are our blood brothers. This I declare to be true."

The circle of both men and women let out a collective, "*Kwey, Kwey, Kwey,*" in recognition of the chief's oration. Then it was Major LeNeuf's turn. After standing, he collected a small portion of tobacco, which sat in one bowl by the fire, and mixed it with cedar from another bowl. Silently, he first held the mixture up to the sky and then knelt to touch it to the earth, before offering it to the fire in honor of the Creator.

The major straightened, broadened his chest and addressed all of those around him in French, which was readily translated for those who did not understand, "*Bazshoo*, greetings my brothers and sisters, I wish to thank the Creator for delivering my brother, Jean, and myself safely to your village, to the home of our brothers and sisters. We come in peace from across the great waters beyond the rising sun, like those who came before us. The prophecies told you to be patient and you have, for we are finally here before you. We ask nothing of you but to share your fire and food over the next few days. In return, we will help you hunt for meat, show your young men how to protect your village in times of need and share our stories with you around the campfires. When the moon is once again full, we will have to leave and ask you to point us to our Shoshone and Blackfoot brothers, for you have already been told the reason for our coming. We are the red and white guardians of the secret you and your brothers and sisters have protected so well. *Chee Miigwich!*"

The circle went quiet, not with awe, but with mutual respect. Chief Bull Bear and the major had properly recognized each other as comparable leaders of men.

The feast carried on until well past nightfall, with the elders regaling their people and the two knights with the stories of the Great Chief who came among the ancient warriors, wearing the white tunic sporting the red cross in the center of his chest. He brought with him many warriors, women, and medicine men, most of whom married amongst the surrounding tribes, to form the Mandan, who are now revered amongst the Native Americans for their wisdom, medicine, and their native skills.

The elders conveyed that those from the far-off lands shared the knowledge of how to grow and harvest the wild crops and berries and to build the wooden wigwam in a circle for greater warmth and protection. They knew how to breed the mountain goat and wild horse to make them stronger and tamer. They shared their knowledge of how to work the metals they dug from the earth, always giving thanks to the Creator and taking only what they needed. They were also skilled in diverting the waters of the streams and raising it from the ground to allow the people to drink all year round.

In return, the native peoples showed those of the red cross how to hunt the buffalo and how use to the natural medicines of the prairies. The native peoples also taught those of the red cross how to follow the ancient trails across the mountains to their native cousins, who live by the great expanse of water. And, when it was time for the Great Chief to die, his Council took him up into the foothills of the mountains, where he would go to fast and to talk with the Creator.

But the prophecies said he lived for a great deal longer on his own, for he was brought food by the Raven, the Trickster, who succumbed to the old man of the mountain's will. When the Great Chief did eventually pass into the other world, his body and his belongings were concealed by Mother Earth herself, nobody knowing where, except for those who showed the strength and courage to be his guardians, for the prophecies told the native people that one day he would rise again to lead them to the promised land.

Both Michel and Jean easily recognized the story and its relationship to Prince Henry Sinclair and those Knights Templar who formed his entourage. Upon this summation, the two knights conferred with one another only for a short while before Major LeNeuf made the decision to share with his hosts the gift that Sacagawea had given them.

When the moon reached its full height in the sky, the major presented to the Mandan chief and the elders the small package consisting of the four elements—tobacco, sage, sweet grass, and cedar—along with the hidden fifth element, the square patch of red cloth. Major LeNeuf also made a purposeful gesture by offering Sacagawea's necklace to the first wife of the chief, who as it turned out, was a cousin of the Indian princess.

As expected, the gifts were received with great humility and appreciation, for they represented a certain magic to the Mandan. In many ways, the elements presented confirmed that the two guardians knew of the prophetic process of "squaring-the-circle" and, therefore, could be trusted and passed on to the Shoshone and Blackfoot guardians. The chief conveyed that his ancestors had been waiting for seven generations for the guardians to return, in accordance with the prophecies, and the Creator kept his word. This meant there was future hope for the continued existence of the Native American.

In return, the chief ordered one of the younger braves, whom both LeNeuf and St. Jean surmised was the chief's oldest son, to go and retrieve what appeared to be a sacred object of the Mandan.

As the son returned, the two knights knew immediately what this object was and what it meant. The chief took the huge broadsword with the Templar cross on its handle from his son and held it out to Major LeNeuf, who very carefully took it with both hands. Michel then proceeded to withdraw the heavy, wrought-iron sword from its handmade leather scabbard and held it up for all of those in the circle to see.

The chief extended his arms wide and proclaimed, "This sword was presented to the Mandan by the Old Man of the Mountain when he left to die in the foothills. He said that his sword would act as a magical talisman to protect the village until a new set of red-and-white guardians would arrive after seven generations." The chief's eyes were welling with tears of joy. "As per the old man's last instructions, we now give you the sword, to protect you on the last leg of your journey."

Both knights were profoundly moved. Here was the absolute proof that the Hereditary Grand Master of the Scottish Templars and his fellow refugees had passed through the Plains Indians' territories on their way to establishing a New Jerusalem further west, in the foothills of the Rocky Mountains.

# CHAPTER 40

Michel and Jean spent the next three days amongst the Mandan people sharing pure wonderment and friendship. The little ones were especially enthralled with the two giants with the pale white skin who appeared to tower over the strongest brave. As a result, the children followed the two around wherever they went, even when the two giants made slipped out of the village late at night to take their readings of the moon and the stars. The excited but tired children at first hid among the rising corn, confident the two giants were unaware of their movements, only to be teasingly scared by the sergeant major, who chased them all the way back to their beds.

The gentleness of the two warrior-monks towards the younger ones did not go unnoticed by the women of the village. This boded well for the two, since the Mandan women had the final say in any decision the tribe would make concerning the future of the two giants.

The two white men were surprised when, on the morning of the third day, a small hunting party of Shoshone warriors rode into the village. The group was led by a proud chief, who turned out to be none other than Sacagawea's brother, Cameahwait. The chief had helped Lewis and Clark on their journey over the Bitterroot Mountains to the source of the Columbia River, and here he was again, wearing nothing but buckskin leggings, moccasins and a loin cloth, having received the news while out hunting the buffalo that the red-and-white guardians had finally returned.

The strikingly handsome and proud Shoshone dismounted from his painted pony with a flourish before the two knights, handing his shield and lance to a brave who stood off to his side. In a mixture of his native language and French, he greeted the two knights, "*Heywha, aaanoo, mes amis, Ne*

*saitungu wahatehwe daiboonehwe bibiide'nnu*—I see that two white men have
arrived . . . *ne ou'est buika—huku dowope'*—looking east, a cloud of dust . . .
*Andebichi-woho'nee?*—Strangers? . . . *Non! Damme newe, damme newe*—No!
Our people, our brothers . . . *Nabidengehdaigwahni!*—Warriors!"

He then did something unheard of in native circles. He enveloped
each knight in his arms and whispered into their ears the password,
"Golgotha," to which the knights instinctively responded with the phrase—
"place of the skull." Upon receiving the correct response, the Shoshone chief
stepped back and howled with laughter like a wolf's cry at the moon. Both
the major and his companion stood in awe, as though struck by lightning.
They were staring at the Native American equivalent of a Knights Templar.

The major quickly regained his composure and said in the same
mixture of French and Algonquin, "Sir Knight—Great Chief, we
acknowledge you as a servant of the poor and the sick, and as having
promised to devote yourself to the defense of the red-and-white bloodline.
The Creator has received you into the number of the brave and faithful, and
while we, the Creator's unworthy servants, receive you with our prayers, may
the Creator grant you the courage to do well, with the will to persevere
always, and bring your people to the happiness of eternal life."

It was Cameahwait's turn to stand in awe at the two men before
him. Even though he didn't understand the meaning of some of the words,
he had been taught the strange phrasing by his grandfather, who was taught
by his grandfather before him. The prophecies were true. The strange
warriors from the east, although they did not wear the type of garb he was
taught to watch for, responded in the appropriate manner.

In full acknowledgement of the enormity of the event, Cameahwait
grandly gestured to his young apprentice, who turned out to be one of his
sons, to retrieve his pipe and medicine bags strung across the neck of his
pony. The Shoshone procession then led the way to the main lodge, where
the Mandan chief and elders waited patiently, knowing they shouldn't
interrupt the private greetings. More formal greetings were made and
Cameahwait gained the Mandan's favour by offering freshly killed buffalo
meat, which lay upon a wooden travois attached to one of the horses.

Both knights were equally engrossed by the many native customs
and traditions observed this morning and lost all of their normal senses by

the time several pipes of different tasting tobacco were passed around the circle. And Bull Bear increased the level of excitement even more when he displayed to Cameahwait the tokens from Sacagawea given to him by the two knights.

With the prayers and formalities completed, the chief issued the command that the noon-hour feast was to begin and both raw and cooked buffalo was presented before the fire in bowls and pots of every size and shape. After ensuring that the elderly and sick, women, and children received their rightful share, the chief stood and took a peace of raw buffalo meat and offered it up to the Creator and gave thanks. He then dashed the meat into the fire to complete the offering and signaled that the warriors could finally eat.

By this time, the air within the lodge was thick with a mixture of wood and tobacco smoke, several different languages and dialects, human sweat and moisture, and the thick aroma of seared buffalo meat and its juices. Michel and Jean were reeling from it all. To top it off, as honored guests, the two giants were offered the buffalo's heart and tongue, as a dessert of sorts. Not wanting to offend in any manner, the two bit into the delicacies with a somewhat reluctant bravado. The resulting looks on their faces brought howls of laughter from around the circle.

Chief Bull Bear held up his hand for silence. He then stood and spoke in Mandan, with different translations happening all around him, "Greetings, my brothers and sisters, we are honored with the presence of the brave Shoshone warriors from the west and the red-and-white guardians from the east. Today, our middle world has been blessed by the Creator in allowing us to bring together the prophecies, which were first promised to us seven generations ago. We were taught by the elders that, on the verge of the mid-summer's eve, when the sun was at its highest between the east and the west, a great buffalo would be offered in celebration of this coming together of the great spirits. Let us give thanks to the Creator once again!"

The crowd murmured, with a number in the circle exclaiming, "Kwey, Kwey, Kwey!"

The Mandan chief continued, "As our grandfathers' stories teach us, when we all come together and share our food and laughter and give thanks to the Creator, this will be the time to pass the guardians on to our western gatekeepers, the Shoshone, so the guardians may continue their journey to where the Old Man of the Mountain rests in wait for them. This being so, we ask the Shoshone to protect these guardians and to see they find the Blackfoot before the sun goes dark."

*Before the sun goes dark?* Michel just stared with his mouth open at Jean, who reciprocated with the same gesture. Michel's thoughts swirled about his head. *The Old Man of the Mountain . . . the Scottish Templar broadsword . . . the western gatekeepers . . . the solar eclipse! I'm hearing it, but I can't quite believe it!* Michel was silently wording his thoughts to Jean, who sat cross-legged next to Cameahwait.

The meal finished, and talk amongst the villagers resumed, Cameah-wait revealed one more thing to the travelers. As a symbol of trust, he moved aside the leggings, exposing one thigh, and there was the seventh symbol contained within Lewis's second parchment.

The lodge fell silent.

Chief Bull Bear would tell the story of what occurred this day around the fire afterwards on many a cold evening. The seventh sign was tattooed onto Cameahwait's upper right thigh. This was done by the Shoshone elders to remind those who had the knowledge to see that the Shoshone chief was himself of the red-and-white bloodline. In body and in spirit, the native prince represented the antient 104-degree west longitudinal meridian in a way nobody could have imagined. It was as if the roseline ran the length of his entire body.

Major LeNeuf had taken in all of the recent information and processed it within seconds. He examined every bit of information he had stored over the past thirty years concerning the lost secret. The pieces to the immense puzzle were being fitted together even as he spoke, "My brothers and sisters, you see before you the seventh sign. Cameahwait is blessed by the Great Creator himself. This proves he is also a red-and-white guardian and, as such, we must go with him immediately, for there is precious time left as the glowing sun makes its way across the great prairies. I promise you that we or other red-and-white guardians will return to protect the Mandan, since they have protected the secret of the Old Man of the Mountain!"

Following this pronouncement, the procession made their way out of the lodge and watched as the two tall men gathered up their belongings and weapons for the trip westward. Two young Mandan braves had run ahead and saddled their horses. The contrast between the white and black horses and their symbolic meaning was not lost on the Shoshone chief.

As Major LeNeuf and Sergeant Major St. Jean took to their mounts, Chief Bull Bear handed the broadsword to the major. Again, Cameahwait's eyes went wide, as the major unsheathed the sword and held it upright to the sky. The sun's rays appeared to concentrate on the shiny blade, and the major turned the blade slightly in order for the reflected light to fall upon the crowd gathered around the small mounted party.

Here was a true blessing from the Creator. The crowd, which by this time was made up of every man, woman, and child in the village, was awestruck and fell silent, for they were blessed as the true "children of the light."

The major silently returned the sword to its leather sheath and laid it across his lap. Cameahwait took this as a sign to proceed and spurred his own horse towards the western gate of the palisade, with the two knights riding in the honored position at his right hand side. The two knights did not fail to notice that the round shield the Shoshone chief carried had a painted red patee cross on it.

The Shoshone chief's son spurred his horse forward in order to ride ahead and prepare for the hunting party's reception at the larger, central hunting camp. It would be a three-day hard ride to the west but the two knights didn't mind. The excitement of the past few days was growing in them in anticipation of finally being able to accomplish their life-long mission. They still had another two months to go until they reached their objective and, during this time, they had to be favorably received by the Blackfoot, but so far all of the signs lined up as Monsignor Lartique had instructed.

# CHAPTER 41

*emplar Express 1* was coming up to the outskirts of Bismarck, North Dakota, when George Artowski's BlackBerry vibrated. The director saw that the caller display showed that blocked number once again—Jean Baptiste. He signaled for everyone in the van to be quiet and then pushed the RECEIVE button. "Mr. St. Jean-LeNeuf, I presume?"

The voice on the other end was cold and efficient. "Have you had a chance to consider my proposal?"

"Yes, we have, Mr. St. Jean-LeNeuf. I want to emphasize it was not my decision to make. The decision was made between Mr. Rose and Mr. Randolph, neither of whom, as you may appreciate, do not condone your methods of negotiation at all!"

"Come now, director, do not feign ignorance at this time. It is not becoming. You and I both know this is all part of the game. Now, what is your decision?"

"Very well, Mr. St. Jean-LeNeuf, the decision is to give you Mr. Randolph. There is one condition, though." By this time, the director was getting anxious, although he showed no outward signs of it.

Jean Baptiste sensed a triumph. "Well, what is the condition?"

"We want Danny Bishop released," George Artowski replied abruptly.

"But, Director Artowski, I was going to offer him to you anyways, as a show of good faith. Besides, his sullenness is getting to me. I must admit, though, he is a brave but stupid man . . . Okay, please tell your driver to turn north off of I-94 at the Highway 83-Twelfth Street North exit. You will soon come to a very large Wal-Mart Superstore. I love you Americans. Everything has to be supersized. Anyways, my sister and I will be waiting for you in the

150

northeast end of the parking lot . . . And please, no funny business. I can assure you several highly-skilled ex-paratroopers will have a bead on all of you. Have I made myself clear?"

"Crystal clear, we're coming up to the exit now." Director Artowski pushed the DISCONNECT button and turned directly to Thomas. When he spoke, there was a certain fatigue to his voice, "Thomas, are you sure you want to go through with this?"

Thomas sighed with resignation. "Yes, I'm sure. I just hope that once I give him what he wants he'll let me go."

Bill Rose picked up on Thomas's sentiments and commented, "Thomas, just cooperate and give him what he wants. Now, don't forget to take your laptop."

Everyone in the van went quiet as Dunk wheeled the van into the gigantic parking lot and maneuvered to the far northeast corner, where they could see Jean Baptiste standing casually next to his sister, Marie Magdalene.

Dunk stopped the van approximately thirty feet from where they stood. Thomas opened the passenger door and hopped out, carrying a knapsack stuffed with some spare clothing, his toiletries, and his laptop. Nobody else exited the van.

As Thomas started to walk towards Jean Baptiste and his sister, he stared directly at Marie, but she wouldn't return his glare. Instead, she moved instinctively closer to her brother, all the while staring at the ground.

Thomas stopped about ten feet away. "Where's Danny Bishop?"

Jean Baptiste replied loud enough for the occupants of the van to hear, "You'll find him in your white van parked about two rows over. I left the keys in the ignition but disposed of all of your equipment." Jean Baptiste was pointing in a southeast direction. "Director Artowski, please stay where you are until we have left."

Rather abruptly, Jean Baptiste walked up to Thomas and took him by the left forearm. He then waved goodbye to the remaining occupants of *Templar Express 1* and, with his sister following closely behind them, they made their way down one of the rows of parked cars and disappeared into the chaos of the noonday shoppers.

George Artowski seethed. Dunk McCormack followed the trio as best as he could out of the front window of the van but quickly lost them in the noonday sun. He was gripping the steering wheel so hard his knuckles were white, all the while muttering under his breath, "The friggin' bitch. Wait until I get my hands on her!"

Bill Rose quickly interjected, "Sir Knight McCormack! That is enough out of you. Obviously, bringing Marie along was to prompt exactly your emotional reaction. If you continue to concentrate on her, you won't be alert to other things within your surroundings. Now, did you notice any possible snipers or how they left?"

Dunk immediately composed himself and responded with military precision, "No, sir. He couldn't have chosen a better spot for the exchange. Any number of the hundreds of people coming and going could be targeting us still. There's no telling how many people he has backing him up."

Director Artowski jumped into the conversation by directing his comments to Bob Ross, who during the entire exchange had just stared across the parking lot to what he believed was *Templar Express 2*. "Okay, Robert. Go and get Danny. By Jean Baptiste's comments, it sounds as though he was roughed up pretty badly. If the van is in good enough shape, bring it along . . . I have to hand it to Jean Baptiste again. The bastard thinks of everything. From the sounds of it, he stripped the van clean."

Bob Ross jumped out of the van and quickly surveyed the perimeter. Although he wanted to rush over to gather his friend and companion, his training told him otherwise. He made a conscious effort to appear as though he was just another shopper hurrying into the store and walked past the van towards the store's entrance.

As he did so, he took in the whole scene and caught a glimpse of Danny Bishop's silhouette through the tinted windows. It appeared as though Agent Bishop was sitting in the passenger seat and Bob Ross could just make out the faint nod of recognition. It also appeared as though Agent Bishop's mouth was duct-taped shut.

Bob Ross strained to control his breathing and continued on to the end of the parking lane, where he swung around to come back up the next parking lane to the back of the van. Everything appeared normal, so he gently opened the driver's side door and hopped up into the driver's seat.

Danny Bishop sat in the passenger's seat with his hands cuffed together with plastic ties and his feet tied to the base of the passenger seat in similar fashion. Judging from the bruises on his face and the dried blood around his eyebrows and mouth, it was obvious he had been worked over by his abductors.

Bob Ross quickly checked the back of the van to confirm that indeed it had been stripped clean.

He sympathized with his buddy's condition but remained professional. Finally sensing that everything was okay, he leaned over to rip the duct tape from Danny's mouth.

Although Danny Bishop had been deprived of sleep and kept in strict isolation since his abduction, his eyes still held their deep intensity. As the tape came off, he gagged a little and sucked in a big gulp of fresh air before he stammered, "Bob, you're a sight for sore eyes. That damn LeNeuf fellow is one sick puppy. It's like he took great pleasure in working me over. He's slick though. The only thing I know for certain is that I was sitting in the van half dosing and then I woke up somewhere in complete darkness with a sack over my head. I think it was a cellar of sorts because I could feel the dampness. The bugger just let me lie there in my own filth, coming in every-so-often and beating the shit out of me. At first he asked me questions about what I knew and then, after he figured I wouldn't answer, he just beat me for the fun of it. The only thing he ever said was that I was helping him lose his aggression. Can you beat the nerve of it all?"

Bob Ross had to laugh out loud. "Danny, do you realize you just said more in half a minute than I've heard you say in the last eight years?"

"Is that so? Then just wait until I get my hands on the bastard. You'll hear me say a few more things."

Danny held up his wrists for Ross to cut the plastic ties with his small all-purpose knife. He then bent over and released his ankles.

As Danny rubbed his wrists, Bob Ross held up his finger to his lips to indicate that the van may be bugged. Ross decided to give Jean Baptiste a little something to chew on if he was somehow listening to their conversation, "Agent Bishop, we'll have none of that. We made a deal— Mr. Randolph for Mr. Rose's life. We're turning around and heading home. We've already lost ten good men in this ordeal."

Danny Bishop played right along but still couldn't believe what he was hearing, "Damn it, Bob, you can't be serious?"

"Yes, we can and we are. You signed on knowing full well that our primary responsibility as Secret Service agents was to protect the president of the United States and then, secondarily, her husband. Let the bastard get what he came for. It can't be all that important!" Bob Ross made the statement but wasn't buying into it. "Come on, let's join the others. They'll be wondering what's going on."

Bob Ross turned the key to the van and the engine roared into life. Heshifted into drive and slowly started to pull the van out of its parking spot. That's when it happened.

The van was surely wired for voice transmission, as the lone occupant seated in the black Mercedes some five rows over had waited to hear the initial conversation between the two agents before he remotely detonated the bomb attached to the van's engine.

The explosion was controlled to take out the two occupants of the van but not to wipe out the whole row of parked cars. Jean Baptiste had even made sure the van's gas tank was almost empty, in order for the extent of damage and kill zone to be minimized. He had a strange sense of honor when it came to protecting innocent Wal-Mart shoppers.

Upon seeing the result of his handiwork, the occupant of the black Mercedes casually pulled out of the parking lot to rendezvous with his boss on the other side of the plaza.

Meanwhile, the three remaining occupants of *Templar Express 1*— Lieutenant McCormack, Bill Rose, and George Artowski, sat in disbelief at the carnage around them. Miraculously, several innocent bystanders only received cuts and bruises, mostly from being blown over by the initial blast or from flying glass and debris; but the effect was nonetheless devastating.

People sobbed and screamed, while the first sirens on the scene wailed away. Everyone milling about appeared to be surmising that the van had blown up due to a gas tank leak. One police officer on the scene had even secured what appeared to be left of the gas tank, which he found several rows over from the immediate scene.

Dunk McCormack was the first one in the van to say anything, "Mother of God! Those guys didn't know what hit them. I can't believe it."

Bill Rose had closed his eyes upon hearing the explosion and now opened them to respond to Dunk's exclamation, "Those poor men. What type of sick person could do that?"

George Artowski always had been the analytical one of the two, yet his eyes had narrowed to two slits. "Sick people just like Jean Baptiste, that's who! I don't think he kills just for the sake of killing. I think he himself has experienced some sick psychological warfare, and it's taught him to throw the enemy off guard. Constant terror of the unknown—this is what he's playing at . . . Well, two can play this game . . . That's now four Secret Service agents he's taken out, plus eight Navy Seals."

Dunk was anxiously waiting for the call to arms but it didn't come. Although the van's occupants were certain Thomas had taken the bugging device with him when he took his laptop, they wouldn't be taking any chances until they could scan the van once more.

George spoke the words he knew Dunk didn't want to hear, "Let's go before the police seal off the scene completely. I don't want them to make an immediate connection to Danny and Bob and the White House, or to who's sitting beside me. I'll contact the Bunker and have them contain the scene. Bill, you'll have to phone Helen. I imagine she'll be devastated and want to pull us out and send in the heavies but you'll have to talk her out of that. We don't want to spook Jean Baptiste after we've come this far. Judging by his character, or lack thereof, if he thinks he's being followed he'll surely torture Thomas for the information and then dump him for dead in a ditch. Let the bastard think he has the upper hand and we're retreating . . . Dunk, please head back east along I-94 until I can gather my thoughts."

Lieutenant McCormack reluctantly pulled the van back onto the highway, all the while surveying the smoke from the bombing through the rear view mirror.

In doing so, he noticed a rented silver Ford Taurus pulling out of the parking lot at the same time, starting to tail him, but not too close.

As Dunk turned east back onto I-94, he silently urged the tail to keep following him. *Come on, you bastard. Keep on coming. It's payback time!*

# CHAPTER 42

Thomas Randolph, Marie Magdalene, and Jean Baptiste St. Jean-LeNeuf had made their way around the Superstore to a pre-arranged spot when they heard the explosion. After the immediate shock wore off, Thomas was going to say something, but the look of sheer delight on Jean Baptiste's face stopped him. By the time Thomas finally got up the nerve to confront him, the black Mercedes had pulled up to the curb.

Thomas was pushed into its backseat, sandwiched between Marie and Jean Baptiste. The car then sped away, followed by the black van, which was still driven by Godfroi—the slightly nerdy communications expert.

By contrast, the driver of the Mercedes was massive, with no neck and broad shoulders and the now-familiar military style haircut. John Baptiste introduced him as Pierre—the head of security at the St. Jean-LeNeuf Estate at Fincastle.

Pierre and two other ex-paratroopers had flown into Bismarck by private jet that very morning, after being summoned by Jean Baptiste, to replace the eight men lost during the incident with Shadow Team 3. Pierre was chosen to drive Jean Baptiste's Mercedes, while the other two provided sniper support during the parking lot exchange and were now tailing *Templar Express 1* in the rented Taurus.

Prior to his present job, Pierre had been the sub-lieutenant in Jean Baptiste's unit, with a specialty in explosives. Unflinching at the explosion in the parking lot, he concentrated hard on his driving. The last thing Jean Baptiste wanted was to be pulled over for speeding, as the police presence in the area had significantly heightened in the last half hour. The frightened look on Thomas's face was a sure sign of distress to any local police officer or state trooper. The fact that Marie was staring straight ahead with the

156

saddest of faces was also a dead giveaway something was amiss within the group.

The first order of business as the small convoy crossed over the Missouri River and headed west, through Mandan, North Dakota, was for Jean Baptiste to assure himself that Thomas wasn't wired. Jean Baptiste ripped the knapsack from Thomas's hands and extracted the laptop. Then he produced from a small compartment on the side door a wand-like device, which he expertly ran over Thomas from head to toe. The wand didn't make a sound until he held it close to the laptop, which produced a slight beeping.

Satisfied that Thomas wasn't wired, Jean Baptiste rather casually put the laptop back in the knapsack and deposited it on the passenger's seat in front of him. Jean Baptiste didn't remove the bug from the laptop because he wanted the communications van to tape the entire conversation about to occur. Thomas concentrated hard not to give away the fact that the bug had previously been discovered by George Artowski.

"So, Mr. Randolph, your supposed friends gave you up in order to assure themselves of Mr. Rose's safety. I must say that was rather in bad form, especially given the fact they're fellow Masons and Knights Templar. I would have thought their vows would have prevented them from abandoning you." Jean Baptiste was obviously gloating and Thomas knew, in an odd way, he had a right to do so.

Up until that moment, the Frenchman had clearly outsmarted George Artowski every step of the way. However, what Jean Baptiste didn't know at this moment was that the director had silently downloaded an application for Thomas's BlackBerry from the White House Bunker, which allowed Thomas's RIM instrument to transmit conversation and continual GPS coordinates without registering on Jean Baptiste's magic wand. As long as Thomas's BlackBerry was on—and the battery was strong—the advantage would go to the Templars.

Thomas wanted to keep the conversation going in the hope Jean Baptiste's plans might be revealed. He decided it was best not to antagonize the man too much and, to that end, he spoke in a slightly conciliatory tone when he said, "Jean Baptiste, I know you know it was my decision alone. I agreed in the hope it would stop the killing. Unfortunately, you found it necessary to eliminate another two innocent men."

Jean Baptiste didn't mind the accusation one bit, as he considered Thomas to be ignorant when it came to the matters at hand. "Mr. Randolph, with the greatest of respect, men who carry arms and who are trained to kill are not innocent. If I had let Mr. Bishop and Mr. Ross live, I'm sure their personal anger alone would have caused them to pursue us. What I did, or rather, what Pierre did, was ensure my current advantage and send a message to your friends—the game is over. Stop playing with the professionals, count your losses, give up and be on your way . . . This means that the old ways of the republic are useless versus the New World Order."

Thomas couldn't help but think he had heard this somewhere before. *Isn't this what Napoleon alluded to before he met his Waterloo?* "Jean Baptiste, do you really think that, no matter what is buried in the foothills, it will allow you to establish a New World Order?"

"Yes, I do!"

He turned his attention to Marie. "You know, I actually feel sorry for you and your brother. You've been raised on all of this *Holy Blood, Holy Grail* background to the point that you think because you are of the bloodline you're entitled to control the world. Let me tell you one thing: Jesus preached above all else, peace and harmony—nothing more and nothing less! Even with this, I seem to remember things didn't work out for him too well."

Jean Baptiste lost all patience. "Enough of this, Mr. Randolph. We have been doing a little genealogical work of our own on your family background. I don't know if it comes as a surprise or not but it appears your mother's line can also claim to be descendents of the Holy Bloodline. It appears that the lieutenant governor of the original 1632 Quebec community of Three Rivers—*Trois Rivieres*, was one Mathieu Michel LeNeuf du Herisson. Yes, he was an ancestor of both of ours. Both he and his wife—a Jeanne Le Marchand—were lesser French nobility, and, as *Trois Rivieres* was a significant Indian trading post under Champlain's rule of New France, it was customary for the governor's son to marry into the Algonquin nation in order to secure the inland trading rights. Your mother's maternal line— Laguarde dit St. Jean, directly descended from that union."

Jean Baptiste let this bit of information set in before continuing, "Thomas, we are offering you your rightful place among us. Come and join us. I know that, although she may appear a little conflicted right now, my sister would welcome this with open arms. She is not getting any younger and would like to have children. With your bloodline and Knights Templar background, you would certainly make a suitable mate."

Thomas couldn't believe what he was hearing. *First I think I'm not going to get out of this car alive, and now I'm being propositioned as a potential husband-to-be. Are these people mad? It now all makes sense. These families have been breeding amongst themselves for thousands of years, but they seem to know enough that new blood, suitable blood, is required every couple of generations in order to keep the bloodline strong!*

Thomas stared at Marie but she was giving nothing away. She stared straight ahead, but Thomas, for a second, thought he discerned a slight turning up of the corner of her lips. If it was a sign of irony or sarcasm, he didn't know.

Thomas turned his head to face Jean Baptiste in order to make his point home. "Let me think about it for a while. In the meantime, you can tell me what it is that you expect in return."

Jean Baptiste was pleasantly surprised and grew a little friendlier to Thomas. "Excellent! Surely, you must know what we expect of you. We're heading towards a small farm, which I've purchased, positioned at exactly 48 degrees north longitude, 104 degrees west longitude, along the North Dakota-Montana border. What you will see there, I think, will certainly intrigue you . . . Knowing what we do, we measured exactly 8 degrees west from this point to a point at 46 degrees north latitude, 112 degrees west longitude, hoping to find the hidden vault. Unfortunately, there was nothing there or, more to the point, there was too much there in terms of underground caves. The limestone and shale is riddled with natural sinkholes, caverns, underground water channels, as well as man-made mine shafts and tunnels."

Thomas interjected, "Therefore, what you need from me is to pinpoint exactly where the vault is located, in accordance with my Templar and Native American background and research." It was more of a statement than a question.

"Yes, Thomas, in less than three days a solar eclipse will traverse North America, positioning directly overhead of the vault at noon, local time, when the sun is at its meridian, as you Masons like to profess." Jean

Baptiste's tone had changed entirely from when they first entered the car. "Join us, Thomas. Together we can change the world and make it a more peaceful place."

"I'll do it, Jean Baptiste. Not because I believe it is your destiny, or mine, but because I want to think that the world needs something to once again believe in. I truly believe the Knights Templar rediscovered something so powerful that it could unite the world in peace and harmony. Call me the eternal optimist, but I also believe mankind can work together for the better good. Over the centuries, thousands, if not millions, of people gladly sacrificed their lives to maintain the secret because they knew that, someday, mankind would be able to receive it with open arms." Thomas wondered himself if he believed his own words or whether he made them up to gain Jean Baptiste's confidence.

Obviously, Thomas's words had the desired effect, for Jean Baptiste laid back, smiled and closed his eyes without responding.

The one person who did respond was Marie. She also leaned back and closed her eyes, but not before her hand slid over to embrace Thomas's.

The rest of the trip was spent in silence and reflection. Meanwhile, George Artowski had followed the entire conversation, as relayed by his people in the Bunker, via his own BlackBerry application. *Thomas, my boy, you've outdone yourself! Let's now hope we can use the information to our advantage.*

# Chapter 43

For the past four hours, *Templar Express 1* headed east along Interstate 94 from Bismarck, North Dakota, in a state of collective shock. Along the way, Bill Rose phoned his wife to convey the news about Danny Bishop's and Bob Ross's deaths. Upon hearing the news, President Helen Jefferson-Rose begged her husband to abandon the mission and return to Washington immediately, but her husband would have no part of that. Bill Rose was adamant that Jean Baptiste be stopped at all costs.

The president was prepared, then, to call in the armed forces, CIA, or FBI to deal with the situation, but George Artowski talked her out of this strategy. His reasoning that it would only drive the Order of the True Rose Croix underground finally won over. The president only agreed on the condition that if the issue wasn't resolved in three days, then the heavies would swoop in.

Of course, George readily accepted this condition, as neither he nor Bill Rose wanted to confirm the fact that if good didn't triumph over evil within the next three days, then all of them, including Thomas Randolph, would most likely be dead.

Lieutenant McCormack was the one to take the deaths of the two Secret Service agents most to heart. To die on the battlefield was one thing a marine could accept, but to be needlessly blown away in your own country was an entirely different matter. Dunk was certainly hoping the director's plan would work but, if it didn't, he wouldn't want to be in Jean Baptiste's shoes. He had made a vow as they drove past the carnage at the Superstore to see to the man personally, if it was the last thing he would ever do.

Dunk was also keeping a constant watch out for the silver Ford Taurus in the rear-view mirror. Whoever was tailing them was good. Over

161

the past four hours, Dunk only caught a brief glimpse of the car on three different occasions. He only told the director about the tail when they stopped for gas, as he didn't want Bill Rose to get more upset than he was at this point. George responded by telling him he had done the right thing and that they would be taken care of in due course.

Having agreed to stop for supper at some out-of-the-way place around 5:00 p.m., Dunk now pulled the van into a small roadside diner just east of Jamestown, North Dakota. He reasoned that the food must be good there, judging by the number of eighteen wheelers and campers parked in its oversized parking lot.

As before, it was agreed all three would don their hats and fishing vests and, hopefully, there would be a relatively quiet table somewhere in a corner where they wouldn't be disturbed. As luck would have it, there was a table for six available next to the broken jukebox, which afforded a full view of everyone else in the diner.

George finally spoke as he went to sit down, "I don't know about the two of you but I'm finding this all too surreal. Here we are in the heart of America sitting down to dinner with the knowledge there's a madman running around out there nonchalantly blowing people up."

Bill Rose seated with his back facing the crowd, said, "Yes, I totally agree, George. You're feeling a little melancholy like the rest of us right about now but you know as well as I do, we have to eat in order to continue. We have to see an end to this business, even if it costs us our lives. What was it you used to say to Michael St. Jean-LeNeuf in Vietnam? . . . There will be time enough to mourn the losses. Well, there will be time enough to mourn Danny Bishop and Bob Ross—our two fellow knights. They died for a just and rightful cause, just like the Knights Templar a thousand years ago."

George picked up the menu. "Of course, you're right, Bill. All the same it won't bring them back."

Before Bill Rose could respond, the trio was interrupted by two men dressed as typical mid-westerners. "Colonel Artowski, sir?" Phil Bloomer had appeared out of nowhere, along with Sergeant Wayne, or so it seemed. In reality, the director had arranged the rendezvous when they stopped for gas.

George Artowski looked up at the two Navy Seals. "Ah, Phil, rank is not important here. Please refer to me as director or, even better, just plain

George . . . And this young fellow must be James Wayne." The Navy Seal tipped his Texas Rangers ball cap as George continued, "May I introduce Bill Rose, who I'm sure you recognize as being the president's husband and Dunk McCormack—Marine Lieutenant McCormack."

Handshakes and introductions were made all around, with Master Chief Wayne providing the requisite wisecrack about marines not being able to swim.

Bill Rose welcomed the easygoing banter. "Gentlemen, you're a sight for sore eyes. I'd very much like for you to join us."

Phil Bloomer was a little hesitant, but Master Chief Wayne jumped right in. "Don't mind if we do, sir. I'm getting a little tired of the rations we have in the back of the truck. I can tell you one thing: I'm going to have a piece of the banana cream pie."

After such a tense afternoon, Master Chief Wayne's easygoing manner was just what the table needed. And, when he called over the waitress to take their orders, it turned into a contest between the Marine and the Navy Seal as to who could best sweet-talk her.

The two laid it on so thick that, after she left, the bet was she wouldn't be able to remember the orders correctly. The immediate result was that the table was firing on all cylinders again, with a renewed determination to stop Jean Baptiste and his colleagues once and for all.

After receiving their food, which astonishingly corresponded exactly to their orders, the director leaned into the group and said, "Okay, here's what we know: Jean Baptiste, along with his sister, Marie, Thomas, and some heavy named Pierre and who-knows-who-else, are heading towards a farm located on the North Dakota-Montana border. Thomas, I think, has gained their confidence by volunteering to help them pinpoint the location of the vault. In two and a-half days, they'll want to have cracked the vault fairly early in anticipation of the solar eclipse revealing the true treasure. Other than Bill, none of you know until now that the eclipse in some manner will reveal the one true secret amongst many others. Don't ask me what this means because we're as much in the dark as the rest of you . . . Now, Bill, here's something I know you don't know."

Bill Rose looked up from consuming a large chunk of homemade meatloaf and set down his knife and fork.

"I'm sorry I didn't tell you sooner, Bill, but we've been followed from the time we left Bismarck. Dunk picked them out and confirmed it." George was looking rather sheepish from holding back valuable information from his best friend.

Master Chief Wayne felt the awkwardness between the two gentlemen and felt best to dive right in. "You mean those two frogs sitting out in the parking lot in a silver Ford Taurus?"

Dunk laughed. "That's exactly who we mean. How'd you peg them?"

"Typical French para-pussies, what with those buzzed haircuts and smoking those French Gitanes non-stop. You can smell those bloody cigarettes a mile away."

George Artowski turned and directed a question to Phil Bloomer, "Phil, is everything now in place?"

"Yes, Colonel Artowski, oops, sorry, sir . . . I mean, George. The funniest thing is they're hiding directly behind our eighteen-wheeler." Phil looked at his watch. "In fact, I'd say they're being looked after . . . right . . . about now."

Needless to say, the Navy Seals timed the operation perfectly. The two French ex-paratroopers, who Jean Baptiste ordered to follow *Templar Express 1*, didn't know what hit them. One moment they were sitting in their car having a smoke and the next thing they knew they were convulsing helplessly after being tasered by two Navy Seals, who'd snuck up on them.

Within two minutes flat, the two were bound and gagged and hustled into the bowels of the red-and-white truck-trailer. The operation went off without a hitch, except that one Navy Seal took it upon himself to give one of the captives a good swift kick in the ribs, in retribution for the ambush on his buddies. Phil Bloomer would see to the incident later but at this moment all he received, via his tiny ear piece, was that the tails had been secured and a bonus had been found. The two ex-paratroopers had foolishly left their encrypted portable phones on the coded channel, so a direct line of communication with Jean Baptiste existed.

This was exactly what Phil Bloomer was hoping for, as he put forward a suggestion, "Gentlemen, we've secured your two tails. At this moment, they're having a little nap inside the trailer. If you don't mind, I have an idea as to how we can buy you some time and assist you."

George perked up at this. "Dunk, please go pay the bill, if you will? We'll listen to what Phil has up his sleeve."

Dunk didn't mind having to get up and pay the bill, as he spied the same waitress seeing to the cash register.

Meanwhile, Phil outlined his plan."I don't know if you know this Colonel, but the trailer's equipped to carry your van. I'm suggesting we run the van up into the trailer to allow the three of you to bunk down with the rest of the crew, while I head west. If I hightail it, we should make the North Dakota-Montana border sometime before sunrise. We could be in front of the prey before they even realize it."

Bill Rose picked up on what was being suggested and responded, "That's a great idea, Phil. I could really do with some sleep, but what about the two Frenchmen? They must be checking in regularly with Jean Baptiste or their communications center."

"This is where Master Chief Wayne comes in, sir. You see, the grinning idiot is really quite intelligent and has a knack for American dialects. It's more entertaining when you witness it firsthand."

Master Chief Wayne sat there feigning ignorance, as George exclaimed, "Then lead on Phil, by all means."

By the time the group reached the truck-trailer, the van had already been run up into the trailer and the big rear doors were shut once again. The few truckers who were coming and going from the parking lot paid no attention to the activity centered on the red-and-white eighteen-wheeler. It was as though it was an everyday occurrence.

What took place next was definitely not something anyone witnessed every day. Master Chief Wayne had been given one of the French encrypted phones and had punched in the first auto-dial button, assuming it was programmed to link into their mobile communication center.

The phone buzzed once before a man's voice came on, saying, "*Oui?*" Jean Baptiste himself answered the other end of the secure connection.

Master Chief Wayne assumed his best North Dakota State Trooper accent and responded, "Excuse me, sir; this is Sergeant Wayne of the North Dakota State Police. To whom am I speaking?"

Jean Baptiste's mind was going a mile a minute but he quickly composed himself. "Sergeant Wayne, this is Jean Baptiste St. Jean-LeNeuf,

CEO and president of St. Jean-LeNeuf World Enterprises. Is there a problem?"

Master Chief Wayne made a screwed-up face to Dunk before replying, "Unfortunately, sir, my men came across a single-car accident. A rented, silver Ford Taurus appears to have been going at a fast rate of speed and missed a curve on 1-94 just east of Jamestown. I'm sorry to say we have two deceased occupants still trapped in the car. They hit the woods going near eighty from the look of it." Master Chief Wayne paused for effect. "The emergency personnel were searching for their wallets and came across holstered Glock revolvers and two encrypted portable phones. Would you care to explain this, sir?"

"Of course, Master Chief Wayne, but first of all, let me say this is a terrible tragedy. Those two men were trusted security employees of my corporation." Jean Baptiste paused for effect. "If you check their wallets, you will see they both have licenses to carry their sidearms. I have a business property here in North Dakota, and they were on the way to collect some very important papers, which I had to have signed by today . . . I am ever so paranoid of corporate espionage . . . I will give you the number of my personal executive assistant in New York, a Ms. Michele Laguarde, who will see to all of the arrangements to bring the two men's bodies back to New York. Would this meet your needs, Master Chief Wayne?"

"Yes, of course, sir. That would be more than suitable. I must apologize. I never enjoy being the bearer of bad news. Please accept our sincerest condolences on behalf of the State of North Dakota. I will personally see to the arrangements and the shipping of their personal property, including their guns and phones."

Jean Baptiste sighed and then responded, "Thank you, Master Chief Wayne. You have been most kind. Now I must say goodbye in order to get hold of my executive assistant. Goodbye."

The Navy Seal NCO pushed the stop transmission button.

Dunk slapped him on the back. "I thought only marines were nut cases. Man, you could go on the road with that act. Come on, I need some sleep."

Phil Bloomer was already revving up the huge truck. Both George Artowski and Bill Rose shook their heads in amazement as the group entered the trailer via the side door, which had an internal collapsible staircase.

After quick introductions were made all around and everyone found a bunk suitable to their liking, the big red-and-white truck-trailer pulled out of the parking lot and headed west. One of the Navy Seals had volunteered to follow in the Taurus until Phil spotted a trooper detachment where the car and captured Frenchmen could be sequestered and remain undiscovered for at least three days. James Wayne would have to wait until the morning to put a call into Michele Laguarde with the news that the bodies couldn't be released until the state coroner had signed off, which would most probably take at least three days.

As soon as the trio's heads hit their pillows, they were fast asleep.

# Chapter 44

It took close to three weeks for the guardians to make their way to a major Shoshone village, located at 48 degrees north latitude, 104 degrees west longitude. Whether the village was located there because of the significant latitudinal and longitudinal coordinates or this positioning was just coincidental really didn't matter to the two knights. What did matter was the fact the guardians were that much closer to their destination.

The ride west from the Mandan village was without any real incident. As such, it not only allowed both Major LeNeuf and Sergeant Major St. Jean to take in the expansive scenery of the vast western plains but also to get to know and better understand their host and guide—Cameahwait, the great Shoshone chief.

The small contingent of riders rode hard most of the time, stopping only to sleep for a few hours each night or to hunt buffalo, in order to deposit the meat at the smaller seasonal camps of the Shoshone.

The two guardians received the royal treatment, in part because of the prophecies and in part because they were the honored guests of Cameahwait. This honor even extended one night to both men being offered the companionship of lovely young women. The two knights delicately declined the gracious offer.

If it had not been for Cameahwait's understanding of the vow of chastity, which the two guardians had taken, the Shoshone would surely have been offended. The two guardian's admiration for their host grew even greater when they came to understand that the Shoshone chief had explained to his people that the two were spirits from the netherworld, and to mate with human beings would bring bad luck on the village. Therefore, in declining the offer, the guardians showered favor on the Shoshone.

As a result, when the two knights finally found themselves as guests in Cameahwait's teepee that evening, the women only offered food and drink, much to the relief of both guest and host. Then they quickly disappeared, leaving the two to rest and reflect.

Cameahwait entered the teepee with his eldest son and one of the village elders, who was carrying with him an odd looking cross made of sticks. The son continued to act as interpreter, now for both of the older Shoshones, and explained to the two knights the elder's name was Nassagaweya, which meant Crossed Sticks. He was the village's shaman. The son continued by saying that both his father and the elder wanted the two knights to follow them and to bring along their stargazing equipment.

Michel and Jean popped up in anticipation of a very interesting evening. After reaching into his deerskin bag for Monsignor Lartique's sextant, the group silently followed the elder, who traveled a well-worn path for the next half hour over a slight rise in the land to the north. Here the group found themselves under a blanket of bright summer stars and the slightest sliver of a new moon.

Having adjusted their sight to the relative darkness of the nighttime sky versus the dancing light of the teepee's campfire, the two knights soon realized they stood in the middle of a wheel formed by a number of small rocks, which had been positioned to form a circle. Cameahwait's son, with some animated assistance from both his father and the elder, explained they were standing in the middle of a medicine wheel constructed by the ancient people, and that the magic of the wheel had been passed down to the current elder, Nassagaweya.

Indeed, the shaman looked extremely proud, as he tried to straighten his withered body to his full height. All the while, Nassagaweya kept up a running commentary in Shoshone, which hardly needed interpretation. It was plain to Major LeNeuf and Sergeant Major St. Jean what the topic of tonight's lesson was going to be. Michel thought, *I wish Monsignor Lartique was here this evening. It would fill the old priest's heart to meet his Native American counterpart.*

Cameahwait didn't need any interpretation either to understand the astonishment on the guardian's faces. His response was nothing more, nothing less, than a self-satisfying grunt. In turn, Michel's response was just a loud chuckle and a friendly slap on the shaman's back as a signal to continue the lesson.

Over the next four hours, the two learned knights remained astonished at the breadth and accuracy of the astronomical knowledge the shaman possessed. Nassagaweya pointed out to the two knights every major constellation in the sky and related them to the animals on the ground. There was the jackrabbit, the horse, the buffalo, and the crab. There was the bear, the deer, the snake, the fox, and the coyote.

The most amazing demonstration that evening was when Nassagaweya literally challenged the major to an astronomer's duel. The challenge was who could most accurately determine the latitude and longitude of the medicine wheel.

Sergeant Major St. Jean laughed out loud and slapped his thigh when he heard the translation of the wager. *This is one for the ages!* Mon Dieu, *we've been involved in many wagers over the years, but never one like this!*

Major LeNeuf was thinking exactly the same thing. He was also laughing out loud. When he finally gained control of himself, he spoke through Cameahwait's son, "You old rascal, you indeed honor us with such a wager. I have a feeling though that the stakes are set against us, for this is your home territory. Before we accept, there must always be a prize when you are challenged." The major thought hard about this. "If I win, I'm going to want that odd-looking wooden contraption in your hand, along with the knowledge of how to use it."

This caused Nassagaweya a little bit of consternation, for the crossed sticks obviously were the shaman's prized possession. Once Cameahwait caught the drift of the conversation, he threw his hands up to sky and proclaimed in Shoshone, "*Kwey, Kwey,* the guardians have chosen wisely. They have judged correctly as to our shaman's most valuable prize." The Shoshone chief patted the major on the back just to rub in the good-natured challenge a little bit more.

But Nassagaweya wasn't to be outdone in the wisdom department. He rubbed his chin as he eyed the sextant held in the major's right hand. The sergeant major caught the shaman's glance and suddenly became deeply worried. If the shaman asked for and won the sextant, the two knights would not be able to pinpoint the vault. Jean looked at Michel, who was displaying the same conclusion on his face, but in all fairness it was up to the shaman to identify his prize.

The silence was golden. Nassagaweya was playing his timing perfectly. When he finally spoke in Shoshone, he interjected just the right amount of sheepishness in his reflection, "Ah, I see the two red-and-white guardians have extended themselves in their wager. I imagine that over the years, the two have wagered with their life on many occasions, but now they challenge an old man to give up his most valuable possession. Yet, when I eye the metal object they possess, they hesitate . . . No matter, I will make their choice easy for them." Michel and Jean stared at each other first and then at the shaman. They had no idea what was in store for them.

After several long moments of silence, the shaman finally proclaimed, "I have decided I will not ask for your metal object if I win. Although I can see it is one of your most valued possessions, I do not think it is yours to give. Instead, I will only ask that, if I win, you take two of the Blackfoot women Cameahwait captured in his last raid back to their people. Indeed, this may help you gain favor with our enemies."

"Hold on, what am I hearing?" exclaimed the sergeant major in French. "Are you saying that if we lose we have to take two Blackfoot women with us as we move west? Cameahwait, we thought the Shoshone were allies with the Blackfoot?"

After the appropriate translation, Cameahwait just shook his head and then replied, "*Kwey, Kwey*, you are wrong. The red-and-white guardians have jumped to the wrong conclusion. Even though the Shoshone and Blackfoot are both of the Algonquin Nation and share the same red blood, we have been sworn enemies for many generations. I promised to direct you to the Blackfoot and this is what I will do. No more, no less." Cameahwait spit on the ground, as if to emphasize his last statement.

This information was unexpected. It changed their plans. The real question was: would the Blackfoot would receive them as graciously as the Shoshone had? Michel's mind was racing with a mixture of emotions. He stared at Nassagaweya's sheepish grin, as he thought through the current set of events in his mind. *Why you old rascal! You know the thing we cherish most is our vow of chastity to God. Although it has no monetary value like the bronze sextant, it nonetheless is what we hold most dear to our hearts. Could this wizard read our minds?*

Michel made the decision right there for both himself and his companion. He turned to Cameahwait's son and proclaimed, "Tell the old coyote we accept his challenge!" But even before the son had a chance to translate the statement into Shoshone, Nassagaweya responded in perfect French, "Who are you calling an old coyote?"

The group of five all roared with laughter. Nassagaweya continued through the merriment, again in French, "Let this be another lesson for the two of you. Never assume anything!"

With this pronouncement, it was almost a foregone conclusion who would win the contest. Major LeNeuf and Sergeant Major St. Jean went first and concentrated hard to determine the latitudinal and longitudinal coordinates of the medicine wheel. Finally, they pronounced their readings as 47.9 degrees north latitude and 103.8 degrees west longitude.

Nassagaweya just smiled and then proceeded to explain how the two sticks were used, much like an angled Celtic cross, in order to measure the relative distance of the northern constellation—Cygnas, to the big dipper—the Bear, and the northern star, all the while keeping the relative distance and movement of the moon in the equation. This was a new set of criteria, which even Father Lartique failed to recognize in his teachings. Finally, the shaman pronounced that the exact coordinates of the medicine wheel were 48 degrees north latitude and 104 degrees west longitude, which he already knew because it had been handed down from his forefathers.

Michel didn't know what to say, but he knew what to think. The old medicine man had fixed the contest even before it had begun. Of course, this was the real purpose of the lesson.

Cameahwait was grinning from ear to ear, as was Nassagaweya. It was obvious from the expressions of the two guardians there were no hard feelings, just bewilderment. The Shoshone chief stood apart from the group, spread his arms wide and spoke in French. "My brothers, yes, you have met the Trickster. He comes in many forms—the raven, the crow, the coyote and the grizzled old man. We do not teach you this lesson out of disrespect but in the hope you will never meet him again . . . Now I already know Nassagaweya wants you to have his crossed sticks. Ah, I see by your faces you are again confused. Do not worry. He can easily make another set. For you have learned it is not the value of the instrument that is most precious, but the value of the knowledge required to work it. We want to make sure your calculations are accurate. As to the penalty you will have to endure as you head into Blackfoot territory, I only wish that the Creator imposed such a penalty on me. But alas, I have too many wives already."

Michel and Jean were once again confused by the chief's statement.

Cameahwait continued, giving some clarification, "When you are about to leave tomorrow, you will discover the true meaning of my words. You will also discover the true meaning of beauty. All I will say now, as we make our way back to our beds, is that you must open up your hearts to find the true treasure. Allow your feelings to guide you in your search for the lost secret!"

The solemn procession fell into silence, as it made its way back to the village and their teepees. In his right hand, Michel carried Father Lartique's sextant. In his left, he carried Nassagaweya's crossed sticks.

# CHAPTER 45

At exactly 5:00 p.m., the black Mercedes arrived at the renovated farmhouse, which for over one hundred years had been owned by the Demers family. After the death of the family's last patriarch, Eustache Demers, the farmstead was purchased by the then-unknown St. Jean-LeNeuf Agro-Enterprises Inc. The locals were astonished when they first heard that such a run-down old farm had been bought by a large international corporation, since the snow was too deep in the winter and the fields were too hot and dry in the summer to grow anything in abundance.

Indeed, they were just as astonished when the huge wind turbines and hydroponic greenhouses went up across the entire 200-acre spread. But they came to enjoy the seasonal employment the thriving industry created, producing hothouse tomatoes and other, rarer vegetables and grains through genetic testing. Besides, the young French aristocrat and his beautiful sister added a certain flare to the otherwise drab surroundings whenever they drove into Williston for supplies, some fourteen miles east of what was essentially the ghost town still called Buford. If it hadn't been for the Fort Buford Historical Site and the St. Jean-LeNeuf farm, the whole county would have died a slow death a long time ago.

The locals also knew enough not to be too nosy as to the comings and goings at the farm. The need for the armed French guards was attributed to potential corporate sabotage, as it had been explained to them that a number of religious groups had already made threats against the corporation because of the genetic testing and alteration programs. Therefore, it wasn't out of the ordinary when the local seasonal workers were asked to take the next few days off due to the arrival of the CEO and president—Jean Baptiste St. Jean-LeNeuf, his sister, and their guest.

174

As the black Mercedes pulled directly into a large, modern-day maintenance shed and stopped, Jean Baptiste was the first to exit the car. He stood proudly, holding the door open for both Thomas and his sister, Marie, all the while announcing, "Thomas, welcome to the St. Jean-LeNeuf Agro-Enterprises and Incubation Centre. I think you will be amazed at our progress in the genetics field by our company within just the last five years. With unique equipment in which we have invested heavily and patented, we are currently producing over fifty strains of modified vegetables, grains, and fruits. Through cutting-edge genetic modification, we are producing disease-free and drought-resistant varieties so fast that we cannot keep up with naming them all."

"Through hydroponic and controlled nutrient techniques, we have increased normal crop yields ten-fold. Everything is powered by the sun, the wind and underground geothermal systems, and we employ on a seasonal basis at least one hundred and fifty of the local population. This is the future you see before you."

Meanwhile, Pierre saw to the luggage and silently disappeared across the inner courtyard to the large, renovated farmhouse, which sported a bank of south-facing solar panels and a large, tinted-glass addition that appeared to be a laboratory of sorts.

Once Pierre was out of earshot, Jean Baptiste continued, "There is another side to the farm, however, a facet I believe will most intrigue you. In the late 1800s, this farmstead was first settled by Benjamin Demers, and how he arrived at this place is a mystery. We do know that when he settled here, he had a young Shoshone wife with him, as this land was still considered by some to be Shoshone territory. Interestingly, it's positioned at exactly 48 degrees north latitude, 104 degrees west longitude, straddling your antient meridian. A major Shoshone village was located here about two hundred years ago."

Jean Baptiste walked to the huge doorway of the shed and pointed in a southwesterly direction. "You can almost throw a stone across the highway there, known as 143rd Avenue Northwest, and hit the confluence of the Missouri and Yellowstone River. Sometimes, at night, I swear I can still hear the war cries of the Shoshone warriors."

"It turned out that old Ben must have known the native history of this place, as he became quite the amateur archaeologist, gathering a rather impressive collection of Shoshone and other Native American artifacts. This collection first came to my attention when the last of the Demers family died. Actually, this is the real reason why I bought the farm. It has become quite profitable in many ways but what I am about to show you now is priceless. Are you interested?" Jean Baptiste knew the answer before asking the question.

Thomas was genuinely intrigued and responded in an enthusiastic manner, "Yes, of course, Jean Baptiste. Please show the way."

Jean Baptiste rounded the maintenance shed and followed a well-worn path to the north over a slight rise in the land for about twenty minutes. Marie fell in beside Thomas without saying a word but once again took his hand in hers. As they crested the small rise where Jean Baptiste had stopped, Thomas looked down into the small valley and gasped. "Oh, my God, it's a native medicine wheel made out of stone. I can't believe it's remained untouched all this time." Thomas paused and tilted his head slightly to one side and then to the other, as though he was trying to figure something out. Both Marie and Jean Baptiste stood silently, each smiling an all-knowing smile.

It finally dawned on Thomas and he exclaimed, "By all that's holy . . . it's the seventh sign in stone! . . . Why, this is magnificent!"

Jean Baptiste was beaming by this time. His faith in Thomas, he believed, had been well-founded and was now confirmed. "Yes, Thomas, it is magnificent. And, by your reaction, I see you also are in possession of a copy of Meriwether Lewis's drawing. I figured that your group of Knights Templar had somehow come into possession of the drawing. I've surmised for a long time that Thomas Jefferson must have made a copy of it when it was shown to him by our ancestors. What I'm willing to wager though is that you haven't deciphered the entire drawing. Nor have you seen the other writing, Le Serpent Rouge? Not to worry. In due time, you will have access to both. But it's time to eat, so let's head back to the farmhouse. Pierre is a magnificent cook, in addition to his other talents."

Thomas obediently fell in behind Jean Baptiste, led by the hand of Marie. His head was swimming, and he was having a hard time breathing. He was suffering from information overload and at the same time, trying to keep his wits about him, as both Jean Baptiste's and Marie's manipulations assaulted his reasoning and logic. *Oh, my God, I can't believe it. They've discovered the seventh sign. According to Native American tradition, the circle is divided into four colors and each represents an element on many levels. Of course, to the west lies the black earth, where the secret lies within the blackness of an underground vault.*

Marie Magdalene moved in closer and spoke for the first time since they arrived at the farm, "Thomas, I can imagine what's going through your head right now. Yes, my brother and I have re-discovered so many wonderful things—things we want to share with the world. I apologize for being angry with you. I know it must be difficult to understand our motivation . . . Please believe me when I tell you that all we want is for the world to be a better place . . . And I want you to share in this world—to share in my world. I know you think my brother and I are ruthless in many ways but some individual sacrifices have to be made for the betterment of the masses. Don't you agree?"

Thomas couldn't quite fathom what he was hearing, but he didn't want to antagonize his hosts at this point. "Yes, Marie, I think I now understand what you're saying. Please forgive me for not totally agreeing just yet, as I have so many things swirling through my mind, which I need to organize. I hope you understand?'

Marie moved even closer, as they made their way down the slight incline. "Of course, I understand. Give it time, and it will come. Meanwhile, let's just have a nice relaxing meal and some easy conversation. I know my brother has many other things to show you in order to help you make up your mind, but he didn't want to overwhelm you. Later on, I will try my best to help you sort a few things out."

\* \* \*

THE FARMHOUSE ITSELF WAS also a pleasant surprise. It was a rambling two-story salt-box design that had withstood the continuous assault of the extreme North Dakota climate for over one hundred years. As they entered through what appeared to be a relatively new addition, which was designed on the outside to harmonize with the historic house, Thomas couldn't help but feel the aura of the original occupants of the home.

The new addition was designed as a large summer kitchen with all the modern amenities, along with a casual sitting area, where Marie kicked off her boots and laid back in one of the oversized sofas. By this time, Jean Baptiste had gone to the fridge and helped himself to a bottle of Perrier water. It seemed the family took on a more relaxed atmosphere away from the prying eyes of the hired help or security team. Pierre was the only other one present, and he was presently preparing what smelled like a mouth-watering French delicacy.

Jean Baptiste had grabbed a stool at the kitchen island. "Thomas, please help yourself to anything you desire—sparkling water, soda? I believe Pierre has laid out some nice cheese and small biscuits and fresh shrimp over by Marie? And, tell us, what do you think of our situation now?"

Thomas felt he should demonstrate that he also was relaxed and comfortable, so he went to the fridge and helped himself to a Perrier water of his own. After casually unscrewing the top and taking a swallow, he responded, "I must admit, this is certainly a mysterious place. Even with the modern amenities and industrialization, the farm has maintained a certain distant aura. You're certainly right, Jean Baptiste. It is almost as though one can feel the presence of the Native Americans all around us. And, to think, the stone medicine wheel is completely intact after thousands of years."

Jean Baptiste smiled. "We were meant to find this place. Now I want to show you Benjamin Demers's private collection of Native Indian artifacts, which I purchased along with the house and land." With this, he gently grabbed Thomas's arm and led him down the hallway into the older part of the house, to what originally had been the front parlor, except that its doors were replaced with hermetically sealed, climate-controlled glass doors.

Standing before them, Jean Baptiste punched a four-digit code into the side keypad and the doors opened with a whoosh of cool, dry air.

Thomas stepped inside and then abruptly stopped. He was flabber-gasted by both the modern technical treatment of the artifacts and the extent of the collection. All four walls of the large room supported floor-to-ceiling sealed-glass shelving, which contained everything from intact lances and hatchets, bows and arrows, shields and blankets, to tiny fragments of clay pottery and leather pouches. There was even a cabinet with Grecian pottery and brass fittings, as well as small iron and bronze axe heads. One particular pouch with intricate porcupine quill work, although it was most-certainly centuries' old, appeared brand new. Thomas just stood and stared. *This is amazing. Here's one of the premiere Native American collections that could probably rival anything contained within the Smithsonian. Yet it's found in this century-old farmhouse. This is just remarkable!*

Jean Baptiste was definitely setting the hook for something bigger. He walked over to a far cabinet and slightly bent down, beckoning Thomas to do the same. "Thomas, I want you to look at what I consider one of the finest and most unique pieces in this collection. I have no idea if old Ben had any idea what he had found, but what do you make of this?"

Thomas leaned over to look at the small piece. At first glance, it looked like nothing more than two crossed sticks tied together with a small piece of leather strip. The wood looked weathered and cracked, with some notches taken out of the cross piece.

Thomas stared at the piece for a while and shrugged his shoulders. "Well, it looks like a crude wooden Christian cross, which was possibly given to a native child by some Jesuit missionary. Jean Baptiste, I'm surprised you would put much value in such a thing?'

Jean Baptiste just laughed and then said, "But that's just it, Thomas! I was the same as you when I first spied this insignificant little artifact. I thought exactly as you do now. But then I came to realize this really is an astronomical sextant in its crudest form. The beauty is its simplicity. Developed over centuries, the village shaman would have been able to measure the relative distance of the stars and moon and, thus, be able to fix both latitude and longitude . . . Thomas, here's the instrument allowing the Antients to fix latitudinal and longitudinal patterns. Once they were able to fix an accurate grid to your specific territory, you know the exact time, distance, and direction of your relative position. This allowed one to map their entire territory and beyond. Thomas, this little insignificant instrument allowed the ancient mariner to circumnavigate the world thousands of years ago! It also allowed the entire Algonquin Nation to understand exactly where their village stood in relation to all other villages."

Thomas was shaking and didn't know how to respond. In the last two hours, all his obscure theories had been confirmed. He couldn't help but be eternally grateful to the St. Jean-LeNeufs for showing him these things, even though they were still monsters in his mind. It generated even more conflict in terms of what he agreed to do through George Artowski's plan. Jean Baptiste was winning him over.

Jean Baptiste stood to the side of Thomas and watched the internal conflict being played out. He was now certain he and his sister had finally won over the modern-day knight who stood before him.

"Thomas, I can hear the gears whirling in your brain. Don't worry, all will be good. Meanwhile, by the smell of garlic, I would say that Pierre has outdone himself in the cooking field. Let's have a nice supper, and then I want to show you some more."

# CHAPTER 46

After the heavenly meal prepared by Pierre, the trio retired to the living room with their heavy Moroccan coffees, basking in the warmth of the meal and natural gas fireplace. As Thomas lay back, next to Marie, Jean Baptiste produced the well-traveled packet of Meriwether Lewis from the inner breast pocket of his jacket. Thomas's eyes widened as Jean Baptiste delicately laid the packet in front of him on the central coffee table and opened it.

"Thomas, I know you've been given a glance at the message Lewis composed during his trip to the Pacific, but what you haven't seen is the two original parchments." Jean Baptiste let the information settle in before continuing, "Yes, Thomas, there are two parchments contained within the packet. This packet was handed down through our family ever since our ancestors, a Major Michel LeNeuf and Jean St. Jean, secured it from Meriwether Lewis himself. The whole story was never conveyed to the family but, as you've heard Marie tell it, these two men were agents for a secret society, which was the inner circle of the French Knights Templar. I am now Supreme Grand Master of this society, which is known as the Order of the True Rose Croix."

Thomas just nodded, as he couldn't take his eyes off of the packet.

"Ah, Thomas, I see you are interested. Very good . . . This first parchment is written in old French and is called, Le Serpent Rouge—The Red Serpent. When you carefully read it, you will see that there is a rich layering of esoteric thought and belief, as well as enigmatic references to alchemical processes, astrology, and religious and spiritual context. The text has driven men mad for centuries, unless one were to realize that embedded in the text is a descriptive journey across North America, which just happens

181

to coincide with your grid of antient longitudinal meridians and a star-chart of sorts. You've heard the Templar saying: As above, so below?" Thomas nodded in agreement. "Well, Thomas, I believe that you have the skills to confirm where the vault exactly lays, if you use the old medicine wheel just to the north of us, along with your antient longitudinal meridian pattern, and the star-chart computer program, which I know that you had installed on your laptop before leaving the White House. I'm going to tell you that we've been searching for close to five years now for the vault and still can't find it. It's like finding a needle in a hay stack. However, I know you have an inkling of where the vault lies, but I need for you to pinpoint it exactly. In two days time, the solar eclipse will be in position to help us identify the one true secret, but we need to have found and cracked the vault before-hand. Time is running out, and we have one shot at this or the secret will be lost for another two thousand years. The question is: Can you do it?"

Thomas thought long and hard, "Yes, I'm relatively certain I can do it. Though there's one thing you've missed in the equation, Jean Baptiste."

Jean Baptiste sat up straight and glanced at his sister before responding, "And what may that be, Thomas?"

Thomas thought for a moment before proceeding, deciding that it was best if he didn't hold anything back, as Jean Baptiste would surely know. "There's the question of how to enter the vault once you've pinpointed it. Jean Baptiste, are you aware of the story behind the ritual portrayed through the Thirteenth Degree of the Scottish Rite, which is essentially the same as the Holy Royal Arch Degree of Enoch, portraying when the workers first discovered the concealed hidden vault of the first destroyed temple of Jerusalem?"

"I'm a little familiar with its religious context outside of the Masonic ritual but why don't you enlighten us, Thomas?" Jean Baptiste knew then that Thomas did indeed hold the final key to unraveling the mystery.

Thomas cleared his throat and began to recite from memory, "At the present time, the Holy Royal Arch Degree is based around the building of the second temple at Jerusalem around 500 BC. What is known for certain is that the Holy Royal Arch Degree appears to be based on the legend of Enoch, one of the legendary patriarchs from the *Book of Genesis* who predated the Great Flood. At some point, the legend forming the basis of this degree was changed from the Enoch legend to the legend of building the second Jerusalem temple at the time of the Jews returning from their captivity in Babylon. Notwithstanding this alteration, the Enoch legend remained the basis of some rituals as late as the early 1800s."

Thomas took a deep breath and continued, "While there are some differences in settings for the story, at least one is set in the time of King Solomon and involves the building of the secret vault and the discovery of the vault of Enoch. In Masonic circles, the story of the Ark of Noah is one of the oldest of all Masonic devices. The story of Enoch is, therefore, intimately intertwined with this story, which leads one to suspect that the Enochian slant also reflects an early version of the myth. Enoch is said to rise to heaven and is shown the triangular plate bearing the name of God, then a vision of an underground vault with nine arches—one on top of the other, within which is a white marble pedestal. God commands him to build this, as well as two pillars of brass and brick, containing all the knowledge of mankind. This he does."

Thomas found this a little disconcerting but continued with the story, "In this version, we are then transported forward to the time of King Solomon, who is commanded to build not only a temple but also an underground corridor, and he is promised that upon completing the temple, the true name of God first revealed to Moses would be restored. According to this version, next to Mount Mariah was another mount called Mount Calvary, which the workmen were excavating in order to lay foundations for another building. They come across the ruins of a more ancient building, upon vertical arches. Solomon then tells his three principal architects to investigate, which they do, lifting each keystone by its ring, and in the ninth arch they discover the pedestal and the triangular plate."

"These three architects, or sojourners, are common to all, as is the idea of them descending by a rope ladder into a place of darkness, finding in the last vault something bright, which in many rituals shines with its own light or is illuminated by the sun at its highest meridian. In most cases, too, the pedestal is a double cube—more of an altar—which means its surface is square, bearing a circle, which contains a triangle of gold: a device familiar to Masons in the Hermetic degrees. Each side of the triangle contains a third of the Omnific Word—the word of God. The end of the story has the three sojourners returning to the surface and reporting their findings to King Solomon, who is the only one with the wisdom and understanding to decipher the three phrases into the one true word of God. Hence, the phrase has been coined—the Wisdom of Solomon."

Jean Baptiste was standing by this time, pacing back and forth and running his fingers through his dark, thick hair. He looked directly at Thomas when he spoke, "Thomas, this is wonderful. You've just confirmed for us the missing pieces. Since its beginning, the vault was constructed on the basis of the story you just told. This way, only certain initiates would recognize the keys to unlocking the vault once they rediscovered it. I was always worried as to how we're going to get in once we pinpointed where the vault lay. We're not going to break in like the three sojourners did, smashing through the top arch. We're going to find the corridor leading to the ninth arch and the vault below it and march right in, avoiding any pitfalls or traps that may exist."

Thomas was proud of himself, and rightly so. There were many layers to the story and no Mason had ever before thought that the rituals actually led to a real place on earth.

Jean Baptiste couldn't stop talking, "Just think: Masonic ritual actually tells us what the one true secret among many others is—it's the one true word of God! It's what Moses learned from God Himself, thus allowing him to converse directly with God. If only I knew this word, the world's three greatest religions would have to answer to my will if they wanted to converse with God. What power! This is surely that-which-was-lost!"

Thomas just received the confirmation he needed. *Jean Baptiste is a certified nut-case!* But before he could react in any manner, Pierre suddenly appeared carrying what looked like a large bundle of heavy woolen blankets and sleeping bags, along with a sturdy down-filled parka and a heavy knapsack.

Jean Baptiste returned to earth, as fast as he had traveled to heaven. "*Oui, Pierre, merci beaucoup!* Thomas, you've exceeded our wildest dreams. However, we need one more thing from you. I hope you don't mind but we think that it's necessary for you to spend the rest of the evening out by the medicine wheel in order for you to confirm your calculations and summations. Pierre has found you the warmest bedding in the place, along with a coat that's good for at least forty degrees below Celsius, which really shouldn't be necessary. As I said, we need to make sure, as we only have two days left. Don't you agree?"

Thomas stammered a little before replying, "Yes, of course, Jean Baptiste. I totally agree." He then got up and moved towards the back door, where Pierre was waiting with his supplies, including his laptop.

Just then, Marie appeared wearing a similar coat to what Pierre was holding. Hers was a little bigger than required and had the effect of turning her back into the little girl that Thomas glimpsed on several previous occasions. She feigned a slight innocence as she declared to her brother, "Jean Baptiste, I know you won't mind if I go along with Thomas tonight. It can get awfully lonely out there at times."

Jean Baptiste just smiled back at his older sister, "Of course not, Marie. You two go and enjoy yourselves! Just make sure you don't distract Thomas too much."

Marie grabbed Thomas's arm and led him out the door before he knew what hit him.

# CHAPTER 47

Thomas dutifully did as he was told and paid full attention to the dark pathway until he arrived at the medicine wheel, all the while trying to ignore Marie, who clung to his arm like a teenaged schoolgirl.

The small valley was eerily quiet yet strangely illuminated by the partial moon reflecting off of the stones. Extricating himself from Marie's grasp for the moment, he made his way into the center of the circle, where he deposited his knapsack on the ground.

Thomas then moved over to a large flat stone some five feet away, where he busied himself booting up the laptop and calling up the star-chart software program. He first checked their GPS coordinates on his BlackBerry verifying that they were located at exactly 48 degrees north latitude, 104 west longitude, and then entered the current time and date into the program. What now came up on the screen was a two-dimensional portrayal of the 360-degree nighttime sky directly above him.

Thomas didn't waste any time adjusting the program's dates and times. First he checked the night and day sky and star pattern on September 17, 1811, then on February 4, 1413, October 14, 1632, and for two days into the future. Thomas eagerly confirmed that Sagittarius, the Archer, was standing atop the hillside to the west in each and every star chart, as though he was waiting to pierce the rising moon with an arrow!

He really wasn't astonished by his findings but, nonetheless, couldn't help but be shocked his theoretical summations had come true. On those four dates, as a full solar eclipse passed over or would pass over his exact position, traveling southwest in a giant oscillating movement around most of the earth, its sighting would register across his antient meridian pattern in a relative time sequence. This confirmed why there was heightened

Templar activity across North America during these periods, first with Prince Henry Sinclair, then Champlain and the Recollets, then Major LeNeuf and Sergeant Major Jean St. Jean, and finally, himself. It was if the sun, moon and the stars were aligning themselves once again to temporarily expose the one true secret.

What this meant was that the Templar astronomers surely possessed an antient knowledge, which allowed them to chart the sky and to predict solar and lunar eclipses and harmonic concordance events. Like the three wise men of old, the Templars knew that these astronomical events could be used as a key to lock away something of value within an earthly vault. They also knew that the key would only be available to those initiates who possessed both the knowledge and understanding of its application.

His research complete, Thomas shut down his laptop and packed up his knapsack. Looking up, all that he could see was Marie standing over to one side with her hands on her hips. Obviously, she was not pleased with the notion that Thomas did not desire her then and there. She had gone out of her way to find a time when they could be alone and, as she thought, consummate their desires. However, Thomas knew the only reason Marie found him attractive was because he represented a new strain of the Holy Bloodline.

# CHAPTER 48

For the past fifteen hours, Phil Bloomer had been high-tailing the red-and-white eighteen-wheeler across the states of North Dakota and Montana, arriving in Helena just in time for breakfast. In the back of the trailer, the seven Navy Seals led by Master Chief Wayne, along with Lieutenant McCormack, Bill Rose, and George Artowski, were just stirring after a solid sleep.

The only ones who hadn't slept right through the entire night were Lieutenant McCormack and Master Chief Wayne. Both the Navy Seal and Marine lieutenant insisted on staying up and listening to the conversations transmitted by Thomas's Blackberry.

The information they gained proved invaluable. It also seemed that both the lieutenant and master chief had gained a newfound appreciation for Mr. Randolph's courage while under fire, so-to-speak.

Thomas had done exceptionally well in secretly conveying the location of the vault, which was determined to lie just west of Townsend, Montana.

The question now was where exactly was the black Mercedes containing Jean Baptiste and Marie St. Jean-LeNeuf, along with Thomas Randolph and the silent bodyguard, Pierre, and what was their destination? Thomas's BlackBerry was giving up the ghost due to a low battery but not before it was determined through the GPS system that the car was heading west along I-94 and then I-90 towards Bozeman, Montana, and then, presumably, north to Townsend or Helena.

At the same moment, Bill Rose was sitting at the prerequisite back corner table in another typical American roadside diner having the breakfast special when he felt as though something, or somebody, passed through his very being. The unseen shadow forced him to shiver, even though he was wearing a heavy flannel shirt and the ever-present fishing vest and hat.

George Artowski was sitting beside him and witnessed the involuntary movement. "Bill, what's wrong? You look as though a ghost just bumped into you."

Bill Rose looked at his friend for a few seconds before responding, "George, I think that's exactly what happened. I think we're searching for something that shouldn't be found. A number of artifacts, if you want to call them that, were hidden away at this one place so the earth's forces could not only protect them but control them. I don't think we have any idea of the power the secret contains. I know this must sound silly, but maybe the Knights Templar never exposed what they found for a very specific reason: They were also afraid of unleashing its power. The Templars knew enough that even just the threat of exposing the secret would rock the earth and destroy the very foundations of the world's three greatest religions. I just don't know if Helen's legacy should be the downfall of organized religion as we know it. George, I'm afraid of the truth!"

The director knew his friend well enough to determine he hadn't come to this conclusion without a great deal of thought. "Bill, I sympathize with everything you've said. I couldn't agree more, but the reality is we have a madman on the loose, and he's looking to take control of the extreme power resting not far from here. In his hands, there's no telling what could happen. You've seen the news: The Middle East is about to explode like a powder keg. The turmoil is spreading every day with places like Egypt, Yemen, Algeria, and even the United Arab Emirates looking to fill a power vacuum created by the movement on the streets. All we need is for Jean Baptiste to fill this void and provide the masses with a common purpose, a historical purpose. As Knights Templars and Freemasons, we're the appointed guardians of the sacred knowledge. We have to stop the lunatic before he forms a New World Order."

Bill Rose shook his head and pushed away his plate of eggs and toast. "Yes, I suppose you're right. We should go on, no matter the outcome. The one thing I really feel badly about at this moment is allowing Thomas to be amongst that band of cutthroats. He has no training and hasn't a clue as to what he's involved in. That witch is manipulating him like dog chasing a bone on a string."

George very seldom did this but he put his hand on Bill Rose's shoulder in order to comfort him. "Bill, you've got to remember he volunteered. I think we have to give him a little more credit. Yes, he seems to be falling head over heels for Marie Magdalene, but, at the same time, he's kept his composure and quite cleverly, via his conversation and BlackBerry's open transmission, kept us relatively informed of the St. Jean-LeNeuf's future plans. We're now in a position where we know their next move. When the time comes, we'll be in position to checkmate them. We've pecked away at Jean Baptiste's resources to the point that he's vulnerable. We'll win out and that will be Helen's legacy."

Just as Bill Rose was about to ask his best friend whether he was prepared to forfeit Thomas's life in order to preserve the American way of life, Master Chief Wayne came into the diner looking somewhat distressed. However, he knew enough not to attract attention and pulled up a chair at the table alongside Dunk and poured himself a cup of coffee before delivering the bad news. "Gentlemen, we just got word from the Bunker that Mr. Randolph's BlackBerry signal has gone dead. They've tried 'pinging' his signal and didn't get a response either, so they figure there's more to it than just a dead battery."

Everyone around the table stared at one another, not knowing what to think. There could be one of two explanations, with the first being that Thomas and his BlackBerry application had been discovered or worse yet, Thomas had been killed. The second alternative was that Marie had succeeded in turning Thomas to their side and he himself had revealed the connection between the BlackBerry and those seated around the table. Either way, it didn't bode well for Thomas.

It was Dunk who broke the silence by proclaiming, "Gentlemen, one thing I know from my marine training is that you always assume the worse. This in all probability means our cover is blown and Thomas has fulfilled his purpose and thus already been eliminated. Given that in all probability this is the case, I suggest we rendezvous back in the trailer and have Phil find us a spot under cover. Once there, we can regroup and evaluate our options. I know we've agreed to go this alone, but we may have to call in reinforcements. Is everyone in agreement, sir?" Dunk was directing the question to Director Artowski. The director reluctantly nodded his assent and moved with the rest of the group to the door of the diner.

At the very same moment as Dunk's reckoning, along a lonely stretch of I-94, a black Mercedes was pulled over to the side of the road. The intricate electronics Jean Baptiste had installed in the car picked up the repeated pinging being directed from the White House Bunker to Thomas's BlackBerry.

As a result, Jean Baptiste was now standing outside the car, grinding what was left of Thomas's BlackBerry into the gravel shoulder of the road with the heel of his shoe. At th same time he was holding onto his hysterical sister, who was screaming at the top of her lungs for Pierre to stop. He, in turn, had Thomas bent over and pinned to the trunk of the car, while he pressed his loaded Glock into the back of Thomas's head.

# CHAPTER 49

When the two young Blackfoot women first appeared, waiting patiently beside Pegasus and Icaria in the faint early morning light, the two knights knew immediately their world was changed forever. With the wily Shoshone chief, Cameahwait, standing off to one side and grinning like a rabid fox, the guardians at first all but ignored the two women while seeing to their mounts and their saddlebags. Yet it was obvious to everyone that the two knights would have to address the situation sooner or later, as the women were not only young and proud, but stunningly beautiful.

Major LeNeuf finally gave into the urge, asking Cameahwait to formally introduce the two Blackfoot women. The Shoshone chief then explained that the taller, lighter one was named Makkitotosimew, which meant "She Who Has Large Breasts," but her Christian name was Marie. The explanation certainly caused the major's jaw to drop. The gruff sergeant major was even more taken aback when he was introduced to the sultry, darker Sinopa Ko'komíki'som, which in its simplest form meant "Fox Moon," with her Christian name being Angelique.

When approached by the major, Marie stood straight and tall and looked directly into Michel's eyes, capturing his heart forever. It was the same with the sergeant major, who had never seen a black Madonna as striking as Angelique. She chose a slightly different tack to piercing the gruff soldier's heart. She decided not to look him directly in the eyes but instead feigned shyness, keeping her head lowered, peering out from under her thick black hair. Even Icaria sensed there was something different at play— something the two horses had never witnessed before in their masters— uncertainty.

192

With their hearts struck for all eternity, the two guardians mounted their horses and prepared to move off, when Marie made a noise in the back of her throat, which sounded like a deep growl of some kind. The major was momentarily perplexed. He had innocently surmised the two young women were going to walk, or rather, trot all the way across Montana.

Looking over his shoulder, he spied Cameahwait giving his best "women—what can you do with them" gesture. In total surrender, the major leaned down and offered his arm to Marie, who adroitly fastened on and with his assistance leapt onto the back of Pegasus. She then settled in and wrapped her arms tightly around the major's lower chest. The same maneuver was repeated between the sergeant major and Angelique, and the party of four headed out of the village, not daring to look back at the smirking crowd.

Though the two Blackfoot had lived with the Shoshone for some time, they were not slaves in any real sense of the word. They had volunteered to go with the Shoshone when their brothers were captured during an ill-timed raid on the Shoshone village. The agreement was the brothers would be released in exchange for the women's labor for one year. As was custom, the women worked hard alongside the Shoshone women and with the year over, were free to return to their Blackfoot territory.

This was something both the Shoshone chief and elder failed to mention to the two guardians. It, therefore, quickly became apparent the real purpose in executing the astronomical wager was to ensure that Cameahwait did not have to escort the two knights or females any further west, since tensions were still running high between the Shoshone and the Blackfoot.

Inevitably, Major LeNeuf and Sergeant Major St. Jean were to learn firsthand how high the tensions had become.

Having traveled across almost the entire length of what would be the state of Montana in their own state of emotional tension, the group of four was relieved to come to what Lewis and Clark first labeled as the Gates of the Mountains Wild Area. The two guardians were greatly impressed by the prominent limestone cliffs running along either side of the Missouri River for several reasons. First of all, by the way the two women became animated after close to a month of silence, it was quite evident the party was near their homeland and Blood Peigan Blackfoot territory. Secondly, the two knights recognized the white limestone as an indication they were entering an area littered with caverns, tunnels, and sinkholes, which was perfect for hiding all sorts of things underground.

Indeed, the first fact was confirmed when the group spied on the next hill to the west a Blackfoot scouting party. From what they could determine at this distance, it consisted of six braves on horseback, all of whom appeared decked out in war paint and carrying all sorts of weapons. At this point though, Major LeNeuf reasoned that the party would recognize the two women as their own and, therefore, they would act as intermediaries on their behalf.

The scouting party remained still on the horizon as the two guardians made their way closer, their horses struggling up the grade of the hill. As they neared, the lead scout started to warily advance. The two knights silently acknowledged to one another that the young brave obviously knew his tactics, as he kept the setting sun at his back.

Major LeNeuf nudged his horse closer to the sergeant major as he whispeed to his fellow knight, "What do you think, Jean? I can't quite tell but it appears to me this young scout is not in a friendly mood."

Jean responded in the same steady voice, "*Oui*, Michel, notice how his painted horse is chomping at the bit, as though sensing his master's intentions. Let's move up to his level and stop, to let him clearly see our two female companions. Hopefully, he will recognize them as belonging to his own tribe."

"I agree," the major replied. "Don't make any sudden moves for your sword or stiletto, as he appears quite capable with his own weaponry."

The major's words were quite prophetic. As Pegasus and Icaria approached a more-level footing, the lead scout took it as aggression, dug his feet into the sides of his mount and charged. The result was both electrifying and deadly. The brave was carrying a shield and a lance, and a bow and quiver full of arrows. Even before the two knights had time to maneuver with the additional weight due to their passengers, the brave had cocked and loosened an arrow with his bow, all at a full gallop. A second before the major felt the arrow strike his left breast, Marie screamed in her native Blackfoot tongue at the brave to stop.

The impact of the arrow drove both the major and Marie out of the saddle, with Michel landing in the tall grass with a solid thud, while Marie managed to land on her hands and feet like a cat. With the major out cold, Marie sprang to meet the oncoming brave and his extended lance with just her gutting knife. At the last moment, the brave recognized his own sister and diverted to his right, still covering the major until he could figure out what was happening. Meanwhile, the rest of the scouting party arrived, surmising that something quite extraordinary was indeed going on, what with another one of the braves recognizing Angelique as his own sister.

The sergeant major wanted to skewer every last one of the Blackfoot right there for the death of his friend but thought the better of it, since it appeared that some strange sense of calm suddenly blanketed the whole scene. Angelique had quickly dismounted and was berating the whole scouting party for being so idiotic, while Marie ran to the major's side. The odd thing was that the arrow didn't lodge in the major's chest but lay broken on the ground, with the major now struggling to raise himself up. Luckily, the arrow struck the one spot where a number of gold and silver coins still remained sewn into the Major's wool shirt. It was a rather expensive knight's suit of armor but it saved the major's life.

The comedy of the situation appeared lost on most of those present because they were fascinated by what was unfolding before them. Upon seeing the major alive, Marie had flung herself on top of him and smothered him with passionate kisses. Oddly enough, the warrior-monk wasn't protesting. In fact, he was quite enjoying the moment. After more than fifty years of celibacy, he finally allowed his humanly urges to burst through to the surface.

The major's lips eventually parted from Marie's, giving him just enough time to exclaim in French, "Marie, please, you're killing me!" Marie refused to stop even after his exclamation, so he tried whatever words he could muster in a number of Algonquin dialects. Still, she ignored his pleas until he somewhat awkwardly found enough strength to roll her off of him.

Sergeant Major St. Jean had never before witnessed such an exhibition of pure love. Having dismounted himself, he leaned down and extended his hand to his long-time companion, relieved that the arrow had not found its intended mark. "Well, Michel, I will say it appears you're engaged . . . And you better say yes, because the lead brave behind me is trying to figure out whether you're his future brother-in-law or just stringing his sister along for the ride. In which case, I don't fancy your odds with the second arrow."

The major grabbed his companion's arm to steady himself. "Here, help me up, you grinning fool." The major wasn't about to be undone, especially just after he had his life flash before his eyes. "By the looks of it, given how Angelique is gesturing your way, I'm willing to wager she's putting her dibs in on you . . . so much for being celibate all of our lives . . . I believe the Supreme Being will grant us a little peace in our old age . . . though I'm willing to wager that, after the honeymoon, you won't be able to ride your Icaria for quite some time."

Jean chuckled and then said, "*Touché, mon ami!* That's a good one. Now let's go meet the in-laws."

Major LeNeuf straightened himself as best as he could and walked under his own steam to where the braves had dismounted. He wasn't going to allow the Blackfoot to sense any weakness, for he knew he would soon need their help. Marie had slowly regained her composure and as a native Blackfoot woman assumed her position slightly behind Michel, but refrained from touching him any further. She knew the bond had already been formed and they would have the rest of their lives to share their passion. She also knew in her heart she had made the right decision and was silently pleased at the strength and warmth of the response she received when she first kissed Michel. It seemed that spending close to a month on a horse together was a rather odd courtship, but it had worked.

Sergeant Major St. Jean was admiring his friend almost with envy until he realized Angelique had silently taken up her position slightly behind him, deftly ensuring the tip of her fingers brushed against his just for a split second. This was all that it took, because as he turned to acknowledge the gesture it was as if a cloud parted from his very being. The glowing aura projected from this man was evident for everyone to see, but he only had eyes for Angelique. She recognized the sign and was now content to assume her earlier role, where she slightly bowed her head in shyness.

Meanwhile, Marie was doing her best to explain to her brother and the other warriors in her native Blood Peigan tongue how the two women had come into the company of the red-and-white guardians of the prophecies. It was quite obvious she succeeded, because the young warriors took on an air of solemn reverence. It was quite obvious to the two at this moment the scouts knew a lot more than they were telling. Both knights were figuring that the six young warriors had suddenly realized the enormity of the possibility that they could have killed the two guardians identified through the prophecies, and now they were trying to concoct a suitable story to tell the Blackfoot chief and elders.

Having more than suitably established their credentials, the group of four remounted and joined the scouting party as they made their way back to the main Blackfoot village, strategically hidden within what the knights understood to be called the Deer Lodge Forest.

Marie's brother's name was Little Head, and as it turned out, he was the first son of the great Blood Peigan Blackfoot Chief—Ugly Head, which made Marie a princess of sorts.

Five years ealier, the Lewis and Clark expedition had discovered that the Blackfoot were assigned as official guardians to protect the secret until such time the red-and-white guardians returned. Initially, Lewis demonstrated to the Blackfoot some knowledge of the signs, seals, and tokens, about which the prophecies spoke, but it just as quickly became obvious that Meriwether Lewis was not one of the chosen guardians. According to their custom, the Blackfoot still regarded Lewis with every civility they could offer until they learned his true intention. To the Blackfoot, the white men intended for the Native Indians to fight among themselves until they were no more in order for the secret to be taken.

The question, therefore, was how would the two true knights be received, given that the Blackfoot's encounter with the Lewis and Clark Corps of Discovery ended in utter disaster?

# CHAPTER 50

"M r. Randolph, do you take me for a fool?" inquired Jean Baptiste, who appeared surprisingly calm considering the circumstances—standing at the side of the highway trying to control his frantic sister, and, all the while, watching his bodyguard, Pierre, slam Thomas down onto the trunk of his black Mercedes while pressing his gun to the back of Thomas's head.

Jean Baptiste had reacted a few minutes earlier to a small alarm in the side console of his car door, which signaled that a high-frequency transmission had just been sent to Thomas's BlackBerry. Some young inexperienced technician, located in the Bunker of the White House, had taken it upon himself to perform the operation when Thomas's BlackBerry's voice transmissions appeared to be failing. The problem was that a test of this nature could be detected by the right equipment, and Godfroi had outfitted the Mercedes with the correct detection technology.

The result was that Thomas was seconds away from having his life ended on a lonely stretch of I-94 just outside of Miles City, Montana. Rather than beg for his life, something strange took hold of Thomas. Deep down inside he found the strength and courage for the first time in his life to truly stand up for what he believed in. Calmly and serenely, he responded to Jean Baptiste's question, "No, Jean Baptiste, I do not. I have no idea what just occurred and, if you kill me, you and I both know you'll never recover that-which-was-lost."

Whether it was the calmness in the tone of the response or the reasoning behind it, the effect was immediate. Jean Baptiste released his sister and called off the threat to Thomas's life. "Pierre, please release Thomas and go sit in the car. I think Mr. Randolph and I have come to an understanding

... Marie, my good sister, I will ask you to do the same. Don't worry. I think Thomas has the best of intentions towards all of us."

Thomas's mind was racing, trying to comprehend what just happened.

What made the scene even more surreal was the sudden calmness that fell upon Marie Magdalene, as quickly as she had earlier burst into hysterics. Incredibly, she even managed to caress her brother's shoulder, as if to silently thank him, before she too took her position back in the car.

Following this exhibition, Thomas thought nothing of the bizarre conversation occurring between him and Jean Baptiste. To anyone passing by, it would appear as though the act being played out was nothing more than a conversation between two friends, who stopped to stretch their legs and take in the increasingly magnificent scenery.

As if in response to the absurdity of it all, Jean Baptiste took on a solemn, almost reverent role. "Thomas, I've witnessed on many occasions the various reactions of men about to die. Most end up weeping and begging for their life, or even worse, soiling themselves uncontrollably just before the trigger is pulled. Only once before have I seen logic and reason come to the surface, along with a calmness and rationale. This tells me, even if you don't realize it yourself, that you have been put on this earth as a messenger of sorts. It's as if your true purpose in life is to convey the secret of the vault, as the time has come for it to be opened and for its contents to be revealed.

*That's it!* Thomas thought to himself. *This confirms it. The whole family is completely deranged, and I'm standing in front of the head lunatic . . . This can't really be happening, can it? . . . Oh, well, if Napoleon here thinks I'm a messenger from heaven, who am I to disagree?*

"You're right, Jean Baptiste." Thomas did his best to appear open and honest. "Everything is meant to happen for a purpose. You must first trust me when I tell you that I have no idea what is going on with my BlackBerry. I completely forgot it was even on."

Jean Baptiste patted the side of Thomas's face, as though he was nothing more than a dog. "Don't think anything of it, Thomas. It's apparent that our good friend, Director Artowski, is up to his old tricks. I knew he just wouldn't give up the hunt . . . Can't you see, Thomas? Mankind is made up of a balancing of two sides—black and white, good and evil, hot and cold. Your friends are now content enough for me to uncover the secret, since they can't. Their reasoning is that once I have it in possession, then they will be able to take it from me. This is the rule of both the playground and the jungle. The Americans have been playing at it for over two hundred years—gunboat diplomacy. In their minds, you always bargain from a place of strength. Well, I can tell you it's not always the strongest, but the brightest, who win. Your fellow knights, misters Artowski and Rose, are going to be completely taken aback when they come to take what is rightfully mine and find that we've already disappeared. Then I'll bargain from the seat of wisdom, just like King Solomon."

"I seem to remember that King Solomon was done in by his love for his Queen—the Black Madonna, Sheba?" Thomas wanted to see to what extent Jean Baptiste's ego and sick love for his sister extended.

Jean Baptiste just laughed. "Now, Thomas, this really is funny, coming from you. It seems to me you are the one who has succumbed to my sister's guiles. Did you really think I was going to have Pierre kill you?"

Thomas just stood there with his jaw dropping, as he could see where the conversation was going.

Jean Baptiste was pleased, because he saw that Thomas had been completely fooled. "Thomas, are you not familiar with the Art of War? Rule number one is to know thy enemy. I expected all along that the White House Bunker would be tracking us somehow. I just needed to know how and whether you were in on it. The Americans just don't give up and retreat with their tails between their legs and recoup their losses. I also needed to know whether my sister was successful in sinking her hooks into you. She's quite the actress, wouldn't you say? I found her quite convincing, although she has a ways to go in order to achieve my acting level . . . Don't worry. I genuinely think she's in love with you. If everything works out as I suspect it will, she will make an honest man out of you and keep you warm at night. Just one piece of advice from your future brother-in-law: She's got some deep emotional problems. At times, you'll need to be more of a father to her than a husband, if you know what I mean?"

Jean Baptiste unleashed a wicked laugh as he made his way back to the car, leaving Thomas to ponder his somewhat dubious future.

Jean Baptiste was more than pleased with the way things appeared to be coming together. After he assumed his seat in the back of the car, he reached across and gently squeezed his sister's hand. She immediately responded and gave him a look that conveyed that the ruse had worked as planned. Deep down inside, though, in her own mind, she honestly regretted having to deceive Thomas. She promised herself that, if everything went as planned, she would make it up to him.

After what appeared to be an eternity, Thomas finally took his place in the front passenger seat, and Pierre stoically pulled back onto the highway and sped up. Thomas searched for the right thing to say, but as nothing seemed appropriate for the circumstance, he remained silent.

Jean Baptiste, on the other hand, had no intention of losing the advantage, and addressed the group, "Wonderful news, everyone. Thomas has most graciously volunteered to show us everything concerning the vault—its layout, how to access it, any traps we have to watch for—everything! Pierre, as we are quickly coming up onto noon, I think we should be on the lookout for a wonderful place to eat—somewhere special I should think. Perhaps Thomas can troll his laptop once more and find us a suitable place up ahead? We'll have a leisurely lunch, and Thomas can enthrall us with all of his findings. Would this suit you, Marie?"

"Yes, it would be wonderful, Jean Baptiste. Thomas, perhaps you could find one of those out-of-the-ordinary restaurants where they serve elk, deer, and other native meats? I'm feeling very American out here in Montana and, as a result, I'm famished. I just can't stand the thought of having to eat in another one of those American diners."

Thomas was finding the conversation more and more incredulous but accepted the double-sided conversation. "Yes, of course, Marie. Pierre, up ahead, in about an hour and a half, I've found a place called Walker's Grill. It's found in the Historic Chamber Building in downtown Billings and is billed as one of the finest bistros in Montana. I think it will more than suit our taste. How does this sound?"

Marie responded as though on a Sunday outing, "Why, Thomas, it sounds marvelous and very romantic. Let's try it, shall we, Jean Baptiste?"

By this time Jean Baptiste's mind was somewhere totally different, deep in the bowels of earth, but he responded anyways, "Yes, it sounds beautiful. Thomas, can you make reservations for us from your laptop? And see if they have a private dining room."

"Already done," replied Thomas.

The rest of the short journey passed in silence. Each of the car's occupants appeared to have retreated to his and her own little worlds. Jean Baptiste was picturing himself seated in Solomon's chair, dispensing verdicts upon the world's three greatest religions. Marie Magdalene saw herself back in Fincastle, where she and Thomas were chasing their young son and daughter across the back lawn on a hot summer's day. Thomas dreamt of the days that he and Sharon would take the boys to the Royal Ontario Museum, where inivitably they ended up in the Roman and Greek section and young Frank and Alexander would marvel at the model of the hilltop Parthenon. Pierre was concentrating on the road and thinking of the moment he was instructed to explode Thomas's head for real, as Jean Baptiste promised.

Coming onto noon, the black Mercedes entered Billings, Montana. Pierre found the restaurant without any real difficulty. Finding a parking spot right around the corner, Thomas, Jean Baptiste, and Marie all headed to the restaurant, along with Thomas's laptop. It was decided that Pierre would stay with the car, as it wasn't everyday that a Mercedes Benz S-Class S65L AMG with New York license plates pays a visit to Billings, Montana. As they moved along the street to the restaurant, Thomas thought it strange that Pierre didn't appear ever to eat or sleep.

If any of the locals had any idea as to what was going to be revealed inside the restaurant that day, it would have started a modern-day gold rush.

# CHAPTER 51

T he owner of the upscale bistro in downtown Billings certainly recognized class when he saw it. Of course, there was no question of providing a small private room for Jean Baptiste St. Jean-LeNeuf, his sister, and their guest, as the family name and the name of their company was well known throughout the western states. The natural inclination of anyone in the restaurant this day was that the family was scouting property in the area. Given this summation, any town in Montana would have welcomed the company with open arms because their successful enterprises had translated into much-needed jobs for the local economy.

Added to the excitement was the fact that Jean Baptiste was stunningly handsome, and his sister was ravishingly beautiful. Many of the upscale locals who frequented the bistro silently acknowledged both their aristocratic manner and their good looks. The news that their sleek black Mercedes was parked around the corner and was being watched over by what appeared to be a rather deadly looking bodyguard added to the mystique.

The meal itself was light and refreshing, a nice change from the standard fare most Montana restaurants offered. After the table was cleared, the owner almost fell over himself when Jean Baptiste asked if they could have the room for about another hour or so, and not be disturbed. He was more than happy to oblige, indicating he would see to it personally that the trio maintained their privacy. When he saw Thomas boot up his laptop, he naturally assumed the money he had sunk into the restaurant was now validated by the interest of the St. Jean-LeNeuf family in the Billings area.

Once the frosted doors to the private dining room were closed, Jean Baptiste pushed his chair back slightly in order to stretch his legs and directed his comments to both Thomas and Marie, "My goodness, I have to admit

203

lunch was surprisingly excellent. Who says the Americans have no taste beyond Manhattan?" Turning his attention to Thomas, he said, "Now, please show us the final pieces to the puzzle as it applies to the vault's location."

Thomas sat there for a split second and pondered the consequences of what he was about to do. *What if they're successful in retrieving the one true secret? Am I going to be responsible for the world's destruction or will it actually result in a New World Order, as Jean Baptiste predicted? God, I pray I'm doing the right thing.*

Shutting out his inner thoughts Thomas spun the laptop around so Jean Baptiste and Marie could see the screen clearly, as he pulled his chair closer to Marie. Then he began by pulling up the first illustration. "What I first want to show you is how I've pieced together Nicholas Poussin's painting, *Et in Arcadia Ego*, with David Teniers the Younger's painting of *St. Anthony and St. Paul*. These two paintings, although in different scales, fit nicely within an antient latitudinal and longitudinal grid pattern. From this, I've been able to not only predict but confirm where the vault is positioned."

Jean Baptiste leaned in to study the illustration. "Thomas, this is absolutely brilliant. I can see where Poussin's work concentrated on the area known as Arcadia—Acadia during the time he completed the painting and how it relates to Tenier's work, which was completed about ten years after Poussin's. The hidden background information must have been gleaned from Champlain's, the Jesuits', Recollets', and other French explorers' early explorations into North America's heartland. This is fantastic. I can only surmise that the overlying grid pattern you've superimposed on the composite is technically accurate and relates to the antient meridians you talk about in your books?"

*If nothing else, Jean Baptiste, you're one hell of a quick study!* Thomas nodded in agreement before responding, "You've grasped the basic premise faster than I first did. Notice how the eastern coastline, the Great Lakes, and the Mississippi and Missouri rivers have all been defined by color variations in the original paintings. Various geographical points within the painting correspond perfectly to the latitudinal and longitudinal coordinates defined through an antient grid pattern."

Marie sat there, awestruck, as Thomas pulled up the next illustration.

"Now here's the official composite map created by Lewis and Clark after their journey. See how in the middle of their map is the depiction of the northerly fork of the Missouri River and the southerly fork, which is the Yellowstone River?" Both Jean Baptiste and Marie nodded, with Jean Baptiste suddenly exclaiming, "Thomas, the confluence of the Missouri and Yellowstone rivers is exactly where our farm and the Shoshone medicine wheel lies. It's the center of Lewis and Clark's map!"

Thomas couldn't help but be pleased with his findings. "That's right, and when you compare the fork in the river to the fork that can be deciphered through Teniers's painting, you'll see that the confluence falls on exactly the same coordinates, where the seventh sign lies."

Marie actually clapped her hands like a little girl before exclaiming. "Oh, my God! Thomas, you've deciphered the paintings! Combined, they're the treasure map!"

"Yes, Marie, but that's not all." Thomas was enjoying himself even more and allowed his last statement to sink in before continuing, "What you have to realize is that the Teniers's painting has another layered composition within it: the background, middle ground and foreground. By deciphering the clues on the various planes, that's how we pinpoint exactly where the vault lies."

Everybody was quiet for a moment, trying to allow what Thomas was trying to explain to become clearer. Finally, Jean Baptiste spoke up, "Thomas, I'm afraid I don't quite follow."

Thomas expected that this would be the case and pulled up the actual Teniers's painting of *St. Anthony and St. Paul*:

"I know it's hard to follow but let me try to explain in a different way . . . See how the general landscape of Teniers's painting forms the background . . . I've already demonstrated how the background—the largest scale, relates to a map of a major portion of North America, right?"

"Yes, Thomas, I follow this easily enough." Thomas appreciated Jean Baptiste's patience, in spite of the absurdity of the entire situation. "Now see how the middle ground depicts the home of the two saints in the wilderness. The doorway to their *hovel,* or underground cave, if you like, is through two pillars, which support an angled roof. On a physical level, this could be a geographical feature—*the Gates of the Rocky Mountains*—located along the

Missouri River, north of Helena. The painting could be showing a natural underground cave with a man-made shaft as its front door."

"Now, let me pull up a map that I'm sure will fascinate you."

When Thomas had the map on his laptop screen, he continued. "I know this may be hard to read, but there are some interesting place names relating directly to the foreground of Teniers's painting. In Teniers's painting, both saints are bald, with long beards, which is suggestive of the original Knights Templar. Well, to the northeast of the vault, you find Big Baldy Mountain, while to the southwest, you find Little Baldy Mountain. In Teniers's painting, St. Anthony is sitting on a rock, on his 'butt.' Just to the southwest of the vault, you find Butte, Montana, which is named after a natural landform. And here, also in Teniers's painting, there is a crow delivering *manna* to the two saints. Very close to where the vault is located, we find Crow Peak. I could go on, but I think you get the idea. Teniers was given the actual location of the vault, not only in latitudinal and longitudinal coordinates, but also in relation to natural landforms, whose names have survived to this day. Indian villages, early mining towns, or city names may disappear or be changed but the names of natural landforms, which are probably translations of the original native names, tend to remain forever! Finally, at the feet of the saints, in the foothills of the Rocky Mountains, through their gateway, we find that 'X' marks the spot."

Jean Baptiste looked at his watch. In just half an hour, he'd learned more than some of the greatest minds in the world had been able to determine in the last four hundred years. *If everything works out as planned, Thomas will surely take his rightful place within the Order of the True Rose Croix. The union between him and Marie will be a holy love.*

It was Marie who broke the spell. "Thomas, you conveyed to us back at the farmhouse that the exact coordinates of the vault are 46 degrees 18 minutes north latitude, 111 degrees 49 minutes west longitude. You don't know this yet, but we've had these coordinates flown over by a private French satellite and its high resonance, infrared photography and ground-penetrating radar confirms the presence of a large underground void, which appears to be accessed by a long underground tunnel of some sort. Our technician also confirmed that both landforms are not naturally occurring and too large to be a mine of any sort. What do you say to this information?"

Thomas was grinning ear to ear. Even though his life hung in the balance, he couldn't help but be ecstatic. "Marie, how should I respond? I can't say I expected it with absolute certainty, but all the signs, seals, and tokens lead me to the same conclusion. And, when I pulled up the topographic map I'm about to show you after I tracked the stars last night, I just knew I was right because of the local place names."

Thomas shrugged before adding, "There is one more thing, which I need to show you. It's the eighth sign, which is waiting in the mire for the sun to release it."

Both Marie and Jean Baptiste sat back down on their seats. As Thomas called up the next satellite photo of the land, both brother and sister recognized the sign of the turtle—the sacred Native American symbol of truth and understanding.

After taking a moment to absorb all they were shown, the only thing Jean Baptiste could suggest was that they should get going, since they were anxious to arrive in Helena by nightfall. His reasoning was that arrangements had to be made, and they would all need a good night's sleep in anticipation of cracking the vault in the morning. As they made their way to the car, it was as if time had no meaning, although the total eclipse of the sun would be happening in less than two days time.

# CHAPTER 52

The occupants of the black Mercedes had been quiet for three hours, trying to absorb all they learned over the last day. Thomas had produced just such a wealth of information that it would take a while for all of it all to sink in.

Meanwhile, Pierre was doing his best to break every speed limit in the state of Montana, as he made his way along I-90 towards Butte, where he would head north on I-15 to Helena. Here prior arrangements had been made to have them hook up with Godfroi, who was at this moment negotiating the services of an outfitter company in Townsend, which provided four-wheel Jeep tours into the rugged Montana foothills. Luckily, Godfroi had quickly developed a rapport with the owner of the company, Johnny Davis, who was not averse to earning a big payday for looking the other way to what was loaded into his Jeeps the next morning.

Jean Baptiste was finally prepared to process the further information he knew that Thomas possessed. "Thomas, there are a few things I want to get straight in my mind before we arrive in Helena."

Thomas swiveled in the front passenger seat in order to face Jean Baptiste. "Yes, of course, Jean Baptiste. What's on your mind?"

Jean Baptiste closed his eyes, as though he was trying to envision the very first guardians making their way across North America with their priceless cargo. "Who do you believe to be the original guardians of the secret?"

"First you have to realize the antient meridian marks the western edge of a great inland lake that once covered most of middle North America. This is why you still find sea shells scattered throughout the Rockies' foothills and the western edge of the Appalachians. This inland lake was Lake Lohatan, which is Algonquin. The Great Lakes formed as the flood waters receded. Here, we find the basis for the Great Flood story told by all Native Americans. So, in answer to your question, I believe knowledge of the high points, or sanctuaries, which correspond to the world's mountain ranges, was first known to those who lived before the Great Flood and survived because of this knowledge."

"Thomas, this sounds very much like the typical standard Mason's story where the two pillars—one made of marble and one of brick—survived the Great Flood, and the rediscovered knowledge is preserved by a number of secret societies. Am I not right?" Marie was now being outwardly contrite.

Thomas sighed. "Yes, that's about the gist of it."

"But, Thomas, you've forgotten one very important group," Jean Baptiste said, interjecting himself back into the conversation.

"And, what group would that be, Jean Baptiste?"

Jean Baptiste appeared extremely calm, almost in an altered state of awareness. "Those who felt they possessed the God-given right, the kings, queens, princes, and princesses of the holy bloodline."

When Thomas didn't respond to this, Jean Baptiste continued. "Thomas, do you realize that throughout the ages, starting with Abraham, Elijah, Noah, and Moses, there have been chosen ones who struck covenants with God and whose remains have never been found?"

"Do we add King David, Solomon, and even Jesus Christ into the mix?" Thomas was afraid of where this line of thought was heading.

"Yes, of course, there are thirteen in all. But if you dig deeper into each and every one's story, it turns out that only one prophet was able to summon God at his will. Everyone else experienced God speaking to them and instructing them, but it was only Moses who could summon God because he knew his true name." Jean Baptiste was glowing by this time.

Thomas picked up on Jean Baptiste's line of thinking. "Yes, it's interesting that Moses had such a revered place as a great prophet in the three greatest religions, Judaism, Christianity, and Islam. I think whoever possessed the true name of God and the original Mosaic Law—God's Law—would once again be able to dictate the Divine Word not only to the world's three greatest religions but to all religions."

"Thomas, if nothing else, you're able to see and understand things where most are incapable." Jean Baptiste wanted so desperately for Thomas to feel a part of his inner circle.

Thomas just wanted to throw up at this point, but to admit that would likely put him back in Pierre's hands. "I think I see clearly now . . ." he said instead. "You believe the vault contains not only the remains of thirteen of the greatest prophetic figures to have set foot on this earth but above all others—Moses, holds the one true secret—that-which-was-lost—the one true name of God; and, the one who possesses this and the original record of His teachings or laws, holds the key to establishing a New World Order. Am I correct?"

Jean Baptiste was pleased Thomas so readily grasped the concept.

Thomas controlled his anger but wanted desperately to find a logical flaw in Jean Baptiste's summations. "I don't think any of the world's three greatest religions will buy it. They all have too much at stake."

"My dear Thomas, this is the beauty of what's contained in the vault. The Christian world will be devastated when they discover Jesus did not rise but that rather his bones stayed on this earth. Jews around the world will discard the notion that the Jewish High Priests and their descendents—the *Cohan*, are the conduits to God, because it is Moses who is considered the greatest prophet and gave the Jewish people the Torah. In the Islamic world, Moses is described in ways which parallel the prophet Muhammad, and his character exhibits some of the main themes of Islamic theology, including the moral injunction that we are to submit ourselves to God. No one will be able to ignore me, especially after we've determined I'm a direct descendent of Moses through DNA testing."

*Bingo. So that's the prize Jean Baptiste is after. He wants to be the High Priest of the World, dictating to all because he'll be the one true conduit to God. Even if he's not a direct descendent of Moses, I'm sure he'll cook the laboratory results to make it appear so.* Not knowing what to say, Thomas just nodded and turned and stared straight ahead, down the never ending highway.

He could almost feel the self-emanating glow off of both Jean Baptiste and Marie Magdalene from the back seat. He knew then and there he wouldn't be able to take too much more of this. *Come on, Dunk, where the hell are you?*

# CHAPTER 53

If Major LeNeuf and Sergeant Major Jean St. Jean had any reservations as to their reception by the main Blackfoot village, they needn't have worried. As soon as they entered the village proper, it became evident their arrival had been foretold for centuries. Besides, the Indian woman Marie, who was riding behind Michel on Pegasus, turned out to be the eldest daughter of the great chief, Ugly Head. This also meant that Angelique, the dark, sultry one, who was riding behind Jean St. Jean on Icaria, was his niece.

Thus, when the small scouting party stopped and allowed the two tandems to ride up to the waiting chief and his council, the swelling crowd went silent with reverence and awe. Not only were there two red-and-white guardians riding the foretold omen of the black and white horses, but it was obvious from the way the two young women held on to the two knights that an otherworldly bond had already been formed.

The knights looked somewhat warily to Chief Ugly Head, wondering how they would be recieved. The answer to this unspoken question was in the chief's face. He really wasn't so much as ugly as being rather unique looking, what with one of the largest and most prominent sloped noses the two knights had ever witnessed. When the chief's toothless grin was added to the picture, it was as though the earth had opened up below a mountain. The crinkled sparkling eyes just completed the picture.

His expression signaled a time of celebration and joy, for the guardians of the prophecies had safely delivered to the chief his two most cherished possessions.

As if to reinforce this fact, Chief Ugly Head stepped forward and extended his arms widely. Speaking in perfect French, he declared to the two guardians, "*Nanabazhoo*, O' Great Creator, you have delivered to us the red-and-white guardians once more. Our thanks go out to you, for you have seen fit to honor our village and the whole Blackfoot Nation by causing their hearts to tremble at the sight of our women. *Kwey, Kwey* . . . My Blackfoot people, we shall let our honoured guests rest while we prepare for a great celebration this evening. *Chee Miigwiich!*"

The whole village disappeared in a wave of the chief's hand, leaving Michel and Marie, and Jean and Angelique, to dismount and to find their own way to their lodges. Both knights were somewhat at a loss as to the village's instant acceptance of the new situation, but the two Blackfoot women were taking it in stride. Michel and Jean quickly gave up trying to analyze the flow and, therefore, were only mildly surprised when both Marie and Angelique disappeared without a word after the two knights had made themselves comfortable in their own lodge.

After taking a spot next to the central fire and stretching out on a some soft furs, Michel rubbed his left shoulder. Jean saw this and said, "Michel, your shoulder must be still stinging. Are you all right?"

"Yes, of course, Jean. It's more of a habit than anything, trying to keep the circulation in the shoulder moving. It gives me time to digest what we just went through. First, a young brave tries to kill me and now it's like we're part of the family. It's the oddest thing." Michel shifted slightly to get at a better angle for his shoulder.

Jean responded in a light-hearted, almost euphoric manner, "I guess this is what happens when your future father-in-law approves of you right off. Did you see the look on his face? It's as though he just saw his path to a long and prosperous afterlife. If I were you, though, I'd watch out before you have about fifty mouths to feed."

Michel was not one to be outdone, thinking long and hard before he replied to his best friend, "If I were you, I'd save my strength and have a nap. Something tells me you and I are going to our own double wedding this very evening!"

\* \* \*

MICHEL WAS ABSOLUTELY RIGHT. Both Marie and Angelique had quietly disappeared because there was a tremendous amount of work and pageantry to arrange. After all, it wasn't every day that a Blackfoot princess married a guardian man-beast, let alone two Blackfoot women marrying two man-beasts.

Throughout the afternoon and early evening, the two young women were tended to by a number of both younger and older women, including their own mothers, who probably giggled the most when trying to explain to their daughters how they should pleasure the giants. Marie pretended to scold the small female contingent, while Angelique was quick to ask them to explain more.

All in all, it was a magical time in the village, as the Creator had truly blessed the Blackfoot in return for their protection of the secret.

The celebration started with the sun setting over the higher mountains to the west and the mock tormenting of the two grooms, who had been shown to their position of honor within the council circle. Apparently, it was Blood Peigan Blackfoot custom to mock the poor husbands-to-be with all kinds of insults with respect to their age, physical stamina, lack of combat skills and hunting prowess, and, worse of all, their sexual inabilities. Michel and Jean probably took it in better stride than most, since they only could decipher about a quarter of what was being said. Needless to say, the two young brothers of Marie and Angelique hurled the greatest insults, since they were probably the most relieved of anybody they hadn't killed the two knights and that the chief and elders were in such a gracious mood.

The merriment reached a crescendo, only to be silenced when Marie and Angelique were led into the larger central lodge by their mothers and grandmothers. The only thing to break the silence were the gasps of astonishment from Michel and Jean, which was deemed acceptable, as they were the grooms. The two young women were radiant with their hair braided in ribbons and wearing their finest beaded deerskin. Tiny bells were attached to their leggings, which gave off small tinkles when they walked to their places opposite the circle from their men.

Michel and Jean only had a few seconds to meet Marie's and Angelique's eyes before mounds of buffalo, deer and rabbit, berries and cooked bitterroot, were produced, along with wooden panels of hard bannock that the early French traders had taught the Blackfoot to make. After the requisite thanks, the women and children, sick and old, were first served by the wedding party, as was the custom. Then the warriors, chief, and council were proudly served and only then did the wedding party itself sit down to enjoy the feast. In accordance with tradition, the four were allowed to drink first from a huge gourd, which contained a soft, mellow liquid tasting like a fermented mixture of honey, berries, and grain. Michel and Jean didn't realize it at the time, but this simple action signaled that they were married.

After this, great cries and songs of joy arose to the beat of the drums. The whole great lodge was in a frenzy of dancing and chanting, with little children running everywhere.

Nearly overwhelmed, Michel stood and held up his hands for silence. As the crowd settled down, Michel cleared his throat and spoke as best as he could in part French, part Algonquin, with a little bit of Blackfoot thrown in. As usual, translations were simultaneously occurring in the background. "*Nanabazhoo*, my brothers and sisters, my heart is full and so is my stomach." That got the wedding party guffawing. "My companion and I are overwhelmed by the greeting we have received. Our emotions are flowing over with the love we have for our wives. I promise you and the Creator that we will forever provide for their needs and comfort. Through this connection, we will always be in your presence, even when we leave the mountains. The red-and-white guardians who came before us also became your brothers. There will be others who come after us to continue to strengthen the bloodline and bonds between us. This I give you as my solemn oath."

The crowd slowly realized the meaning of his words. The mixture of red-and-white blood would continue forever.

Michel slowly continued, "Now I would like to present my new father-in-law, Chief Ugly Head, with a token of our dedication and a gift for allowing me to join together with his eldest daughter and my companion to join with his niece. I know it is Blackfoot custom for us to present a gift of horses . . . but we have something just as special to give."

Instead of the usual frenzied response during any gift-giving, the crowd went silent, as Michel produced his knife and proceeded to stick the tip of it into his left breast. Most of the crowd naturally believed the gift that the man-beast was going to produce for his father-in-law was his own heart, but he only worked the blade far enough to tear the outer lining of his heavy wool shirt.

A number of gold and silver coins fell from the tear into Michel's hand. As he did this, he turned to look at his young brother-in-law. Realization slowly fell across Little Head's face, and he nodded in acceptance that he had been tricked. From this time forward, Little Head would challenge any brave who dared to question the red-and-white guardians' honor, for the young brave had just been taught to appreciate knowledge and understanding as well as bravery and courage, especially when it came from his brother-in-law.

Chief Ugly Head took in the subtle exchange between his son and new son-in-law with great pleasure. He grunted in great joy and readily accepted the gold and silver coins from Michel as a token of appreciation for his daughter and niece. The coins would hang around the Chief's neck until he died and then be passed on to Little Head.

The party was really beginning to shake after Michel's speech but both Marie and Angelique had other ideas.

Both woman had somehow managed to slide up to their men and whisper in their ears that it was time to go. This time they were allowed to take their new husbands by the hand and to lead them silently out of the central lodge and out of the village.

The night air was slightly warm, with a faint mountain breeze. A mixture of older pine and younger maples and birches was blowing in the wind, making a rustling sound as the couples went their separate ways. The hoot from an owl in the distance appeared to be mocking the two grown men, since they were the ones shaking in anticipation of what the night would bring.

That afternoon Marie and Angelique had gone into the forest and prepared their wedding beds, under framed canopies of willow saplings and cedar branches covering stretched hides. Small fires smoldered at the entrances to the cozy dwellings, with small clay pots of water and food set off to one side. Silently, the two young women entered their individual lodges and disrobed, only leaving on the leggings with the tiny bells attached to them.

Jean readily accepted what was about to come and disrobed quickly and joined his Angelique. Michel, on the other hand, had to be gently encouraged by Marie's soft purring. Eventually, though, it all worked out in the best way possible, and it was said among the Blackfoot for a very long while that the bells tinkled among the rustling of the leaves for two days and two nights.

\* \* \*

215

On THE THIRD DAY, both knights arose before the sun. Their young brides were still sleeping peacefully, as the two companions quietly met on the pathway leading back to the village. Jean just smiled and lightly slapped Michel across the back, as if to say, "Well, that's what we've been missing all these years."

In response, Michel whispered, "Yes, Jean, I believe it is the closest to the Supreme Being we've ever been. I think both of us have been to heaven and back . . . Now let us return to our mission . . . I think that it is the sixth, and we only have a few days to be in position."

Before Jean could reply, Ugly Head stepped out from behind a tree. He quickly sized up the two knight's contentment and then said to them in French, "Ah, I see that the two guardians are pleased. I pray to the Creator these unions will produce strong and healthy children, and not deformed man-beasts." This comment got Jean looking towards to Michel, but the chief continued, "Come, it is our custom that before the man-beasts can return to the village as humans they must spend some time in the sweat lodge cleansing their new bodies and minds."

Both knights had heard of a sweat lodge before but had never experienced such a thing. Indeed, they had partaken as young soldiers in the ritual of baptism by fire but never in their wildest dreams did they ever dream of such a solemn tradition.

In good faith, they followed Ugly Head, who was only dressed in a loincloth, down another path, which veered back into the woods. Coming upon a small clearing, they were greeted by a group of approximately thirty similarly dressed natives, of all size and shape and age. Both Jean and Michel recognized a number of braves and elders, including their young brother-in-laws.

Indeed, it was the brothers-in-law who instructed Michel and Jean to take off all their clothing in preparation of the sweat. As they complied, both knights noticed that a hot fire was burning outside of a low, rounded structure, which resembled a turtle shell.

Before either of the two could question as to how so many men could fit into such a small enclosure, they found themselves being hustled inside through a small opening that pointed due east. The result was immediately overwhelming. Although there appeared to be some organized chaos to the arrangement of men into two circles around a central pit, the smell and touch of naked bodies was already stifling. Then Chief Ugly Head, who had entered first and assumed the head position, cried out to two younger helpers who remained by the fire. With deer antlers, they carried the glistening, red hot rocks from the outside fire to the inner central pit before they covered the entrance with hides and boughs and maintained their outer guard position.

The result was both fascinating and terrifying. The artificial womb was absolutely devoid of any light, except for the strange, red glow from the rocks.

Chief Ugly Head then spoke in a mixture of Blackfoot and French, in deference to the two honored guests, "Welcome back, my brothers. We come together to give thanks to the Creator for the delivery of the two red-and-white guardians to our care. They have mated with our Blackfoot women and now are human. Now, let us pray that they are successful in their chosen mission."

With this one of the elders produced a large wooden bowl of water and with a cedar branch proceeded to chant and, at the same time, splash the cold water on the rocks.

It wasn't just Michel and Jean who instantly lost their breath. The waves of heat and steam were so shocking as they moved outward from the central pit that gasps were heard around the confined lodge. However, the first waves of shock were soon followed by grunts of euphoria, as everyone in the lodge gave into its warmth and comfort. It was as if every one of them had been transported back to the safety of their mother's womb. This ecstasy brought forward songs and chants, which over the centuries had been designed to slow the rhythm of breathing in order to allow the initiate to withstand the onslaught of water upon the rocks.

Ugly Head's next pronouncement took the two knight's breath completely away.

"*Kwey, Kwey, Kwey*, it is good to be inside the belly of Mother Earth once again, for she provides safety and comfort where we can share our secrets . . . Many generations ago, our ancestors looked east towards the rising sun and saw a cloud of dust roll across the prairies. It turned into a group of proud warriors, who were all mounted on their black and white horses and who wore the red-and-white hide and lambskin loincloth. The sun sparkled off their heads and weapons, which our people would learn were molded from the earth herself. Strangely, the hair on their heads had slipped to their chins and grew in many cases to their big leather belts. This is why these mountains that we sit upon are known as the Big Belt Mountains. Their leader, although old and frail, was just and wise, and taught the Blackfoot many things in exchange for our wisdom. "

Michel LeNeuf's and Jean St. Jean's hearing had become amplified. The chief's words resonated to their very souls as he continued. "The man-beasts desired to be shown what they called the Well of the Prophets, where the giants' bones are kept. Having formed an eternal bond, they were shown where the dark pool lies and it was here the warriors left gifts in thanks to the Creator that the giants could sleep in peace. And, when their leader, a prince among men, passed away, he too took his place among the giants, making the number thirteen. Those who came with their leader stayed to guard the well until they too passed beyond, but not before they mated with our Blackfoot women and became human. The Blackfoot stayed as the guardians because the prophets told us to do so . . . Even when the two white captains arrived several seasons ago with their magic guns and possession of some of the signs, the Blackfoot protected the secret at the cost of several of our brave's lives."

The sweat lodge was totally silent, even when the remaining water was dashed upon the smoldering rocks.

Chief Ugly Head spoke even more reverently than he had done before, "And now, just as the prophecies promise, the red-and-white guardians have returned to strengthen our bloodline. In return, in a few moon's times, when the moon hides the sun at its highest spot in the sky, we will give thanks when the two guardians conduct their own ceremonies in the Well of the Prophets. The prophecies tell us they alone have the knowledge and understanding, which enables the giants to continue to sleep safely, and the Blackfoot should follow any wisdom that the guardians share to make sure the Trickster is kept high in the sky—until it is time for the giants to wake once and for all!"

Everyone within the sweat lodge murmured their acceptance of the chief's sacred pronouncement, and the door of the lodge was flung open to reveal the first light of the glowing sun rising in the east. Michel and Jean followed the glistening mass of bodies to the nearest stream and jumped into the shocking cold water, thus allowing all those who had occupied the sweat lodge to be reborn.

# CHAPTER 54

Lieutenant McCormack stood at the open doorway to the warehouse and stared vacantly into the darkness. Phil Bloomer had managed to pull some strings and find a suitable building in the industrial section of Helena where he could hide his big rig and set up a command center. But Dunk failed to acknowledge any of this. He had given Bill Rose his word to look after Thomas Randolph, and after what happened to agents Bishop and Ross, he felt doubly responsible for Thomas's well-being.

Reflecting this concern, his thoughts wandered back to the first time they met one another at the White House. He smiled when he thought of Thomas's wide-eyed introduction to the president. *Come on, Thomas. You've overcome so much for being so naïve. Give us a sign. I can't believe you've succumbed to that witch's charms—give us a sign!*

Just then, as if by magic, he heard George Artowski's BlackBerry ring. One of Bloomer's Navy Seal techs had patched the director's BlackBerry into a tracking device, and it was displaying a call from the Hampton Inn in Helena.

Dunk ran over to where George Artowski was about to receive the call and positioned himself behind the director. Bill Rose, Navy Seal Lieutenant Bloomer, and Master Chief Wayne were all gathered around the director, just as anxious to receive any news of Thomas's whereabouts and of the St. Jean-LeNeuf's plans.

George pushed the RECEIVE button after the technician indicated with a thumbs-up that the recording of the conversation would begin automatically. "Hello?" George offered.

The response was crisp but came through in a whisper, "George, this is Thomas. I haven't got much time. Jean Baptiste destroyed my BlackBerry, but I had to call you. They've got the suites on both sides of mine so I'm virtually locked in. We just had supper and now we're turning in early. Tomorrow morning we're heading out at 7:00 a.m. to Townsend, where we've been outfitted with a number of four-wheel Jeeps. Jean Baptiste has a communications specialist by the name of Godfroi running the operation. He was already at the hotel when we got here. With Pierre, their bodyguard, that makes five of us. I haven't seen anybody else."

George sensed the urgency in Thomas's voice. "You've done well, Thomas. Hang in there. It won't be much longer. We'll get you out at the right time, I promise." With that, Thomas's end went dead.

George didn't panic. He was too acquainted with novices being melodramatic.

What he did do was instruct Phil Bloomer to pull up the Hampton Inn and its surrounding area on the USGS aerial photo series. "Here's the situation. As far as I know, Thomas is still on our team. He's camped out at the Hampton Inn in Helena with Jean Baptiste, his sister, a fellow named Pierre, who's apparently their bodyguard, and another fellow named Godfroi, who Thomas describes as a communications specialist. I'm going to assume both Pierre and Godfroi are French ex-military . . . Phil, I want two of your team to get over there and see if they can get a positive ID and photos of all of them. I want to make sure Thomas is okay and functioning under his own steam. Let's also see if we can identify their transportation and whether they have any other support. But tell your guys not to engage, even if discovered and provoked. Thomas also said that they're using an outfitter in Townsend. Let's see if the Bunker can identify likely choices."

Bill Rose jumped in, "George, what are you thinking?"

George cleared his throat before responding, "What I'm thinking is that it's all too easy. Why would they leave Thomas alone, even for a minute, so he can contact us? Jean Baptiste is one slippery sucker. He knows we wouldn't give up that easily. He's using Thomas to try to expose us. I have a feeling he has something in his back pocket, which could explode if we get too close."

George turned to the Navy Seal with the headset, who was sitting at the portable table set up outside of the truck's trailer. It was strewn with a myriad of electronic gear and laptop computers. "Son, were you able to determine if the call was traced from the other end?"

The Navy Seal specialist knew his work, although he looked no older than eighteen. "No, sir, it wasn't. The call was just routed through the main switchboard. Somebody could have been listening in, but they wouldn't be able to pinpoint our location, sir."

George patted the young Seal on the shoulder before responding. "There, at least some good news. Our location appears safe, for now."

George was pacing back and forth at this point. "Phil, we can't be driving this big red-and-white rig around the foothills of Townsend. Let's think of some way we can get up into the foothills without being too conspicuous.

Dunk had also listened anxiously to the entire conversation and now had an idea. "Horses!"

Bill Rose piped up, "What did you say, Dunk?"

Dunk grew excited about the possibilities. "An old marine buddy of mine, Scot Lindsey, came back to the family farm in Townsend and set it up as a dude ranch, complete with outings into the Helena National Forest, above Townsend in the foothills. He makes a killing with the tourists, and his only competition are the Jeep outfitters and some companies taking people on tours of some of the old gold and silver mines. It's real wild west-type stuff."

George Artowski stopped pacing and responded, "That's brilliant, Dunk! Try to get your friend on the phone. We'll need horses and supplies for the four of us by 4:00 a.m. tomorrow morning, if we're going to outflank them. Your friend shouldn't be involved except to supply the horses."

Bill Rose quickly did the math and didn't like what he was hearing. *George and Dunk—that's two. Phil Bloomer is from Texas, and Wayne is from Utah. I imagine they can ride.* "George, make that five!"

George knew it was coming but wouldn't hear of it. "Bill, damn it. As a friend, I'm asking you not to do this. You're the husband of the president of the United States. Besides, you're my best friend and, hell, you're over sixty years old. And, technically, you're a civilian!"

Bill Rose held up his left hand, palm forward. Dunk, Phil, James, and the techie froze and watched the drama play out between the two companions. "George, I can't pull rank here because, yes, I'm a civilian. You know how I feel about all of this. While you were off in Vietnam fighting for what we believed in, I was at graduate school partying. All my life, I've been the one who's relied on you to protect both Helen and me. We've lost twelve good men on our own soil in the last eight days and now we have a fellow Mason and Knight Templar who needs both of us. We're the ones who got Thomas into this mess in the first place. You can't deny me this!" Bill Rose was almost pleading.

Begrudgingly, George answered, "Okay, Bill, okay. But you better not get yourself killed. Your wife can strip me of all my medals, you know. Hell, if something happens to you, she'll have me beheaded. Just do me a favor and hang back behind the professionals, will you?" George was regretting his decision even before he made it, but Bill Rose had won the privilege by serving his country in a different way. "And, Dunk?"

"Yes, sir, Colonel!" The marine lieutenant snapped to attention to show his admiration for the director's decision.

"Cut out the bullshit and help Mr. Rose with one of the titanium vests. Hopefully, he can stand behind a tree and not get shot!"

* * *

As THOMAS TALKED TO THE DIRECTOR on the phone, he heard a light knock at the door between his and one of the adjacent suites. This was the reason he'd hung up the phone so quickly. The effect was he was a little shaky as he unlocked the door and opened it, only to discover Marie standing there somewhat sheepishly—wearing what could only be described as a very short, see-through nightgown.

Before Thomas could react, she threw her arms around his neck, embracing him so hard he almost fell backwards. It was as if she had shifted personalities again. "Oh, Thomas, I've longed to feel you all day. I've found your intelligence and honesty so enlightening that I've ached for you. I want you to stand beside me when the New World Order becomes a reality."

Thomas really wasn't in the mood for any more of the New World Order rhetoric. "Marie, do you honestly think the possession of a single word and an old scroll, which may never be proven to be genuine, will cause billions of people to abandon their faith and follow a new religion, where peace and harmony reigns throughout the world? A thousand years of hatred between the world's three greatest religions is being played out in the Middle East right now. A thousand years is hard to forget. Besides, the Israelis will never give up Jerusalem. They believe it is their God-given homeland."

"But, Thomas, that's where you're wrong." Marie was almost pleading with Thomas to understand. And then, it slipped. "Thomas, at the exact same time the solar eclipse exposes the true secret, a small nuclear device will go off under the Dome of the Rock and destroy the entire Old City of Jerusalem. Jean's closest friend, Robert Dumas, has seen to it."

Thomas stood stunned, almost unable and definitely unwilling to comprehend what he was hearing.

Marie saw the shock on Thomas's face but continued. "After that explosion, people will have to listen to my brother. Can't you understand? The people will feel their God has abandoned them. Because Moses wrote the Torah and is deemed comparable to Mohammed, people will have to obey his original teachings and laws over the many generations of copies and interpretations, which have corrupted the true meaning of God's words. My brother will be the true conduit to God, and God will speak directly to the people through him. The priest, rabbis, and imans will all have to obey if they want to maintain any semblance of leadership."

Thomas recognized Marie's rhetoric for what it was—pure insanity—but it was too late. He felt the prick at the back of his neck and knew immediately it was a hypodermic needle. In the shock of hearing Marie's pronouncement, he failed to notice that Jean Baptiste had silently slipped into the suite from the opposite doorway. But, in a moment, everything went black.

As Jean Baptiste carried Thomas to the bed, he commented rather sarcastically to his sister, "Marie, I told you that you could have your way with Thomas as long as you didn't tell him about our plans."

Marie worked to cover herself as best as she could. "But he's with us all the way."

Jean Baptiste shrugged. "I hope so. I need to know who I can count on at a time like this. Now we have to be up early tomorrow morning, so you should get some sleep. I'll see the two of you at 6:00 a.m."

# CHAPTER 55

Michel's new father-in-law, Chief Ugly Head, gathered the two Frenchmen, the village shaman, and the two brothers-in-law well before dawn, with the purpose of showing the two knights where the vault was located in time for the predicted eclipse.

Prior to leaving the village, the two knights had instructed their wives to spread the word that the entire village was to remain in their lodges when the sun was about to reach its meridian. He warned that they were not to look directly into the eclipse, even when the sun was hidden.

The vault was only about an hour's ride from the main village, located at the end of a fairly deep, dry gulch. The gulch ran by a prominent limestone promontory, which could be seen for miles across the Missouri River and open plains. The vault was a natural sinkhole formed ages ago when an underground stream carved its way through soft shale and undermined the porous limestone.

The dramatic result was a gigantic wormhole, located within a circle of oak trees mixed with softwoods. It was forty feet in diameter and one hundred feet deep. Over the centuries, the underground stream had dried up, leaving only a small pool of still water at its sandy bottom. The pool itself was only twenty feet across and ten feet deep and had the appearance of perfectly smooth black glass.

The blackness of the water was due to the high level of titanium and manganese leaching out of the surrounding limestone rock. Thus, the raw energy of the pool, as the living heart of the vault, was sustained for time immemorial. This notion, which coincided with the Native American belief that the vault was the inner soul of Mother Turtle, ensured that her stomach would only be penetrated by the red-and-white guardians, as the natives were superstitious of being swallowed up by the giant turtle.

As guardians, Major Michel LeNeuf and Sergeant Major Jean St. Jean would be the first ones to access the vault since Prince Henry Sinclair had been laid to rest alongside the other prophets of the true faith. In preparation, the two knights had been shown a cache of materials, left by the previous red-and-white guardians, which was stored in a nearby cave.

The two knights at first were puzzled by the cave's contents until they realized it consisted of a rolled-up chain ladder, made from metal ringlets and metal rungs, and several large clay jars, which were filled and capped with a distilled bear grease. Obviously, the previous guardians were skilled metalworkers, working laboriously to construct a ladder that, if properly maintained by the oil, would last forever. Judging by the smile on the two brothers-in-law's faces when the knights admired the tenacity with which the metal was maintained, it became obvious that it had been their task to do that for some time now.

Taking the ladder with them, the small band made their way to the vault. In no time, the two knights found themselves standing safely on the sandy floor of the hole.

The sight greeting them was simply amazing, even to hardened veterans like themselves. Carved into the wormhole's rough, circular wall were thirteen niches. Oddly, the rock itself held a golden translucent light, as if bathed in a holy golden aura, so no torches were required. The luminescent glow came from the ever-growing bacteria from sea crustaceans, which at one time denoted the western edge of an ancient inland lake.

Each niche had a rounded ceiling, which allowed a person to stand under its roof. In the center of each cell stood a perfectly shaped limestone block or plinth, upon which rested a single limestone ossuary. On each carved plinth, they saw the carved symbol of the original Royal Arch Mason and, on an opposite side of each ossuary was carved the name of the occupant.

The problem was most of the rough-carved names were at best shallow and faded, confirming the antiquity of the ossuaries, if not their contents. To make matters even more complicated, many of the names were in Aramaic, a couple in Norse Rune, a few in ancient Hebrew, some in Egyptian hieroglyphic, and one was even in what appeared to be the earliest Sumerian script.

The two knights were humbled to be in the presence of such greatness, yet they were perplexed as to how a solar eclipse high in the sky was going to reveal the true secret, as the final resting places of the thirteen prophets looked roughly the same. How were they to find the ossuary containing Moses' remains and the original scroll of the Mosaic Laws?

As Major LeNeuf's head started to spin, he conjured up the fourth ritual of the French Blue Lodge. That contains the culminating mystical lecture to the supreme degree of the Holy Royal Arch of Jerusalem . . . *On top of the Pedestal is an equilateral triangle which has ever alluded to the Deity. In the days of Pythagoras it was esteemed the most sacred of all emblems, and when any oath was required, it was always administered thereon . . . On the sides of the triangle appears that sacred and mysterious Name of the Deity which you have sworn never to pronounce unless in the presence, and with the assistance of, two or more companions of the Order. The first part of the word is the Chaldaic name of God, signifying His essence of majesty, incomprehensible; it is also a Hebrew word, signifying I am and shall be, thereby expressing the actual, future and eternal existence of the Most High. When the Almighty commanded Moses to go into Egypt to deliver his brethren Moses said: Behold, when I come unto the children of Israel and shall say unto them, the God of your fathers hath sent me unto you and they shall say unto me, what is his name? What shall I say unto them? And God said unto Moses, I AM THAT I AM, that is I am from eternity to eternity . . . The second part of the word is an Assyrian word, signifying, Lord or Powerful; it is also a compound Hebrew word from the preposition Beth, in Heaven, or on high; therefore this word means Lord, in Heaven or on High . . . The third part of the word is an Egyptian word, signifying Father of all; it is also a Hebrew word signifying strength or power, and is expressive of the omnipotence of the Father of all; taken together they will read thus; I am and shall be, Lord in Heaven or on High, Father of all, the all powerful Jehovah, Jove or Lord.*

The Major thought he just might have the answer but, as he spun around in a wide circle, he could not see any golden triangle, either literally or symbolically.

What broke him out of his spell was the sergeant major yelling, "Michel, look! Look at the water." Jean pointed towards the pool, trying to keep his arm from shaking.

Michel stood to one side and peered down upon the reflective surface, which showed a faint reddish glow due to the movement of the eclipse into the area above the hole. It was as though the glow was resting on the surface, yet penetrating the whole pool at the same time. The two knights froze at the sight of the glow expanding and consuming the entire pool, mimicking the advancing total solar eclipse above.

When the sun reached its meridian, a strange effect took hold of the entire vault. It was assumed the eclipse would travel directly overhead of the wormhole, but its oscillating path around the world had taken it slightly to the north of the vault. This meant that the eclipse's reflection in the pool was caught at an angle, causing the strongest concentration of the sun's rays to deflect off of the pool's surface. This resulted in one cell taking on an intense, lozenge-shaped glow, temporarily blinding the two knights.

Just as quickly as it occurred, the brilliant flash of light disappeared into itself, leaving the two knights on their knees and holding their faces in their hands, as the blackness of the hole and sky quickly dissipated.

Major LeNeuf gently raised himself up and opened his eyes to discover that his eyesight was completely restored. Looking at the sergeant major, still on his knees, still cowering from the sudden spectacle, he yelled, "Jean, rise up and open your eyes. It's gone and I can see again!"

The sergeant major did as instructed and felt an immediate sense of relief when he discovered that he too could see. "*Mon Dieu*, Michel, am I dreaming? Were we just shown the one true secret by the Supreme Being?"

Both Michel and Jean moved over to the still-glowing cell and stood around its central plinth and ossuary. Almost reverently, Jean nudged the limestone box with his finger. "The box is still warm. It must be the one."

"Let's wait a few seconds for it to cool before we see what we have." Michel wanted the time to collect his wits. "There's a faint carving of a name on this side but it's in a language I don't understand." He then touched the box himself, with his index finger. "There, it's cooled down enough for us to move it. Here Jean, help me lift it off its plinth."

The ossuary wasn't overly heavy but Michel didn't want to take any chances, especially as it appeared the box still held some kind of strange energy. As Jean and Michel each took an end of the ossuary and lifted it off its plinth, a gold triangle—a perfect equilateral triangle inset into the top of the limestone plinth, was exposed. On each side of the triangle, a number of different antient characters were lightly carved into its surface.

Upon seeing the golden triangle, Michel's face went white, and he instinctively crossed himself. "Oh, my God, Jean, it's that-which-was-lost! It's the key to the treasure itself. We are standing in the direct presence of the Lord."

Jean became solemn and reverently crossed himself. "I am almost afraid to see what is contained within the ossuary. Do you think we should open it, Michel?"

"Yes, Jean, we will open it up to see what is in there. But we must put everything back as we found it and devise some way to seal up the hole at the surface." Michel had gained an extraordinary sense of the Egyptian Deity's—Ormus's—wisdom within the past two weeks, in addition to the higher knowledge and understanding he already possessed. "What we have seen here today we will take to our graves. I feel eternally blessed and I know, Jean, you share the same feeling. We'll let Thomas Jefferson know we discovered and sealed the vault for future generations but I have to tell you, I'm scared by the raw power exhibited before us today. Jefferson will be content enough with the Templar sword. I'm not even going to hazard whose remains are in the other twelve ossuaries . . . Jean, today, we have set one foot in heaven . . . Quickly now, let us see what lies in the ossuary."

Jean already had the lid half open. What stared out at the two knights was almost anti-climatic, but the two knew the real value of what the box contained. There was a single skull and accompanying two legs bones, as well as what appeared to be a large scroll encased in a leather wrap and bituminous seal.

Upon looking at each other for a second without any apparent outer emotion, the two knights replaced the limestone lid and placed the entire ossuary back upon the plinth, in its original position.

Without saying a word, the two made their way back up the suspended metal ladder where they found their Blackfoot companions waiting. As they mounted their trusty steeds for the return journey to the village, not a word was spoken. Even the two younger, usually boisterous braves had been awed into silence by the eclipse and the sudden flash of light from the sinkhole. Only the Blackfoot shaman who accompanied them had any real idea as to what had happened down in the vault, as the story of the previous red-and-white guardians' journey into the hole had been conveyed to him by his predecessor and by his predecessor before him, going back to the time of the last guardians.

As they turned their horses to ride away from the sacred turtle, Michel LeNeuf suddenly realized they stood atop the shining brow—Taliesin, the white limestone promontory that the Blackfoot called in their own language Little Hogback, as the natural landform resembled the razor-haired back of a wild boar. Michel stood high in his stirrups, looking at the reddened, flood-swollen Missouri River making its way to the east.

For two days afterwards, both Michel and Jean spent time alone with their wives in their lodges, trying to find peace of mind in the arms of their loved ones. Major Michel LeNeuf was the first of the two to emerge and, in doing so, approached Chief Ugly Head and the Blackfoot council for their help in sealing the vault and becoming its protectors. On behalf of his people, Chief Ugly Head acknowledged the request as the Creator's wish and that Mother Earth had spoken.

# CHAPTER 56

Thomas's head was splitting and his mouth was beyond dry when he woke, due to the drug Jean Baptiste had administered. He also woke to find that his hands had been secured by plastic cuffs.

He attempted to raise himself up into a sitting position but even this small movement was difficult, as his shoulder also ached. *What was it they shot into me?*

Marie Magdalene entered through the side door she had used the night before. This time she was dressed in tight jeans, ankle-high hiking boots, a thick wool shirt, jean jacket, and down-filled vest, and carrying a tray of hot coffee, tea and juice, along with muffins and fruit. It was as though nothing unusual had happened the night before, even though Thomas's wrists were still secured and he was naked.

Marie Magdalene put the tray on the small round table next to an armoire and poured Thomas a cup of hot Earl Grey tea. After adding lots of milk and sugar the way Thomas preferred, she carried the cup over to the bed's side table and bent over Thomas to give him a kiss. Thomas instinctively pulled his head back and exclaimed, "Marie, what the heck's going on? My head's ready to fall off, and you're acting as though drugging someone is a natural, everyday occurrence."

Marie took it all in stride, as the previous evening's events actually were an everyday occurrence where she came from. "Thomas, don't be silly, Jean Baptiste just wanted to be sure you wouldn't try to make a run for it when we're so close. I needed to get you some breakfast, so the plastic ties were insurance that you wouldn't go anywhere."

Thomas couldn't believe what he was hearing. "Marie, do you mean to tell me that you undressed me and then tied my hands?"

Marie feigned innocence, all the while sliding her hand under the covers. "Why, Thomas, my darling, I'm hurt you'd think I handcuffed you. That'll come later, if you like? . . . Actually, Pierre's been watching over you while I had a shower and got dressed. I imagine he just wanted to make sure you wouldn't attempt something silly like trying to put your clothes on and go for a long walk."

Before Thomas could respond, Pierre walked around the open door and stood there smirking. If looks could kill, Thomas would already be dead.

Thomas jumped at the sight of Pierre and tried to maintain some semblance of decency, but it was hard while Marie was doing what she was doing. Finally, she turned and spoke to Pierre, "Don't worry, Pierre, he won't go anywhere while I have hold of him. Please leave us alone and shut the door behind you. Thomas is going to have a shower and then put on his clothes and have something to eat. Then we'll join you and the others down in the parking lot in thirty minutes. Is that clear?"

Pierre withdrew without saying another word.

Marie then reached into her jean jacket and produced a little pocket knife, which she used to cut the plastic ties binding Thomas's hands. She then bent over and whispered into his ear, "Thomas, don't do anything hasty. I'm sure they're listening. Let's go into the bathroom for your shower."

Thomas stared at Marie rather incredulously but obeyed her anyways. He first wrapped one of the bed sheets around his waist and walked over to the bathroom, with Marie following him. Once in the bathroom, Thomas turned the shower on full blast before quietly confronting Marie, "Okay, what's this all about? One second we're wrapped up in each other's arms at the doorway and the next thing that I know I'm waking up with a drug-induced headache?"

Marie looked around as though she expected Jean Baptiste to burst through the door any second. "Thomas, Jean Baptiste was listening in last night. He heard me when I told you about the bomb. Obviously, you weren't supposed to know. The only reason you're still alive is that he needs you to verify if anything is out of place once we access the tunnel. Now quickly, let's act as though nothing's out of the ordinary. Have a quick shower and I'll lay out your clothes." Marie leaned forward and gave Thomas a quick kiss on the cheek, and then she was gone.

* * *

T HE SMALL CARAVAN that made its way to the outfitters in Townsend consisted of only two vehicles—the black Mercedes and Godfroi's black van. The arrangements had been made ahead of time, so it took no more than ten minutes for Pierre and Godfroi to transfer all of the necessary equipment from the van into the three Jeeps secured for the occasion.

It had been decided ahead of time that the first Jeep was to be driven by Godfroi, since he had earlier programmed the route into a hand-held GPS unit. The second Jeep was to be driven by Jean Baptiste, with Marie in the passenger seat, and the third would be driven by Pierre, with Thomas in the passenger seat. Prior to leaving the outfitters, Pierre had silently bound Thomas's hands once again with another of what appeared to be an endless supply of plastic ties.

Following the transfer, the Jeeps formed a line out of Townsend and onto a local road leading west to an area known as the "Limestone Hills Range," where they continued going upwards along a dirt road, a trace that zigzagged up and around the prominent limestone outcrop known as Little Hogback, to a small plateau. From there, it took the convoy no longer than half an hour of following a dirt track to a point where they were directly in front of the small wooded area which represented the turtle's head.

As if circling the wagons, the three Jeeps came to rest in a semi-circle. Godfroi was the first to jump out of his Jeep. He rummaged around under the canvas at the back of the Jeep until he produced a hand-held instrument that resembled a shovel. As the others stepped out of their Jeeps, Godfroi pressed a number of buttons on the unit, which turned out to be the latest in ground-penetrating radar, and proceeded to sweep the immediate area until he got the reading he was hoping for. "It's right here," yelled Godfroi excitedly.

Thomas hadn't noticed but Pierre had retrieved a large shovel and deadly looking pick-axe, which he was now swinging over his head. As it sunk into the ground, there was a sharp thud, as though it hit wood six inches below the surface. Pierre yanked the pick-axe upwards, and when it came away it had what appeared to be a rotten piece of log stuck to its end. Pierre swung again with renewed vigor and the "mouth" of the turtle opened completely.

Having succeeded this far without any real obstacle, Jean Baptiste slapped Pierre on the back and gave him the first bit of praise Thomas had ever heard come from him towards one of his men, "Well done, Pierre, this is easier than I suspected. Godfroi, you've outdone yourself also . . . Now grab me three of those flashlights from the Jeep. I want the two of you to stay here. If I need you, I'll call you on the portables . . . Sweep the area every so often to make sure we don't have company, but make sure you keep your weapons out of sight. If any innocents come upon you, just indicate some tourists are checking out an old mine shaft."

Pierre handed the lamps to Jean Baptiste, Marie and Thomas, but failed to release his hands from the plastic cuffs. Thomas looked at Jean Baptiste in a questioning manner, but the only response he got was a curt one, "Mr. Randolph, you go first. So far there haven't been any surprises and I want to keep it that way. I would think you're the best one to recognize any signs, seals, or tokens that your fellow Knights Templar, my ancestors, left when they carved this tunnel. The satellite photos show it extending downwards to a large cavern one hundred feet below the surface. I can't imagine any pitfalls or traps, but one never knows. Shall we?"

With this small oration, he gave Thomas a rough shove into the tunnel. It had a height of about six feet and a width of about three feet, which made the going easy. Thomas quickly figured that it would have taken an experienced mining crew only about two months to dig out the tunnel, due to the relatively soft and porous limestone.

He also figured that the tunnel was built to facilitate access to the vault—not to kill anyone who accidently stumbled across it. Only the truly initiated would know where the entrance to the tunnel lay in the vast wilderness. Besides, Thomas figured Major Michel LeNeuf and Jean St. Jean didn't have the time or inclination to booby-trap the tunnel.

As a result, Thomas made the journey down into the center of the vault in a relatively short time. When the trio entered the vault, its majesty took their collective breaths away. All three were almost moved to tears, since the vault represented a belief that all three shared for a lifetime.

After turning their flashlights off, the translucent aura of the cave itself only added to their awe, as did the intricate wooden scaffolding appearing to encircle the central pool, extending upwards to the artificial roof of the cavern. Thomas gasped when he realized the octagonal scaffolding contained nine arches—one built on top of the other.

Upon witnessing this unique feat of human engineering, Thomas exclaimed to Jean Baptiste and Marie, even though his life hung in the balance, "This is truly amazing! Have you looked around you?" Thomas waved his hands, which were still bound, in a wide arc, illustrating the thirteen carved cells containing the carved limestone plinths and ossuaries.

Surprisingly, neither Jean Baptiste nor Marie had fully taken in their surroundings, as they were too fixated on the central wooden construction and black reflecting pool. However, they were now even more awestruck by the significance of what they found around the perimeter of the cave. The knowledge and understanding of the raw power lying within the thirteen ossuaries could have been overwhelming, if it were not for the distorted comprehension that Jean Baptiste and Marie shared. Where Thomas was humbled beyond comparison to be in the presence of spiritual greatness, the St. Jean-LeNeuf's viewed the relics as agents of universal power and world dominance.

Jean Baptiste was satisfied that Thomas had served his purpose and, therefore, now considered him expendable. Taking the semi-automatic from his jacket pocket, he pointed it at Thomas and said, "Mr. Randolph, we are in your debt. Thank you . . . But I must now ask you to get on your knees. Every re-consecration of a sacred site requires a sacrifice and, unfortunately for you, you're it!"

Thomas couldn't believe what he was hearing, but he did as he was told. He thought of rushing Jean Baptiste, but he knew it would be futile. This way, at least, he could say a silent prayer to his family. *Frank, Alexander, I'll love you always. Please forgive your father for being an old fool. Sharon, I'll be seeing you soon, my love.*

Jean Baptiste grunted his disapproval of Thomas's apparent easy acceptance of his fate. He had admired Thomas earlier for his defiance but now he only had disdain.

He quickly glanced over to Marie, who had stepped back to be beside her brother. "Here, Marie, take my gun. You need to do the deed in order to cleanse yourself. I know you love this man, but our fates are melded into one. Michele will have my children in order to keep the bloodline strong, but you will rule at my side as my queen."

Thomas didn't know what to expect next but wasn't really surprised when Marie took the gun and assumed the firing stance. Her face showed no emotion, even when she took a bead on Thomas's chest and slowly started to pull the trigger. In return, Thomas's eyes locked onto hers.

The silence was broken by the deafening roar of the gun in the enclosed environment, but instead of Thomas feeling the searing pain of the bullet entering his chest, the side of Marie's head exploded in a sickening display of blood and bone fragments.

Jean Baptiste screamed, "No!" before his paratrooper training kicked in. In an instant, he rolled away from Marie's limp body that was falling and disappeared into the shadows in a flash, leaving his gun in the sand where it had fallen.

Thomas was just cognizant enough to catch out of the corner of his eye what at first looked like a walking robot. In reality, it turned out to be Marine Lieutenant McCormack decked out in full combat gear, complete with bullet-proof vest, wireless headset, and night-vision goggles. As he swept the immediate area with his futuristic-looking sub-machine gun, since he half-expected a charge from Jean Baptiste, he calmly noted to Thomas, "I told you never to trust her. Man, she was one crazy lady! She would have killed you without even thinking about it!"

Thomas slowly raised himself up from his knees. The tears swelling in his eyes were quite genuine, "Dunk, you asshole, what took you so long?"

"I'm sorry. You're welcome for me having to save your sorry ass . . . I didn't expect the cavern to have this glow about it, so I had to pop up my goggles and wait for my vision to adjust." Dunk had a funny smirk on his face but he knew he had cut it pretty close. "Now pick up the handgun lying beside you. We still have to take care of that crazy bastard."

Thomas, in shock from the death of the woman he oddly loved, had just enough sense about him to say, "If I'm correct, there must be another way out of here. There was once an underground stream flowing through here, so I imagine there's a tunnel of sorts . . . By the way, where are the others, and what happened to Pierre and Godfroi?"

"Phil Bloomer and James Wayne took them out before they even knew what hit them. Actually, we were in the trees to the north even before you pulled up." Dunk was expertly clearing every sector of the vault as he spoke. "After we took out the two lookouts, Bill Rose convinced Artowski to call in the cavalry. Three Black Hawks full of rangers are heading this way from Hill AFB in Utah . . . Hang on for a minute."

Dunk pressed the transmit button on his wireless headset, "Colonel Artowski, it's all clear down here. Ms. St. Jean-LeNeuf is dead, and Thomas is secure and well. Jean Baptiste has made a runner for it down a natural tunnel heading west-southwest. I don't think he's armed but when the rangers arrive tell them that we'll need some tunnel specialists with dogs to try to sniff him out . . . Colonel, you and Mr. Rose are not going to believe what is down here!" Then he signed off.

Without saying another word, Lieutenant McCormack walked over to Thomas and extracted a knife from his boot. Thomas held up his bound wrists, and Dunk deftly sliced the plastic cuffs

Thomas cleared the moisture from his eyes before saying to Lieutenant McCormack, "Dunk, there's something I've got to tell George and Bill right away. God, I pray that we're not too late."

# CHAPTER 57

It took a little over ten minutes for George Artowski and Bill Rose to join Thomas and Dunk in the Well of the Prophets, where they quietly spent another ten minutes trying to comprehend what they were seeing.

Meanwhile, Phil Bloomer and James Wayne stayed on the surface to await the arrival of the US Army Rangers. Master Chief Wayne had scouted out a suitable landing zone and dispersed flares around its perimeter, while Lieutenant Phil Bloomer established a direct satellite link-up through his portable communications center within his big rig, with both the White House Bunker and Hill Air Force Base.

The tractor-trailer was now in position in a large parking lot in Townsend, having been driven from Helena by one of Bloomer's Navy Seal Team members. Only this once would Phil Bloomer forgive the driver for touching the steering wheel, as he had more pressing matters to deal with.

Within the big rig, four of the Navy Seals were suiting up to join Bloomer and Wayne, with specific instructions that they were to bring four body bags as soon as possible—for Pierre, Godfroi, and Marie Magdalene, with the hope Jean Baptiste would soon be occupying the fourth.

The information concerning Jean Baptiste and his escape was already being relayed to the Rangers, along with a digital copy of his photograph and vital statistics. Another two Black Hawks with specialized sensing equipment, men and dogs had been requested and were already dispersing from Hill AFB. The Rangers in these choppers were specially trained in a specific anti-terrorism scenario involving underground and tunnel spaces, following the bombing of the Manhattan tunnel. If Jean Baptiste was still underground, then flushing out and capturing him would be the responsibility of these men.

237

The coordination of resources had been swift and efficient, and already the president was informed of the situation by the Bunker. The Secret Service's personal army was also coordinating the dissemination of misinformation to the local and state authorities, with the objective of sealing off the area as quickly as possible. If Jean Baptiste managed to make it to the surface anywhere in the near vicinity, the trap would be set.

George Artowski and Bill Rose had finally absorbed enough to understand they stood in what could be the most exciting spiritual discovery since the Knights Templar first dug under the Temple site in Jerusalem some one thousand years earlier. George and Bill nodded to one another in recognition of this and moved over to where Thomas was now standing.

Bill Rose was the first to extend his hand to Thomas, saying, "Right Eminent Knight Randolph, your fellow knights salute you and congratulate you. I know this is a very difficult time for you, but I want you to know that what you have done is not only a great service to the United States but to the entire world. The historical significance of what exists here is beyond comprehension at this point; but I hope and pray that, if properly disseminated, it will lead to a better understanding of the origins of all religions. I'm also hoping that through my wife the promise of access to this material will bring together all of the great religious scholars and leaders of the world in peace and harmony. Of course, you will be suitably rewarded."

Thomas stared at the two modern-day knights. At this point, he was totally disillusioned and exhausted. *My God, where have I heard this before? Outside of Jean Baptiste and Marie Magdalene spouting their New World Order rhetoric, the result of this whole fiasco will essentially be the same. The Dead Sea Scrolls have been controlled by the Vatican for some forty years and the same will happen here. Of course, quid pro quo!*

Thomas then remembered what he had to tell George Artowski and Bill Rose. He ignored the nagging feeling in the back of his mind and spoke quietly, "There's something you need to know immediately. Marie told me last night that Jean Baptiste's best friend, a Robert Dumas, has managed to plant a small nuclear bomb in a cave under the Dome of the Rock. Its detonation is set to coincide with the exposure of this vault to the total solar eclipse happening tomorrow at noon."

Bill Rose gasped and then exclaimed, "Oh, my God, this must explain the present turmoil in the Middle East. Someone or some group must know something? George, something like this would cause a Holy Armageddon. Can we stop it?"

George was already on his BlackBerry, but told whoever he had on the other end to hang on for a few seconds. "We'll try, Bill. I'm going to have Helen call in the Chiefs of Staff and CIA on this one . . . Thomas, think hard, is there anything else Marie told you that can help us?"

Thomas closed his eyes and went over the conversation from the night before. The tears were once again welling up but his memory was working. "She said the bomb was planted in a recently-discovered cavern, which led from a cistern to right under the site of the First Temple. She also said Robert Dumas was an old paratrooper comrade of Jean Baptiste and that he's now in Paris, waiting to hear from him."

George didn't need to repeat Thomas's comments to the person at the other end of his BlackBerry, as the anonymous person was listening in on the conversation. Instead, George just posed the question to the faceless voice, "Got that? . . . Okay, move on it fast and do whatever, I repeat, whatever, has to be done. Keep me and the president informed on a need-to-know basis"

George recognized the symptoms of shock in Thomas and realized they needed to get him to the surface. "Dunk, what do you think are the chances of Jean Baptiste doubling back?"

Lieutenant McCormack took a second to mull over the question, also recognizing that the director realized what was happening to Thomas. He also knew the director and Bill Rose needed to be alone inside the vault before the Rangers arrived.

"I expect the odds are nil to none. He'll have realized by now that all of his plans have gone awry. I think he knew that he had a backdoor beforehand. He was too quick to vanish. My bet is he won't give the death of his sister a second thought." Dunk paused to allow his comments to sink in. "If I was him, my best hope would be that the bomb isn't discovered in time. The resulting chaos could still work in his favor and, if there's such a thing as the Holy Bloodline, he still could make some interesting claims, once what's here is exposed to the world."

Thomas stared at Dunk almost in disbelief, as though to say: That's a pretty astute assessment for a hard-headed Marine!

Dunk looked back at Thomas and winked, before saying to the trio, "Might I suggest, colonel, you take my sub-machine gun, and I'll see that Thomas gets to the surface. I've got my sidearm. This way, I can co-ordinate with Phil Bloomer and his Seals, and also the incoming Rangers. We're also going to have to open up this wormhole in time for the eclipse tomorrow. I have an idea as to how we can accomplish this but I'll have to see if we have the right equipment."

George just had it confirmed to himself and Bill Rose that they certainly made the right choice when they sponsored Lieutenant McCormack to become a Knights Templar five years ago. "That sounds good, Dunk. Let's do it! A Colonel Steve Sinclair is in charge of the Rangers. He's a good fellow. He'll take over field operations on the surface once he gets here. Tell Phil Bloomer that his Seal team has jurisdiction over the vault and the bodies. Anybody who sets foot down here will be served with a presidential order, which means they'll carry this secret to their grave. Now off with the both of you and make sure a medic checks out Thomas."

With a nod to both men, Thomas and Dunk vanished back up the tunnel, leaving only George, Bill, and Marie Magdalene's lifeless body behind.

George Artowski and Bill Rose stood over Marie's body, trying very hard to understand the meaning of it all and the global repercussions. "We have some pressing issues here. I hope to hell your fellows are as good as you say they are and can discover and disarm that bomb. I also haven't a clue as to how we're going to open up this hole in time. I wonder what Dunk is thinking?"

Dunk was on the surface thinking that the immediate area looked like something out of Iraq. The first three Black Hawks had already touched down within the landing zone and purple smoke was gently floating on the wind. US Rangers had spread out to form a first perimeter, with a command center established between the three Jeeps, next to the tunnel entrance. Phil Bloomer's Navy Seals had also arrived and were pouring over satellite photos of the site.

Thomas was sitting in one of the outfitter's Jeeps, being attended to by one of the Rangers' medics. From his right arm protruded a rubber hose, connected to an IV bag. He was more dehydrated than anything else, but the IV would combat his mild shock. Standing beside him was Colonel Sinclair, who appeared to be a gentle giant, yet it was quite obvious that even Phil Bloomer was deferring to him. All was in order, and Dunk had every confidence Jean Baptiste would be caught and hopefully join the two occupied body bags that already lay to the side of the Jeeps.

Dunk took advantage of the time to go through the contents of the Jeeps to see what the Frenchmen had planned and discovered what he already had in mind for the wooden scaffolding. Tucked into a military carry-all were a number of phosphorus incendiaries, bricks of C-4, other explosives and various remote-control devices. Dunk figured this must be Pierre's personal collection of explosives, some of which had been used to blow up agents Bishop and Ross. Dunk looked over at the body bag containing Pierre's lifeless body and smiled a wicked smile. *I hope you roast in hell, you bastard. I wonder how many other innocent men, women, and children you've killed. I only regret that I didn't pull the trigger myself.*

The sound of the other two Black Hawks could be heard in the distance. Dunk grabbed what he needed and moved over to Colonel Sinclair, who was now talking to Phil Bloomer. "Excuse me, sir, Marine Lieutenant Duncan McCormack at your service." Dunk smartly saluted the colonel, who returned the salute. "Colonel Artowski extends his compliments, sir."

Colonel Sinclair liked what he saw in the Marine. "Ah, lieutenant, it's Dunk, isn't it? No need to be formal here amongst us Fraters, especially after Phil tells me how things went down. I must say that Mr. Randolph over there looks like the most unlikely hero, especially with the blood splattered all over his clothing. Quite remarkable—a modern-day Knights Templar, you say? . . . Anyways, down to business. We'll have the tunnel team and dogs on the ground in exactly two minutes. Meanwhile, we'll have the three Black Hawks do a recon of the surrounding woods with their heat-sensitive cameras. We'll find this bastard, whether he pops up out of his hole or stays underground . . . I understand you and the Navy Seals are heading back down to be with Colonel Artowski and the president's husband."

Dunk liked what he saw in the colonel. "Sir, I'm to tell you that anybody who enters the tunnel will be bound by a presidential order . . . I should also tell you, in the Jeep over yonder, there's enough explosives to take out this whole plateau."

The colonel raised his eyebrows at this.

Dunk continued, "Just to make sure you understand the situation, sir, this immediate area will need to be cleared by 1600 today. If someone in Mr. Bloomer's team is handy with explosives, there'll be quite the interesting fireworks display at 1700."

"Thank you, lieutenant. We'll see to the stuff on the surface and look after Mr. Randolph for you. We'll also make sure the perimeter is extended to two kilometers by 1600. One question if I may: How long are we expected to maintain this position?"

The marine lieutenant smiled before replying, "Sir, at least until tomorrow's solar eclipse, sir."

Dunk and the Navy Seals were in the tunnel before Colonel Sinclair could respond in any fashion. All the colonel could do was stand there, staring up into the sky looking at the sun.

# CHAPTER 58

R obert Dumas and Angelique Martine had been inseparable since Robert's return from Israel, spending their time in the Paris flat or taking leisurely strolls along the Seine. For the first time in their lives, they were truly happy. However, Robert was also becoming slightly anxious, as the big day was closing in. As a result, he told Angelique he was just going to pop over to the corner café for a cognac and a cigarette with the locals. He never made it.

As he was about to cross the street in front of the apartment, he spied a pretty young lady with shoulder length brunette hair walking towards him. She looked like any other American student studying in Paris, with skin-tight jeans tucked into knee-high suede boots, a short beige leather jacket and bright tangerine scarf. She was also carrying an over-sized Gucci handbag and seemed to be absent-mindedly searching for something in the bottom. Robert wasn't overly concerned but casually felt for his Berretta, tucked into the small of his back and covered by his own leather jacket.

He relaxed when he noticed the girl extract a small pack of Gitanes and select one. It was obvious to him she was going to ask him for a light, as it appeared as though rummaging through her bag again would be too much of an effort. Ever the gentleman, Robert had already produced his prized lighter with engraved paratrooper wings from his jacket pocket and was waiting with a smile. "*Madememoiselle*, if I may?" he questioned as he held up the lighter.

She smiled back, then nodded and, having put the cigarette to her lips, she tipped her head slightly to take the light. The cigarette flared as she drew a puff and then looked up. Robert immediately noticed that both of her eyes were almost pitch-black in color. Before he could remark, she responded, "Ah, *merci*, thank you. Do you speak English?"

Robert was surprised he could feel the flush of his cheeks. He quickly regained his composure and replied, "Mais, oui, but of course. You are American?"

She took another puff on her cigarette and then coolly replied, "Actually, darling, I'm Israeli."

Upon hearing her response, Robert's training immediately kicked in, but even then it was too late. In a split second a non-descript white van roared to the curb. Its sliding door was already open, and the occupant in the back already pulling the trigger on his high-voltage taser. At such a short distance the effect was totally disabling. Two strong hands reached out of the van and dragged Robert inside. The young lady then nonchalantly threw her cigarette onto the pavement and squashed it with the toe of her boot before jumping into the van and sliding the door shut. The whole operation took less than a thirty seconds to play out.

Inside the van, two sturdy young men with olive complexions ensured that Robert was gagged and hogtied before the van pulled away from the curb to melt into the early evening traffic.

When Robert woke from the shock, he found himself in what appeared to be a dimly lit, abandoned warehouse. His hands were tied and he was suspended from a horizontal beam somewhere above his head. He was also stripped to the waist.

Standing in front of him was the young lady, who was talking to two middle-aged men. The shorter one was dressed sharply in casual evening clothes, while the taller one was wearing an expensive two-piece suit. Listening closely, he could make out the Israeli accent of the shorter one, while he thought that the other had a somewhat mid-west American accent. He recognized the extent of his predicament immediately, as he realized that his captors hadn't bothered to gag or blindfold him.

The girl noticed he was starting to stir and nodded to one of the two men—the one with the Israeli accent. He grunted his approval and turned to face Robert. The sight of the man's face almost caused Robert to throw up, although Robert had been a paratrooper in some of the roughest places on earth. This was different. The man's face was almost angel-like in its demeanor, except that one-half of his face had been ravaged by an intense fire. The skin on that side was so bunched up and livid red that Robert actually felt sorry for him, especially as he could see that the eye on that side of the face was obviously useless.

The one-eyed angel stepped closer to allow Robert to take in the horror of his face, before speaking in English, "Ah, you are awake, Monsieur Dumas. This is very good. It wouldn't have done anybody any good if your heart had failed just yet . . . I'm sorry, please allow me to introduce myself: I am Major Lazarus Eisenberg of the Israeli Mossad. The young lady you found so charming is Lieutenant Elizabeth Cohen. The others shall remain nameless. Now, as we don't have much time, I need you to tell me everything about the nuclear bomb, the one you planted under the Old City."

Robert mustered up every bit of courage he had. He spit into the major's face and said, "Why don't you go and stick your taser up your ass?"

The major quietly took a handkerchief from his pocket and gently wiped the spittle away from his face, before deliberately folding it and putting it back into his pocket. Then he said, "Yes, I see you are a proud young French paratrooper and hero of the Republic. It would give me a great deal of pleasure to flay you alive over hot coals like the Bedouin do, but I don't have the time. Besides, I don't think you would talk, because you truly believe in your cause. I believe you and your girlfriend are committed to the Order of the True Rose Croix, is this not so?"

Robert didn't say a word, but it was obvious the major knew much more than he was saying.

To prove his understanding, the major snapped his fingers and out of the dark came the two young Israeli men who had kidnapped Robert. At first Robert couldn't quite make out the shape suspended between the two until he realized the limp mass was an unconscious and naked Angelique. Robert gasped at the sight of his beloved Angelique. It was quite obvious she had been brutally beaten and repeatedly tasered.

Robert dropped his head and sobbed before the major grabbed his hair and yanked his head back. Robert already knew that, for Angelique, he would tell them everything.

The major also saw the look on Robert's face and smiled. "Mr. Dumas, we Israelis are not the barbarians many make us out to be. I deplore this type of violence but we are at war, make no mistake about it. We, therefore, do what we must, even though we also appreciate rare beauty. I

therefore promise that your girlfriend still has a chance to remain beautiful
. . . Now, we know you held a French work visa as an archaeological assistant
to Professor Chevalier and that you returned from Jerusalem without him
several days ago. You also fit the description of an Israeli sniper who caused
a great deal of upheaval in Palestinian neighborhoods around the same time.
We found the true owner of the uniform with his neck expertly broken in
an orchard just off the highway into Jerusalem . . . Now I'm going to ask you
the question one more time and, if I do not receive a satisfactory answer,
you will be responsible for the torture and death of your girlfriend. Do I make
myself clear?"

Robert knew he was a broken man and quietly croaked out, "*Oui!*"
He then went on to explain every last detail of how he used the Templar
tunnel and cavern and how to find the doorway behind the cistern. He
confessed to the murder of the professor, the Israeli soldier, and the
subsequent deaths of at least five Palestinian youths.

He also described in detail the Middle Eastern sect who provided
him with the nuclear bomb, their contacts and whereabouts. He described
Jean Baptiste's New World Order plan in detail and listed all of the members
of the Order he could remember. In between sobs, he even disclosed a
number of the European aristocratic elite, who had quietly supported the
Order both financially and politically. He even went so far as to implicate a
number of high-ranking Jesuit priests and their contacts within the Vatican.

In fact, there was almost too much information flowing forward, as
the tall middle-aged American gentleman, who was wearing an immaculately
tailored, blue Gabardine wool suit, stepped forward from the shadows and
addressed Major Eisenberg, "Lazarus, it's good enough for now. You better
get going and relay the information to your headquarters. Do you really think
your experts can disarm the bomb once it's found?"

Major Eisenberg let go of Robert's hair before calmly replying, "Yes,
most certainly. We have some of the finest nuclear minds in the world. I will
leave my two men with you. What do you intend to do with Mr. Dumas and
Ms. Martine?"

The American gentleman shrugged, while he balanced Robert's
Berretta in his hand. "Oh, I don't know. I'm going to stick around a while
and hear the rest of Mr. Dumas's story. It's quite fascinating. Afterwards,

fate will show itself? Perhaps they are a young couple in love, strolling along the left bank at night, hopelessly exposing themselves to a number of bad things? I'm sure I can come up with something suitable. Actually, I'm getting quite tired of all of this constant intrigue . . . Lazarus, you'll make sure you brief James on the situation, won't you? He and his colleagues can prove very useful as go-betweens among the various religions."

Major Eisenberg was about to leave but stopped and addressed the American, "Yes, I'll make sure your James is fully briefed . . . Do not forget your end of the bargain though . . . My people receive exclusive access to the ossuaries and their contents before they are released for their collective examination."

The American was examining Robert with a detailed eye and nonchalantly waved the major on his way. "And, Lazarus, please do not forget the other part of the bargain, my friend. If the cavern does indeed contain the thirteen original pillars of the Templars as our friend here claims, then my people will receive exclusive rights to them and all of their possessions, whatever this might entail."

Major Lazarus mockingly saluted the American before saying, "You Americans are all alike. Everything is *quid pro quo*. So be it. I will not touch your Christian knights. Let's hope we can keep them in one piece. If not, then we will not be seeing each other ever again. *Shalom*, my friend!"

In a wink of an eye, Major Lazarus, along with Lieutenant Cohen at his side, was gone.

\* \* \*

WITH THE DETAILED INSTRUCTIONS that Major Eisenberg provided to his central headquarters in Jerusalem, the Mossad team had little trouble finding the Templar tunnel and ancient cavern beneath the Dome of the Rock. The team itself was made up of two highly skilled nuclear scientists from the University of Tel Aviv and two equally skilled special operations agents.

Even with their collective skill level and experience, they were still awestruck by the contents of the cavern. The two agents appreciated the historical significance behind the thirteen desiccated knights who stood guard over the now-empty cavern, while the two scientists genuinely appreciated the perverse art which had gone into the construction of the nuclear device lying before them. None of them gave the shriveling mass that was all that was left of Professor Chevalier, who lay to one side of the carved Templar cross and the bomb, a second glance.

One agent, Fred Baker, was taking a video of the cavern's contents and streaming it back to Mossad headquarters, while the other one, who appeared to be in charge, delicately probed the silent sentries as they stood their ground. Both were as cool as could be in a situation like this, but deep inside they could also feel the adrenaline rush, which was something they lived for since being removed from front-line military duty.

The leader, Jack Mannheim, quietly said to the two scientists, "Well, gentlemen, what do you think? Can it be disarmed?"

The older of the two scientists, Professor Stein, casually replied, "Yes, I think so. It is actually a rather ingenious yet simple device of Serbian-Russian design—a small dirty bomb. What we need to do is remove part of the explosive lens shell, which, when detonated, sets off the larger plutonium reaction. Once this is done, we need to deactivate the lens shell itself by separating it from its timer."

Jack Mannheim was trying to maintain his patience with the scientist. "Thank you, professor, for that rather interesting dissertation, but can you do it? We don't have much time."

The professor wasn't the least bit put out and replied as though he was giving a lecture at the university to a class of disinterested students, "Yes, but in doing so, we'll all be exposed to a fair amount of low-level radiation. I imagine that whoever first constructed this is dead by now. Indeed, I hope he is dead by now."

Fred Baker quietly chuckled at the morbidity of it all, even though all four knew the personal risks involved before they volunteered for the job. The risks, however, were tempered by the thought of what the global repercussions would be if they failed in their mission.

Upon receiving no objection, the professor set to work with the help of his colleague and long-time friend, Professor Uri Solomon.

# CHAPTER 59

Exactly one year after Michel LeNeuf and Jean St. Jean first penetrated the Well of the Prophets, they returned to Thomas Jefferson at Monticello. They had spent the winter months living among the Blackfoot with their wives, and it was during this sojourn the two knights secured the vault for future generations. Of course, this amazing feat couldn't have been accomplished without the help of the entire village, but the Blackfoot were as much committed to the cause in their own way as were the two knights.

It was Major LeNeuf who provided the brains to the operation, while Sergeant Major St. Jean provided the logistics and management of the construction. In both instances, the two guardians demonstrated a commitment and understanding that could only have come from what they witnessed on September 17, 1811, and the belief they were on a direct mission from the Supreme Being.

Luckily, the previous guardians had left another cache of equipment, allowing them to complete the seemingly impossible task of securing the vault on time. Again, it was the two native brothers-in-law who proved their worth when they showed the two knights another hidden cavern, one that had served as a foundry for those Templars who had come before them. Perfectly, the cavern contained the underground face to a coal seam running under the Tobacco Root Mountains.

With such a handy source of fuel and the necessary iron, copper, and limestone deposits located nearby, it was obvious the previous guardians had anticipated what would be required to seal the wormhole.

When first shown the cavern, both Michel and Jean recognized the neatly stacked, molded axe-heads, adzes, and timber-linking brackets, which would be required in order to construct the wooden scaffolding intended to support the artificial roof of the vault. The two guardians also recognized the pick-axe and shovel-heads required to dig the access tunnel to the surface. Michel and Jean had earlier found the natural underground stream tunnel on the floor of the vault, which ran for nearly two miles before any access to the surface could be gained, but they quickly dismissed this way as being inappropriate to bring the immense quantity of timber and other supplies to the floor of the vault.

So, while Michel set about calculating the appropriate angle for the proposed access tunnel running to the surface on the edge of the wooded circle and drawing up the plans for a nine-arched scaffold, Jean set about showing the strongest braves how to chop down western pine and spruce and to delimb and square the timbers. Of course, in accordance with native custom, the knights were always sure to give thanks to Mother Earth for her generosity in providing the timber and other raw materials necessary to carry out the unique engineering feat. Tobacco and other gifts were always offered up, as were the prayers of the ever-present Blackfoot shaman, who ensured that everything was carried out according to the oral prophecies.

Even Chief Ugly Head tried his hand at swinging the largest axe and became quite adept at dropping a tree in the proper direction. The chief's many wives and children were indeed impressed by the chief's newly acquired skill as a forester, which led to the chief good-naturedly demanding a say in almost every detail of the construction.

The village people worked in harmony and peace alongside the man-beasts who had become their own flesh and blood. Food was plentiful during this time, as the snow during the winter was relatively light, and the elk and deer came close to the village out of natural curiosity, allowing the braves to cull the older animals at will.

With their pots brimming over and their bellies full, the women and children merrily worked day-in and day-out, processing meat, hides, and bones. Nothing was wasted and Michel and Jean even received full buckskin suits from their new wives as presents when the winter solstice came. In return, Michel and Jean took advantage of being able to melt down several of the gold coins they still possessed in order to create good luck amulets for their wives. Marie received one in the shape of an owl while Angelique's was in the shape of a sea shell, both symbolic of the goddess's wisdom. Thin leather strips were used to secure the amulets around their necks and the whole village was in awe of the skills the red-and-white guardians possessed.

The village was not only blessed with an abundance of food and its resulting good health but with six pregnancies among the villagers. It appeared to be coincidental at first, but the shaman prophesized it was because of the presence of the two red-and-white guardians. Chief Ugly Head attributed it to his newfound logging skills, while the village women saw it as a challenge to demonstrate their love for their own mates in a fashion comparable to the outwardly compassionate love Michel and Marie, and Jean and Angelique, shared for one another. No matter, the only unfortunate situation was that neither Marie and Angelique were among the newly pregnant women. Both Michel and Jean attributed it to their age, but this didn't stop them from continuing to try to conceive.

With the calculations completed, it was around the first of November when Jean stripped to the waist and swung his pick-axe into the north side of the cavern to mark the first cut into the soft limestone. It was completed just three days before the winter solstice ceremonies, which made the celebration all the more poignant, as the southeast sun penetrated the vault for the first time ever via the entrance tunnel on December 21, 1811.

After this, the transporting of the vast timbers and other equipment to the bottom of the vault went fairly quickly, allowing the scaffolding and artificial roof to be completed within the next three months.

The design Michel perfected for the eight-sided, nine-arched scaffolding, which surrounded the central pool, was based on a similar design Michel had seen as a youth in Paris.

Having completed the task at hand, it was with mixed feelings that the foursome left the Blackfoot village in the same manner they arrived. Marie once again took her position behind Michel, atop Pegasus, while Angelique assumed her position behind Jean, atop Icaria. The whole village chanted and sang in tribute to the departing warriors and their mates, as they headed down towards the vast prairies and rising sun. The Blackfoot were sad, yet content with the knowledge that they were chosen to continue as the guardians of the Well of the Prophets.

Marie and Angelique could not look back on the land of their birth and home of their parents for fear the tears would come. Instead, they took solace in the strength and warmth of their two knights, with the inner knowledge the Creator had chosen them to melt the man-beasts' hearts.

Indeed, they showed no outward remorse whatsoever, even when they re-entered the main Shoshone village at the confluence of the Missouri and Yellowstone rivers. Not surprisingly, their arrival had been foretold, for none other than Cameahwait himself stood dressed in his finest ceremonial garb in the center of the village to greet them. As usual, he had his arms spread wide and howled like a great wolf at the sight of the two knights dressed in their new buckskins, with their new wives sitting behind them.

Both Michel and Jean anticipated the rather unusual reception they would receive, as Cameahwait's prediction had come true, and the great chief wasn't going to allow anyone to forget it. The resulting feast would be whispered about for years afterwards in Masonic circles, as it just happened to have been witnessed by two French-Indian traders—Masons both, who were in the village at the time for the spring trading.

Legend still has it that the great chief was almost brought to tears when Pegasus and Icaria were presented to Cameahwait as a gift in return for his unusual matrimonial introductions. In return, Cameahwait promised that the guardians' horses would be set free to roam the prairies with their wilder relations, as Cameahwait pronounced that the black and white beauties had earned the right to be among the wild painted horses.

As fate seemed to have taken a direct hand in the lives of Michel and Marie and Jean and Angelique, it was indeed fortuitous the two French traders were present this day in the Shoshone village, for they offered to convey the foursome down the Missouri River on their giant raft, which was piled high with bundles of winter-kill furs, to St. Louis where Brother Dumas himself would be handling their fur trade.

The raft was an unusual mode of transportation to the foursome but it was swift and comfortable, as the fur traders were sensitive enough to set up two tents at the front of the raft in respect of the newly married couples. The traders also suspected the two older Frenchmen, who were now as deeply tanned as any French explorer and decked out in native buckskin from head to toe, were the two who had been whispered about over the past winter in Masonic Lodge #111.

* * *

THOMAS JEFFERSON STOOD at the same spot on the front porch as the last time the two knights had arrived at the estate. As the wagon with Michel and Marie and Jean and Angelique, came to a stop, the president bounded down the steps, all the while exclaiming, "By all that is sacred, welcome, welcome! Major LeNeuf, Sergeant Major St. Jean, you are indeed a sight for sore eyes. I had not received any news of you for over nine months. Indeed, it is a relief to see you on many levels . . . But I can see you are not alone. Pray tell, who are these ravishing creatures?"

Major LeNeuf was the first to descend from the wagon and extended his hand to the president, who took it with great vigor. He then said, "Mr. President, it is indeed good to be back. I'm pleased to be able to tell you that our mission was a success. We will talk later. In the meantime, may I introduce to you Mrs. Marie LeNeuf and Mrs. Angelique St. Jean?"

The president stood in awe as Jean helped the two ladies, dressed in their native finery, from the wagon. Then he broke out laughing, "Do you mean to tell me that my two celibate knights gave into temptation after all? Why, this is wonderful. This calls for a celebration! But where are my manners?" The president then moved forward and in turn took each of the ladies' hands and formally bowed before them in the French fashion. "Mrs. LeNeuf . . . Mrs. St. Jean . . . may I formally introduce myself. I am Thomas Jefferson—former president of the United States. May I welcome you to my humble estate?"

Much to the surprise of everyone, since the two ladies had been quiet since leaving the Indian Territories, Marie responded in English after curtsying in front of the president, "Mr. Jefferson, on behalf of the Blackfoot Nation, my cousin, Angelique, and both of our husbands, may I say it is an honor and privilege to meet such a great statesman."

The president was dumbfounded. His initial summation was that the two women would be subservient to their husbands and their English would at best be halted.

Michel LeNeuf laughed out loud at the president's preconceived notions. "I'm sorry Mr. President. I can see you are at a loss for words. What you do not realize is that the Native American puts us to shame when it comes to statesmanship and majesty. The two ladies are of noble blood and are quicker to pick up languages than either the sergeant major or myself."

President Jefferson quickly regained his composure. "I envy you, my knights. Your wives' intelligence and beauty makes me speechless, which is not good for any politician, more so when the politician is a widower. We were just about to have lunch. It would indeed be our honor and privilege for you to join us."

Thomas Jefferson extended each of his arms to Marie and Angelique, which they readily accepted with grace. With the major and sergeant major in tow, the president escorted theladies up the steps and into the shaded coolness of Monticello.

Inside, greeting them was an attractive, mixed-race woman of about forty years of age. Her skin was very fair and she had straight, dark-brown hair flowing down the back of her European-styled dress. Although she presented herself as one of the estate's head servants, it was obvious to all she carried herself as the mistress of the house.

The president gently took her hand. "Gentlemen, ladies, may I present to you Ms. Sally Hemings? Sally has filled the void since my wife passed away, and I am in her debt for her assistance in seeing to the ongoing operation of the estate. We were just about to sit down to a light lunch when I received news of your arrival from one of the field hands."

The major without hesitation stepped forward and took Sally's hand, bowing formally. "Ms. Hemings, it is indeed a pleasure. I'm Major Michel LeNeuf, originally of Paris, France. May I introduce you to Sergeant Major Jean St. Jean, also of France, and our two wives of the Blackfoot Nation? I present to you Mrs. Marie LeNeuf and Mrs. Angelique St. Jean."

In turn, Jean and the two ladies took the hand of Ms. Hemings and further introduced themselves. Thomas Jefferson nodded in delight and addressed the entire group, "If everyone would be so kind. I believe the dining table is laid out already, and Mrs. Peter has made a hot squash soup, which I believe you will enjoy."

As everyone was in agreement, they all made their way into the dining room and assumed a chair, with the president at one end of the table and Sally at the other end. The head servant, Peter, appeared and presented lunch as though the two knights had never left the estate some two years earlier.

It was a magnificent lunch, what with the two knights telling the entire tale of their journey. They left out no detail, from their first meeting with the St. Sulpician priest in Montreal to their first encounter with their wives-to-be. But they didn't stop there. With the president's nodded approval, the two knights enraptured both the president and Sally with their tale of discovery and the wise decision of not disturbing the vault's contents. The only piece of information the two omitted to tell the president was the true coordinates of the Well of the Prophets. The lunchtime gathering continued well into the afternoon, with a reluctant collective agreement to break until suppertime, which enabled the foursome to retire to their quarters to freshen up and unpack.

It also afforded some time for Ms. Hemings to take the guardians' wives aside to ensure their every need could be accommodated. As a result, when everyone met on the front porch for a pre-supper drink of apple cider, the gentlemen were dumbstruck to witness the radiant beauty of all three women, who were dressed in the latest Parisian fashions. The low necklines of the dresses were perfect in showing off the amulets Marie and Angelique had received as gifts from their husbands. Both ladies were beaming with pride, not only in their own appearance but because of the easy acceptance of their presence by both the president and Sally.

While Sally had stolen away with his wife, Michel had taken the opportunity to retrieve Prince Henry's sword from its hiding place among their rolled bedding. The sword and its sheath were carefully wrapped, and now, the large package lay upon a small side-table.

The president had repeatedly eyed the package ever since the major brought it out from the house but he knew the two knights first wanted to finish their story, so he waited.

Finally, as the sun was about to set, after the recounting of a few minor details the two knights had failed to convey through mere oversight, Michel cleared his throat in preparation of what would be a once-in-a-lifetime presentation. "Mr. President, on behalf of Sergeant Major St. Jean, myself, our wives; and the entire Algonquin Nation, the Ancient, Free and Accepted Masons, and the Masonic Knights Templar, and in honor of those who came before us—from the Antients to Prince Henry Sinclair and his Scottish Knights Templar, to our fellow Brothers, the late Captain

Meriwether Lewis and Brigadier General William Clark—and, in eternal thanks to the Almighty Creator, the Supreme Being, the Great Architect of the Universe, I would like to present to you and to the Republic of the United States of America, a sword of peace given to us by the Mandan, the White Indians, in recognition of the bonds of friendship forged since time immemorial between the red and white people of the world."

Everyone on the porch that evening went silent as the president solemnly accepted and unwrapped the sword of peace.

Having done so, he unsheathed the sword and held it up so the last rays of the sun could reflect off of the glistening blade. As the reflection of past secrets danced across the estate's porch and upon its pillars, the president pronounced, "Major and Mrs. LeNeuf, Sergeant Major and Mrs. St. Jean . . . indeed, the entire nation owes you an immense debt of gratitude. Your rediscovery and concealment of that-which-was-lost will not go unforgotten within the halls of power. The true secret will remain as such, until there is a more-appropriate time for it to be unveiled to the world."

# CHAPTER 60

A s Phil Bloomer, James Wayne, and the rest of the Navy Seal team followed Lieutenant McCormack down the entrance tunnel, they could swear the marine was humming the theme from *Snow White and the Seven Dwarves*.

It was becoming clear to everyone that the marine lieutenant didn't take anything seriously, which was probably why he had survived so long.

Even after having shot and killed Marie Magdalene at point blank range, Dunk showed no ill effects whatsoever. Phil Bloomer could reason that Pierre and Godfroi were soldiers of fortune and, therefore, deserved to die; but killing a young woman, even though she had drawn a direct bead on Thomas, was another thing. Unfortunately, the question as to whether Marie would actually have pulled the trigger had gone to the grave with her. Unless, of course, her brother could shed some light on the subject, but this wasn't likely, since it appeared Jean Baptiste was long gone.

However, in acknowledgement of the slight probability that Jean Baptiste still lurked somewhere nearby, Dunk called over his shoulder as they approached the opening to the cavern, "Look alive, you frogs, we might still have a hostile bogey running around down here. Aside from this little nuisance, be prepared to be amazed at what you're about to see, and appreciate it even though I know that none of you have anything beyond a sixth-grade education. Also, remember you'll carry this secret to your graves."

Like all soldiers, Dunk took every opportunity to put the dig into his compatriots, even at a tense moment such as this.

In muted response to Dunk's odd sense of humor, the eight-man team ignored the remarks and professionally fanned out as soon as they reached the cavern opening. Besides, everyone knew there would be time for wisecrack rebuttals later on after the job was done and they settled into a few beers.

In the meantime, the only two living bodies they encountered were George Artowski and Bill Rose, standing by one of the thirteen ossuaries. Somewhat strangely, they had almost assumed the same golden glow of the cavern, making them blend into the background. Even Dunk was more amazed the second time underground, with the translucent, almost transfiguring quality of the cavern walls and its thirteen pillars.

George was the first to acknowledge the lieutenants' and Navy Seals' arrival. "Lieutenants McCormack and Bloomer, we're over here. Have the team assume defensive positions and secure both the tunnel entrance and the entrance to the stream tunnel. There must be another underground tunnel leading away from here, so find and secure it also. There's been no sight or sound of Jean Baptiste, so he must have taken a runner."

Dunk responded in a clipped military tone, "Yes, sir, Colonel! Seals, you heard the colonel. Let's move it!"

The Seal guarding the tunnel entrance suddenly shouted, "Lieutenant, we've got company coming down the tunnel. I think it's the Ranger team because I can hear a couple of dogs."

Lieutenant Bloomer jogged around the central pool and wooden scaffolding to be in position when the Ranger team emerged from the tunnel. He didn't want the team and their dogs to be startled by the cavern's contents or its strange glow.

Emerging first from the tunnel was a rather small and wiry Ranger, when compared to some of them Bloomer had encountered either in the field or in some of the rougher bars around the world. The Platoon leader's name was Dave Levesque, and he seemed to be having a hard time keeping an oversized German shepherd from tearing his arm out of its socket, as the dogs had already sensed death in this cavern. Levesque quickly came to a standstill and sharply saluted Phil Bloomer before quietly whistling, which caused the dog to stop in its tracks and sit motionless.

Sergeant Levesque then addressed Lieutenant Bloomer, allowing the seven other Rangers and another German shepherd that made up his squad to congregate in a semi-circle behind him, "Sergeant Levesque, sir, US Ranger Team 8 at your service. Colonel Sinclair sends his compliments, along with the instructions that we are to follow your directions to the letter. He also indicated that whatever we saw or what took place down here was immediately to be forgotten. Sir!"

Phil Bloomer liked what he saw and heard in the sergeant, realizing Levesque's size was probably best suited for some of the specialized tunnel work that the squad had been trained for. "At ease, sergeant!" Phil Bloomer extended his hand to Levesque. "Colonel Sinclair is correct on both counts. Now here's the situation: We have one ex-French paratrooper by the name of Jean Baptiste St. Jean-LeNeuf running around somewhere underground, if he hasn't broken to the surface. I need you to split your squad in two and explore both the entrance and exit tunnels. But you need to be on the surface by 1700 hours at the latest. That's when the fireworks will be starting."

Phil Bloomer pointed to the two different directions—tunnels' entrance and exit—and then continued. "And, gentlemen, make no mistake about it. This Jean Baptiste fellow is deadly—a nasty piece of work. We don't know if he's armed, but it doesn't matter. He'll be additionally pissed because the body over there is what remains of his sister. If possible, I want this man alive, but the level of force is discretionary. Keep in constant radio contact with me, Channel 13. Do I make myself clear?"

Sergeant Levesque spoke for all of the Rangers, "Perfectly clear, sir!" He then quietly dispensed his own instructions, and the two Ranger squads quickly dispersed to their respective tunnel entrances, where they donned night-vision goggles and released the dogs. Within a minute, the cavern once again went silent as Phil Bloomer rejoined George Artowski, Bill Rose, Lieutenant McCormack and Master Chief Wayne, with the foursome gathering near where Marie's body was being zipped into the body bag by two Navy Seals.

Dunk acknowledged Phil's return with a slight nod and an easy grin. "Phil, those Rangers look like they know what they're doing, so let's concentrate on our next task." He turned to face George and Bill. "Colonel Artowski, Mr. Rose, here's what I propose we do. One of Phil's Navy Seals is an expert in explosives and controlled demolition. Thanks to the French, we have the necessary specialized incendiaries, plastic explosive, and remote-control detonators. I think Jean Baptiste had the same idea, so it tells me that it should work. The timber scaffolding is so old and dry that, with the right primers and settings, each of the eight supports to the nine arches should simultaneously burn so hot they would virtually vaporize the entire scaffolding and the wooden roof. The key is for it to implode in on itself. The dried grass on top of the roof and what little soil there is should also disintegrate with the intense heat. The result essentially would be the raining of small particulate matter and carbon dust onto the cavern floor and pool."

The other three pondered the suggestion and then Bill Rose spoke up, "Dunk, I think your idea just might work. How long do you think it would take?"

Lieutenant McCormack was all business when he responded, "I imagine, sir, it shouldn't take more than half an hour to set up and, if I'm correct, the implosion itself would take less than five minutes, maximum. I've already requested that Colonel Sinclair establish a two-kilometer perimeter in anticipation of the fireworks going off at 1700 hours."

George Artowski was once again impressed with the marine lieutenant. "Dunk, it appears you've thought of everything. Good lad! Then get to it, but there's one thing . . . if anything happens to any of these ossuaries, then I'll have your head on a platter."

"Just like John the Baptist, sir?" Dunk retorted.

"Just like John the Baptist!" George replied, but Dunk was already walking away towards one of the Seal team, who were laying out the necessary explosives and equipment on the cavern floor.

Dunk approached the Navy Seal explosives expert and said, "I take it you overheard the conversation? This cavern really magnifies the sound."

The Navy Seal looked up from his bent knee and responded, "Yes, Lieutenant, it looks like a piece of cake. Those Frenchman sure have the right stuff. I'll time the incendiaries to burn first, in order to set the entire scaffolding and roof on fire before I blow the base supports with the C-4. You were right when you indicated the whole structure will implode. If it happens as we envision, all we should be left with is a fine ash."

Dunk slapped the Seal on the back. "Good man. Let's do it. The cavern will be cleared by 1650, and we'll blow it from the surface with the remotes."

The Seal confirmed the instructions, "No problem, Lieutenant! We'll be ready."

Dunk walked back to the group. "Colonel, we'll be all set then by about 1650, where everyone should be back on the surface. Might I suggest that you and Mr. Rose start making your way back to the surface now? You can grab Thomas and make your way to the extended perimeter with Colonel

Sinclair. Once we blow this wormhole, I think the best thing to do is to retire to the truck and trailer where we can spend a secure night regrouping for tomorrow's big event. The Rangers will have the entire area locked down, so there's no chance of anyone accessing the cavern."

Phil Bloomer at this time interjected, "Here comes the Ranger squads now. It looks as though they've turned up empty-handed."

Sergeant Levesque left his Ranger group over by the tunnel entrance to the surface and came to report to the main group. Saluting smartly, he responded to the groups' inquiring looks, "Sirs, unfortunately, it appears our little mole has broken through to the surface. My dog picked up the scent right away, and we followed it underground for about two thousand meters where the tunnel gently rises up to the surface along an old stream bed. The prey could have easily climbed the slightly inclining tunnel wall and broken through to the surface. I had one of my team do exactly that, and they tell me it breaks through just past the edge of the woods. There's no telling where he went from there, but I'm pretty sure he could have hightailed it out of the area before we arrived by helicopter."

Phil Bloomer was the first to respond, "That's okay, Sergeant. I half-suspected as much. If you would be so kind, I'll ask you to escort these two men to the surface and report to Colonel Sinclair. With the extended perimeter, we might catch him yet."

The sergeant saluted in acceptance of the lieutenant's instruction. He noticed for the first time that one of the gentlemen looked an awful lot like the husband of the president of the United States. His eyes grew wide, but he said nothing except, "Absolutely. Please follow me, sirs."

\* \* \*

THE NAVY SEALS WERE PREPARED to move out with five minutes to spare. Lieutenant Bloomer nodded his satisfaction at the demolition preparations, looked around the cavern one more time, and then gave the order to move out. The body bag containing Marie Magdalene's body accompanied them.

Lieutenant McCormack was the last to leave for the surface. But before he exited the cavern, he stopped for one last look at the thirteen pillars—the very foundation upon which all of the major religions of the world were based. He said a short prayer to himself in acknowledgement of the prophets that lay before him. *God, I hope the collapse of the scaffolding in no way damages the cavern's contents. After all of the effort and sacrifice over thousands of years, to lose that-which-was-lost would be unthinkable.*

There was no time to second-guess their strategy, since Dunk knew better than anyone they had less than twenty-four hours to be in position to witness the solar eclipse. With a salute to the thirteen prophets and everything they represented, Lieutenant McCormack made his way back up the tunnel that Michel LeNeuf, Jean St. Jean, and their native Indian brothers had carved out of the limestone some two hundred years ago.

At the surface, he was greeted by Lieutenant Bloomer and Master Chief Wayne, who inquired, "Lieutenant McCormack, is everything secure?"

As was his practice, Dunk slapped the master chief on the shoulder and replied, "Yup, we're ready to go. Let's join the group and your demolition man and have ourselves a party."

The trio hopped into the outfitter Jeep, which had been left next to the entrance of the tunnel. With Master Chief Wayne driving, they high-tailed it over to where Colonel Sinclair had established a mobile command center to the wider perimeter.

The master chief slid the Jeep sideways to a stop right next to the two other Jeeps. All three hopped out and approached the small group composed of George Artowski, Bill Rose, Colonel Sinclair, and Thomas, who appeared no worse for wear after his ordeal.

Also present was the Navy Seal demolition expert and a US Ranger radio operator, who had established his communication center in the back of one of the other Jeeps. The two specialists were awaiting the command to proceed.

Dunk checked his watch. It was 1700 hours right on the mark. Not saying anything, both Colonels Artowski and Sinclair nodded their assent to Dunk, who then nodded to the Navy Seal who had placed the remote-control switches on the hood of the nearest Jeep. Taking his cue, he flipped up the guards to the two switches, which resulted in two blinking green lights indicating the system was activated.

For the sake of those Rangers manning the perimeter, the communications specialist then said into his mike, "Fire in the hole!" This was quickly followed by the Navy Seal flipping the first switch, which detonated the incendiaries. After what appeared a lifetime, but in reality was no more than a minute or so, the Seal flipped the second switch, which set off the C-4 at the base of the scaffolding, causing the inferno to implode upon itself as it collapsed.

The timing was perfect. The scaffolding disintegrated with a giant "whoosh" when a rush of oxygen was drawn into the wormhole by the collapsing structure. The result was a fine particulate dust that settled to the cavern floor, while a golden plume of dust rose from the wormhole, having caught the late-day sun's rays.

Everyone in the group reacted in the same manner, in that they solemnly stood and stared at the rare spectacle. It was as though the Egyptian god Ormus, himself, had just coughed up an alchemical mist of gold and silver.

Even Jean Baptiste, who was lying hidden within a large pile of leaves and cedar boughs just within the edge of the surrounding forest, stood up in reaction to the controlled demolition. He had surfaced from the underground stream just prior to the arrival of the US Rangers and Black Hawks but decided to stay around in order to assess the situation.

He was also conflicted because of the death of his sister. Even though he saw her death as the extreme necessary sacrifice, he had promised himself he would extract revenge on both the marine lieutenant and Thomas. He had enough pride to try and maintain the family honor, even though it was quite obvious all else had been lost.

He was too wrapped up in thought to notice the camouflaged Ranger who had snuck up on him from behind. It was apparent the events of the past few days had affected him more than he was willing to admit.

The young Ranger trained his weapon on Jean Baptiste as he moved in. "Don't move a muscle, buddy . . . Now slowly turn around and place your hands behind your head."

Jean Baptiste tensed as he slowly proceeded to do what he was told. However, as he turned slowly around to face the soldier he extended his arms outward, not upward, as if in confusion and feigned ignorance by saying, "Excusez moi, je ne parle l'anglais . . .?"

Unfortunately, the young soldier was a bit too anxious and had moved in too close. In one fluid motion, Jean Baptiste saw his opening and deflected the barrel of the soldier's weapon with his left hand, causing the weapon to discharge harmlessly into the soft earth. During the same flowing moment, he flicked the stiletto resting up his right sleeve into his right hand and thrust the blade upwards into the soldier's chin.

As the soldier fell face-first, Jean Baptiste deftly caught the weapon and was on the run away from the Well of the Prophets within seconds of the encounter. With the sun setting and the woods closing in around him, Jean Baptiste figured the probability of his escape was highly likely.

At the same time, the sound of the gunshot echoing across the plain startled the central group. Within seconds, the cackle of the radio increased ten-fold and the communications expert exclaimed, "Colonel Sinclair, sir, we have a man down on the perimeter."

Sinclair immediately stepped into action, "Tell everyone to maintain their position. I want a medical team responding to the required position within thirty seconds. I also want a three-man squad trying to pick up the trail of our prey. And I want all three Black Hawks in the air scouring the identified sector as soon as possible. Maybe they can pick him up with their heat sensors. Tell everyone the level of force has been elevated. I want that man—dead or alive! Now move it!"

"Yes, sir!" The communications specialist was calm in relaying the orders and the area became a beehive of activity in no time. All of the Rangers were itching to go after their prey in retaliation, but they realized if they broke the perimeter there would be hell to pay.

George Artowski also realized the ramifications of what had just taken place. *Damn, it must be that bastard, Jean Baptiste. Surely that black cat must have used up his nine lives by now!*

George grabbed Bill Rose by the elbow and started to lead him towards one of the Jeeps. "Bill, Thomas, we need to get both of you to a secure place. We need to move out now! Lieutenants Bloomer and McCormack, we're moving out to the truck. I want your Seal team providing escort for our priority one and Mr. Randolph. Colonel Sinclair has everything in order here and will maintain the position overnight. We're taking the outfitter's Jeeps. Let's go!"

# CHAPTER 61

E ven though Jean Baptiste had escaped capture, everyone in the eighteen-wheeler slept soundly, knowing that Phil Bloomer's Navy Seal team had secured the immediate area surrounding the tandem truck and trailer and the US Rangers had doubly-secured the area surrounding the Well of the Prophets. Besides, everyone was so exhausted that, at this point, Jean Baptiste presented no significance at all.

Thomas had also resolved that, even though he had fallen in love with Marie Magdalene, she was obviously deranged. Whether it was from issues during her childhood, or whether it was due to the belief her family was of the Holy Bloodline, it really didn't matter. What really mattered was a global Armageddon had been adverted and the priceless depository of ancient relics and writings had not fallen into the possession of the Order of the True Rose Croix.

With this knowledge, Thomas and the others were excitedly eating a hearty breakfast prepared by Master Chief Wayne, who had surprised everyone with his culinary expertise, when Colonel Steve Sinclair pulled up in an army-issued Jeep. He appeared crisp and shaven, though it was apparent by his red-rimmed eyes he hadn't slept during the past twenty-four hours.

There was also a spring in his step, as he practically vaulted the side stairs to the trailer and entered via the open door. Upon seeing Colonel Sinclair arrive, George stood to greet him and extended his hand, "Steve, it's good to see you this morning. What's the situation?"

Steve Sinclair eyed the four-cheese omelet Thomas was digging into, as he and his men were surviving on field rations since they arrived. "Everything is nice and quiet and secure. I brought in another thirty Rangers late last night and dispersed them around the perimeter. The Montana State Police have been most cooperative, especially after I told them the plume was the result of a controlled demolition required to bury some exposed low-level radiation. That's the story leaked to the press also. Nobody will want to get anywhere close to the wormhole, as I've also had a military hazmat team running around pretending to take readings and samples. The look on the state troopers' faces when a couple of my men showed up in full hazmat gear was priceless."

Bill Rose laughed. He too was digging into an omelet, along with plenty of toast and coffee. "That certainly is worth the price of admission, Colonel Sinclair. Tell me: What condition is the vault in?"

"I have to tell you that in the light of my flashlight, everything seemed unreal. The significance of what is down there almost brought me to tears. I'm pleased, though, to be able to tell you everything is in order and that other than a fine ash covering everything, the demolition didn't damage a thing, from what I could tell." This, in part, explained the exhilaration and raw energy the colonel appeared to possess this morning.

Dunk came from the far end of the trailer, where a fully functioning bathroom and shower had been built into the trailer. He was casually wearing a towel around his waist and using another to rub his closely cropped hair. "Colonel Sinclair, sir, that's indeed good news. My head was on the line if we damaged the ossuaries. Any sign of the murdering lunatic, Jean Baptiste?"

The colonel hesitated a little before replying, "Unfortunately, no. From what you've told me, I expect he's had considerable wilderness training and also extensive training in avoiding capture. He's pretty handy with a stiletto, too. I lost one of my best men and would have really enjoyed capturing the bastard, but there's no telling where he is now. My Rangers are still on high alert, and we're using the dogs, but the trail went cold last night."

George Artowski jumped in, "No need to blame yourself or your men, Colonel. One thing this Jean Baptiste fellow is, is resourceful. I've notified all federal agencies and had him put on the wire for suspected murder and terrorist activities, so he's on the no-fly list. We've also frozen any assets he has here in the States through a presidential order. We'll get him if he tries to leave the country via any normal channels. There's virtually nowhere he can hide. Now, tell me: Have all your men been prepped for the solar eclipse at noon today?"

Colonel Sinclair was relieved to hear the report on Jean Baptiste. "Yes, Colonel, everyone is fully aware of their duties. We'll maintain the two-kilometer perimeter while you're in the vault and I'll make sure the Black Hawks are grounded. I've checked the weather report and the sky is going to be clear. Is there anything I should be worried about?"

Bill Rose caught the uncertainty in Colonel Sinclair's voice and jumped in to reassure him, "No, Colonel, nothing we know of. To be honest, we're not completely sure what will happen, but I can tell you that previous discoverers of the vault have experienced it and lived. Isn't that right, Thomas?"

Thomas was just finishing his breakfast and pushed his plate away. "Yes, that's correct. I really don't think any of us have anything to worry about, as long as we don't look directly into the eclipse. What I'm thinking will happen is the image of the eclipse will be reflected in the central pond. All I know is that somehow the eclipse will reveal something. What happens next is anybody's guess."

Dunk had managed to get dressed while the conversation was taking place and now returned to catch Thomas's comments. The cockiness in him was never too far from the surface. "Perfect, Thomas! You sound really convincing . . . Don't you remember the teachings relating to the Masonic Companion's Jewel of the Royal Arch? The jewel is depicted as a double triangle in the form of the Seal of Solomon within a circle of gold. At the bottom is a scroll bearing the words: *Nil nist clavid deest*—Nothing is wanting but the Key. Beneath this is the Triple Tau, which not only signifies God but the temple of Jerusalem, *Templum Hierosolyma*. It also means *Clavis ad Thesaurum*—A key to a treasure—and *Theca ubi res pretiosa deponitur*—A place where a precious thing is concealed, or *Res ipsa pretiosia*—The precious thing itself. In other words, the key leads to a Temple of Jerusalem where a treasure lies. Or, the wisdom and truth gained through the discovery of the Temple is, in itself, the treasure."

Everyone was awestruck at Dunk's recital, which was not only in English but also flawless Latin. Once again, the marine lieutenant far surpassed expectations.

Thomas was almost brought to tears with laughter. "Dunk, I swear, what comes out of you at times amazes me. Yes, I well remember what the Jewel of the Royal Arch stands for. Maybe the eclipse will in some way open our minds and provide the key to where the true treasure lies within the vault."

Bill Rose had also just finished his breakfast by this time and was pushing his plate away. "Thomas, both you and Dunk have surpassed our wildest dreams and expectations time and again. There is one thing, though, that I've been meaning to ask you. Were you able to decipher Lewis's second parchment in its entirety?"

Thomas smiled and reached to grab his laptop. As he booted it up, he said, "As a matter of fact, I have! I admit it had me stumped for a while. Captain Lewis was certainly a resourceful fellow. I would have loved to meet him in person. I would also have loved to have met both Michel LeNeuf and Jean St. Jean. From what I've pieced together, those two knights almost transcended time and space. I've also wondered what took place between the two knights and Lewis, but I don't think we'll ever really know. Here, let me call up Lewis's progression of symbols once more."

The sequence of circles and squares once again appeared on the laptop's screen.

Everyone, including Colonel Sinclair, moved in a little closer to get a better look at what Thomas's laptop displayed.

Thomas collected his thoughts and began, "Do you remember the notion the Templars believed, that there is order in nature and, therefore, they could control nature? Order from chaos?"

"Of course!" Bill Rose piped up. "Jack Whyte recently wrote a trilogy concerning the medieval Knights Templar, and the third book is *Order from Chaos.*"

"That's right," Thomas replied, "Many of his ideas about what happened during the initial two centuries' initiation and existence of the Order were correct. What was most interesting was his grasp of how the original families of the Order were descended from Moses and the Jewish High Priests, who realized that to survive they would have to convert to Roman Catholicism. But this was, in reality, the beauty of the whole situation. The cabbalistic knowledge that the High Priests of the Temple, including Moses and his brother Aaron, possessed, was passed down throughout the generations. This cabbalistic knowledge is said to have been derived from the original knowledge contained within the Book of Enoch, meaning that first developed from before the Great Flood."

He continued, "What I'm talking about are the secrets lying in all things—secrets that can be distilled through applications like numerology. Each number had tremendous significance and above all-else, the numbers 3, 4, 7, 8, 9 and 11, and 13 held the most significance . . . 3 stood for the three-sided triangle or the trinity. 4 stood for the four-sided square. 7 could only be divided by 1 and, therefore, was considered to be in harmonic concordance. The number 8 is what is achieved by following this harmonic concordance to a higher level, thus achieving infinity. 9 is 3 times 3, which represents moving from one dimension to another. The number 11 represents the start of a higher level still and is also considered mystical because it is a mirror-image unto itself. And, finally, the number 13 was considered to be good luck to the Templars."

Dunk jumped right in on that one, "Thomas, I thought the number 13 was considered bad luck. After all, it was on a Friday the 13th when the Templars were decimated."

"I lot of people look at it that way, Dunk." Thomas responded. "But you have to think like a Templar. Remember, Order from Chaos. The Templars survived Friday the 13th and went underground, where their beliefs and resolve were strengthened. They actually believed the Church had done them a favor, in an odd sort of way. It's like the saying: What doesn't kill you makes you stronger. The chaos generated over the next two centuries allowed the Order to regroup and to establish their New Jerusalem in the New World."

Thomas knew he had the group's full attention and, therefore, continued. "Okay, let's apply the idea of numerology to Lewis's symbolic progression. If you read it from right to left, east to west, you'll see a progression of 8 symbols, which correspond to the 8 lunar phases. Eight phases or the 8 inner pillars of the Temple—however you want to view it.

Dunk cleared his throat to give Thomas a subtle hint he was rambling again.

Thomas picked up on the signal. "Uh, thanks, Dunk. You're right: I am getting off topic. I'll get to the point. When I saw the eight letters immediately below the symbols, I knew I'd seen the sequence before. When I originally researched this, I found a cipher relating to a secret society known as 'The Illuminated Ones,' which existed in Britain during the seventeenth and eighteenth centuries. The relative numerical values of this cipher assigned to the letters are V equals 20, A equals 12, S equals 18, O equals 14, and U equals 20."

Thomas allowed what he had just said to sink in a little before continuing. "So, the first four letters—V.V.A.V.—add up to a value of 72 and the second set of four letters—S.O.U.O.—adds up to 66; for, a total value of 138."

Bill Rose immediately grasped what Thomas was getting at. "Thomas, 138 can be viewed as 13 and 8—8 being the number of lunar phases necessary to find the 13th pillar. Eight is also the number of longitudinal degrees between each antient longitudinal meridian. In the composite of the two paintings, we've followed 8 phases from 56 degrees west longitude to 112 degrees west longitude. "

Everyone was impressed by Bill Rose's immediate grasp of Thomas's application. The president's husband continued. "Meriwether Lewis, by 1804, must have been aware of The Illuminated Ones' code. Lewis was certainly quick to apply it. This is utterly fascinating in itself."

George saw the need to interrupt with his own summation, "The eighth symbol appears to be the most complicated one. I see it suggesting that only when there is a solar eclipse, when the moon comes between the sun and the earth, are we able to complete the square. In my mind, the three-dimensional square in this case is the underground vault. So, we have to be there at the precise moment when the circle—the eclipse, penetrates the square—the vault. Gentlemen, I suggest we get going and be in position when the sun reaches its meridian. I don't know about you, but I can hardly wait to see what happens."

George's excitement was infectious as all of the trailer's occupants prepared to move out.

# CHAPTER 62

Marie was having a tough time throughout the delivery. Both she and Angelique had long ago determined that she carried twins but, even still, something wasn't right. The bleeding and pain was unlike anything that either one had witnessed either in the Shoshone or Blackfoot villages. Even Sally Hemings, who had come over from Monticello to act as midwife, was showing signs of concern, as she attempted to shift the position of the twins, which had dropped but were refusing to come out.

Marie's screams were also causing Michel a tremendous amount of grief, as he waited in the second-floor hallway of the estate, which had just been completed the year before. Michel sat with Jean and tried to keep his mind off of his wife's distress, but it wasn't working.

"In the name of all that's holy, Jean, what's happening?" Michel leaned toward his friend while posing the question.

Jean really wasn't sure, but moved closer as if to reassure his companion, he said, "I don't know, Michel. Angelique says even though Marie has fairly wide hips, her birth canal is somewhat obstructed. We'll just have to wait it out. Sally has sent for a doctor, but it'll be at least a day before he makes it."

Jean wasn't much on humor but tried anyway to make light of the situation. "Damn it, Michel, who would have thought you would be so virile beyond the age of seventy, especially after being celibate for the first fifty years of your life! And twins at that!"

Michel smiled faintly until another one of Marie's blood-curdling screams came through the door.

Just then, Sally opened the door and stepped out into the hallway. She looked grave and almost ill as she addressed Michel and Jean, "Michel,

I know you know that it isn't good. I just can't stop the bleeding. Marie's amazingly strong and spiritual but even with that, I think, we can't save her. She wants you now by her side."

Michel couldn't accept what he was hearing and rushed to be by Marie's side. There, in a big, four-post bed, laid a weak and distressed Marie. The entire bed was soaked with blood, but she had her eyes open and was trying to extend her hand to her husband.

Over to one side sat Angelique, holding a tiny baby wrapped in a white cotton blanket. The baby was quiet but alive. Jean moved to be with Angelique, who was was quietly weeping and chanting the death song in honor of her Indian cousin, once he saw what was about to unfold.

Michel quickly embraced Marie's hand and gently sat down on the bed beside her. An angel-like calm had overcome Marie, as though she was resigned to the fact she would soon die. When she spoke, it was in a faint whisper. "Michel, my darling, we have one son, I pray to the Almighty Creator he will grow up to be big and strong like you. Oh, darling, please do not cry. I want to name him James Louis LeNeuf, in honor of two French kings. He will have to earn his Blackfoot name. Our other son, Michael, is stuck inside of me and he's already dead. I tried so hard but it just wasn't meant to be. Please, forgive me . . ."

With those final words, she let out one last gasp and was gone. The Supreme Being took her spirit quickly. Save for Angelique's quiet crying, the room was silent.

Before Jean could reach his friend in order to comfort him, Michel shot out of the room, past Sally Hemings and down the stairs. He bounded like a madman across the central foyer, past the newly installed thirteen pillars, and shot out through the front doors. Jean was trying to catch up with him, wondering where his distraught friend was going, but Michel ran aimlessly, as though trying to outrun the devil himself.

In what seemed an eternity but was really only five minutes, Michel found himself atop a small hill, which lay behind the estate and could be seen from the main second-floor terrace. It was here Jean finally caught up to his friend, who was lying face down in the soft grass, sobbing uncontrollably.

Jean didn't know what to do, so he just sat down beside his friend and put his hand on his shoulder. After Michel shed all the tears he could muster, he rolled over and sat up next to his friend. Staring aimlessly towards the estate, Michel finally said, "Marie loved it up here. She said it reminded her of home, what with the trees rustling and the long grass swaying in the wind . . . Jean, do you think the Supreme Being has punished me for all of the killing I've done and the fact that we entered the inner sanctuary?"

Jean was at first startled by the question but responded with a higher understanding, "No, Michel, the Supreme Being is not punishing any of us. Remember, you yourself told me that God granted man the ability to reason and, therefore, the ability to follow his own path. You and I chose a path we believed was holy. The Supreme Being rewarded us by bringing Marie and Angelique into our lives. You also have one son who is alive. What happened with Marie is just one of life's mysteries. Did you not tell me that as Templars, we are not to regret any of our actions, for we are on a life's mission from God?"

Michel found tremendous comfort in Jean's words, and his body appeared to shed all of the stress and tension. Later, Jean would confide to Angelique that Michel's face had taken on a translucent quality, as though he was looking into another world.

Michel nodded with resolve and responded to Jean's words, "Jean, we've traveled a long way together. You have always been my conscience and my comfort and, as I've often said, what with the spark the Supreme Being has provided to me, along with your companionship, I have lacked for nothing in my life. And when Marie came along, I felt as though I was truly blessed . . . Jean, I have asked a great deal of you over the past fifty years and now I have one more favor to ask of you."

Jean, puzzled, knew he would do anything for his friend. "Of course, *mon ami*. Tell me what you desire, and I shall see that it happens."

Michel lay back into the long grass and looked up into the sun. "Jean, first I want you to promise that you and Angelique will see to James Louis as though he was your own son."

"You have my word and bond as a Brother. It goes without saying." Jean was concentrating on this request but couldn't help but think what the second request would be.

Michel closed his eyes and felt the warmth of the sun on his face. "Secondly, I want you to promise me that you will see to having me, Marie and Michel buried on this hill. Marie would like it."

Jean continued to be puzzled by his friend's melancholy but again responded in the positive. "*Oui*, of course, Michel, I will see to Marie and your unborn son. It will be my honor and pleasure to serve you once again. And, when you pass away, if this happens before me, then I will see to your skull and crossbones are buried right beside your wife and child after the Masonic and Templar funerals."

Michel reached out and gripped his friend's right forearm. "Jean, my last wish will be the hardest for you but the Supreme Being will absolve you of all guilt. Right here, right now, I want you to dispatch me to Arcadia with your stiletto, so that I can be with Marie and my son, Michel!"

Shock registered on Jean's face but Michel would not let him go.

Michel continued, "My Brother, you once saved my life and now it is in your hands again. You know, as well as I do, that our eternal rules require you to do my bidding. I absolve you of all responsibility and our past sins. Quickly, now, before you have time to think."

Jean knew that he had no choice. Their eternal vows required that much of them.

Michel let go of Jean's arm and lay back in peace, exposing the soft underbelly of his chin. He heard the soft click of the stiletto popping from its hidden sheath and being palmed. All he felt was the tiniest of pin pricks tickle his chin, as he whispered to his friend, "*Merci!*"

# CHAPTER 63

What surrounded George Artowski, Bill Rose, Duncan McCormack, and Thomas was awe-inspiring in one sense and humbling in another. Certainly, it was Thomas who best understood the suffering and sacrifice required in order to bring together the remains of thirteen of the greatest prophets who ever walked this earth.

But like those who had gone before him, Thomas felt as though he was somehow trespassing on sacred ground, where heaven and earth came together. And, like those who had come before him, Thomas did not feel worthy enough to be witness to what was about to happen.

The only uncertainty in the whole scheme of things, other than Thomas's own thoughts, was what effect the eclipse would actually have on the thirteen pillars. Thomas had a pretty good idea but, until it happened, wasn't totally sure what would take place.

Given this much, the foursome gathered as one just inside the tunnel entrance to the vault and silently counted down the last seconds before the eclipse reached its zenith. As it had done two hundred years earlier, the sun positioned itself slightly to the north of the sinkhole at its meridian.

Thomas could hear his own breathing as he struggled to control his internal emotions. *Just think, the Wisdom of the Antients is about to be revealed.*

Dunk tapped Thomas on the shoulder, disrupting his thoughts, and pointed towards the central pool. A reflection of the total eclipse was caught by the dark surface of the water, transforming the pool into a giant mirror. Deep within the pool itself, there beat a luminescent heart of translucent fire and then, just as suddenly, a piercing ray of light bounced from the pool's surface and angled its way towards one of the thirteen ossuaries. It was as though a prism of light was struggling within itself to gain some semblance of order.

The walls of the sinkhole sparkled with refracted light as the chosen ossuary consumed the energy from the beam. The limestone box took on a translucent, glowing appearance. Thomas and the others could just make out the image of a triangle coming from what appeared to be underneath the box itself.

Just as suddenly as it happened, the moon continued its path across the face of the sun and the beam of light shrunk back into itself and disappeared below the surface of the water.

A few seconds later, as the foursome moved out of the safety of the tunnel entrance, Bill Rose was the first to exclaim, "Sir Knights, I believe we have just witnessed the hand of God pointing the way to the one true secret! I will be forever grateful to be offered a glimpse of the true power and majesty of the Supreme Being, and I am humbled by the experience. This is what the prophets must have felt. I only wish all of mankind had the opportunity to witness such an event."

George put his hand on his friend's shoulder in confirmation of experiencing the same profoundness. "Well said. Now let us move over to the ossuary before we lose track of which one was pointed out to us."

Dunk was already standing beside the identified ossuary. "Over here!" He called. "The box is still hot."

The rest of the group solemnly congregated around the ossuary and bowed their heads in reverence. To disturb the box was almost as if they were to disturb the heavens. Nobody moved until Bill Rose finally spoke up, "Thomas, beyond any of us, this is your journey of discovery. In my mind, this ossuary contains the relics of Moses, along with his writings and teachings. It's up to you, but I believe you deserve the honor of opening the box."

Thomas sighed and then responded, "Thank you, Bill, it is most kind of you but in witnessing this spectacle, I appear to have gained a greater insight and wisdom than I previously possessed. Do you not remember the warning contained within Le Serpent Rouge? . . . 'Under the thirteenth sign of Ophiuchus—The Keeper of the Secret: Take Heed my friend, do not add or take away one iota; think and think again, the base lead of my words may contain the purest gold.' I think Michel LeNeuf and Jean St. Jean possessed the wisdom to understand the meaning of this some two hundred years ago and I think we should heed the same words. However, I want to see if I'm right in my summation. Dunk, would you mind carefully shifting the box away from its plinth in order for us to see what is underneath?"

Dunk nodded and grabbed hold of the ossuary, which by this time had lost most of its heat. As he shifted the box, two gold triangles with unusual markings became evident. They were positioned between the underside of the ossuary and atop of the plinth, almost as a conduit between heaven and earth.

Both George Artowski's and Bill Rose's eyes grew wide. It was just as the thirteenth degree of the Scottish Rite foretold. Both of them thought the same thing: *Here is the secret knowledge alluded to within the Thirteenth Degree of the Ancient and Accepted Scottish Rite, which the antient prophet, Enoch, is charged by God to preserve for future generations.*

Thomas could almost read the others' thoughts and confirmed their summations by saying, "Within the Thirteenth Degree, it is said that Enoch was granted a vision, after which he constructed on the Temple Mount a crypt nine levels deep, where he placed the great secret and a key to its discovery on two engraved triangular plates of gold. When King Solomon began construction of the Temple, the workmen found the crypt and brought its contents to Solomon for his interpretation, because of his knowledge and understanding. Solomon proclaimed that the one true name of God was to be found on the triangles. Solomon then assembled the two triangles within a gold circle into a symbol, which is still known as the Seal of Solomon, and received from God an understanding of all things."

Thomas continued. "Gentlemen, my suggestion is that Dunk replaces the ossuary to its original position and we leave this place, since I for one cannot fathom such power. Billions of people go to bed at night with the absolute faith their prayers reach God directly. I do not want to be the one charged with changing this faith. I believe Prince Henry Sinclair and his Knights Templar understood this also. It's just a shame the New Jerusalem they established here in the wilderness did not survive."

Dunk countered Thomas's last thought by saying, "Thomas, what makes you think they failed? Here we are, modern-day Knights Templar, continuing their very cause, ensuring what they preserved will continue. I'm sure some good will come out of this. If nothing else, we prevented it from falling into the hands of a lunatic who would have used it for his own purposes."

Bill Rose jumped in on the reflections, "Dunk is right, Thomas. I would guess that my wife will be thinking along these same lines. I'm hoping she will also realize that these thirteen pillars need to remain where they are. I'm sure the sinkhole and the entire site can be secured and its content be studied over time for the good of mankind by all religions. This vault should be turned into a center of global learning and debate."

As if on cue, Master Chief Wayne stuck his head out of the entrance tunnel and yelled in the direction of the foursome, as though he was back on a schoolyard. "Hey, you guys, what's up? We're a little worried up here. We just got word the president is on her way, and I would hate to have to tell her that the four of you got fried like some chicken in a pan of oil."

The master chief's easy manner was just the thing to break the seriousness in the cavern. Everybody laughed in relief of the situation and made their way over to the entrance of the tunnel. Without looking back, Thomas indicated to the Navy Seal he should lead the way.

When the group re-entered the real world, the master chief was waiting for them. "Hop into the Jeep and we'll head over to Colonel Sinclair's mobile headquarters. Oh, and I'm supposed to tell you gentlemen the president's plane landed at Hill AFB and that she's enroute as we speak, via helicopter, with an ETA of 1600."

The foursome was quiet at that news and hopped into the Jeep. It was a little crowded, but it was only a few minutes' drive to the perimeter, where Colonel Sinclair had moved his mobile command center.

All of a sudden, Jean Baptiste appeared, out of the woods where he had been laying in wait for the crew. Eyes blazing wildly, he let off a couple of shots as the master chief swerved and slammed on the Jeep's brakes, allowing Phil Bloomer to reach the rifle stowed by his side. Too late, the group heard a sickening crunch. Sidearms at the ready, Dunk and Bloomer hopped out of the vehicle. Thomas shuddered as a single shot dispatched Jean Baptiste, Dunk's vow to avenge his friends having been carried out. "Crazy bastard," muttered Bloomer in satisfaction.

# CHAPTER 64

The twin-blade military helicopter containing the president and her entourage arrived shortly after Jean Baptiste's fatal assault. By this time, the air was thick with hovering Black Hawks, and higher above were the two F-18s providing an escort for the president's helicopter.

News of Jean Baptiste's attempted assault reached the president prior to her lift-off from Hill AFB, along with the message that her husband, as well as George Artowski and Thomas Randolph, was safe. Relieved, Helen Jefferson-Rose made a mental note to reward Major Chief James Wayne and lieutenants McCormack and Bloomer in some way, as news of their quick-thinking actions had also been conveyed by the Secret Service.

With the helicopter making a smooth landing, the president stared across the aisle at James and his three companions and smiled. Everything had been sorted out as much as possible with respect to the Middle East crisis, with an added bonus. The remains of thirteen of the original Knights Templar guardians had been spirited from the cavern below the Dome of the Rock to an undisclosed location by the mysterious CIA agent.

The president and James knew the historical significance of such a find would yield priceless information. Indeed, the Jerusalem discovery was almost as significant as the Well of the Prophets, in that there were remaining clues as to where other treasures such as the Ark of the Covenant and the Temple Menorah could be found.

She also knew the geopolitical favors gained by preventing the destruction of the Old City, including the Western Wall and the Dome of the Rock, were priceless when it came to negotiating a lasting peace. When combined with the promise that all religions would have controlled access to the Well of the Prophets, the president knew that she not only controlled the world stage, but had also confirmed her re-election.

With the door opening and the several Secret Service agents scrambling to secure a small perimeter around the helicopter, the president let out a contented sigh as she rose to exit. She was the first to descend the steps, followed by James and the rest of her entourage.

Strategically, the president had also invited the grand chief of the Blackfoot, Merida North Star, a direct descendent of Chief Ugly Head. The chief was specifically flown to Hill AFB to confer with the president during the helicopter ride. The president felt it was important to share the re-discovery of the vault with the Native American people, as they had as much right to its contents as did the Knights Templar.

Waiting for the president was her husband, along with Thomas and George, Lieutenants McCormack and Bloomer, as well as Colonel Sinclair and Master Chief Wayne—seven Brethren in all.

Upon seeing her husband, the president was visibly moved, but quickly regained the same elegant composure she had displayed when Thomas first met her. Addressing everyone present, "Gentlemen, I understand you've had a very interesting fishing trip. The whole country, as well as the entire world, will forever be in your debt."

She then turned to Thomas and spoke to him directly, "Thomas, I understand a great deal of the credit for the discovery must go to you. Please accept my personal heartfelt thanks for your many sacrifices. I know it certainly wasn't easy."

Thomas smiled and nodded in recognition of the president's kind words. "Thank you, Madam President. I must say, though, it was a joint effort. George and Bill, Dunk and Phil Bloomer here, as well as Colonel Sinclair and Master Chief Wayne, deserve as much credit as I do . . . probably more. At one time or another, each and everyone here saved the day, as well as the lives of the others."

The president nodded but was growing impatient to see the vault, as James, the Blackfoot chief, and the others had moved to the tunnel entrance. Thus the president quickly replied, "Yes, Thomas, I realize this, and there will be time enough for individual accolades. Now, I must insist you personally show me what the group of you has discovered."

Thomas quickly realized this wasn't the time to recount the past ten days' events and fell into step with the president. The entire group, along with twelve Secret Service agents, just as quickly fell into the procession.

As the group entered the vault, James and the others gathered around the ossuary identified by the eclipse. It was apparent a solemn ceremony was being performed by the Blackfoot chief, who was holding tobacco up to the sky and the Creator in thanks for what was before them. He also held a juniper branch in his left hand, shaking it as he was chanting. Thomas reckoned this was to scare away any remaining evil spirits.

Meanwhile, the president had stopped dead in her tracks to take in the vision of the entire Thirteen Pillars. With the rays of the setting sun playing off of the walls of the sinkhole, the contrast between light and shadows added even more depth to the individually carved niches and their contents. Everyone else moved discreetly about but remained silent, in reverence to both the president and the ossuaries lining the walls.

Finally, after the president satisfied herself as to the true significance of what lay in the vault, she quietly summoned Thomas once again. "By now you have probably figured out that I used you through your fraternal relationship with Bill and George. The secret presidential file written by George Washington alluded to this priceless secret, but I didn't truly believe it until now. It's a heavy responsibility for the United States to bear, but I believe that with wisdom and foresight, and with the cooperation of the Native Americans, we can use this knowledge and understanding to bring peace and harmony to much of the world. "

Thomas was somewhat stunned by what he was hearing but he recovered quickly. "Madam President, I always had the nagging feeling there was a silent hand playing me as we went along. I understand why you had to do this, although I still don't approve of it. Unfortunately, I was a fool and fell under Marie Magdalene's spell. I know this now."

The president moved closer to Thomas and shocked those present when she gently put her hand on Thomas' forearm. "Thomas, if you allow me, I want to say I'm sorry . . . I truly am. I don't know if this makes it any easier, but it was obvious Jean Baptiste was manipulating his sister to his own twisted ends and that she, in turn, was manipulating him. I believe theirs was a complicated relationship that we'll never truly understand. I know you loved her, but she played on your vulnerability."

The president slowly led Thomas off to one side, away from the group and quietly whispered, "Thomas, I can understand that you might want to go home to your sons now, but there's going to be a time when you need the adrenaline rush you've experienced over the last ten days. When you do, I want you to know you can come and work for me directly, as an historical advisor, if you will? There are so many secrets to sort out here and in Jerusalem. I plan to keep the Thirteen Pillars here and to create an international center for learning. We have also uncovered a remarkable trove of medieval Knights Templar relics and artifacts in Jerusalem. I hope that, when combined, this treasure trove of knowledge will enable us to bridge the gap between certain religious sects. This talk of modern-day crusades and jihads has to stop. The Knights Templar at one time were mediators between the world's religions and I want this to happen once again. James and his three companions are beyond wise but are extremely old. It's time they had new blood. George and Bill will help guide you."

"That's very kind of you, Madam President," Thomas replied. "I will have to think your offer over. I've had my heart broken for the second time in my life, and it will take some time mending."

"I know, Thomas. Take your time. If you need anything in the meantime, please ask. I have a feeling I won't be going anywhere soon. And, I have a feeling you'll come back to me."

In response to the incredible offer, Thomas knew he had to ask the president for one immediate favor. "Madam President, there is one thing you can do for me."

The president raised her eyebrows. "Yes, what is it, Thomas?"

Thomas cleared his throat. "Madam President, I want you to promise me that both Marie Magdalene and her brother will be buried at the family cemetery on the St. Jean-LeNeuf estate in Fincastle along the antient meridian. Marie would have wanted this. She told me herself."

The president reached out again and lightly touched Thomas's arm. "Yes, of course, Thomas. I promise you the two of them will be buried amongst their own bloodline, under the sign of the cross."

*Veut Dieu Saint Amour—God wills holy love!*